ORIGIN, SONGS

CREIGHTON, HALBERT

Foundations Book Publishing

4209 Lakeland Drive, #398, Flowood, MS 39232

www.FoundationsBooks.net

Origin Songs
By
Creighton Halbert

ISBN: 978-1-64583-009-2

Published in the United States of America
Worldwide Electronic & Digital Rights
Worldwide English Language Print Rights

These stories, a dozen less three,
Seem unconnected to me.
Yet each man's position,
I have the suspicion,
Has bound him in bad company.

A.

EON 10 - THE REINCARNATION OF AGENT AFTERSHOCK

The rain started as a gentle mist at first, but it grew to a steady thrum against the pavement as the streetlights buzzed and flickered to life. Mark drew his heavy duster closer to shrug off the spatter and the wisps of New England winds that threatened an early winter. Even when he wasn't running around as Agent Aftershock, Mark enjoyed the security the duster's built-in armor offered. The glob of hair gel with which he had tamed his short hair threatened abandonment, so he threw his long legs into full drive as he jogged from the bus station towards the address scrawled on the letter he had folded neatly into his hip pocket.

And he marveled at the rain. This Earth was both like and unlike his birthplace of Methaldian Earth. He smiled a little.

The directions in his letter were simple enough to follow—his mother was proud of her ability to communicate efficiently, honed by decades of technical writing. All too soon, Mark found himself on the step of a modest Tudor-style house in the heart of suburbia. He hadn't written ahead. He hadn't written them at all in the past months. The Majhran Confederation's finishing touches on the Ihcheldrin War had required all hands on deck, leaving no time for anything but reorganizing their devastated ranks, preparing Mekrro to withstand any attempts by the enemy against the Parthon, and tracking the remaining shifters. By the time he had remembered to reply to his growing stack of correspondence, he was sitting on his first vacation in the two years since he had joined. So he hopped on a porter instead.

Mark's uncertainty slashed a narrow frown into his rugged features. As the doorbell squawked into the depths of the house, he reflexively checked his face for stubble with a brush of his hand. Nothing. Naturally. The mutation within had changed a lot, but faster hair growth was nothing against the military rigidity of his morning routine.

Scratching and scraping sounds heralded the release of a dead-bolt, and he stood up straighter. He ran a hand over his short blond hair to keep it combed back as best he could.

His mother peered out behind the screen door. Spots of sauce speckled her sleeves. She wore her wire-rim glasses. Blonde hair with hints of silver woven in hung past her shoulders.

"May I help...?"

She trailed off and sagged at the knees without warning, startling Mark. She clutched at the door frame and the lines in her face dissolved in an expression of agony. "No. Oh no, no. No, don't say —no!"

Stunned, Mark watched as tears began leaking down her Germanic features. Her husband rushed to the door and held her, staring in horror at Mark.

"No, my Mark. Oh, Mark... I told him not to go! I—I..." Mother stammered.

Dad clutched her and glared up at Mark.

Mark...in his full agent attire, holding his densely-packed briefcase in hand. As he pictured himself, understanding jarred him out of his shock.

"Mother!" he yelled. Embarrassed and distraught all at once, he couldn't think of what else to say. "Mother, Dad! *Seriously.*"

They visibly jumped a little at the familiar boom of his voice.

The Confederation's genetic retooling had given him height, muscle, a clearer complexion, and the face of a general, but it hadn't bothered his vocal cords any more than he had bothered to send his family a photo of his new identity.

Oops.

Killed the poor little—

"Mark?" Dad gaped at him. "Our Mark? What—?"

Mother, however, took one look at Mark's blue eyes and threw open the screen door, smacking him in the shoulder. She smacked his arm a few times with waning ire and sniffed a little, finally relenting and giving him a tight hug. "Mark? Oh, my boy."

"Remind me not to stop by for dinner again," Mark stated, stuffing his embarrassment behind a placid face. "I was hoping for more stollen and less weeping and gnashing of teeth."

"If you wanted Christmas cake, you should have come during Christmas," Dad laughed and wrapped him in an iron embrace. "That, and let us know you were coming. Or alive, for that matter! Come on."

"We heard about what happened on that one desert-y planet. They said people in dusters were fighting those monster things! I told your father, 'That's them! Our son is over there with them!' And you don't even write us three words since?" Mother demanded, wiping her face.

He tried to apologize, but she smiled through the tears and held him more closely. Dad guided them both to the kitchen table, where two more familiar faces were staring in amazement at the scene.

Like the small entry hall, the kitchen was warm and dark: stained wood panels on the wall, a nice new table and chair set, and cushions, pillows, and rugs that shrunk the room while also dragging at his eyelids in an invitation to relax. A fern grew on the windowsill. Dishes sat around on the counters and stovetop with the remains of stroganoff still clinging to them.

Gif had grown. His blond hair was a shaggy mess, appropriate for a high school senior. He wore a baggy sweatshirt that read *Motorheads Basketball* and had his patented manic Gif gleam in his eyes as he piled his stroganoff into two separate mountains on his plate. He was scrawny and a few inches shy of even pre-mutation Mark, but something in the face was markedly similar to Mark—at least to the old Mark.

As if born to contrast, Sarah looked as dignified as usual and had yet again revised her brown locks, this time into a bob. When they were much younger, Mark had always teased his sister about having the only brown hair in a family of blonds until his father had spanked the habit out of him. Only later did he realize how much it had hurt her. At the moment, Sarah wore a veneer of calm as she read from an open tome the size of a small dictionary. Her one blue eye and one green eye shone vividly in the light.

Mark's chest relaxed at the sight of his siblings, and a grin wormed its way across his face. "I see you two haven't changed," he teased.

"Dude!" Gif yelped. "It's Mark—I mean you're Mark. I mean… What'd you do to yourself?"

"It's, uh, a very long story."

Sarah folded her legs up underneath her as she sat, eyeing him without expression. "It's been two years, idiot. Two years of not knowing where you were or if you were coming back and how dare you just come in here and sit down—"

"Sarah," Dad cut her off. "He's had a long trip. At least let him eat first."

Mark's sister growled, while his brother kept gawking at him. Mother dashed about, setting an extra place for him. He tried to help but couldn't find anything in the strange kitchen, and Mother ordered him back to his chair to take his wet things off.

He slipped the heavy leather duster off and draped it over the back of the chair. The pounds sliding off his shoulders felt like cool water on his trapezius and neck, and he stretched. He noticed Gif gaping at him.

All murdered—

"What?" Mark said, and then glanced down at his tight grey undershirt and the muscular form it failed to hide. His face flushed.

"Oh. Yes. I'd like to say I bench-pressed my way to this point, but I'd be lying. It's part of that long story that I…would just love to save until after dinner."

He glanced questioningly at Mother.

She slid a warm plate in front of him and handed him a glass of water. "At least get a few bites in you first. Talking with our mouths full is a Jager tradition," she added, raising her brow at her husband while he whistled and looked away.

Mark smiled. Then, as the smell hit him like a brick, he began to shovel beef stroganoff down as politely as possible.

"How is it, living on a different Mirror Earth?" he asked after the first truckload.

"Besides the fact that people here call butt burps 'farts' and 'lame' means tepid, not that different from the old world," Gif said. "Oh yeah, and more clean space and less random nukings."

Mark nodded solemnly and turned toward his parents. "I thought I'd be getting here around Christmas, but it looks like my time zone has been running a bit faster than yours. So, two years?"

Dad and Mother glanced at each other briefly.

"About two years, yes," Dad said slowly. "Besides the hours, being factory foreman has been a nice change from the world of weapons development. Almost as much stress, though, if you can imagine. And your mother has won many victories in the campaign against the house."

She blew air at the strands of blonde falling on her face. "When I fix one thing around here, something else gives out. I'd say there's nothing left of the original house but the bones, but termites took their turn on the bones, too."

"So, you two got a good price on it, I hope?"

"After immigration fees, immigration physicals, immigration coding and filing, and whatever else they could come up with, the house *did* fit nicely into what was left of your…of our moving budget," Dad replied, correcting himself at the last moment.

Mark shot him a wary look. Gif and Sarah didn't know about

his financial help, and he preferred it that way. Mother saw and quickly continued.

"For his last year of schooling, I picked up Gif's education where it left off back on in Arkansas. Methaldian Earth, Arkansas, I mean. Not Arkansas here. Do you know they have government schools here? And everyone is forced to attend!" she exclaimed. Her eyes never stopped studying the new, unfamiliar face of her firstborn.

Gif broke in. "Yeah, but they were stupid. That's why Mom taught me. I blew them out of the water on the tests, of course. 'Cause I'm awesome." He high-fived himself.

Mark and his sister snorted in unison. Mark turned and smiled at her, finding strange solace in reliving their old, shared exasperation with Gif's antics. She looked up. Scrutinizing his features, she offered an unsteady smirk in return.

He said, "Speaking of outscoring everyone, did you find a university here, Sarah? They were probably fighting over…"

Too late, he noticed Dad's "red alert" glance.

Sarah stiffened, her eyes narrowing at the bowl of fruit in the middle of the table. She said, "Tuition is really inflated. They don't take higher learning seriously. I wouldn't waste money like that."

Mark took the chance to take a few more reasonably-sized bites of the beef dish and licked the sauce off his fork. He glanced sideways at Dad.

His family knew very little about his job, his physical transformation, or his life now. The only thing he had shared was how much money he was earning, and then he'd only told his parents so they would accept enough to move out of the deathtrap that was their birth planet—it was easier to risk his life knowing that his family wasn't in danger of waking up some night to the roar of a hydrogen bomb.

But his siblings didn't know, and he preferred to keep it that way. He was strange enough to them as it was. Information would trickle down on a need-to-know basis.

So he tried to be discreet and pointed when he said, "Come on, you're too good at making everyone else feel like idiots not to go. I'm sure there are scholarships out there."

"Yeah. You'd think so," she mumbled, her thin lips somehow both curled and shaking at the same time.

Mark stared meaningfully at his father. "I'm sure Dad could dig up—"

"I have my own job and my own plans, Mark. I'm fine," Sarah interrupted. "We're not on the same team here anymore. You left. That's fine. But we have our own lives, too. We can handle ourselves."

Killing him he didn't—

Mark shook the blurred image of the bodies out of his head and focused harder on his sister. Cursed memories.

"Sarah," warned Mother.

Sarah held up her hands as if she had just finished a written test. She plastered on a neat imitation smile and handed Dad the bowl of corn, saying, "Since we're trading stories now, what about you? How is your life lightyears away, traversing space with your new religious friends?"

Mark stared stupidly into his sister's heterochromatic eyes. Keeping up with her myriad lines of thinking had long since proven to be an unachievable goal.

"Uh," he said, "where do I even start?"

"Start with the weirdest thing," Gif said. He glanced around. "What? That's what I would do."

"That's not as easy as it was during my last job," he remarked.

As their children spoke, Dad and Mother kept exchanging glances and watching Mark when they didn't think he was looking. For the moment, they seemed to be content in letting them chat. Or maybe they were still catching their breath from the heart attack he had handed them at the door.

"Okay. Then what the crap happened to your face?" Gif said, grinning. "And why are you ripped? If you didn't *sound* like my swell-headed bro, I'd tell you to come back with the real deal."

"Are you saying I was scrawny before?" Mark demanded,

forcing a glare. "You don't get to be lab security by *sleeping* on those weight benches, you know."

"Well excuse me, Your Sweatiness! But really, dude. What gives?"

Mark glanced around at the food still piled on his brother's plate. "It's not great table talk. Maybe later."

"Everyone's adjourned to the living room!" Sarah leaped to her feet. "I'll clean dishes later. Mr. Hero is going to explain himself and you don't want to miss this once-in-a-lifetime opportunity."

As she physically shooed everyone out of the kitchen, Mark realized that his sister could be very, very sarcastic when she wanted. And he was beginning to wish he was back hunting down the surviving shifters instead.

Killing him he didn't even try to avoid why not why didn't they—

He repressed an angry burp and smiled through the pain.

UNLIKE THE KITCHEN, THE LIVING ROOM HAD PALE BEIGE DRYWALL AND white couches to keep it bright and inviting. There was no over-head light, so lamps stood guard in every corner. A fat old tube TV perched on an even older table, where it impassively observed the family of five all take their seats on couches that nearly swallowed them. Between the cushions, throws, and pillows, "sitting" felt more like "nesting."

Killing him—

No. Mark grunted as he twisted his neck to elicit a satisfying pop. Felt better. The memories died back again.

He looked around at the older man, older woman, younger man, and younger woman, who were all looking around as well. No one knew where to start, apparently. Not having Gif try to seize control of the conversation or Mother ply everyone with ques-tions…unusual and uncomfortable. This might have been his fami-ly's home, but by the way that they were acting, you would have thought they were sitting in some grand court's parlor across the Local Network.

Dad finally coughed.

"Son," he began, straightening the wrinkles in his trousers.

"You only call me that when I'm in trouble," Mark said. "The last time, I think I had just told you that I didn't want to go into military research, that I wanted to join the Timberwolves."

Dad laughed slightly, his voice rumbling. "You were so sure that American football would make a comeback. Hah, you would like it here. They have games on television every Sunday. Though you always said—"

"Always said watching isn't like playing, yeah," Mark smiled. Then the mirth vanished. "Sometimes playing isn't what you thought it'd be either."

A small clicking sound came from where Mother sat in her corner, watching him with worry outlining her features. Mark saw Sarah glancing back and forth between him and her as if trying to read their minds.

So he turned directly to her and Gif. Well, as close as he could to them both. Sarah was on the same couch he was while Gif was balancing on a corner of the TV table for who-knows-what reason.

"So, how much did Dad and Mother tell you two?" Mark asked.

"Apart from the fact that you joined a dinosaur cult—which is a cool deal, by the way—not much," Gif said. His arms were flung wide to help him balance. "They said you found better money and left. But that's all they knew."

"You 'joined a religious organization called the Majhran Confederation,'" Sarah recited. "That is literally the extent of what they told us. I couldn't even find anything on this Confederation until the news came about some crazy robot rebellion on Mekrro. Now, you hear all kinds of things and can't trust any of it. So knock off the hedging and just tell us."

"You hate not knowing something," Mark sniped.

"You do, too," she protested. "Shut up and talk!"

"Oh, play nice, you two." Mother fixed them with a stern eye. "Mark, you know we've been through a lot; and Sarah, you know he probably has as well."

"We're teasing," Mark said. "That's all. And fine, I guess I should start with the obvious."

"Like why you look like you've been taking 'roids?"

"Taking what?"

Sarah grunted. "Steroids are used on Mirror Earths for muscle enlargement. So it's actually a fair question, despite the fact that it came from the twerp. Was it drugs?"

Dad leaned forward with bright eyes, and a few loose feathers spat out of one of the pillows threatening to bury him. "No, no. Not drugs. Too many variables with the added height. That's bone growth, organ development…not just some muscle mix, at least. Unless the Confederation has found a way to throw eternal life into a syringe?"

Killing so many and killing him that one—

"No, but it is true that I won't be aging much either."

He might as well have told them that Congress had just banned throw pillows. Four blank faces blinked at him. So much for it being better to jump off the cliff than to roll down. But now he was committed, so he drove forward.

"Look. When I left, I was six foot tall to the hair and twenty-seven years old. Now I'm six-three... and twenty-seven years old. Yes, I did live and experience the last two years, but it will take years for me to physically reach twenty-eight years, and I may never experience the kind of mental degeneration that comes with age, if I live that long. I've seen veterans who look like they're four hundred going on forty. It takes some adjusting to get used to it."

His father licked his lips nervously, but his gaze was steady and curious. Almost hungry. Mother gave him the same look she had when he had fallen out of a moving train at age twelve and insisted he could talk to animals for the next three hours.

Sarah sniggered—then replaced it with a small smile when Dad shot her a look.

"So, you *can* die or you *can't* die?" Gif asked. "Just curious."

"Depends."

"Aw, tepid answer! What do you mean, 'depends'?"

"Depends on how," Mark said. "I can still get shot or poisoned or run over by a train, same as anyone. I'm just more...stubborn. No jokes, Sarah. I haven't gotten a cold in the past two years, and a good surgeon would have a much larger window to save me if I was critically hurt."

He scoffed as he saw their faces. "You don't believe me, do you?"

"Anything could be possible," Dad said.

"We believe that you're trying to make your family feel better about the kind of work you do," Mother said gently.

Sarah sat up so fast that three pillows bounced to the shag carpet. She stared torrents through their parents.

"The kind of *work*? 'That's all he told us, Sarah,'" she quoted softly. "'He's allowed to live his own life without sharing everything, Sarah.' Without sharing everything *with* Sarah, you meant."

Mother's frown ignited. "Sweetie, his recruiter said the Confederation was at war and there would be fighting. Mark told us that much. We just didn't think there was a point to telling you when we didn't know anything more. Especially with how close you two—"

"So that's it?" Sarah said. "'*Parva primatum tenens principia parva sunt*'? What about '*timendi causa est nescire timoris*'?"

Gif blew a raspberry. "You read more than us—we get it. Doesn't mean you're right."

She turned on him. "You agree with them?"

Mark checked the orbiri in his pocket as it translated Sarah's phrases. For once, he wouldn't be caught flatfooted. Plus, he didn't want any part of this argument.

Gif slid off his corner and stumbled over to an easy chair facing the TV. Sighing, he fell into it with the grace of a meteorite. Dad clucked his tongue at his treatment of the furniture, but Mother nudged him and offered Gif a warm smile.

He stared at his shoes as he replied. "No, you're right. Just not because you know some stupid dead language."

"Your mom and I handled it as best we could," Dad stated. "I am sorry if we weren't as forthright as we could have been. I promise we can discuss it later, but could we please return to Mark? Genetic splicing like the Methaldian United States did is one thing, after all, but—"

"Maybe it's just super Botox so you don't *look* like you're getting older…" Gif broke in.

"I remember the days of civilian calisthenics," Mother said. "Those runner highs can certainly make you feel ageless…but *Mark*. You can't deflect bullets! Don't go running into danger unnecessarily."

He was getting whiplash looking back and forth—never in time with a retort before someone else spoke up. Sarah, at least, just sat and looked skeptical.

"Perhaps there is some merit to slowing the aging process," Dad inserted. "The DoD had some major money flowing into a few projects like it back in my day, and I'm sure they've only advanced since. Days when you were on duty in the labs, did the genetics boys have anything building steam for us?"

"Dad, I bet this Confederation is light-years ahead of any one planet anyway. They have more money, at least," Gif said.

"Just a moment." Mark left.

"Mark, where are you—?"

In a few swift strides, Mark bounded back into the living room with his dinner fork in hand. He stood with hip cocked, preparing himself.

"Look, the lifespan thing is just a side-effect," he announced, mouth pulled grimly at the corners. "We have…abilities. Power from above, you could call it."

"Dude! Don't lie to me now. Agents have superpowers?" Gif demanded, a manic grin shining.

"I don't…" Sarah stopped.

This time it was Mother's turn to lean forward intently, eyeing him in a way he knew and disliked most. Her eyes were carefully narrow, her worry lines aging her, and her mouth quirking with a hundred thoughts beyond voicing: the same way she looked when he had joined the military's laboratory security force. She thought he was going to get himself killed.

Mark twisted the fork in his mouth, cleaning off the last sauces from dinner. They had no flavor. All he tasted was metal—smelled metal, bit metal. He wiped the semi-clean utensil off onto his shirt.

Killed and dead so many of them how when all he—

He winced and shut out the deluge again. What felt like lifetimes of weight threatened to smother him these days.

"What are the psychological impacts of your 'augmentations'?" Mother murmured. "Can you be sure you've never suffered manic episodes while working?"

"You can't just ask someone if they're crazy!" Sarah cried. She straightened her spine like she usually did when getting defensive. Seeing the small gesture made Mark smile a little.

Mother looked taken aback.

Mark peeled his shirt off.

Glancing at him, Sarah said, "Well maybe you can."

Gif wolf-whistled and said, "Save it for the bars, dude."

He ignored his family and slowly turned, his arms outstretched. "Do you see any hidden wires, tricks, traps, whatnot?" He waited for a response but only received blank, if curious, expressions. "No whatnots? Good. I'll make my closing statements."

He bent over to the wall near the TV. An electric socket with the bottom spot empty was half-buried by the table.

Killing him he didn't know but—

He blocked out the painful echoes in his head…and jammed the tines into the socket.

The lights in the room dimmed slightly and Mother yelped.

A moment passed as Mark held the fork steady. The familiar vibration humming through his arteries was warm and welcoming, an old friend he had ignored for months. Instead of his muscles seizing at the invasive current, they relaxed when he found he could easily keep the power from leaving him at any point but the fork. The metal utensil popped and sparked loudly, though.

He turned around to see Dad holding his wife down to keep her from running to her little boy. Sarah gripped the arm of her chair. Her fingers were bone white.

Mark yanked the fork out and the plethora of lamps brightened again.

"I rest my case," he said. He had planned to throw the words out suavely, yet demurely. But it came out flat. Dry. To lighten things up, he spun the fork deftly between his fingers and shoved it in his pants pockets like a gunslinger. It popped loudly one last time. Mother jumped.

He waited.

"Dude!" Gif finally gasped. "I knew powers were real some-where! What's yours? Are you, I don't know, invincible?"

"Did you have resistors of some kind? Were you grounded, just then?" Sarah interrogated.

Mark stared at them. This was what a grand gesture bought these days? Skepticism was a disease. Truly a tragic symptom of their time.

"No!" he said, groaning. "One more show and done, understood?"

He let his frustration whitewash the rising trepidation. Before he could think twice, he held out his hands as if playing cat's cradle and focused on the sensation he had felt when shocking himself at the outlet.

Then he flexed. He flexed a muscle that hadn't been there before the mutation—one that humans shouldn't have. Like a sneeze, his arms twitched. Visible arcs of power, raw electricity, flickered between his two palms.

You killed him you killed her you killed him you—

The doubt that had been hovering as a fog in the warm living room had just been ionized, and it was evidenced in the faces he saw gaping at him.

"'I am become death, the destroyer of worlds,'" Mark said, ending the current.

"The *Bhagavad Gita*," Sarah mumbled, more out of habit than choice.

"Well, I was quoting Oppenheimer, but yes," Mark stated. "I haven't stopped telling myself that since I heard my mentor quote it in my first year of training. I just wanted you to know, I'm not all human anymore. My boss is even less so. And my enemies…"

He stopped. They got the idea.

"How?" his father breathed out.

Mark sat down on the floor and pulled his shirt back on. He wouldn't bet that he would be welcome back on one of the comfy couches now.

"Everyone in the Confederation just calls it mutation. But even the operatives who regulate the chamber where it happens don't seem to understand the details. Humans go in. Agents come out. I am Agent Aftershock of the Majhran Confederation. And I'm afraid I have to ask you to call me that in public from now on," Mark stated. He took turns meeting the gazes of Dad, Mother, Sarah, Gif, looking for…something.

"But—I mean, *how?*" Mother asked weakly. "My little boy."

"Still yours, Mother. Always yours," Mark said. "This has more to do with magic than science, and even more to do with physics itself, like the fulcrums."

"Fulcrums?"

Mark kicked himself mentally. "Ah, that may have been classified. Ignore that. And before you ask," he said, turning to Gif, "my specific 'powers' include electric generation and limited manipulation. Like nearly a third of our agents, I'm also faster and, supposedly, more flexible. Just don't ask me to do the splits."

Sarah let slip a short laugh at that, to Mark's relief.

Then Dad startled him by lunging forward and throwing his arms around Mark. No question about whether it was *safe* or anything. Following a moment of confusion and two moments of embarrassment, Mark returned the embrace.

Dad finally pulled back, his eyes watery.

"You need to know, son," he murmured, "how proud we are of you. And we'll help you get through anything. No matter what you look like, no matter how many amps you produce—" there was some nervous laughter here "—*you* are our son. Nothing changes who you are except you."

"I..." Mark trailed off. He was overwhelmed by conflicting embarrassment over the children'sbook idealism and desire to accept it as truth. He sat backward hard.

Mother followed her husband's example. After letting go, she wiped at her eyes and added, "Of course. I always knew you were capable of more than just a security shift."

"I'm not going to hug you, idiot," Sarah said. The corners of her mouth twitched as she tried to remain straight-faced. "But maybe I can live with this. 'Aftershock'?"

"Yep," Mark said.

"As in an 8MO Aftershock landmine?"

"See! You get it," Mark exclaimed. "Basic Methaldian Earth warfare. But people keep asking me if I can control earthquakes."

He grinned up at Gif, expecting to at least get a laugh out of him.

Gif smiled and stood up proudly. The look in his eyes, though? Danger.

What was he doing? Mark's smile faded. Stop, Gif.

"Dad, Mom?" he said. "I'm going to be an agent, too."

The room went quiet yet again as all eyes turned to the youngest member of the Jager family.

No. *Killing so many many—*

"Don't be daft, Gif," Dad said. "Mark told us how selective the process is. You have to be singled out of billions, then tested, and then approached—"

"...approached by a recruiter," Gif finished. "Though I guess they call themselves missionaries, not recruiters. Missionary Gainsong gave me the green light three weeks ago. I was waiting for the right time to tell you guys that I'm going to say yes."

"No!" Thought exploded out of Mark faster than he could contain it. "No! You can't...It's a terrible idea. Don't be stupid. You wouldn't last a week."

He didn't care how demented he looked. He had to shut this down.

"Mark!" Mother cried. Her glare bounced back and forth between her two sons. "Gif! Are you telling me the truth?"

"Following your brother is admirable," Dad said slowly, standing up. "But to invent a story about being invited?"

"No, Dad," Gif insisted, eyes huge. "It's legit! Mark, I didn't mean to steal your thunder—heh, *thunder*, right?—but we'll work together and everything. Tell them it's legit. You know it's legit! The Gainsong lady said she recruited you too. Tell them!"

So many dead and all—

"Use your brain for the first time in your life, Gif!" Mark hissed through gritted teeth. Blood pounded in his head. How did things fall apart this fast? "Do you know how many agents survived the war last year? Less than half! Of everyone! Two of the three people I apprenticed with were slaughtered with the rest on Mekrro."

"Don't yell at him!" Mother demanded, tears welling in her reservoirs.

Mark hated for her to hear this—for any of them to hear this, but especially her. He wanted to convince them all he was safe. But if Gif followed the same siren song he had, his little brother would be as far from safe as Mekrro was from Khodnuu.

"You'll die, or worse, you'll mess things up," Mark continued. "And while you're telling people, 'my bad,' some innocent person will be lying on the floor bleeding to death, and you'll never be able to erase that! Is that your big heroic plan?"

Dad's hand gripped his shoulder in warning as Mother cried, "Mark, stop it!"

Gif's face screwed up like it hadn't in nearly ten years. And Mark hated himself at that moment. After being bullied by other kids as a child, Gif had always quietly prided himself on growing out of crying.

Then Gif ran out of the room, anger and pain flickering across his face in the brief glimpse Mark got of it. The sound of a door slamming hard and a short, agonized howl were all that returned to the room.

"Gifford, wait," Mother called, going after him.

Mark groaned and lay back on the carpet, staring at the lazily circling ceiling fan. The floor smelled vaguely musty—no doubt another gift wrought from the previous owner's neglect.

"I'll go speak with your mother," Dad said after a moment. Then he was gone, too.

By the time Mark sat up again, Sarah had her People Shield up. Somehow the girl always had a book on her to hide behind when things became rough. Finding himself alone in an unfamiliar house, Mark let his feet carry him back to the kitchen.

He glanced around at the piles of dirty bowls, utensils, and bakeware dripping all over the counters. It's not that his family was messy. They just had their priorities straight: food first, cleaning later. Well, now was later.

Chilled by the slight breeze of the fan, he grabbed his duster and slipped it on, rolling the heavy sleeves up as best he could and buckling the front closed. A few turns and squirts later and the left half of the sink was filling with steaming water and soap bubbles.

Killed him killed them all—

Drum, drum, steady drum. The rain beat down on the window alcove above the kitchen sink. Darkness prevailed outside, except where the back porch light shone down on a modest backyard and garden of shrubs and ivy vines. A tall brick wall surrounded the property.

The poor fools…

The shushing sound of the faucet ended as he wrenched closed the tap and took a deep breath. He plunged his hands into the suds, a sponge in one hand and a pot in the other. He attacked the caked waste with a vengeance. Splashing sounds filled the quiet. Small splashing sounds now. He tempered his motions. Simple, precise. Pot done, move it to the right side, wash the lid next.

Killed so many more than he needed to. Why had they fought back?

Now the lid was clean. Now he used the soft rag on some tableware.

...too easy. Didn't even try to avoid...He had seen him stun the first rebels, hadn't he? Why had they still threatened him? He should have surrendered before Aftershock had to shock him too.

Too many things were piling up. He rinsed. Placed on a towel to dry.

That level of power shouldn't have killed any of them. He had trained for two years to measure the voltage of each current, use the right amount of resistance before each blast. They should have been stunned. Not his fault. Not! The rebels that hadn't survived must have been weaker. Older.

But how likely was that, really?

"Oh, you didn't have to do the dishes, Mark," said a voice—Dad, in the doorway. "You're a guest!"

"Force of habit," Mark replied, elbows deep in soap suds. "Like riding a bicycle. You wouldn't believe how hard it is to get a dishwashing fix in the Confederation."

"Well, who am I to stand in the way of a dishwashing fix," Dad said with a small smile.

For the next minute, Mark settled himself into the stoic scrub-rinse-move routine. The hot water flushed the chill out of his hands. His dad wordlessly joined him at the counter with a dry towel in hand.

"Do you constantly feel like the last man standing, or is that just me?" Mark asked, throat dry and raspy.

Dad said nothing.

"For the record, I am sorry for yelling like that at him."

"Shock and awe is often the first resort in warfare," Dad stated.

"Come on. Our house is not a warzone," Mark retorted. "That was just panic. Not even panic. That was an overreaction from a boy who likes to think he's an adult just because he's twenty-eight. It's just...You and Mother have enough problems with one son out there fighting, getting shot at, and forgetting to write home."

"You're talking about yourself as if it were some *other* guy who had done all those things," Dad said as he placed a stack of clean spoons in the drawer.

Mark grunted, his face feeling warm. "That's my point. You don't need a second kid doing that to you."

"Your mother is of the same opinion."

"Hmm. Dad...since I doubt I can dig my grave any deeper at the moment..." He took a long breath, looking at his father out of the corner of his eye to test the waters. "Do you think Mother would be running after Sarah if she were the one who had just announced she was going to join?"

Dad stopped. He set down his towel and waited until Mark looked him dead in the eye. Mark had to glance down, which was unnerving and odd in and of itself.

"Now that's not fair," Dad said quietly. "You know what Gifford means to us. To all four of us."

"You can't live in this family and not know," Mark countered. "You can't talk to Mother for five minutes and not know."

"She is very protective of you all," Dad stated. "If she occasionally favors him, it's just because we tried for so long. He was the son we were told we could never have, and she felt responsible."

Mark paused—actually paused with his arms half-buried in bubbles as the heat crawled up his skin. "'She felt responsible'?"

"This stays between you and me, Mark," Dad said. "Your mother is an exceptionally giving woman, and she hates to be a disappointment to anyone, even just an imagined disappointment. Every time I tried to convince her that you were more than enough, well. It has nothing to do with you. It has nothing to do with Sarah. It doesn't even really have anything to do with Gif. But you can't hope—you can't want something for that long and not become—"

"—overprotective?" Mark spoke so that his voice would not carry.

"At times."

"Sarah and I may have noticed on occasion."

He scrubbed the last of the scum off the main pot and rinsed it.

Steam and dragon-hot spittle splashed into his face. The pipes on the left sink gurgled as the brackish water drained from it.

As Dad continued to dry, Mark walked around absent-mindedly, wiping the counters with a hot rag. The motions would have been more automatic after decades of cleaning up the dinner mess, but finding his way around the strange kitchen slowed him. A realization hit him: he would never again sit around the old kitchen with Sarah and Gif while Dad made pancakes on Saturday. He wouldn't get to push his younger siblings on the train wheel hanging from the ancient oak in the old backyard. Granted, Ye Olden Days would have been behind them anyway since both he and Sarah had moved out of the nest, one farther than the other.

"I do agree with her, though," Mark spoke up. "Gif, that far from home, doing who knows what? Bad idea. He's still a minor by American law."

Dad sighed, thinking holes through the opposite wall. After a moment, he resumed putting away plates and answered.

"I only had one older brother growing up, your Uncle Garrison, and we're only eleven months apart. Best of friends. Inseparable troublemakers, growing up. I've told you some of the stories."

Mark waited for the point. There was usually, if not always, a point.

Dad continued. "So I have never been an older child. I certainly didn't have the age gap that you and Gif, or even you and Sarah have. Back in the day, you were more like their uncle than a brother, at times. Certainly a bit overprotective, yourself. Remember that one goose at the New Statesmen Expo?"

"I try not to, thank you," Mark said with a slight shudder. "But trust me when I say I'm not being 'overprotective' at the moment. You don't want Gif in the Confederation."

"Are you saying that because it's dangerous? Or has something changed with the Confederation since you joined?"

A fly beat against the window in erratic bursts.

"I don't...I have stories about my life now that never need to be told," Mark said. "But even the normal work can be grueling. I studied under two different mentors while I was being trained, and the second one was a man whose idea of cardio was to run until you actually collapse. Don't get me wrong, I learned a lot from him. I quartered my mile runtime. But can you see Gif training like that? Having his day planned down to the minute?"

Dad grinned. "You always had the fortitude and the focus to throw yourself into a task even when the only payoff was self-improvement. And yes, Gif is the closest thing the Jagers have to a free spirit."

"Exactly," Mark agreed. "And beyond that, the Majhran Confederation is about religion as much as charity or missions. Once you're in, you're in for life. I don't see how he can understand that at his age."

Sarah's voice bounced into the kitchen. "I agree. Military, sure. Military for four, eight years would help chill out the little spaz. But he'd regret a lifetime membership as soon as they tell him he can't play guitar until midnight."

Her owlishly stoic face appeared in the doorway. She gave a tiny jerk of the head back towards the hallway, where the sounds of classic Earth rock music wailed. Sure enough, a second guitar was wailing along with the song.

"I see Mother's talk with him goes well," Mark said.

"Door's locked. Think she went into her bedroom. Hope she's okay," Sarah added with a soft frown.

"Ahh…" Mark groaned. He glanced around the kitchen, but there was nothing left to occupy his hands. "I'm sorry, guys. Dad, want me to apologize to her now, or should I head to the hotel and come back in the morning?"

"Hotel?" Dad scoffed. "Do you want to send her into fits? No. I'll grab some comforters and pillows out of the closet and we'll get the extra bed made up. Your mother would kill me if I let you pay to sleep on a hotel mattress."

"You're sure?" Mark queried. "You're not afraid I'll catch the bed on fire while I sleep?"

"You can do that?" Dad asked.

"Unbelievable," Sarah breathed.

"Well, I haven't yet."

"How about under induced stresses?" Dad asked, a familiar gleam brightening his face again. "Sleep deprivation? Hunger? Confusion? Drug influences? Anger?"

Killed them all…

"Okay," Sarah broke in, grabbing Mark's arm and dragging him out of the kitchen. "Dissection at 8:00, Dad. I want to show Mark my book before bed."

Dad's laugh followed them down the hall until it was drowned out by sounds of…someone. Some band. Whoever Gif was blasting in his room. Mark knew Offenbach and Chopin better than what Mirror Earth composers had done. On Methaldian Earth, the nuke-fest had ended the entertainment revolution that other earths had enjoyed. It was a little sad. Although listening to the screeching voice of the lead singer now, Mark could see a small upside to nuclear war.

"Does he do that often?" Mark asked as he followed Sarah into her bedroom.

The small room had a bunk bed against one wall, and only the top was open for sleeping. The bottom had been converted into a sort of reading den with a nest of pillows and crumpled sheets centered in a sea of books. A writing desk on the opposite wall was piled high with stuffed folders, papers, and office supplies. Her Methaldian-Earth laptop sat humming on the desk, its geometries as harsh and sturdy as the environment from which it had come.

Sarah plopped down in the yellow metal folding chair in front of the desk. "No, Dad only gets that way when something reminds him of his lab days. He misses them more than he tells us."

"I meant Gif," Mark responded, glancing around at the clothes draped over the furniture, the floor, and framed pictures on the walls. "Hey, didn't you get your own apartment somewhere downtown?"

The laptop powered up with a warm *rah-ding*.

"*Gifford* blasts that garbage whenever Mom and Dad let him, or when he's too worked up to care," Sarah said, flicking her hand dismissively. "And Mom hates my new place. Says the neighborhood is unsavory—her words, not mine. So she invites me over for late dinners all the time and tells me just to stay over. Ergo…"

She motioned around the room and then scoffed. Which, for her, was the equivalent of a belly laugh.

"Nice gig if you can get it," Mark said with a grin.

The glow of the computer caught his attention as Sarah logged into her account and her hands flew across the keyboard. She could do more with keyboard shortcuts than Mark had ever been able to do with a mouse. The application Pensoft opened to a massive document with hundreds of pages and a few appendices thrown in for flavor.

"Writing a novel?"

"Yes, actually. Surprised?"

"It's a murder mystery with a psychopath in solitary confinement as the victim, isn't it?" Mark asked, eyebrows lifted.

For a brief but glorious moment, his sister was visibly startled. Then she rubbed her nose ruefully and said, "I told you about wanting to write this. But that was years ago!"

"It's going to be the 'ultimate locked-room story.' Of course, I remember," Mark said with a grin. "Now: synopsis, list of characters, and themes, stat."

Sarah hesitated and then jumped into a nearly half-hour explanation of her mostly-completed book. Mark listened patiently through the parts she stuttered out as her brain analyzed and revised the book as she spoke. Once he had to stop her from jumping back to a whole section and deleting it entirely after she had second thoughts while describing it to him.

"Sounds like you have everything done, then," Mark surmised, genuinely impressed by the work.

Sarah leaned back in her chair and flicked a few bills off her desk as she wrung the warmth out of her mouth. Mark sat on the one clear spot of the book nest under the top bunk, half-listening to the guitar riffs wafting from down the hall. Surprisingly, the racket was only half bad.

"I have the climax and falling action, but those are the easy parts," she grumbled. "I can't explain how they got there."

"Sounds tricky," Mark said. "But it doesn't all have to be interesting. If you start with interesting and end with interesting, people expect the middle to drag a little."

"That's the reasoning behind every movie sequel they have on this planet."

Mark's chuckle tasted like stroganoff. Not for the first time that night did he wish he had a frosty mug of real whisky. He patted his sister on the shoulder.

"You'll figure it out. You figure most things out," he said.

Sarah recoiled at his touch and Mark yanked his hand back.

For a moment, nothing was said. He tried to keep his face passive and pretend he hadn't noticed. She looked back at him. The brief panic faded from her expression and a studying, scrupulous gaze replaced it.

"I'm sorry," he finally said. "I know I'm not the Mark you remember."

"You're not Mark at all."

"What? No, I am. I promise you."

"You're Agent Aftershock," Sarah stated. "Mark doesn't yell at me or at Gif. Mark only ever yells about his job and his life, if you annoy him about it."

Mark's eyebrows furrowed.

Without giving him time to retort, Sarah continued, turning back to her laptop. "Mark only yells when Dad pushes him to work harder at a real career. Or when Mom asks him what he wants for his future. Mark only yells when he cares enough."

"What?" he repeated, flustered. "You're saying I did not yell at you because I did not care for you?"

"You sound bizarrely archaic now, you know that?" Sarah commented. She still paid more attention to her laptop than to him. "And sure you cared…in your own way. But not really cared. Not life-and-death care. You didn't yell because our problems back in the military base weren't life-and-death to you. But the son of a famous researcher stuck just working on the brute squad? That was life-and-death to Mark. That's what Mark screams about."

She slowly swiveled around, head tilted down and her big, demanding eyes aimed at him. "So why is Agent Aftershock different, hmm? What's life and death for him?"

Mark stared at the far wall, trying to piece his thoughts together. He was failing.

"Hello?"

A gentle knock on the doorframe preceded Mother into the room. Her cheeks were a touch blotchy, but she carried herself smoothly.

"I see everyone's calmed down out here. Has anyone thought about calming down my youngest?" she asked.

"If he plays that '80's junk any louder, he'll take out a window. Or an eardrum," Sarah said with a dark look.

"That's not funny, young lady," Mother snapped.

"Of course not. None of this is funny. It's bizarre."

Gif's song ended, heralding a ceasefire. The ceasefire was immediately violated by a drum kit and a singer's insistence that he wasn't going to take "it" anymore, whatever "it" was.

Mother sighed and wiped her glasses on her sleeve. She mopped her forehead with the back of her hand as she scraped the topmost layer of books off the bed next to Aftershock and plopped down on the petrified deposits beneath. Aftershock coughed and wondered if he had imagined the eddies of dust that had just sprung out to play in the streaming beams of the overhead light.

"Why did you have to yell at him?" Mother asked him, her tone barely audible over the muffled guitar wails. "He looks up to you! I mean, God knows you should talk him out of it! But—"

"Don't," Mark barked. "Please, Mother. Just…don't say God's name like that around me, okay?"

"I thought you believed in that Crown Mind now," Sarah queried. "What do you care?"

"Different names, same fame, I think," Mark replied. He regretted even bringing it up, but the flippant use of His name sounded strange after years of tiptoeing around it. "And I'm not sold on it. Just, for now, say something else. Okay?"

"Linguistics, theology, they're not exactly the pressing matter here," Mother retorted. "Mark, please go apologize to your brother! And try it without yelling this time."

Sarah gave him a pitying look and turned her back on both of them as she fidgeted some more with her story. As usual, she wasn't about to fight any battle that she hadn't already been thrown into. It was her *modus operandi* in the family. Always had been.

Mark hugged Mother around the shoulders. "You're right. I am sorry. And I will tell him that. But I will yell, threaten, whatever it takes to keep him from following me down this path."

She glanced at his face and it seemed to take some of the wind out of her turbine. "You knew what red market work would look like. But he's innocent and doesn't realize—"

"It's not red market work!" Mark frowned. "It's…"

So many dead…Ruined a man's reputation. Made a deal with the devil. Loosed the elements…

He inhaled meaningfully, willing the oxygen into his brain faster to clean out the thoughts and wash away the guilt. Too much guilt for one life.

His face turned as unmoving as a Renati mask as he heard Mother and Sarah continuing to talk. The thoughts wouldn't leave him. The memories stung here, then there, like wasps going in for exploratory stings on a fat, slow target. Flashes from the caverns, fighting, clenched muscles, and sweat.

Don't think about it. Don't think about it.

Big mistake. Rookie mistake. In picturing what to avoid, he opened the floodgates.

That college kid, Stephen, bleeding and dying. Angry masks. So many masks. Scared and betrayed and angry and in it for blood now. His rifle, useless. Half-melted staff now. So many bearded, ugly masks. Poor

Jinnrose. Monjuan. Furious. Unyielding. Falling apart. Aftershock couldn't help. Agent Bier butchered. Ihcheldrin to blame. Masks to blame. Masks screaming at them. Saw blood. Saw sweat. Felt thunder below. Threats. Screams. Threats. Jinnrose threatened. Stephen dying. Poor Bier. Poor Jinnrose. Poor Stephen. Poor Aftershock.

Poor rebels.

Masked enemies on the ground now. Staff breaking teeth and shattering noses. Fists splintering ribs, driving out breath. Lightning everywhere. Smell of ozone. Watts and amperes and voltage hitting the ones that were too far away. Now hitting the ones in front of him too. Masks, broken, discarded. Monjuan down. Others down. All down now. Salt in sweat. Salt in tears. Orders given.

Some would stay down. Didn't take orders. Didn't hear. Never heard. Never got up. Why not? Why not? Wasn't I careful? Wasn't I careful, Agent Tepht? Taught to be careful. You taught me. I was careful, I was, I had to have been, so why aren't they getting back up, I did it right! I did everything right! Everything! I—Oh-God-save-them-they're-dead-those-are-all-dead-that's-why—Not moving again. Not getting up. Smoking hair. Singed, dirty clothes. They were broke and desperate. Not moving again. Not getting up. Broke now. Smoking now. Not moving—

His neck hurt. Someone was shaking him. Mother was calling, "Mark? Mark!"

"What's wrong with him?" Sarah screamed.

Did she? No. Sarah never screamed. But it sounded like Sarah, if Sarah were loud and shrieking. Now he could see Mother, huge eyes. She looked at her son and was tearing up again. And he was crying too. She looked so terrified.

He had been sobbing and shaking and saying everything out loud in a frenzied mumble, his anger and helplessness and regret wrenching his face into a hundred horrid expressions. All in front of his mother and sister.

He closed his eyes as brine flooded past them. He couldn't look into her face. Another failure. There's always one more person to destroy, isn't there?

Mark-who-was-Aftershock remembered the worst of the fight

on Mekrro. And in that moment, he felt he would for the rest of his life.

HE DIDN'T FEEL ANY BETTER. THEN AGAIN, HE HAD SOME BITTER BEER in him thanks to Dad, and he wasn't crying in the fetal position either, so he took that as an improvement. At least Gif had rocked out through the entire event and didn't know. The rest of the family hadn't been as lucky, and it had taken a while for anyone to calm down enough to make sense of it. Dad called it PTSD. Sarah called it "completely horrifying."

But as Aftershock had still been shaking, he had been the one who was all but smothered by sympathy—after explaining what he'd been hissing and spitting about. His part in the Mekrro War required more context than he expected and left him hoarse.

Now it was a relief to barge into the room of the brother he had yelled at earlier instead of sitting still for more psycho-therapy with his parents. The shudders in his muscles were fading. His breathing had settled.

Aftershock let himself into Gif's bedroom and grimaced through the roaring of the album that his brother had blasting. His knocks were either ignored or drowned out, so he yelled, "Oi! Gif!"

Sprawled out on his twin bed's red comforter, Gif jumped at the intrusion and stared at him with wild eyes. He relaxed after a moment.

"Expecting a ghost?" Aftershock said, his voice still raspy.

"Ghosts aren't half as pale as you," Gif quipped. He peered closer. "Hey, what happened? You look like *you* just saw a ghost."

Aftershock started to shrug. His muscles tensed, and he released them.

"I did. You never stop seeing them, you know."

Gif's old sweatpants caught and dragged an album off his bed as he put his guitar back on a wall hanger and turned down his stereo. He didn't offer Mark a seat, but there really wasn't a seat in the room besides the bed anyway.

The place was bigger than Sarah's room but emptier. His guitar gleamed from the wall now, a keyboard sat silently under the window, and shelves with various albums and cassettes were everywhere. A battered white skateboard jutted out from the closet like a shipwreck, but there wasn't a desk or a computer of any kind in the place.

"Never stop seeing what? Ghosts?" Gif's voice dropped to a murmur. "Can you see them, like, now? In this room? Can all agents see them?"

"Yes we can," Aftershock said. He forced eye contact and imagined it was just as uncomfortable for Gif as it was for him. "The instructors teach us how not to kill. Our training, our conditioning —it's extreme so that we can fight without killing. With abilities like mine, there's no excuse for it. I'm strong enough to avoid it.

"But it happens. It happened. And then you see the dead again and again and again. 'Cause no matter what you do now, it only took seconds to fry a living body into a burnt-out husk and let the ghost out."

Gif's mouth quirked to the side, as if in disappointment. "So it's just a metaphor."

"Not all metaphor. Memories can possess you, too."

"If you're trying to scare me, you should have stuck with your hissy fits," Gif said with a snort. "Ghosts. *Very scary*. You just don't want me to be as cool as you. Or, or what? You think I'd get a little power and turn dark? I'm a good guy, just like you."

"I know you are," Aftershock said. "That's—"

"Better, even!" Gif flung at him. "You had your lab job, you know. A life you could have worked with. Me? I always knew it was 'go big or go home.' I was made to do crazy stuff like that. A normal life would have killed me."

"A life in the Confederation can literally kill you," Aftershock returned. He leaned against the wall and slid down it so that he had to look up to meet his brother's gaze. "The war with the shifters almost had us. And a lot of people who survived the diversion teams or the Battle of L'hera lost parts of themselves they may never regrow."

"Look around you!" Gif threw his arms wide. He then frowned at the walls around him. "Figuratively. *Figuratively* look around at the galaxy. The war's over, bro! They need people to rebuild, people to watch over Ihcheldrin, sure. But Missionary Gainsong told me about new plans. You guys have ideas to help people, like heroes. One-on-one fights. Saving people from fires, beating up muggers, that jazz. That's me, dude!"

Aftershock sighed.

"A young guy, an agent, he just had a nervous breakdown," he stated, voice flat. "Months ago he made a choice to save his own skin by slaughtering some locals who carried knives and sticks, and now he can't live with his decision. Tell him about your jazzy plans."

Gif stopped.

He looked embarrassed as if Aftershock had just described a rendezvous he'd had with a girl in some crummy club. Then again, Aftershock supposed no guy wanted to hear that his brother was a killer and traumatized to boot. Okay, that was actually far worse than the girl analogy.

"For real? Why?" Gif mumbled.

"Because they were threatening me and some friends, and because I wasn't in control like I should have been. That's why," Aftershock snapped. "Yes, we all make mistakes, blah blah, thanks for that gem, Mother. But if you make the pledge and the mutation takes, then you'll have to live like I do now. You'll make horrible mistakes and have to live with them for centuries. And *those* mistakes won't mean a bad grade, or a broken nose, or—"

"I get it," Gif interrupted, though he didn't sound hurt. "I may not get it like you get it now, but I get it. Okay? That wasn't my question. I meant 'why,' like 'why can't you live with your decision?' I mean, sounds like you didn't have a choice. You or them. Fight or die. Right?"

Aftershock frowned up into the face of his brother. Outside the house, a dog barked from somewhere in the rain.

"I killed people."

"Did they kill people?"

"What?"

Gif rolled his eyes. "Did. They. Kill…"

"Okay, yes. No. Well, yes, but only indirectly, that we know of."

"Don't end on a preposition around J. R. R. Sarah," Gif said, mouth twitching.

"She misuses Latin and I have the recording to prove it, so she can't say anything," Mark returned. He tried for a smile and almost made it. "What was your point?"

"Were the people you killed bad guys? That's my point," Gif said. "And don't give me the 'there are no bad people, only bad actions' speech that Dad throws at us."

"What do you want me to say?" Aftershock felt his neck boiling beneath his undershirt. "That they deserved it? That I did the world a favor? We're not supposed to be talking about me anyway, just your brilliant plan to sneak off to join the Majhran Confederation."

"Which you are *totally* ruining!" Gif cried, leaping up and looking as if he'd just won the argument. "If you believed in me, like you really should, you know, Mom and Dad would be fine with it. And why are you ruining it for me? Because you think you're a horrible person now and none of it would have happened if you stayed home like you want me to do. Right, bro?"

Aftershock grunted.

"Right. So we're still on subject and you're the one trying to avoid it, ha!" Gif beamed. His smile faded, however. "No, look, sorry. This is apparently huge to you and I can't fix it. But maybe I can make you realize that you're acting nuts."

"Gee, really? That's it? Thank you, Gifford."

"Just don't waste your tears on those losers," Gif said. "Did they absolutely have to die? Guess not. But I know that my brother wouldn't kill a rat if he thought he could bag it and release it. What'd you tag them for? Looking suspicious? Loitering? Weird word, loiter. Fun to say. Loiter, loiter, loiter…" He shook himself and continued. "No, they got toasted because they were trying to do the same to you and other people."

The memories of the cavern had not hit him again yet, but he felt hollow. He knew he was in a bad way if his brother actually sounded serious about something. Still, he was being dismissed by a kid ten years younger.

"So I should just reason with my trauma? 'Go away, man, because I had my reasons!' Just like that?" Aftershock said, smirking slightly.

"Dude…" Gif rolled his eyes. "If you're going to tell your pet trauma anything, tell it to do the math."

The room was quiet except for the rain on the roof and the low tones of Bon Jovi over Gif's speakers. Gif looked him in the eye with something weirdly like maturity.

Gif continued. "Lives saved minus lives lost. And divide something by who was trying to unleash a shapeshifter Armageddon on who, too. That's gotta count for, what, a couple thousand trillion lives?"

Aftershock rubbed his brow with closed eyes. Fingering his grandfather's silver dollar in his pocket, he listened to the last strains of the old rock song drifting through the room. He finally looked up at his brother. Gif stared out at the rain, a mental distance clouding his expression.

"Thanks for trying. Seriously," Aftershock eventually said. "Where do we go from here, though?"

"If Mom has her say, to an early bedtime," Gif said. "Another reason to get out of this house."

For the first time (if Aftershock was honest with himself, at least), he thought about Gif's side of this thing. A dozen questions surfaced in Aftershock's head. How long had Gif been in touch with his missionary? What had been his morality test? Was he just being recruited because the Confederation had already successfully vetted Aftershock? Did Gif really believe in the Majhran religion of Crown Mind, or was he just in it for the adventure?

But what Aftershock asked was, "Do you really think you can commit the rest of your life? You get to the battlestations through a one-way door, you know."

Gif lay back on his bed and grinned.

"At least you realize that you can't make up my mind for me. Besides, I was born ready, dude."

Aftershock groaned. "If we work anywhere near each other, you have to stop using those stupid kid sayings. There was no 90s in interstellar space."

Gif sat up and started bouncing in place on the bed with his usual rambunctious energy. "Hey, that's right. It'll be like a family business there! Can you imagine the three of us standing in a doorway after blasting the door to pieces, smoke swirling every-where, fire behind us, like—"

"Three of us?" Aftershock asked.

"Uh, yeah. You, me, and Sarah. Didn't she tell you that she got recruited, too?"

Aftershock slammed his head against the wall behind him and groaned. "Our parents are going to kill me."

EON 1 - WAKE-UP CALL

When visitors came to the Ninth River-Garden, they came with recommendations. It was simply Policy. The mason Hu had presented the wax-pressed signet of Guardian Difex. So did a weaver named Ra. And just fifty or so years ago, Mi the husbandman had brought the signet of Guardian Drekihjrol.

So why did this Shepherd Ve not have any?

The late afternoon sun gleamed off the river behind the two cave bears wrestling at the bottom of the hill. Their grunts and playful growls punctuated Ca's thoughts for him.

"You understand I am happy to see you, goodman," Ca said, smiling at Ve. "Visitors are as rare and treasured as Du's vintage wines. But I must admit that I am unused to one outside Policy."

A handsome, pale-skinned fellow with startling blue eyes, Ve seemed quite at home on the shaggy carpet of zoysia grass. At Ca's proclamation, he threw back his head and laughed. His small teeth gleamed whiter than even his skin.

"I certainly apologize for throwing you off your horse here, Ca," he said. "Have you really never seen a stranger without recommendations?"

Ca shrugged, his own dark eyes trolling along the undulating horizon, lulled into sluggishness by the warm heartbeat of the sun. He stretched his lithe, dark body across the grass, yawning and shaking some debris from his long hair. "There used to be, a few hundred years back. But by the by, I cannot remember what their reasons were. Last time my family decided to indulge a pinch of wanderlust, Guardian Jhradilnon gave us his signet press. We still have it on the fireplace mantle."

Ve winked. "Does it not melt?"

A slow, rolling laugh boomed from Ca. Something about the visitor demanded joviality.

"Nay. We assumed that if the Majhran can keep the world together with just Policy, they can keep wax together through a little heat on winter nights," Ca answered.

Ve stood and stretched his back. Eyeing the pomegranate tree above them, he walked nearly all the way around it before scuttling up the thick trunk and picking one for himself. Patting the tree as if in thanks, he dropped back down next to Ca and went to work on the fruit with a narrow, shiny stone from his travel pack.

Ca leaned over, fascinated by the ease with which he split the pomegranate and discarded the inedible parts.

"Which bothers you more this far North?" Ve asked, inspecting a plump seed up close with a slow smile. "The winters or Policy?"

"I..." Ca trailed off, perplexed. "The— The winter chill does little more than give us and the garden a reason to nap through one month out of ten. But why would Policy bother us? Or anyone?"

The man wore an expression—such an expression!—as he replied.

"Ah-ha-ha, you mean to jest, goodman! Or perhaps you do not? Either way, it is a good one. For who has not chafed under a reign like my field comrades, the horses? And we humans are far superior to the animals that must bow to law. Policy and other such rules are to be obeyed, yes, but always resented! You have been walking through life with your eyes closed, goodman. You've been asleep. Have you never dreamt of flying freely?"

He laughed again as if he had made a jest of his own, and then requested a tour of the Ninth River-Garden. That crushed that conversation, and Ve did not bring it up again for the remainder of his visit.

For years afterward, Ca would reimagine the man's huge, reflective grin as it cut through his cheeks, the exultant wrinkles in his nose and under his eyes, and the teasing arch in his bristly eyebrows. He would recall the man's expression and wonder what it could have meant.

Eleven years later, Ca's family had a much-unexpected second visit from beyond the northern lands.

That winter was a mild one, yet still chilly enough to keep them around the fireplace smoldering in the heart of the garden vale. The green and red glow filled the stone structure that Guardian Jhradilnon had given to the family when they had migrated up to the Ninth River-Garden—an eternal flame, he had said, crafted by Crown Mind especially for them. Ca kept it in the center of the small, shaded vale where they slept and kept items of value on the carved mantle. The fire burned throughout the year, warming them when the sun rested and allowing them to bake bread during the day.

The morning of the visit, Ca was woken from a heavy slumber by Gi, his young son. Gi was about four decades old and did not yet reach his father's elbows. He had, however, put on some good weight and was more noticeable when he jumped on Ca.

"Oof!" Ca gasped as Gi drove the breath out of him. He rolled over and wheezed for a moment.

Fe ran over, snatching up her son in her strong arms. The love of his life, a short-haired, short-bodied beauty with sparkling eyes, held the other love of his life, the squirming mass of shaggy hair and baby pudge that giggled loudly.

"What have I told you about waking him up like that?" she

scolded, her eyes twinkling. She turned to Ca as he sat up. "Are you alright, love?"

"Ah." He smiled through his groan. "You know I only feign pain to hear you ask me that."

"Sorry, Fath," Gi squeaked, his eyes wide.

"I do miss the days when I could just take your wake-up calls in stride and wrestle you to the ground without blinking," Ca laughed.

"I am bigger now," Gi proclaimed, stretching his arms like Ca did for Fe. "Soon, I will wrestle you and win!"

Fe gave him a squeeze and set him down, guiding him towards the river. "Fetching water for morning juice would help you become even stronger."

"You just want me to fetch water." Gi's face scrunched up under his light, scraggly locks of hair.

"Yes, Gi."

"I will, Muth."

Gi flounced off, snatching the large clay water bowl before disappearing over the ridge that led down to the river.

"I wager the first gulp of juice that he goes straight to that nest of great turtles before remembering the water," Ca teased.

Fe turned towards him with a mischievous squint. "No, he loves his muth! I wager he visits the new panther cub first."

"Wagered," Ca agreed.

The two of them leaped up to the ridge in a few giant bounds. There they lay in the fern growth, peering down towards the river. The clutch of great turtle eggs was just in sight. Each glistening white orb was larger than Ca's fist. Gi was still hidden from the couple's position by the lower fruit trees.

Ca felt the slight warmth of his wife's arm pressed against his and he smiled. Out of the corner of his eye, he watched her lips puff out as she breathed, her striking emerald-colored eyes fixated on her son's progress to the river, her nostrils flaring slightly in the brittle morning air. She seemed oblivious to his stare.

His hand slipped into her curls of hair. Her dark lashes blinked once and then her eye was set squarely on her husband.

"What are you doing?" she asked, a slight smirk on her lips.

He thought a moment. "Would you believe that I just brushed a leaf off your lovely head?"

"No."

"Or that some of your curl left in the night and I am simply twirling it for you?"

Fe's eyebrow rose and she bared her teeth in a lioness's smile. "No, I do not."

Ca leaned toward her.

"Would you believe that I was just thanking Crown Mind that he saw fit to reward me with you?" he asked in a low growling tone.

"If you were not, I would suggest it."

Ca leaned closer to her. Then, without warning, she turned back towards the river and chuckled.

"His mother's son, he is indeed," she said.

With a whisper of a sigh, he followed her gaze. Gi wandered from tree to tree as if he had already forgotten his chore. He carried the bowl in front of him as he trotted.

Just then, the sun rose over a distant cloudscape, revealing the scene more clearly. Ca's sigh blustered into a triumphant laugh.

"And there he goes, his *father's* son, straight to call on his friends, the great turtles," he crooned.

Sure enough, Gi was petting the great turtle matriarch on her shell, which could be mistaken for a mossy boulder if not for her lumbering legs and scaly face. He then slid into a large depression in the dirt of the riverbank where the eggs warmed in the rising sun.

"I believe I would like my blackberry juice in the new clay mug," Ca trilled in his wife's ear.

"Perhaps tomorrow, my love," she said, running her finger through his own long locks. Both her voice and her gesture held too much confidence.

Ca frowned. "And why not this morning?"

"Look who Gi is introducing to the turtles."

Ca looked again. He grunted his disappointment as he saw the tiny black form of the panther cub roll out of the water pot and bump her nose against the nearest egg. The panther's parents came up behind Gi, keeping an eye on the situation and begging for attention from the boy. The mother great turtle ignored them all and went back to sleep in her shell.

"But he did go to the turtles before getting water," Ca protested weakly.

Fe just smiled at him.

"I am sorry, but at what are we looking?" asked a deep, smooth voice.

Both husband and wife jumped and turned. A tall bald man with orange-brown skin stood bent at the waist, his hands behind his back as he peered between the two of them towards the river. Bright colors stenciled over his body contoured muscle and highlighted the natural curves of his chest and legs. His face was full and his eyes large and expressive.

Behind him rose the monolithic body of a Guardian. Its skin glowed like the winter moon and its eyes cast shadows on anything it watched. The Guardian stood as still as a mountain, filling the vale with its thrumming presence. Huge fingers of gleaming crystals spread from its back like a bird's wings. Like a human, and yet not. A living being, yet not.

"You have a beautiful son, Gardeners Ca and Fe," said the man. "He appears to have a future in shepherding."

Ca and his wife stood and bowed in respect. Taking in a bowlful of breath, he found his voice.

"Thank you, goodman. Forgive our surprise, but we were not expecting visitation again for several years, at least. Do you have recommendations?"

The man laughed and stood to his full height. "Perhaps. Guardian Mehan?" he said, turning towards the giant being.

The guardian focused its luminescent gaze over the couple. Ca squinted.

"Peace, Ca. Peace, Fe. We do not require food, shelter, or teaching from you," Guardian Mehan rumbled. "We three journey simply to witness the world that Crown Mind provides us."

"And to visit family," cried yet another new voice.

A woman with hair down to her calves glided over to stand by the man from the foliage nearby. She held a freshly filled jug of water.

"Greaten-five-father Az?" Fe asked, her smile brightening as she recognized the couple. She slung her arms around the man, an embrace he heartily returned.

"And Zi," added Ca. He bowed respectfully to the stately woman. She scoffed and strode the distance between them in a breath's time, hugging him as well.

"You know I hate formality, child," Zi chastised. "But you did remember not to add all the greatens before my name, and I thank you." Her stern expression dissolved in a soft smile.

As the four exchanged embraces and bows, Fe spoke.

"The father and mother of humanity, visiting us! You ask for nothing, but Gi will be back with the water soon and then you must try this year's blackberry juices. They have been remarkable!"

Guardian Mehan shifted its ponderous mass from foot to foot. "We had hoped to visit the Silver North Cathedral before snowfall."

To Ca's shock, Az waved off the guardian's comment and smiled.

"Nay, we have time for both worship and blackberries in our travels, Mehan. You worry overmuch, which is good and proper but unnecessary today."

Guardian Mehan nodded, its face unmoved. Bits of daylight in its stretching wings sent a waterfall of color across the ground.

"Child, have you considered exchanging fruits while yours have this 'remarkable' year?" Zi asked Fe, changing the subject with a sharp look at Az. "My husband and I have noted that many beautiful gardens in First Reach have great success in diversifying through exchanges with each other. I personally try to collect whatever I can for the First Central Garden. Now, I already have giant blackberries, sweet blackberries, and blackberries that bake well into bread, but I must try yours if we are to dine with you this morning."

She glanced deferentially towards Guardian Mehan, who answered by glancing around and then sitting back onto the grass of the vale with a thump that Ca could feel through his heels.

"Splendid!" cried Az. He then dropped a hand onto his great-great-great-great-great grandson's shoulder and led Ca towards the orchards. "Now, gardener to gardener, you must show me the famed Ninth River-Garden. I have heard stories from other northern men that they would give your family a few extra decades of life for a tub of your ecthagrates and pomegranates."

Fe set about the task of prying stories of First Reach from Az's wife, and Guardian Mehan continued to sit impassively, so Ca allowed himself a flare of pride as they left. The words were high praise coming from the original gardener.

Their stroll took them through the citrus orchards, where they enjoyed the warmth of the steam vents that opened between the trees during cold months. Trees were shorter here. The morning sun crept through the green, swaying leaves to fall amongst the breeze-tossed tuffs of ramgrass. The lemons, grapefruits, and limes were flowering, but not producing at the moment. The oranges were more prolific, and the two men sampled one of the larger fruits as they walked.

A family of parrots called noisily from the orange trees. Occasionally, one of the jewel-toned birds would dive down to shake itself vigorously in a steam blast. They and many of the other birds preferred the citrus orchards during the chillier months.

One of the parrots, a fowl with a headdress of glistening green feathers, swooped low and landed on Az's head. Gi had named the bird Turtle after its bright river-colored plumage, or so Ca assumed.

Turtle hopped about the father-of-all's hairless dome, seeking purchase on the smooth, copper surface.

As she gave up and settled on Az's shoulder, Ca held his breath to avoid laughing at his ancestor.

Az had no such reservations and chuckled, tickling Turtle's head feathers. He asked, "This flier seems particularly familiar with us. Does it have a name?"

"My son calls her Turtle. She plays hide-the-berry with him during the summer days. Do not let her near your ears, though, or she shall nibble," Ca replied, inspecting a lime blossom and flexing the branch to show it to him.

"She is a sweet thing," Az acknowledged. He held out his wrist and Turtle jumped to roost there. "Some fliers are bold and friendly, like your Turtle. Others appreciate solitude and they take counsel only with their mate. And yet others once associated with us humans, but now take counsel with whom we could not guess. Perhaps one must be a flier to truly be close to the Flier? Perhaps it is not for us to know such answers."

Ca thought for a moment about that, but in vain. He admitted, "You speak of mysteries to me, Greaten-five-father Az. Of what flier do you speak?"

Az grew silent and his eyes widened, allowing light to seep into the mournful corners of his mind. Dimness seemed to leak out between the dark lashes as the ancient man stared up at the sky, although whether the flickering shadows were fleeing from the encroaching sunshine or testing new teeth out in the world of day and night, Ca could not tell. The petulance that had crept up on Az held no answers for him.

The conversation severed, the two walked side-by-side in silence among the steam vents. Ca paused twice to warm himself in one of the damp, earthy-scented blasts. During the second such break, Az leaned into an adjoining geyser as well. He showed little enjoyment in it, however, and his spirit clearly wandered elsewhere.

As they stepped out of the citrus groves, Ca led them through more dense underbrush around berry bushes burdened low with fruit and tall, preening trees that threw up a canopy against the elements far above their heads.

Ca preferred these forested paths of the Ninth River-Garden. As much as he loved the cultured orchards and open fields, the woods sheltered him and Fe and Gi more intimately, as if Crown Mind had cultivated those trees specifically to keep them nestled away from the enormity of the world. The boughs cast everything in a starry twilight. Tongue-entrancing fruit grew everywhere. Fliers perched and nested and performed acrobatics just for fun, and countless beasts of the ground and the trees filled the paths with a presence that spat upon the very idea of loneliness.

In such winsome, winding corners of his home did Ca spend his days. Gi would often join him and learn about the animals and plant life that teemed in the garden. Their family would take what they needed for the day from the world. And in return, they would study and tease and play with it, wrenching out life from the days and the nights as they wrenched Fe's blackberry juice from the fruits of Crown Mind's labors.

He wondered how things could possibly be better in the First Central Garden. They surely *were* better, of course, because that blessed home was the original, the grand plan, the field upon which Crown Mind touched the Earth.

But Ca had difficulty imagining anything more nearly perfect than the Ninth River-Garden.

As Greaten-five father Az bent to inspect a tiny sugar maple, he broke the silence. "When I visit places, people ask about Crown Mind. 'What is he like,' 'does he ever mention me' or 'does he ask about my home,' and most often, 'has he planned anything new?' Curiosity among the created is natural, but I often cannot help but long to hear questions about my life, my wife, or my garden. Why not ask the guardians about Crown Mind? It is they who serve him —oh, we all do, but the guardians care for nothing more than Crown Mind's will. Whereas I and the rest of humankind exist to care for the creation."

Ca remained silent. Az spoke like a man who sought to straighten jumbled thoughts rather than initiate a conversation. Sure enough, Az continued to talk to the sugar maple without prompting.

"And yet during this trip of ours in these past years, the questions have changed. The people no longer ask after Crown Mind. They finally show pride in their gardens, their pastures, their lakes. Now people want to display their own knowledge and accomplishments and they ask me how they could further improve their craft and their lives.

"Yet you have asked me nothing, goodman. May I ask why?"

Ca turned to see Az standing at his full height again, watching him. Ca shooed away the long lizard he had been tempting with berries and cleared his throat.

He offered a little bow.

"I apologize for not making better conversation," he said. "I am a simple gardener, and our plot is a quiet one this far north. We receive visitors only once every few decades, so we have become used to the solitude. And now I have had two uncommon guests in a short time! I am afraid that I have little insight to offer unless it is about my wife, my son, or my life here in my garden."

Az grunted. "Ah. 'Don't look away when your life is right here'...Interesting. And apology denied: I was commenting on it as I would the weather, goodman, not chastising you for a lack of hospitality."

The trees parted ahead of them on the edge of the garden. They stepped out to see the vast southern plains before them and the river winding away to the west. Ca took the lead and they walked along the garden's rim towards the river.

He laughed ruefully, feeling foolish. Guardian Jhradilnon made Crown Mind's wishes abundantly clear concerning admiration that verged on worship. It was not to be spent on anything they could see or touch, be it beast or statue or fellow man. But Az was, well, Az. He was the original human. A bow had seemed respectful.

"And right now, you are quoting the guardians' rotes of

worship to yourself, are you not?" Az inquired with a small smile. "For all the countless years I have walked the step of life, I still find myself tripping over my own clumsy feet. It is all right. We are only human. Immovability and stone-like steadfastness are best left to the guardians."

"I do not envy them their task," Ca replied. "But come, let us speak of things less lofty and more proper for a humble gardener."

"Indeed!" Az cried, a full smile shining through his coppery face. "Let us speak of berries and turtles and birds named as such for a while! My last few visits have been at the homes of herdsmen and potters. It will do my gardener's heart good to hear of more familiar trials and triumphs. Come. I shall wash the road off in the river as we discuss our trade."

THE SUN BURNED HIGH IN THE HEAVENS BY THE TIME THE MEN returned to the hollow for midday meal. Az still chuckled at Ca's stories as they spotted their wives. Little Gi ran up to them and tackled Ca, who obliged him by falling over and feigning defeat at his son's hand. Gi giggled at his victory but squealed a moment later as Az snatched him up in one hand and swung him in a wide arc up onto his broad shoulder.

"I am tall, Fath! I am tall!" Gi crooned.

"And I am small because you knocked me to the ground," Ca retorted, feigning a pout.

Zi sashayed over, her waterfall hair splashing everywhere with each step. Fe eyed the mother-of-all as if contemplating adopting her grooming habits. Unconcerned, Zi kissed her husband on his stenciled chest and smiled slowly as she glanced up at the boy.

"I do miss having children that age," she said with a humming sigh. "They are so lively and sweet."

"Did Crown Mind ask you not to have any more?" Fe asked.

"Nay, child," Zi replied. "Although the guardians do remind us to increase in measured numbers, as the beast and bird do. Nay, we have not heard an edict, a warning, or so much as a conversational word from Crown Mind since before our last tour of the world."

What? Ca realized his mouth was hanging open like his wife's and he shut it.

Az tromped over to where Ca and Fe prepared the meal of fruit and tubers near the fireplace, waddling from leg to leg so as to swing Gi back and forth more. He was rewarded by a fit of giggling and two arms wrapped around his forehead for support.

The flame in the stone fireplace crackled and hissed pleasantly. A row of the trimmed tubers sizzled on a stone slab that glowed crimson over the flame. The smell of the spicy dish brought a small smile stuffed wide with memories to Ca. But Az's face had lost its impish smirk, and now he gently lowered Gi to the ground, ignoring the protests.

"Crown Mind has not abandoned us," he rumbled, "but he no longer seems to take interest in us like he once did, either. I—I! the eldest of man!—have only rarely seen the Great One. And even on those blessed days, he walks in on the twilight and vanishes again with the dusk. Where he lives and to what he plies his trade mystifies Zi and me alike."

"He's gone?" Ca demanded. "Surely the Great One does not simply disappear."

"Have you ever met Crown Mind, Ca? Fe?" Zi asked, lifting an angular eyebrow with practiced ease.

"Yes, but only when I was young," Fe answered. "When I still lived with my parents in the Golden Lanes, he visited me. I had never seen something look so magnificent and could barely talk to him, but he was kind and quiet and said how much he cared about me."

Ca nodded. "I had a similar experience when I first arrived from the Eastnears. He showed me every corner and every cranny of the Ninth River-Garden and told me how much every part of it meant to him, and how I should treat the beasts, how to encourage the fruit-bearers to prosper, and other such things."

His voice softened as he remembered the sheer hugeness of

Crown Mind. Not even the northern mountains had a presence like the Great One. These days, he could not recall exactly in what form Crown Mind had appeared, but he seemed to remember something more human than beast, fish, or bird. And there had been bright silver light that had filled everything nearby.

He caught Az watching him reminisce. His greaten-five-father nodded as if he could read his thoughts and agreed with the raw feelings he found.

Zi took a sip of her blackberry juice. "You have seen his glory only once. Have you ever felt abandoned by him?" As they shook their heads, she pursed her lips. "Just so. And why not? Because when one sees a river or a hill, one can remember and be sure it is still there. Even if millennia pass, it remains there, out of sight."

"Even rivers can change course, and hills crumble and shift," Fe countered.

"Very true," Zi said with a small smile. "But what is a river but moving water? What is a hill but earth and stone? Even through change, they will exist somewhere in some form until the end of creation, and who is to say that you will not, in one midmorning stroll in some future year, find the same dirt rising again as a hill? Or see the water you once bathed in, now a river returned to its old course?"

Gi lost interest in the big-people conversation and wandered towards the downs in the north garden. Ca watched as he spotted a small white hare and sprinted after it into the bushes. The father felt a little jealous. Lofty ideas were wasted words unless one acted on them, he felt.

Fe continued to question the matron, and Az and Ca sat back and ate as they watched their quicker-witted counterparts duel.

"Your metaphors are as pretty as a moonflower, Zi, but not as perfect as one. Crown Mind has thoughts and travels under his own volition, does he not? He is more like a human than like a hill or a river. Choice is available to him. He *could* choose to abandon us, unlike a feature of the lands."

"Child, do not presume that he is like us simply because he is not a river or a hill," Zi warned. "He is not a mountain, a bird, or a human. He is Crown Mind. We share some characteristics with him, but he is as far beyond us as we are beyond that red squirrel that is eating your apples."

Ca turned. So it was.

Az roared with laughter as Ca took a diving leap to stop the apple-snatcher. He missed by a mile, and the red squirrel was staring at him from a high branch of a nearby larch by the time that he had landed, pulled himself back up, and brushed the dirt out of his face. Fe smiled down at him and he fought the urge to stick out his tongue at his wife.

"And that was a perfect metaphor for how we humans react to life," Zi said with a straight face. "We see a bit of how things are, we take a flying leap in our assumptions, and we generally receive a faceful of dust for our troubles."

"I do not believe I like your metaphors either, greaten-five-mother," Ca said.

This time Zi beamed, her shoulders shivering in silent laughter.

"She is right, you know," Az said, wiping sprinkles of mirth from his eyes. "When I get an idea fixed in my head, even the guardians rarely convince me I am wrong. Only Crown Mind or my own foolish mistakes slapping me in the face do that. It is not any fault of ours, but simply how we must treat our knowledge of the world as humans. If we doubted everything we know, we would be too paralyzed to do more than debate and question."

"Not that all doubt is bad," Zi augmented. "Because, again, the faceful of dirt."

"Right," Ca said through a grunt. "Speaking of which, I find myself with a sudden need to wash. Does anyone need more drinking water?"

A chorus of no's met him, so he tromped off to the river, sans water pot. The sounds of the garden purred in his ears. He welcomed the familiar murmur of the land and its inhabitants as a reprieve from the talk. Now he had time to make sense of his thoughts.

The river water was cool but not cold, a flash of lightning in his body that brought life and revival in an instant. His teeth chattered for a moment and he had to laugh at the funny sound.

A stuttering giggle erupted from a massive fern that grew near the tree line, a stone's throw away.

"Come out, fern," Ca called. "I am certain you need a bath, too."

"No!" the fern squealed. "Ferns like dirt better!"

Ca swallowed his smile and struggled to adopt a look of serene wisdom. "Ah, but ferns are garden plants, and all of our garden plants like water."

The fern suddenly went quiet. With two quick steps, Ca appeared behind it and snatched up his son.

Gi squealed, a wriggling mass of leaves. Apparently, he had decided to play Ambush the Bunnies again and then tried for a bigger target. Lithe in his youth, he managed to squirt out of Ca's grip and bound down the river–bank with a string of excited hollers.

With his best bear roar, Ca charged after him. He lagged behind but made sure to look like he was trying, with straining arms and exaggerated steps.

Gi laughed as raucously as Turtle the parrot. Splashing himself with mud at every jump, he quickly changed from fern to pondweed. He glanced over his shoulder and beamed at his father. The sun on his boy's smooth, straight teeth bounced around Ca's insides, lightening each step so that he thought he could run forever.

Then the little escaped weed leaped on top of the great turtle matriarch, crying, "Swim, swim, swim, Boulder! He is going to catch us!"

The great turtle glanced up to stare at the man on her back and then jumped into action. She tucked into her shell and left Gi out in the cold.

"Aw" was as far as Gi got before Ca executed a diving tackle that took both of them nearly to the middle of the river. Gi whooped. Ca turned so as to absorb the jolt of the landing.

They hit the water and sunk a moment before flailing to the surface. Ca played with Gi, enjoying the sounds and sights and smells of the bit of river that Crown Mind had entrusted to his family.

THE TWO SPLASHED EACH OTHER WITHOUT MERCY UNTIL THEY WERE both glistening, clean, and a tad waterlogged. Then, Ca floated on his back with a gut full of pent-up air. Gi sat on top and rowed them back to the great turtle nest with a scrap of drifting wood that he had found and now clung to happily.

Ca watched the clouds float past, blinking out flecks of water splashed into his eyes. The heavens soared overhead: the final expanse that man had not yet explored. Crown Mind had told them all to spread over the heavens and the Earth. And they had, almost. Men lived on the ground, under the ground, and there were even stories that the magnificent seas were being tamed with help from the Majhran guardians. The mandate to improve and enjoy the world was not far from the heart of Policy. Crown Mind had ordained it.

He loved his garden, but Ca thought he might not mind being one of the men picked to first explore the heavens. Living up there was so far beyond his comprehension that it had to be wondrous.

His head bumped into the beach. Gi had rowed them faster than he had expected. Ca looked up and witnessed a unique view of Zi, who stood right overhead. He stood up as soon as his son had scampered off his chest and offered a small bow.

"Need a drink?" he asked, gesturing widely to the cool, gently tossing river.

A smile crawled up Zi's face.

"No, thank you, Ca. You have a lovely garden and I simply hoped you would show me more of it. I never turn down the chance to learn," she replied.

"Ah, indeed. 'Grow knowledge, grow wisdom,' I believe some

say," Ca replied. He ignored the mumble of discomfort from his stomach. Food could wait. Visitors were rare.

"I do not believe that is a phrase," she answered with a slight lift of her nose and eyebrows. Then she glanced at Ca and changed the tilt of her face to a more demure angle. "Perhaps it should be, though. I do believe I enjoy the sound of it."

Ca smiled and nodded towards her, surprised that the mother-of-all approved. To himself, he wondered if he had not accidentally just made up that phrase on his own. He would have to remember it.

"In which part of the garden were you interested?" he asked.

"Although Az cares most for the fruit easily reached, I have always been fascinated by the lower side of the garden," Zi said, walking north along the riverbank. "It is the roots, the grasses, the warm water flowing through deep culverts that nourishes the great trees and allows them to pass their seeds back to us. The complexity of our world is marvelous, yes?"

With no response to the flowy words, Ca remained silent and let Zi lead the way. He glanced around to snatch up Gi and bring him with them, but his son had found a newborn rabbit nestled in a ginkgo tree's roots and gently caressed the fragile creature. Boy and beastie disappeared behind a curve in the river a moment later as Ca and Zi continued.

Zi, meanwhile, gently pulled on Ca's arm until he walked beside her, and then released her hold on him.

"I could show you the berry brambles if you wish," Ca suggested. "Or the apples. We have some spring-fed irrigation trickling through that entire area. The springs are one reason the river is so wide here."

Zi smiled amicably and agreed. She listened with rapt attention as he rambled through his descriptions of the plots and the techniques they had learned to maximize the growth and fruitfulness of the various plants in them. Sometimes he would feel that he was blabbering and faltered. But she would nod at him to continue, and he would launch into another story about the berries or a tale of their orchard misadventures.

She only occasionally spoke up, and then only to ask a question.

Finally, Ca found himself out of breath as they climbed the hill and found themselves winding between the berry tangle and the mostly wild stand of apples. He sat down and leaned against an old apple tree with drooping branches, giving him a small bower near the path. Only some curious squirrels broke the silence, shaking leaves and branches as they scurried nearby.

"I believe I talked too much," Ca apologized between breaths. "I do wish the apples were blooming now so we could inspect them."

Zi stood quite close, so that Ca had to look up her torso to make eye contact. For the first time, he noticed that Zi's curtain of hair was not the only part of her more voluminous than his wife's.

Unexpectedly, Zi laughed. It was a soft sound, more like water than Az's earthen chuckles or Fe's breezy giggles.

"Like my husband, you are overly interested in hanging fruits," she accused with a sly smile. She sat down nearby and crossed her muscular legs.

"We could look at the streams and soil instead," Ca offered, searching for what he had missed in her comment.

Zi shook her head slightly. "Guardian Mehan will wish us to leave soon, and the Majhran are always correct. I wish I had the time to explore every corner of every garden in this world. But, alas, our own garden is ours by Policy and we must return before long to tend to it. I suppose it is enough to meet the fascinating children of our children's children."

At the mention of ancestry, Ca felt a strange twinge of disappointment. He felt as if his relation to this remarkable gardener somehow diminished...things. The feeling was fleeting and impossible to grasp, though.

"I do hope you will return soon," Ca found himself saying. He placed a hand on her warm knee. "You are a legendary gardener and make an equally fine visitor."

"You are as sweet as your blackberries. But Policy is Policy, and the First Central Garden will need attention for a good many years after we return," she answered, swirling a long finger over the gnarled knee of the tree's roots.

"Do you—do you ever resent Policy for restricting your travel?" Ca's curiosity faded to regret, and he shut his mouth.

Zi looked up, her mouth startled into a cute circle. "'Resent Policy'…"

The idea was obviously beyond her, but that she had not questioned it or dismissed it immediately sent slivers of cold into Ca's skin. Again, the sensation was fleeting.

"Please put a gibbering gardener's query out of your ears, goodwife," Ca pleaded. He glanced down and realized he was still holding her knee. He quickly pulled away. "The idea was simply something I heard from our last visitor."

"Fascinating!" Zi exclaimed. "Who was this visitor? Did the visitor know a Man who did feel bitter about Crown Mind's law and orders?"

"He was an odd man named Ve, I believe. Ve had a good many ideas about it, so many that I wondered if he himself disliked Policy," Ca squinted his eyes as he recalled the discussion. "He believed that everyone hates Policy, but does not like to admit it. Asked me if I ever thought about escaping from myself, said I was asleep and must wake up. As I said: he was very odd."

Zi frowned in thought and Ca respected several long moments of silence. The squirrels seemed to have retreated to the taller trees nearer the center of the Ninth River-Garden, leaving the tense murmurs of the high winds through the apples to their ears. The sun shone less brightly as it slowly abandoned them. Its warmth, however, was stronger than ever.

Zi spoke.

"In every garden, every pasture, every home in which man resides is a fireplace, such as yours. In each fireplace is an eternal flame, such as yours. Ours in the First Central Garden is grander than the others. It was the first, and it burns with bright golden flame from Crown Mind's own mouth.

"I myself was there when Crown Mind lit the fire. He told us that it was a small tool inside the fireplace that would give us heat and let us cook our food. But he also said that, should the flame ever be removed from the fireplace, it could be much more powerful and much more dangerous. He said that trust was at the heart of Policy and trust was in his heart as well. We should never remove the flame. That was his decree."

"Why not?" Ca asked. He was unsure what the point of the story was, but was fascinated by the thought of a more powerful flame. "Did he not entrust it to you? Surely you and Az could use it safely."

"He entrusted us with the safety of our garden, and because of that, we would not do anything that could bring our plants and animals to harm," Zi answered. "Besides, a test of trust is no test if restraint is unwarranted. But Crown Mind gave us that single order for the sake of giving us an order, with no other real consequences. That way, defiance is a reasonable option. Without the option to defy him, we cannot choose to obey. I believe he likes knowing we *choose* to obey…"

"I understand, Zi. You should make your own choices."

"But your visitor Ve could be correct," she concurred after a moment. "Resentment is a strong word. But I admit that when it comes to the flame, I might bring myself to question Policy. After all, Crown Mind also told us to hold dominion over the world. And the flame is in the world… Perhaps I have misjudged the test."

She shook her head hard, wincing. Hair whipped about the bower. "I do not know what to think. Perhaps I will find this Ve and speak with him myself. Then I can put this question to rest."

"Only you can make it right," Ca agreed. "Use your own good judgment."

At that, Zi smiled. Really and truly smiled.

Relieved to be out of the uncomfortable situation, Ca nodded and frowned to appear sagacious. He was not simple-minded but did prefer to dwell on the physical world. The hypothetical, the spiritual, they were best left to the elder men. Giants like Az and Zi had the wisdom to consider such thoughts.

Meanwhile, he would consider root and leaf, great turtles and tasty tubers.

As if by an unspoken command, he and Zi stood. Ca had to duck slightly to avoid knocking his head against the apple branches.

"I must go. My family's journey shall continue," Zi said. "But thank you for allowing us this long rest in your lovely home. Crown Mind has smiled upon you."

She took a step closer. "And so do I, Ca. Thank you for expanding my mind."

They embraced closely. Then Ca found his and Zi's lips pressed tightly against each other's. The farewell felt oddly comfortable— more so than normal. When they finally separated, Ca immediately went about remembering it in detail so as not to lose it to long-term forgetfulness.

The sensation was strange, but wasn't every human family with every other human? He kissed his wife as family. Surely this was no different. This was fine.

Zi turned away, her strong features shadowed with what Ca could only assume was the same dusky uncertainty that he had felt. But the moment passed.

So did the day, and he and his wife and son waved farewell to their two esteemed visitors.

So did the months, and the plants and animals of the garden continued to grow at their glacial rate.

So did the year. Year, but not years. Before singular could pass into plural, a night came when the flame had been extinguished.

CA AWOKE WITH A START AS A CHILL SPIKED THROUGH HALF-WRITTEN dreams of green fields and playing children's games with dragons. Fe stirred beside him, rolling out from under the thin woven blanket they had just received from Guardian Jhradilnon.

He did not at first understand why the air seemed colder. The night was full and inky around them, but it was not even winter anymore. At this time of year, the garden was bustling underneath the warm bloom of spring. Yet, that was not so tonight.

"The fireplace is out," Fe whispered.

Ca swung around to follow her gaze. She was right. The stones were cold and as dark as the rest of their vale.

He cautiously slid his hand into the hole but felt a chilly bite of heatless rock rather than the gentleness that the eternal flame had once given. He leaped to his feet and listened.

"The night beasts are silent," he mumbled. "Why? Let me check the apple groves, love. Perhaps they are gorging themselves there."

"What of the fire?"

"We can ask Guardian Jhradilnon in the morning. Would you mind checking the southern citrus groves for the animals while I walk north?"

Fe inclined her head, looking regal in the faint silvery rays of starlight that seeped through the foliage above their heads. He fought off the urge to throw her to the ground and enjoy the strangeness of the night.

"I will," she said, smirking as she read his expression. She cocked her hip and his breath caught. But then she frowned. "I will also look for our child there, love."

Ca glanced around, embarrassed that Fe had noticed Gi's absence first. He shrugged and nodded.

They quickly parted ways, fading into the trees. Ca had just made it to the top of the hill where the apples and blackberries grew, when he met an impossible sight. Frost—silvery fingers of beautiful ruin—lay over all but the nearest apple trees. The vast majority of the orchard stood black and stunted under the star-streaked canopy.

Ca waited there for something he could not quite give voice to. But there was no answer as he rocked back and forth on his toes. No explanation came from the Earth or the greenness left on it.

A crack sounded as a branch fell, and Ca jumped. The branch

had fallen off a tree very nearby, one that had still been green a moment ago but now was black and frozen like the rest. And then a bitter wind danced by, slamming into his bare skin. The cold was creeping closer. The decay was actually advancing like an animal.

From the hill, he had a view over the rest of the Ninth River-Garden to the far south lands. They did not seem as icy and black as the world to the north did now. Yes, the south held safety and warmth.

But he squinted. A faint glow like the dawn throbbed at the horizon. Unless the sun now rose in the south, there was an odd new light in the world. It must be massive to be visible from so far away. A thick black cloud slowly grew over the area, just barely visible in the unusual glow.

Well, a glow meant fire. Fire meant heat. Heat was life and happiness.

He ran back towards his vale at the heart of the garden. Several times he noticed a bird or nocturnal beast, but they fled when they saw him.

When he met Fe, she was in tears. "I cannot find Gi. And Turtle would not land on my shoulder like she used to! Ca, what happened to the fireplace? What happened to the animals?"

"I do not know," he answered tightly. Why did she expect him to have the answers? "But we have another issue. Winter has returned without mercy to the north. The apples are probably all lost now, and the blackberries will be soon. By Crown's decree… The whole garden may soon be lost to the ice. We need to leave."

"Leave? We never leave unless we have somewhere to go!" Fe said. She wiped her eyes.

"Then…then…then we will go to the home of Ra the weaver. He does not live far from here, and he left us an open invitation when he visited last!"

Fe snatched the wax signet of their Majhran guardian from the lifeless fireplace. But a sudden burr of red flared in Ca's head, and he snatched it from her, throwing it to the ground.

"Policy is dead until my entire garden is alive again," he snapped. "Jhradilnon can give his permission later."

Fe curled her lip at him, nursing her hand as if Ca had bitten it. "Fine. But we will not leave without my son."

They stared at each other for a moment, the heat in their expressions fading. Simultaneously, they said, "The turtles."

They ran down the long slope to the river, the breeze around them growing less and less forgiving. Ca wondered about finding some way to cover up, soon. A covering like the beasts had with their fur. He regretted not bringing the blanket.

Sure enough, they saw Gi's small form hunched over in the nest, his back to them. He seemed to be working something in his hands. As they approached, they saw him throw back his head, holding something round to his lips.

"Gi, what are you doing awake?" Fe asked softly.

He jerked around with a strange glint in his eye as if he were embarrassed...or frightened. Then he pouted.

"The flame was gone and I was ready to be awake," he offered.

"Well, we are going visiting, Gi. We will visit that nice weaver who visited us. Does that sound good?" Ca asked, moving closer. He wanted to see what Gi had been doing with the rock in his hand. Had he crafted a whistle of some sort?

"Okay, Fath," Gi said with a lopsided grin. Something stained his teeth. "I want to finish eating first, though."

Eating?

"Ca..." Fe hissed.

He leaned forward. The mother great turtle was still nowhere in sight. Neither was the father. But half a dozen eggs were smashed. Emptied. Devoured like fruit. Nothing would ever hatch from them.

"They taste good, Fath!" Gi insisted, holding up another two eggs. He handed them to his motionless parents. "You never said turtles hid food in here."

Ca thought of several things to say, but no words trickled up his throat.

Fe put a hand on his shoulder. "We do need to keep up our strength if we have a long journey ahead of us. Just this once, we should try it."

"If you find a yucky slimy thing in yours, throw it away and get another one," Gi cautioned.

With a nod, Fe accepted an egg.

Ca thought for a moment. Then he followed. It was delicious.

EON 2 - GET OUT ALIVE

A man called Arssen awoke on his towel on the floor, still almost able to touch his wife and child. But the dream had vanished into the nether, unreachable, and his life smothered him again.

The sun rose on a land of exquisite carnage outside the small, abandoned house. The world was on fire, but the gaze of a young sun blunted the spears of flames and cast even the husks of the burnt-out neighborhood into glistening art. Not that they couldn't still smell the acrid fumes of the wreckage in their nostrils. Not that they weren't still hit with occasional quaking, huddled in the cellar and listening for monsters. But even Arssen had to admit it was beautiful.

Salik of Wold, Vanders and her family, and Arssen and his mother were the last ones in their little group. The others had parted ways back at the crossroads. The original group's leader had insisted that the highland with its quarries and vistas would provide more protection than the fields. Salik had disagreed. He said the Gray Ones held the plateaus of the highland and would pick them off one by one before they ever reached the security of the East lands. So Vanders' and Arssen's families had followed Salik to the south.

The south: where they had found more of the Possessed, more foaming mad animals, and what the war had left of a once sprawling collection of neighborhoods just north of Melimard. Like so many other towns that had teemed with people before the last great battle, the city of Melimard itself was completely unapproachable.

"We shouldn't have gotten this close," Vanders' son, Marx insisted. He was still short, not having hit his growth spurt yet, but his legs and arms were starting the slow trip through adolescence ahead of his torso, making him lanky. The boy's nose seemed permanently wrinkled into a sneer.

Arssen's mother sniffed, her own wrinkles deepening in annoyance as if to irrigate skin baked red by months of travel. "Do you really think repeating yourself makes you sound smarter?"

"Please," Arssen said, ducking his head at her audacity. "Let the boy complain if he wants."

"Ursa's right, honey," Vanders chastised Marx. "Your father and I trust Salik to help us all reach the East lands, so trust us."

Vanders frowned with tired eyes at her son. Although she and her husband John were Arssen's age, she always sided with his demanding, griping mother. Apparently, the two women were friends now. As if someone like his mother could have friends.

"I told you, I heard a gray one out there!" Marx hissed, his squinty eyes flickering about a cracked hole in the foundation. "Melimard's streets are crawling with them. My friend Abram said everyone knows it."

John gently pulled his son back and swung shut the strip of heavy oilcloth they had pinned over the hole. His brown bangs dripped sweat into his ruddy face. "Don't let the heat in, please. Salik will be back soon."

Grumbling under his breath, Marx flounced off to one of the dirty corners.

In a low tone that wouldn't carry back there, Arssen asked the others, "Think we'll really be safe until he gets back? This is the only hovel on the street that's still standing. We might as well have a sign on the roof."

"My son's always been inquisitive," Ursa said, glancing to the heavens as if for patience. "Too bad he has no grasp of building or sapping, or else his father and I could have been safe in some rebel barracks during…"

It was like a strike to the gut. Arssen cringed as if struck and became very interested in sharpening the edges of the shovel he had weaponized. Everyone in the group had heard his mother tell the story before and knew to feign deafness. But not a human left alive on Planet Earth would have wondered how her thinly-veiled snipe ended.

During the last battle.

That fight was only the latest in the millennia-old War. It had wracked the continent of Pangaea and destroyed their home, and still, the Gray Ones advanced. Some feared the monsters would finally win the war. Every day, there were more stories, more reports, more whispered warnings that featured the gibbering things on the move. They didn't look much like men. But they were too clever and intentionally cruel to be beasts. And only the truly unfortunate ran into a Gray One.

Now the beasts, they had seen. Everything from cats and birds to apes and jaguars had become violent to the point of being suicidal. Yesterday, before they had made it to this house, John had had to behead a howling mutt that had charged them one time too many. With smaller animals, normally a blow or two to the head would knock them senseless. But this mutt, with cracked and bloody teeth snapping and slobbering, had refused their gift of sleep and forced them to put it down. Vanders had cried. Marx and Arssen had dry heaved at the sight.

If the insane beasts weren't bad enough, the lunatics running around in human skin were. No one in their group had known a person to go crazy like that, yet it seemed that more and more of

Earth's population were devolving. These people had lost their humanity completely.

No speech, just screams and gibbering. No rational thoughts, just shambling sprints and beating. Their finer motor functions seemed to remain, though. Arssen's dad had learned that when one of the Possessed had impaled him with garden shears in his sleep.

That was the first time Arssen had sent a crossbow bolt into a living thing.

A dry rattle spun every head in the room as someone or something pushed against the barrier they had thrown against the cellar door. The metal shelves, piles of forlorn junk, and bags of junk scraped against the stone foundation. Salik slipped into the room. The group let out a collective sigh of relief while Arssen rushed to help their leader close the door again.

"The good news," Salik murmured, "is I found a berry thicket in what used to be someone's garden. When we head out, we'll pick all we can and take it with us. Breakfast is served."

Arssen joined the others in crowding around and snatching the berries as fast as Salik could hand them out. Marx was stuffing them into his pimply face with both hands.

"What's the bad news? Oh, ladies first, dear," Ursa interjected, pushing back Arssen with one finger and picking out a particularly fat berry from Salik's basket.

Arssen obediently sat back, face flushed.

"There is no bad news," Salik said. "Just old news. From the signs I've seen, the war is raging south of Melimard. Maybe the angels are attempting to retake the city from the Gray Ones. Maybe the rebellion is making a move against the Possessed. Either way, we're too close to the fighting."

"Move?" Marx asked through a mouthful of fruit. He looked excited for the first time in a week. "I thought we'd want to be close enough to get into the city when the Gray Ones are driven out. I don't want to go all the way east. Let's stay here!"

"But will they be driven out?"

Salik frowned at Vanders' question, his dusky, boulder-like face the picture of calm.

"Vanders is right. The war has left Pangaea in shambles. Cities almost never change hands these days, not with this century's developments. All we can expect from this battle is more death."

"Then let's go fight with the angels or rebels," Marx proposed, his eyes flashing in the dim light of the cellar. The boy changed his tune faster than a drunken skald.

"Don't you want to reach your 18th birthday, boy?" Ursa said. Her voice crackled and popped worse than a bonfire. "Use whatever bit of a brain the gods gave you."

Arssen glanced at Marx's parents, but neither jumped on his mother for jumping on their son. What kind of parent lets another adult pick on their child?

Ursa had this bizarre magnetism about her that made people accept her. At least, people accepted the things she did. Personally, Arssen suspected she had a special power: guilt. She could just make you feel like you deserved whatever dish of superiority she felt like serving you that day. Her tone, her crossed arms, even her gaze did the trick. So you took it quietly. That was the best explanation Arssen had for Vanders' and John's silent approval.

That and the fact that Marx just threw Ursa a rude gesture and turned away. It was hard to feel bad for the boy.

John grunted, not having seen his son's response. "Are we still sure there are safe houses in the eastlands? Perhaps we should take shelter here if the Armies of the Human Rebellion are redirecting their forces to the area."

"Melimard is a gamble. The eastland's sanctuaries are fact. And we do need to move now," Salik stated. "When I headed back here, I heard something yowling in the distance. Big cats of one kind or another. We need to fill our packs with the food we can carry and head out *before* they get close enough to identify us."

Salik had spoken. Without a word, the rest went to their corners and started throwing their towels, blankets, and other meager possessions into the sacks they used to carry their lives. Moving had become so routine that it was almost as comfortable as staying. No one argued out loud, although Marx and Ursa both grumbled under their breath.

When their hometown had fallen last year, they had become nomads in an increasingly desolate land. More and more cities in Pangaea were either destroyed or overrun by the Gray Ones. The remaining cities and towns were overcrowded and unwilling to accept more refugees, so all that remained was to wander eastward toward the fabled sanctuary cities until one of three things happened.

They could find a cell of the rebellion and stay with them...assuming they could prove themselves useful.

They could trail behind a war party of angels, letting the supernatural warriors clear the way...and hope that they wouldn't be asked to join in the war effort directly, like most humans that the angels met.

Or they could die.

Option three was the easiest, held the most possibility, and was ultimately the most likely. The thing about life was that you couldn't get out alive.

They had been running for months and months, and Arssen had become convinced that their luck wouldn't last much longer. In a journey that was measured in weeks rather than miles, every careful step forward could kill them. Safety only existed in hiding under rocks.

Good carts had long since disappeared, along with their drivers. Beasts of burden couldn't be trusted not to turn, anymore. So Arssen, Ursa, Marx, Vanders, John, and Salik tied another wrap of cloth over their tattered shoes and crept out of the sad, crumbling house on foot.

A few minutes later, Marx broke the silence with a barely audible mutter. "I'm hungry."

"You just ate, dear," Vanders said softly.

"Not enough."

"You and me both, pal," Arssen said.

"Soft now," Salik cautioned from the front of the line. "Possessed."

The six of them all dove for cover behind an intact wall to another house. Flattened against the ground, they were mostly hidden by the tall thistles around them. The same painful thistle patch upon which they were now lying. A wheezing sound from the street kept anyone from whimpering.

The once-human monster had two friends. The three staggering Possessed were emaciated and clad in stained garments. Two had the darker skin of the northerners, but all three had an odd, moon-like paleness to their skin in the morning light. The fairer-skinned one wore a sweater that was once white, and she kept cackling to herself. The other woman just kept wheezing loudly—the sound that had saved the group from being seen. The one male among the Possessed silently walked forward with his head dipping and snapping one way after another, eyes huge and nostrils flared as if he were sniffing the street for normal humans.

Arssen shivered slightly at the sight. Morbid. Unnatural. His hand tightened around his shovel.

Salik dropped his hand on the end of the shovel handle in warning. Arssen had no interest in fighting, though. John, Salik, and even Vanders were better at it than he.

Ursa just peered at him through narrow eyes. He got the message: a true man would protect his mother anyway.

Meanwhile, the Possessed walked past. Unlike the stragglers that the group had hidden from in the past, these three walked quickly. Purposefully. If Arssen didn't know better, he'd say they were on patrol. Maybe their nearness to a Gray One city galvanized the local Possessed into more military forms of slaughter. Or maybe these monsters were just angrier than the usual walking nightmares. Either way, Arssen hoped they had a set destination. Particularly if it were a very important destination somewhere else that required their immediate attention. That would be best.

Wheezy turned towards them...and noticed the prone humans. She greeted them with a mouthful of fangs. Not broken teeth. Not sharp teeth. Actual fangs. Teeth that were too big and roughly the shape of pruning shears…

In less time than it took to blink, Arssen had adrenaline burning in every finger and every toe. He roared and lunged to his feet, double-edged shovel in hand.

He stumbled.

Wheezy the Possessed was on him in a flash. She boxed him in both ears before he managed to stagger back out of the range of her flailing limbs.

Thudding pain rocked his head. He struggled to regain his footing as Wheezy used her momentum to keep him off balance. She kept flashing those horrible teeth.

John and Salik flew by Arssen on both sides. John swung his family's old broadsword towards Wheezy's arm, but she twisted. It became buried in her shoulder instead. Salik was smaller than John but quicker. His long, thin knife found her heart even as she continued to press toward Arssen.

Her surprisingly large pink tongue whipped around her fangs as she fell to Salik's blade. The two milky-blue orbs in her head were wide and didn't blink. Disgusted but still buzzing with hate, Arssen swung his shovel overhead with all the might he imagined he would need to bisect a tree. He found his mark.

He let out a gurgle of nausea at the sight, and it took all his will not to release his stomach contents back into the wild. Too late, he remembered Wheezy's cohorts.

Salik was the only one who could slide his weapon free in time. Then, the two other Possessed hit him. He went down under the other woman, but Arssen glimpsed his knife doing its work as he fell. That left the big, snuffly one to the rest of the group.

The Possessed threw John to the ground and drove his foot into John's face, eliciting a pained cry from the poor man. Vanders dove in to protect her husband, slinging a worn boot up into the stomach of the Possessed. She made the mistake of kicking a second time after he had doubled over, and he caught her foot and gave it a vicious twist. Vanders yelped and collapsed.

"Get away from Mom!" Marx howled from where he still lay, next to Ursa. He seemed paralyzed, though, and thankfully didn't rise to try to help.

So Arssen was left to face the Possessed onslaught with no shovel. No knives. No skills. The sniffling ex-person charged him, arms outstretched to strangle the last man standing. Arssen staggered backward and saved himself a split second, but the Possessed was in full motion. Arssen punched the attacker in the face.

Whether because of the creature's own momentum or the adrenaline of the moment, Arssen's strike actually stopped him flat. Arssen was shocked. The Possessed was shocked. For a humid moment, neither moved.

Then Salik ended the moment. His blades disappeared into the Possessed back, and with little mess or pomp, the last burly creature dropped.

John and Salik took a moment to ensure the Possessed were dead.

Chest rising and falling lightly, Salik glowered. "Arssen. Why did you force their hands?"

"What?"

"Are you out of your shriveled mind?" Ursa screamed. She was staggering to her feet in the thistle patch, her face pale and her dirty dress stained green. "You could have died! You could have gotten us all killed!"

Arssen stood thunderstruck. Desperate, he swung around to where John and Vanders were picking themselves up and spread his arms towards them.

"You two saw, right? That wheezy one had spotted us!" he cried.

Nobody else had noticed it and nobody believed him. He could tell by their reactions. None of them could read people as well and as quickly as he could, and right now that stunk.

John silently helped his wife up with one big hand and cradled his bloody nose with the other. Vanders, however, let her eyes burn Arssen's hope to floating cinders. She stomped towards him and leaned forward until she was inches away from his face, forcing him to retreat a step.

"I saw you try to be a big man and nearly get my family killed," she seethed.

"My son has a knack for panicking," Ursa said, shaking with outrage or fear. "Ask his wife and daughter."

Red. Then white, then blue, all in the span of a breath.

"Enough: he understands," Salik interrupted, his face paling as he watched Arssen. "I'm certain Arssen is sorry. There is no need to kill the dog over the dead cat."

Arssen's teeth were clamped together so hard, he couldn't speak if he wanted. Vanders blushed and turned away, pulling back to her husband and Marx. Shuddering, Arssen turned and ripped the shovel out of the corpse of the first Possessed.

"Idiot woman. Idiot, useless bag of worthless..." he hissed under his breath, tears threatening the gasping, twitching remains of his pride. "Stupid me. Stupid, stupid."

He knew he sounded like a child, but no one could hear him. Even in his current state, he made sure they couldn't hear. He had almost gotten them killed, just like they said, and his past wasn't their problem. His mother could conceivably be right. His father? Not Arssen's fault no matter what the old crow might claim. But Arssen's own family? Angels knew he was to blame for Jemma's and Sara's deaths—himself, and this thrice-cursed war. He might as well have torn them apart himself for all the good he had done them.

Ursa was still playing the wounded old lady when Salik finished cleaning his weapons. The rest had gathered in silence as the morning sun baked the desolate neighborhood street in a breathless sky.

"Plans haven't changed," Salik said with a grim pinch to his mouth. "If anything, we need to move faster than before. There's no telling how many more Possessed are out here. We grab the berries we can pick and we keep moving east until we get out of the Melimard area. Rebels in the area can give us better directions to the sanctuaries in the eastlands. So, as expected, I was right to come south."

"South, North, East, or West, we're going to need more water soon," Vanders cautioned, weighing the large bags that she used to carry the group's supply.

"Which means we stay near houses and their rain barrels," John added. He sounded congested. A foot to the face had that effect. "But we're still too close to the city, Salik."

"We got to fight. They're coming after us anyway," Marx grumbled.

The adults ignored him. Arssen passed him a look of pity, but Marx was too busy blowing his nose in his baggy shirt to notice.

"First things first," Salik stated, holding up a pair of sadly deflated food sacks. "Berries."

THEY WOULD HAVE PICKED THE OVERGROWN BLACKBERRY PATCH CLEAN, but more and more Possessed were marching down the street. The back wall of the house in front of the patch still stood, protecting the backyard garden and its pillagers from the baleful gaze of the monsters. But each patrol frightened them into longer bouts of silence. Eventually, Ursa's nerve broke and she insisted the group move on, refusing to pick another berry. Arssen couldn't disagree with her this time. Nor did the rest of the group.

Besides, just to the north of this house was a long, wide field that had been farmed by the residents years ago when Melimard was still held by humanity. Just beyond that were untouched woods that spread out and up into the highland. As they had picked blackberries, occasional yowls drifted to them on the stale air: howling and snarls and hisses of wild animals driven to madness by the Gray Ones.

Now was a good time to leave.

With their food rations fuller and their thirst sated at a surviving rain barrel, they continued their trip eastward one yard at a time. The sun's rays burned crimson in the poisoned atmosphere. Arssen had heard stories about a blue sky once but had grown out of such fairy tales decades ago. Shadows were short and stubby and the heat could reduce spit to steam before long.

The terrain became hilly and they were always either trudging up one hill or picking their way down another. But at least once an hour, they would find a hiding place in the shade and wait out another collection of the Possessed. Arssen longed for each break and would rub his swollen feet, enraptured when he got to sit.

When the sun was midway through its descent in the sky and the air practically burned around them, Arssen heard John lean forward to whisper to Salik. John's raspy voice was clearly audible to him, but that was doubtlessly unintentional considering the topic.

"These Possessed—patrols, would you call them?—are getting larger."

"I noticed," Salik murmured back, barely moving his mouth. "Keep it to yourself, if you will."

"We're leaving the Melimard lands. Shouldn't we be seeing less of them?" John hissed.

"Yes."

"What should we do?"

"Continue carefully. Do not worry the others yet. If we have to change direction, better to risk the woods than the farming communities farther south," Salik said. His eyes closed, he leaned back against the wall, looking as tired as Arssen felt.

"But this city is the last obstacle," he continued. "I used to travel before the last great battle. I know the old trade routes, which is why I refused to go north and die with the rest. They think they'll be safer crossing through the mountains, but there is no path east that way. They will starve, or else be eaten. Not us."

"At least we'll be safe after Melimard," John whispered.

"Safe? No. The great plains will take months to cross, and will likely offer little food except meat taken from the wretched beasts. The rebels might show us a path through it if we can find them."

Arssen stopped listening and began worrying. He had thought

that he could never worry again after he lost his family. What mattered in a world without them? And then he lost his father after the most recent wave of fighting between angels and Gray Ones. The Gray Ones' latest weapon, these Possessed, had done it. And again, Arssen thought there was nothing left to lose that was worth caring about.

But the farms of his hometown had been overrun. The nearby city had been all but razed by the fiends, leaving thousands to flee.

And each day on the run proved Arssen wrong. Each encounter with a Possessed or the beasts reminded him that he had plenty of blood, bones, and flesh to lose. And as hopeless as he felt, his sorrows could not extinguish his terror when death leaned over and hissed in his face through a smile of broken teeth.

So yes, Arssen worried. He worried about how much it would hurt to lose the game of survival. How had humanity lasted this long?

As the sun beat down, the group continued to slink on in silence. Everyone was acutely aware of the presence of the Possessed, who were now marching in packs of eight and nine regularly. At one point, they had to hide from a veritable swarm of the creatures. If Ursa, Vanders, and Marx hadn't noticed the increase in the Possessed before, they did then.

One other detail differentiated these monsters from the Possessed they had seen in the past. These carried maces: flanged metal heads on the ends of short wooden hafts. Whatever they were doing, wherever they were headed, they were prepared for a battle.

The last horrible footfalls of the patrol had long since died against the burnt stone and gritty earth when Ursa managed to retrieve her voice from wherever the Possessed had taken it.

"What have you led us into, Salik of Wold?" she asked, her voice a pitiable mouse squeak.

"We'll risk the north now," John murmured. His eyes narrowed at their leader. "I will not lead my wife and child into a slaughter!"

Salik frowned and squinted. Arssen recognized the expression as contemplation, although he didn't know what about running for their lives needed to be contemplated. It seemed fairly straight-forward.

So he sidled up to Salik and asked.

"Back is too dangerous," Salik answered slowly. "We found few enough supplies in the past few days in the farm lanes, and it would bring us nearer to the city again. Traveling south presents the same problems. But north? North takes us into the highland. Cold nights, no shelter, and no path east. We'd trade in our quick deaths for slow ones."

"We have enough food to last us a day or two," Arssen whispered. "That should be plenty of time to skirt around this battle."

"And if the battle isn't here? What if the Possessed are simply marching towards their masters in Fosallom or another eastern settlement? Instead of passing the Possessed, we would walk alongside them for miles. And when we came south again and found them, we'd be softer targets."

"We need to do something," Arssen said.

"We could find shelter and wait..." Salik mused.

"No!" Vanders hissed, nostrils flaring. "Moving now is our only safe option, and north is the least terrible choice we have!"

She had apparently been listening, along with the others. Their concerned stares were broken only by occasional, twitchy glances towards the road. The long, low, L-shaped stone house offered some protection from prying eyes, so they had a corner to hide in for the moment. No one dared to explore the safety of the place. Not after seeing the last troop of the damned.

Salik breathed heavily as he hefted himself up. In the burning light of midday, Arssen noticed the sprinkling of silver in the man's dark beard and hair.

"Very well," Salik sighed. "Perhaps we will find my fears were for nothing."

Ursa shook her head. "I hope not. If we do find the highland isn't as horrible as you warned back at the crossroads, then we'll know we followed a fool."

"Mother, please show some respect," Arssen begged, wincing. "He's trying his best."

"Responsibility comes with leadership. You knew that when you decided to play king," Ursa told Salik with a scowl, ignoring her son.

At that, Salik narrowed his eyes. But he bowed his head slightly in acknowledgment and said nothing. Ursa wrinkled her nose in response. Why had Arssen bothered to support Salik if he wouldn't stand up for himself?

"Can we go now?" Marx groaned. He wore his angry mask again, which meant he was probably scared out of his little head. "I hate it here. All these old, dead houses are creepy, and those monsters could come back."

"Well said, child," Ursa said, with a nod and frown.

John hoisted his wife's load and started walking as if the rest of them didn't matter. Vanders grabbed Marx's hand, to his dismay, and followed. Ursa shuffled after them, and Salik and Arssen trailed behind the pack. Arssen made sure to stay near the man with the knives.

"Do you think you could teach me to use knives?"

"Not now, Arssen."

"Sorry."

The dead air carried murmurs of something in the distance as they hiked up the tall hill, away from the farmlands with their burnt houses and empty fields. Arssen couldn't make out what they were hearing, but it wasn't the crazed howl of battle. That was good. But the distant whispers and whimpers still left trails of raised hairs on his arms as they passed.

Like most of the people from his hometown, Arssen had never wagered much time on thoughts of evil and good. Life was filled with success and failures, starvation and survival, bountiful crops and famines, what worked and what didn't. Morality was too relative. Such thoughts were better left to old men and skalds.

But everything since the last great battle had reeked of evil— violence and bloodthirstiness beyond even the worst humanity had to offer. Senseless acts of terror and rage, like the one that had left him a childless widower, had battered his shrinking sense of self. He had gained a nose for evil in these past years. Maybe someday it would save his life, but today, right now, it just gave him the heebie-jeebies.

He smelled evil wafting off the land, and the fumes only grew worse as they walked northward.

The landscape grew more mountainous, and there were few signs of life besides some prickly brown grass underfoot and a sprinkling of coniferous trees across the hillside. The sky was huge here. It spread off the hills into a wide, red oblivion. The broken stumps of what had once been great trees had left more and more sky open. The last great battle between the angels and the Gray Ones had devastated western Pangaea. The proof was in the ravenous beasts, in the new barrenness of the soil, and in the countless seaside cities like Melimard that were now unapproachable glimpses of the Pit.

Arssen also hated how the air felt in these past years. He remembered a time when the air had moved in gusts and breezes and great gales. Now, it simply pressed down on them with the added weight of an arid heat.

"Water," he mumbled.

Vanders gave a cluck of sympathy and passed him one of the water skins. From the pounding in his head and throbbing in his feet, Arssen knew he needed a rest as well. But if his mother wasn't begging for a stop then he wouldn't either. He took a large swallow from the skin, then one more for good measure.

"Don't gulp it all," Vanders said. She snatched the waterskin back from him.

He flushed. Maybe Vanders was just in a bad mood—weren't they all? But it was hard not to take the attitude personally from the one person in the group who didn't act like he was a nuisance.

As they approached the gentle peak of the hill, he stomped ahead of the rest to hide his embarrassment. "Can't a man quench..."

The sound died in his throat and he collapsed to the ground, sending a plume of dust into his dry face.

"What are you doing?" asked Ursa.

"Quiet!" he hushed his mother. "Get down! Everyone down!"

Naturally, they ignored him until they too had crested the hill and could see into the deep valley just to the east. Then Arssen heard a series of thumps as they all dropped to their bellies behind him. He didn't look back to make sure. He couldn't.

Hundreds of men and women in patchy armor marched past the bottom of the hill, heading south. Many were equipped with glinting steel weapons: swords, axes, scythes, and flails. Others nearer the front carried long metal poles with short spikes on the end. They actually had muskets. Weapons of fire and metal like that were rumored to have replaced crossbows as the greatest equalizer in the fight against the Gray Ones and their ilk.

An army. The rebels.

And here Arssen's little band were, about to wander merrily into the very battle they'd tried to flee.

THE ARMIES OF THE HUMAN REBELLION WERE THE COLLECTIVE FORCES of guardsmen, mercenaries, and the fractured remains of the old nation-state armies. In the past age, before the last great battle several years ago, there had been few organized fighting forces. Pangaea had been locked in a cold war against the "haunted" cities like Melimard that the Gray Ones were said to keep, and construction and revitalization of human settlements had taken priority over training up soldiers to poke the proverbial wasp nests.

But in the wake of the last great battle, anyone who couldn't fight learned from those who could. And most of those who could fight banded together into any one of the furious militias springing up with a single goal: kill Gray Ones. Those with other useful skills could join the rebels' bunkers with their families, but most people joined because they had a few dead reasons to tear the monsters some new nostrils.

It was a mob unified to throw off the reign of terror the Gray Ones had placed on them—a rebellion of sorts, with a little imagination.

This was the closest Arssen had ever come to one of the rebel armies. He had expected the soldiers to look more frightened. What they did look like was hungry. Food and water were scarce enough for roving bands of wanderers like Salik's, so a whole troop of marching, active young people must have been all but impossible to feed. The soldiers would have had to be satisfied to fill their bellies with anger instead of grains and meat. Most wore scowls.

Arssen felt he could relate to that look. He saw it in every rain barrel before he drank. Life cleaved more than it mended, and any way you could return the favor was up for grabs. A man might as well rip back a little satisfaction before he died.

"Halt!"

The order drifted up to Arssen and the others from the front of the army's ranks. A powerfully-built man stood a shade taller than the rest. He strode out to the front with a broadsword slung over one shoulder. Then the man turned and faced his men, revealing the hard lines of his face.

"Well, here we are again," the leader called to his troops. Some chuckled, but the sound was tired. "We've lost good men and women—good fighters, good human beings—but we've always taken more than they have. And it's time to do it again! The long-lost brothers and sisters in Melimard demand their pay in kind, and we will wash their memories in the thin blood of the Gray!"

A louder response met him this time, roared from more throats.

"Can you believe that man?" Ursa whispered.

"Shut up, I wanna hear," Marx grumbled, immediately catching a cuff in the ear from Vanders for the backtalk.

The leader paced as he talked, and lowered his voice so that it was almost inaudible to them. "Messengers bring troubling news from the south. Our brothers and sisters on that march are faltering, they say. But they die well, I say! Their distraction clears the northern approach for us! We will sweep down like a plague and be in the city before the Gray Ones can send more of their blade meat to stop us. Scouts have reported fierce fighting back west. Let us prove ourselves worthy of the same title that those who fight there hold: warriors of the Human Armies!"

Arssen let out a long, trembling breath. They would be squashed, these rebels. They didn't know of the roving bands of Possessed, but the once-human monsters seemed to be aware of them. Surprise was a deadly ally. The humans would all die, one at a time or in one quick massacre. It was safer to avoid violence as Arssen did. Security was found in swift retreats, not in death-or-glory attacks.

Because if it was, then there was hope to be had. And hope had died with the light in the eyes of his four-year-old daughter.

He tore his glance away from the juggernaut of a man at the front lines and he picked specific faces out of the crowd. Few wore helmets of any kind, and most of them were ancient relics. From this distance, he could only see the strongest of expressions. That expression was visible in shifting jaws, clenched faces, and upraised arms. The scowls from earlier were deepening with every word from the leader. The man was feeding their disgust, their fury, their fears. What else could compel a man to throw his blood and bones into battle with no goal but to destroy an enemy with his last breath?

The thought was...intriguing. Horrifying and depressing, but intriguing. To throw everything away like that...

Arssen glanced back at the others. No one seemed inclined to move. Ursa and John were carefully fiddling with their clothes and packs. Salik's eyes darted back and forth across the scene in a tactician's analysis. Marx stared at the leader, enraptured by the man's speech.

Vanders was the only one to notice Arssen and met his gaze blankly. He didn't look away. She didn't look away. Whether they were intimidating each other, courting each other, or just staring out of exhaustion, Arssen wasn't sure. He always figured that he and Vanders would be the last ones alive. Arssen, because he was smarter than the rest of them. Vanders, because she was the perfect balance of strength and wisdom and, unlike Salik, could cut the rest of them loose to save her own life.

He took a deep breath. A sickly sweet smell pervaded his nose and made his eyes water. Then the war found them.

The sun roared into full power as screeches filled the air. The Possessed poured into the valley from the south, wailing and screaming as they sprinted towards the small rebel force. The human soldiers were outnumbered already, and more of the Possessed kept arriving. All of them were waving the crude maces like children with sticks.

The rebel leader managed to belt out "Attack!" a second before his vanguard was engulfed by the enemy. Confusion wreathed the fighters in a blur of flailing limbs and weapons. A satisfying artificial thunder echoed against the hills as the musket men sent metal death into the swarm of the Possessed, but if they had had much effect, it wasn't evident. They were still struggling to reload when the fight came to them. Those who didn't abandon their guns were overwhelmed by the rising tide: trampled, not to rise again.

"We need to help kill monsters!" Marx said, edging forward.

John dragged his son back, his face pulsing redder than usual. Vanders covered Marx's mouth and held him close.

Arssen barely noticed. He felt like the dry, prickly grass beneath him had melted with his dirty clothes. Piles of earth had risen to engulf him. It all crushed him. He couldn't move if he wanted. Thirst, hunger, and sunburn vanished as he watched the tragic comedy play out before his eyes.

The rebels didn't wait at the bottom of the valley to be overrun one line at a time. Those in the back scrabbled up the steep dirt slopes on either side and flung themselves at the oncoming wave of the Possessed. The battle evolved from two narrow sword points clashing to two broad edges slamming into each other.

One by one, the rebel soldiers with their masks of rage fell, buried under the twisting, bloody bodies of the Possessed. The piles of sliced, hewn, shot, and broken enemies swelled, but not fast enough. The gibbering slaves of the Gray Ones waged a war of attrition, and that was a fight they wouldn't lose.

The screams of pain rent at Arssen's ears. The inhuman howls of the Possessed nearly drove him to claw at his head. He turned his eyes away and began to crawl away from the slaughter. It was all just gory proof that anything standing up was that much easier to hack down to size.

Arssen froze. Behind Ursa at the back of the group, visible to no one yet except him, walked a pair of creatures that he normally would have never given a second look. But now he could feel the blood drain from his veins.

Goats.

A buck and a nanny glared at the group through their unsettling rectangular eyes. They were wild creatures, with yellowed and matted hair. Both were stamping at the rocky soil with their front hooves, and they began making chuffing noises now that Arssen was watching them. Flecks of foam grew at the corners of their mouths.

Then, the buck took a step forward and began bleating for its life. A little blood dripped from its long tongue. Mad. The pair had the madness.

By now, the rest of the group had rolled away from the goats. John tried to shush the buck, but the nanny began screaming and the buck joined in, the cries sounding unnaturally human. For a terrible moment, Arssen was struck by the fantastic idea that maybe all the turned animals had once been people, just like the Possessed, before being changed by the Gray Ones. He tried to shake the uncanny notion.

"Silence! Shush! Quiet, quiet, quiet!" John hissed at the goats, his face turning as red as the sun. The goats just screamed louder. Arssen hadn't thought that was possible.

He drove the morbid thoughts out of his head. He had no doubt that some of the Possessed had heard the alarm by now and would be coming to silence it.

Worse, his mother Ursa had been paralyzed by the bleating. She had been closest to the pair of hooved beasts and she hadn't so much as turned around in fear of triggering a charge. Rightly so, but now she was the only target. And they looked about ready to charge anyway.

For the second time that day, Arssen dove forward before his better sense could slap him down.

The buck charged when he did. Arssen almost reached his mother first, but not quite.

Fortunately, his shovel beat both him and the goat to the punch.

Unlike the Possessed, the goat was not particularly immune to the sharpened metal edge of the tool. Arssen managed to get under the horns and strike upwards, drawing a red line into the creature. Yet the goat was deterred from its original target and fixed an unsettling eye on the shovel-wielder as it regained its footing.

Still screaming, it turned slightly to lunge at Arssen. At this range, the bloody spittle at its mouth was confirmation enough of its sanity—as if its attack were not.

"Arssen!" Ursa moaned, fear and accusation blending together. No doubt she blamed him for triggering the goat attack.

"Goodnight," Arssen muttered.

Tong. Tong-tong-tong thunk.

The goat collapsed. Four blows to the head from the business end of a farming implement had that effect. It was motionless and quiet, except for its heavy breaths.

The nanny goat was not going down quietly, especially after seeing its mate bludgeoned into a stupor. It bleated and wailed, bouncing back and forth and flailing with its hooves while Vanders and John tried to circle it. It screamed louder and bounced to Vanders' side. Maybe the goat took her for the lesser threat. Maybe it was just avoiding John's long blade. Either way, the goat chose poorly.

"My knife!" Salik yelled, startling the rest.

Vanders turned first, and her glare dissolved into horror.

"Marx!" she screamed.

The little fool was stumbling downhill towards a phalanx of

nine of the Possessed that were approaching the group. One was missing an arm and another her hand, but all still had their maces. Some of the ex-humans even had ragged iron and leather armor protecting their bodies. And they were confronted by a single boy with a stolen knife.

Marx waved the blade threateningly and seemed unshaken by the number of enemies. "Die!" he screeched. "For humans!"

And then the boy tackled the lead Possessed. Marx actually managed to bowl him over.

A wordless cry tore out of Vanders throat and she ran towards her son. Agony spread across John's face like army ants, but he turned and threw himself at the nanny goat as it used Vanders' distraction as an opportunity to strike. The goat was stopped by 200 pounds of muscle and five feet of tempered steel.

Arssen had heard life-and-death stories around the cooking fire from others in the original group, dozens of them. Man after man had sworn that when a mad beast was charging or the Possessed attacked, time had slowed down and let them make just the right decision to save themselves. That was either a skill that others had and Arssen didn't, or the stories had been embellished.

Either way, Arssen had no such extra time to prepare. He had to follow his first instinct. John was stuck with his sword buried in the nanny goat's neck. Salik was too many long strides away from the rest. Vanders was running towards her son, who had three of the Possessed on top of him. And this wasn't a cookfire story. Marx wasn't a headstrong young hero, surviving against all odds. He had screamed once and moved no longer.

And Arssen had been haunted for too many years by the sight of looters standing over his wife's unblinking form. He had no time to make a decision now. He just acted.

Arssen tackled Vanders. The two of them tumbled to the side and he rolled in the air so that he took the brunt of the impact. Something hot and wet dripped onto his neck as she sobbed.

There was no time for mourning. The Possessed ones had finished with Marx and were nearly to the hilltop. John had his sword and Salik would not be taken easily. But they were outnumbered, and that never ended well. The rebels that still could walk were struggling to retreat now, but the swarms of the Possessed filled the valley. The sight of so many insane, howling people turned the stomach and stained the eyes red in despair. More and more of the Possessed noticed the group on the hills and rushed in for the kill.

Arssen went limp. They might have successfully fled from nine crazed murderers, but the escape of the remaining human soldiers would initiate a hunt, and their little group was fair game for every last one of the Possessed.

Then he got a glimpse of a figure amidst the rolling ocean of the Possessed. Hopelessness hardened into something worse and more solid: a block of wordless fear that stopped the breath and stilled the heart. There in the valley was… Something. Something pale, something formless, something strong.

Something wrong.

For a brief moment, it was visible. It was there. It seemed to stare straight towards him through pinpricks of blue light, as if it could pick Arssen out at that great distance. Almost immediately, his line of sight was obstructed by more of the Possessed trudging towards the frontlines. And after they moved past, the…thing, it was gone.

No air remained in Arssen's lungs. His limbs lay where they were, numb and motionless. He lay beneath Vanders' shaking form and watched with unfocused eyes as the Possessed crested the hill.

Thirty steps away.

Twenty-five steps.

Twenty.

A roar.

Beastial shouts echoed from the south. Every eye, human and ex-human, turned towards the southern hills. The Possessed seemed to have lost some of their driving spirit.

Running faster than bears or even horses, forty or so figures like giants sprinted into the valley. They stood twice as high as a man and blazed with clean, white light. No weapons sat in their hands or lay sheathed on their backs.

The strangers closed the distance on the Possessed and started, for lack of a better word, destroying them.

The giants didn't just kill the creatures. They disemboweled, dismembered, delimbed, decapitated—and all that just with their hands. As outnumbered by the monsters as they were, the giants were steadily pressing forward.

Arssen couldn't understand how until he noticed that they also appeared to be using sound and fire-like physical weapons. The Possessed burned and flew through the air and scattered under the assault of thunderclaps and blinding flashes. Several of the strangers walked behind the rest like some sort of cleanup crew, torching the tattered remains of the monsters. It was like nothing Arssen had ever seen. He couldn't turn away.

The Possessed that were still on the hill turned and rushed back down towards the giants with renewed ferocity, their mouths open in ghoulish, sharp-toothed grins. They panted like dogs as they ran. The monsters threw themselves at the blazing strangers with maces swinging and hands clawing.

Vanders let out a whimper and scampered over to the still form of her son, but what she found elicited a tortured moan. John joined her, stumbling as if wounded. The rest of the group waited and watched.

Three or four of the giants were knocked down by the hordes of Possessed, and their falling bodies sounded like great trees crashing upon rocks. But after what felt like an eternity, the blood-stained valley fell silent as the last of the drooling creatures was crushed under the foot of the lead stranger. Then two massive, sparkling triangles expanded from each giant's back, like wings from a swan carved of diamond. They roared again.

The sound forced its way into Arssen's mind, singing his memories and ransacking his despair until the process of elimination left only startling bursts of pride, relief, and confidence. Their cries stole his identity and left a different man, and at that moment, the new man loved the giants for it.

As the echoes faded, he felt the glowing light that lined his eyes and burned his nose and throat fade with it. But also gone was the twisting fear of the unknown that he had felt when he'd seen that unnatural pale thing. He felt scoured. Balanced again.

He stood uncertainly and cleared his throat. Perhaps some of the others had also felt the strange effect of the giants. The wrinkles in Ursa's face were less pronounced, and Salik's mouth, normally bunched into a tight line, had loosened into a relieved smile.

But Vanders spared Arssen a different look, tearing her red eyes away from Marx's body. Her eyes were burning with hate beyond momentary anger, her gentle mouth open to bare her teeth like one of the Possessed. Arssen looked away. But the look still burned so intensely that he glanced around for a way to step out of her line of sight. There was no shelter on the bald hilltop.

A giant appeared near the group, her skin radiating a pale luminance. At this range, her aura noticeably ate away at the burning heat of the sun, cooling Arssen's cracked skin like mist. She was also beautiful beneath her glow. Skin like white marble glided over gentle curves, belying the power that the giants had shown on the field. She stood several lengths taller than even John.

Had she and her kind saved them by slaughtering the Possessed? There was no question. But there was no salvation without a price. What trick exactly they had played to create the noises and lights that they used against the enemy, Arssen didn't know. Perhaps those that practiced voodoo in the dark corners of Pangaea were not complete fools. Maybe dark magics were at play. Or maybe the giants simply had better muskets and weapons than humans did.

Regardless of their intent, regardless of their abilities, these huge people were strangers in a land where trust was a luxury. Arssen kept a tight hold on his shovel handle.

The giantess did not smile, but no one would have believed a smile. Instead, she wore an expression of acute pain as she beheld Vanders, John, and their son. She made no attempt to approach.

"I am Guardian Difex," she said in a rich voice like far-off thunder. Even her own crystalline wings shook. "Please, attend to us for a few hours and afterward you may continue on your way unhindered, unless you accept our offer."

Arssen traded looks with Salik. Guardian?

Then the giant padded with surprisingly light steps to where Vanders and John knelt, spoke to them for a few moments, then gently lifted Marx in her arms. The time for questioning had passed. With slow steps and watchful eyes, the group followed her down the hill towards the survivors below.

"YOU'LL BE FINE, BOY. YOU KNOW, MY SON IS SWEET LIKE YOU. IT'S just too bad he wasn't good at building things, or else we and my late husband might have been with your army now," Ursa was telling one of the rebel soldiers resting on a mat as she gave her head a sad shake.

Arssen sighed and felt a little more life escape between his dry lips as he did. He tried to appear deaf as he passed by those soldiers in the healer's tent, padding through a now-overflowing guard post of the Armies of the Human Rebellion at the heels of Salik and two of the angels.

And angels they were. Any doubt had been scrubbed away in the last hour. If the angels really did exist as an antithesis to the Gray Ones, they existed in the forms of these giants. Even when they were calm, lightning seemed to pulse through their veins and march across their flesh. Their battle cries still thudded in Arssen's own heartbeat. There had not yet been an opportunity to suss out whether or not the angels were, in fact, holy creatures. But that they could decimate a swarm of the Possessed several times their number had made them friends with every poor soul in the rebels' post.

This station was a small network of trenches and shallow but tall caves dug out of a hill to the northeast of Melimard. From the entrance of the place, the sprawling curves and the multi-storied turrets of the great city's wall were visible in the cinders of sunset across the great southern plains.

The tall man who had led the rebels on the field had survived. His name was V'lair, and he was the last remaining leader in this compound. Most of the soldiers who had finished the day with breath in their lungs were torn and bleeding on pallets. The civilian populace of the bunker scurried about in a head-spinning effort to keep the living alive, and the dying comfortable. The bunker was not the haven of peace Ursa had painted for them. It was a white-washed tomb where men hid among the dead as they waited their turn.

But every time an angel strode past, such thoughts seemed petty. Hopelessness was the excuse of a weak mind. Arssen felt a lingering, throbbing shame for the corners of his heart, and he banished the thoughts of tombs and death as insignificant. Following directly behind Guardian Difex and her companion now, his spine felt straight, his head felt clean, and the world was bathed in the gentle glow of the angel's presence.

The whole experience was vaguely unsettling and distinctly unpleasant.

Salik, Arssen, and the two angels walked through the dim, earthen tunnel between the healer's cave and the deepest of the caverns, V'lair's station. The man himself stood waiting in that chamber with two human lieutenants. One of his men had his arm in a makeshift sling, and the woman on his left had angry red scratches across her face and throat. V'lair himself was covered in black welts and stitched gashes. He watched the newcomers with angular eyes as they strode into the candlelit interior of his chamber.

The cave had been furnished like a simple room. An old four-poster bed had been dragged all the way down here into the far corner, along with a few boxes with clothes draped over them. In the middle of the cave was a table with a motley collection of seats around it. The dark space smelled wet and ancient, and the light cast by the angels revealed segmented worms and nervous crickets with bulbous eyes scattering out of their path. Arssen both heard and felt a crunch underfoot and vowed to choose his steps more carefully.

"Our saviors," V'lair rumbled, bowing at both waist and knees in eastern fashion. "We who live today do so because of your generosity."

Guardian Difex bowed her head in return and stepped forward as spokesman.

"We have you to thank for gathering so many of the pitiable creatures into one place." Her voice filled the room, even though it was softer than V'lair's. "But you paid a high price for your campaign. Have past attempts against the Gray Ones left no impression on the armies of men?"

"These monstrosities that protect their makers are abominations and insults to us as human beings," V'lair responded without batting an eye. "They are traitors. We cannot and will not suffer the lives of the Possessed any more than you allow that of your own traitors."

Arssen couldn't see either of the angels react from where he stood, but one must have flinched because V'lair smiled slowly.

"Come," he said, "is it such a surprise that the Armies of the Human Rebellion should know our enemies?"

"Would it surprise you to learn that you do not know as much as you believe you do?" she asked mildly.

V'lair glanced at his lieutenants. The man and the woman must have been in pain, but it wasn't evident on their faces. The woman nodded encouragingly and the man kept his face steeled.

"It would surprise us, actually," V'lair answered. He scratched his smooth chin. "We do not have your might or our enemy's numbers, so we use our heads and our eyes. Test me! I can tell you how many Gray Ones are in Melimard, the manner in which the Possessed defend themselves, the names of some of your fallen, Guardian. And no, I do not mean deceased. We also know that you do not experience death as we mortals do. I mean your *fallen*: those who are to blame for this war. All this and more, men like us have slowly collected years before the last great battle began. Intelligence is our steel and our shield."

Arssen watched the proceedings quietly from behind the angels. Despite both his own cynicism and the failure on the battlefield hours before, he found himself impressed by this V'lair. Perhaps the rebels did stand a chance. Marx was right.

Marx. At least, he had been right. If he had been here, he would have cheered. His face would have lit like the red sunrise in a smaller version of John's. He would have begged his parents to let him join. Would have, would have, would have. *Never would*, was more accurate. Arssen felt a nauseating lump drag his stomach towards the Earth harder than usual at the thought. And for some reason, the angels weren't staving off these particular pangs.

"We have all lost much," the second angel said. Although the same size as Guardian Difex, this one seemed younger. For a second, Arssen thought the angel had read his mind. "But that does not let you cast your blame off like a coat onto the nearest available peg. Make no mistake, Man's great abandonment of Crown Mind made all of this possible."

"Yet it is funny how it is only men who are dying in droves," V'lair said in a conversational tone.

The second angel huffed.

"Peace, Varrador," Guardian Difex said to her companion, laying a hand on Varrador's shoulder. She gazed serenely at V'lair. "The whole Earth groans from the weight of these times. Waters are soured, the sun smolders, soil burns, gentle animals slaughter, people turn against people. This is not a good time to be alive, even for us."

From Marx's group, Salik cleared his throat and stepped forward, catching the eyes of the rebel leaders. "But live we must," he said. "If you don't mind me saying so, sirs, philosophy is not for me while we can yet save the dying."

"Philosophy..." Guardian Difex began, but V'lair chose the same time to say:

"Well said! I confess that I do not know your name, soldier, or the name of your silent companion, although you know mine."

"You wouldn't know us. We are only travelers who chose the wrong time and place to travel," Salik replied. "But if it pleases you, I am Salik of Wold and this is Arssen. Our companions, Ursa, John, and Vanders, currently enjoy your compound's hospitality as we mourn the loss of one of our own—a boy whose bravery may well have saved our lives."

Pity for the boy aside, Salik's memory was certainly kinder than Arssen's.

"Bravery often ends thusly these days," V'lair replied with a grunt. "You and your friends are welcome to spend the night here. We have more than a few empty pallets to offer, I'm afraid. Meet with Nehemia when you can. He's our scoutmaster and you should be able to find him in the forge if he isn't in the barracks. You may be able to update us on the situation around the city."

Salik nodded and said, "Thank you. We will not linger here. My people seek refuge in the far east, where Pangaea has not succumbed to the Gray as it has here."

"Another reason to speak to my scoutmaster," V'lair said. "You have a long, treacherous journey ahead, but Nehemia knows those roads. In fact, it was not so long ago that I myself trained in the east. There are still strong, proud cities with tall walls and flourishing trade there. Farms. Pastures. Working mills and running rivers. They would be happy to receive news from the west."

Salik bowed his head in wordless thanks and stepped back, apparently satisfied to leave it at that.

Arssen was less so. He had had it with his mother's disingenuous accusations and Vander's silent blame. If he wanted respect, then it was time to stand up for the group.

"Excuse me," he blurted out, stepping forward.

Both rebels and angels turned towards him, and he imagined

that they were annoyed by the interruption. He blundered forward before he lost his nerve.

"It's not that we don't appreciate your offer—the beds for the night, I mean. We do. I do. But is there no *job* we could do here to earn our stay? Until the end of the war, at least. I mean, you do have a lot of openings after today."

The air in the room grew thicker as V'lair's face tightened. Salik cringed.

"Many wish safety, but who will sacrifice for it? Many wish for peace, but who will die for it? Send me such a man," V'lair said as if quoting someone, the crags in his countenance dark and ominous.

Arssen's breath caught. Ursa would renounce him as a son if he didn't try again, however, so he drove forward.

"Just because I'm not a fighter doesn't mean I'm useless," he clarified. "I'm good with fortifications, construction, scouting maybe."

"But are you willing to get your hands bloody?" V'lair's lieutenant with the clawed face asked. "Are you willing to bleed while you build us these fortifications? Even our leader walks amongst our vanguard!"

"And they're all dead!" Arssen yelled, feeling his ego battered once again. "You can't afford to turn us down. We can help!"

"Quiet!" V'lair demanded, his eyes on fire. "Spurning an offer of sanctuary is one matter. But the bodies of our brothers and sisters command respect from even you. Yet you dare use their lives as leverage. Where's your humanity? Get out of my sight, *Friend* Arssen, and you may take your companions with you if they will follow."

Still scowling, V'lair turned towards his lieutenant with the sling wrapped around his arm. "Garen, escort him out."

Arssen stood stunned, looking on at the scene in horror. Garen the lieutenant grabbed his arm and marched him out of V'lair's cave into the tunnel beyond. Yet even then, they kept walking.

"I'm sorry. I am. I didn't mean…" Arssen stammered.

"Then you shouldn't have spoken," Garen stated with a voice like stone.

Arssen realized they were still marching. "We're out of his sight now, you can probably let me go."

Garen didn't even spare him a glance.

"V'lair said *get out*, and he meant it," he said. "I'm here to make sure you leave the caves. You will fend for yourself tonight."

He gave his head a small shake as if enough of his heart remained to feel some measure of sympathy for Arssen. "No time for goodbye, my friend. You really shouldn't have spoken up."

No one in the group came out to check on him.

For what must have been half an hour, Arssen stood shivering in the last dying hour of the day. The heat that had seared the Earth during the day was already escaping back into the sky and would soon leave the surrounding hill country in the grips of an icy night.

There were no more signs of civilization here. No towns or cities were within walking distance, no farms offered the relief of a rain barrel and some shelter. Small creatures like foxes yelped and wailed as they scampered in and out of sight. Burrows and the small, scruffy shrubs of the hills offered homes enough for them, but nothing around was big enough for a human. The ground was littered with as much jagged shale as dirt. Shards of rock bit at unprotected feet and would doubtless make the night all but unbearable, even if chance smiled and the night was a warm one.

In all this, Arssen son of Ursa waited. When the waiting amounted to nothing, he walked away until his body shook without his permission. Wracked with self-pity, he let his legs fail him and he dropped to his knees, somewhere on the craggy hillside. The only rain the desolate country had seen in months fell now from his hazel eyes.

He *was* going to die. *He* was going to *die*. He played with the words numbly. There was no food in his pockets, no water in his shabby pack. Starvation and dehydration were lumbering predators at best, though, and it would be the flesh and blood carnivores that caught him first. Mad beasts, the Possessed, human raiders that looted and killed for their dinner... Cannibals, even. The monsters of the world had been unsettling enough while he was surrounded by other travelers around a cook-fire. Now, he had two blurry eyes to his name. He was going to die. Murdered, eaten, gone.

"Why!" The cry was strangled, croaking. Pent-up frustration constricted his lungs until the shout slammed into the hills around him. "Why! Why? Why? Why does—did...? Why!"

Hot with the unfairness of it all, Arssen screamed his defiance to the world. Nobody would answer his questions. Nobody noticed how hard he tried. No one would care. And in return, he didn't care who heard him. The warmth of the angels was long gone, so he'd inject his own blaze into the cooling land around him. He savored the painful rawness of his throat and listened to the form-less echoes of his scream returning from distant hills.

He breathed in a lungful of dusty air as his chest heaved. The quiet around him was no longer stifling. He kneeled in the dirt and breathed and thought.

If that tyrant V'lair and his cronies had souls, they would send someone back to fetch Arssen and return him to the safety of the caves. Then he might survive the night.

His dreams of staying in the rebellion's safe caves had crumbled, yet Salik's promise of sanctuary in the east remained. Perhaps V'lair's man actually did know the way. The group would have a path forward, at least.

A stinking, deadly, sweltering, months-long path.

So if by some miracle Arssen did manage to fend for himself until morning, he would have to reconnect with the group. His mother and the others would be escorted out in the morning by the worthless rebels just like he had, and likely to the same place. Again, that meant he had to stay in the area.

Being visible could kill him or save him.

Arssen tore off a scrap of the faded red cloth tied around his shoes to muffle them and hold them together. He tied the fabric to the tallest shrub in the little valley: a sign for any rescuers in case he was asleep when they came. Maybe they would actually look for him this time.

But he still needed a place to hide. A small section of hill had fallen away, leaving a mound of earthen debris to hide behind and an overhang out of the steep hillside to provide some margin of protection. It was a pathetic excuse for a shelter, but as much as he could hope for in the circumstances. At this point, solitude sounded nice. Maybe a few hours of uninterrupted sleep would help the world look more rosy and less bloody.

He turned around to make sure there was nothing else better. In the fading twilight, he noticed a pale, bulky shadow patched onto the darkness of another bush.

The shadow blinked.

Arssen's stomach twisted and plunged, and he gave a hoarse cry. Something gray. Something stunted. Something.

He swore he didn't so much as blink, but the Something he had seen from the battle crossed the distance between the shrub and him without so much as taking a step. It was breathing on him.

He smelled it: carrion and saltwater.

Now, nothing.

"*Huunhhhh…*"

Arssen's life restarted with a desperate clamor for air. As the oxygen hit his lungs, his eyes blinked open. He quickly came to the conclusion that that was a bad move.

At first, he thought he was on a stony hilltop at night, because nothing was visible outside of his small patch of light. But Arssen could feel the distance spreading out everywhere. The air filling his nostrils was damp, earthy, and heavy. He was underground, somewhere.

This was not a shallow, candlelit cave like those of the rebels, but a monstrous cavern so deep that the weight of the earth overhead pressed on every inch of Arssen, and so enormous that the sounds of his wheezes didn't return.

Lying on his back on the cold stone, he propped himself up on his elbows. His hands brushed the floor and felt smooth, solid rock. If there wasn't even soil here, he had to be somewhere deep. He glanced around, but an angry drumming in his head forced him to move slowly. A single, flickering flame sprouted out of a single finger of stone in the ground, no longer than his hand. The sole source of light hissed quietly. But the strange, pale fire disquieted him. It was an aberration and failed to comfort.

No sign of life interrupted his isolation.

A thought ignited in Arssen's mind and brought a shadow of a smile to his face. Maybe he was in an elaborate test designed by the Armies of the Human Rebellion for recruits. Perhaps V'lair's anger, Arssen's eviction, the creature, and now this room were all designed to try his resolve.

Arssen sat up fully now, braver, but still not willing to stand. His heartbeat had returned to a more temperate patter and he wrinkled his nose at the stench of mildew he had just noticed. He turned around and stopped, hesitant.

The Something skulked in the long shadow Arssen cast. It was close but nearly invisible in the faint light. It was little more than a smooth, dark gray lump on the cave floor. It could have been asleep, or dead.

It opened two orbs with pulsating blue centers and stared at Arssen. The something emitted a tiny, pitiful moan.

Just like the angels' roar, the Something's soft cry slithered into Arssen's ears and bit hard.

The cave was gone. Pain roared in his ears like the ocean off Pangaea's coast. He saw his wife and daughter lying dead at the feet of humans. Blood. His father was murdered. Darkness. The distant, terrible clashes between angels and Gray Ones tore his old home apart all over again.

His thoughts returned to the cave as his body rattled against the stone floor. His head was still swimming with raw longing and fear that belonged to someone else. Arssen wasn't sure when he stood up, but he knew he was running away from that terrible Something.

Underfoot, the ground seemed to pitch and churn as he fought to find footing at that speed in the unforgiving darkness. He briefly considered the possibility of running into a bottomless chasm in his blindness, but he had no choice. He stumbled and nearly fell. Only the mad scrambling of hands and feet kept him up and forwardly mobile.

Another hiss sounded ahead, and another finger of flame appeared in the floor. He dashed into the light and back out the other side, afraid of being visible to the Something. The light disappeared behind him.

His panting, gasping, weeping rush ended against something warm and surprisingly soft.

Arssen staggered backward and finally collapsed. Yet another finger of light sprang up next to him, revealing a small host of Somethings on every side.

They were ringed around him. Only the foremost were visible in their entirety, but over their sloping shoulders, he could see the heads of more. Many more. None moved, but they shivered and faded in his vision as if he were badly drunk. Sometimes they looked doubled with each Something crouching next to a twin, and other times they were barely there. His eyes refused to look directly at any one, instead sliding around to either the darkness above or the earthen floor below. The Somethings seemed to be nothing but textureless, gray skin. The only feature Arssen could pick out was their huge eyes, which glistened a dazzling azure. The beautiful sapphire color seemed profane in their setting.

The smell of sweet nectar flooded his nostrils as he saw the eyes. The taste of a bitten tongue filled his mouth at the same time, seemingly from nowhere. He mumbled to himself and tried to look away from the Somethings, but they were all around him. A distant roar, like a waterfall draining the oceans in the end days, hissed into his ears and began washing away his thoughts and scouring his mind clean of reason. He licked his lips to try to taste something other than iron. His tongue felt numb and heavy, and the sensation barely registered.

And he supposed he was still standing there. He could see himself as if peeping from a second-floor window nearby. Then he saw his own wide eyes staring blankly ahead. He tried to blink and found he was inside his own body again.

The Somethings were the Gray Ones. Arssen's heart skipped beats and a lack of air nearly plunged him back into darkness. People didn't know what the Gray Ones looked like because people didn't see the Gray Ones. Those who assumedly did were murdered, or they vanished, or worst of all they became another ghastly member of the Possessed.

But these monstrosities surrounding him seemed so thoroughly opposite to the angels that Arssen was certain he had found the enemy.

One of the Gray Ones cried: a lost, longing sound. As it did, Arssen thought he noticed not one but three open mouths. He couldn't, wouldn't look close enough to make out details. But he got an impression of gleaming ivory fangs—toothy daggers that made those of the Possessed seem like poor imitations.

Arssen shuddered and pulled himself into a ball, hiding his face. A second Gray One answered the call of the first. More joined. In seconds, a harsh cacophony stabbed Arssen again and again and again, so he was certain he would feel blood oozing across his skin. He couldn't so much as put a coherent thought into words, as even the sanctity of his head was scourged with acid.

The noise ended. Arssen's muscles relaxed in exhaustion.

"Peace, cleaners."

The voice rumbled through the ground, and Arssen felt it as much as heard it. A pair of soft hands picked him up and unfolded him like a father with a fresh towel. They set him on his feet. He would have fallen immediately, but one hand remained and held him in place until his knees started working again.

Arssen looked up through numb, aching eyes. Before him stood an angel among the Gray Ones, his skin gently glowing and humming with power. The angel smiled.

Unlike the other angels, this one had cracked skin that looked painfully dry beneath its aura of light. When a bend of an arm or leg opened one of the cracks particularly wide, faint blue light snaked out of the split in lazy tendrils that flowed like smoke. And strangest of all, a soft *thump-thud, thump-thud* filled the silence around the guardian. Its heartbeat pounded the air around it loudly enough for Arssen to hear over his own raging pulse.

Whether his thoughts were his own or the perverse toys of the Gray Ones, Arssen didn't know. But he beheld the angel, and Arssen hated it. Any true angel in such close quarters to the enemy should be throwing its life away in an effort to destroy as many as it could. This one was false, a trick or worse. Arssen's face twitched once, twice, and then contorted while his chest heaved and he bent almost double.

"Traitor!" he roared at the giant. "Filthy, worthless son of slag! I hope your friends tear off the least important parts first and let you bleed!"

But his venom seemed trite. So he screamed and threw himself at the angel.

The angel grunted and pushed Arssen to his knees with one hand. The pulsating heartbeat throbbed through the touch. "Peace and joy to you, as well," it said. "I am Guardian Pejhrafer."

The ease with which the angel rebuffed him fueled the maelstrom in his head. Arssen threw himself up again, but the angel firmly pressed him down again without hurting him.

"Stop treating me like a child, I'm not a child, I will not be helpless, I'm not weak!" Arssen screamed in one breath, spittle rolling off his lips on his chin.

"Prove it then, and speak from your heart and not the heart of the Cry." Guardian Pejhrafer motioned to the Gray Ones.

Arssen felt angry tears stumble down his cheeks. He wanted to pulverize the calmness off the traitor's face, then use his limbs as flails on the Gray Ones until their numbers finished his sad, pathetic excuse for a life. He could do something right before the end. Swallowing the shakiness in his throat, he looked up into the luminescent face of Guardian Pejhrafer and spoke, carefully pronouncing each word to make sure they each tasted like his and no one else's. They did.

"Kill me now, or I do the same to you."

The Gray Ones began to agitate, ululating at his words.

"Well, you have pleased them, at least," the guardian said. He, and it seemed to be more he than she, shifted his ponderous weight on his feet. "Do you know what they are, child of Man?"

Arssen felt confident that the guardian was expecting an answer like *Gray Ones* or *animals*, so he spited Pejhrafer with a well-earned cliche. "Evil."

"Oh. You *do* know what they are," Pejhrafer said as if genuinely impressed. "These 'Gray Ones' as you humans call them are, quite literally, the essence of evil. The very fact that Crown Mind allowed them to exist and torment us all is proof of his...fallibility. Has the war brought us peace? Comfort? The fighting must end, and so I refuse to fight them any longer. A simple solution, child of Man. Take note."

Arssen grunted without commitment.

Pejhrafer pressed forward, his eyes softening as his arms fell to his sides. More whiffs of the bluish lights trailed from the cracks in his skin at the motion.

"You feel it too," he said, "but the only end you can see to the war is death. I was created slightly taller. I can see an end to these torturous times that does not include our deaths, Arssen, son of Uruh."

Flinching at the sound of his father's name in the profane pit, Arssen continued to stare ahead without any other acknowledgment.

"Let us live! But the fighting must cease. The war must cease. These savage things around us, they feed on our misery and fear. It is why they played with you instead of ravaging your spirit and corrupting your body, as they are wont to do. It is why they run, unchecked, through this world. But they bathe in our hate and rage with just as much relish. They love it until the moment they cease to be."

"So we help them on their way out," Arssen growled.

"Admirable," Guardian Pejhrafer conceded. "Futile, though. It will not lead to real happiness. How can you enjoy revenge on a monster that cannot feel misery like you do?"

"The only real happiness in the world died years ago." Arssen's breath shook as he spoke, and he waited until he felt his thoughts were his own again before he continued. "Any end will suit me fine, so end it! And quick, too, if you please. Let's get this over with."

He threw out his arms and thrust out his chest, presenting himself as an easy target. Slowly, his eyelids fell shut. He waited.

No one spoke or made so much as a sound. Only the slight whisper of the candle jet broke the oppressive nothingness of this infernal hole. There were no teeth or claws burying themselves in his unprotected body.

The waiting became unbearable, and finally, he opened his eyes.

"Lost your—?" he started, before his jaw snapped shut. And then it gradually dropped open again.

Every last Gray One was gone. They had vanished as immediately and silently as they had appeared. Although Arssen could imagine that they were simply behind some ethereal veil, invisible but there, he was also sure he would have still been able to sense their suffocating presence. The taste of sugar and blood had disappeared from his mouth. They had left.

There was more light now. Spouting up from the ground from a pair of tiny craters were two tall columns of white fire, much like the other candle flames. Except each of these was about the size of a tall man. And within them flickered a pair of bipedal images that were at the same time both alien and familiar.

"Jemma," he moaned, quaking at the sight of his young daughter in one of the flames.

She looked just as beautiful as she had years ago, but she had grown. She stood almost up to his shoulders now, and her face had lost much of its childish roundness: a young woman mere months from blooming into adolescence. Her blonde hair had been cut shorter. He had always liked it long, but Sara had never cared.

Sara.

The image of his wife flickered in and out of view in the other white fire. Her bright eyes were alive and blinking, and he could feel his mind lose its grip on the horrible memory of them frozen open in death. The old, wretched image slipped away at the sight of her now. She looked healthy and happy, if a touch frustrated at something.

He reached forward to touch her shoulder. He had to. The feel of her would… It would do something. He wasn't sure what. But the need for it blotted out everything else. The heat of the flame gnawed at his hand at his approach, and it bit down harder with each passing inch. He pushed through the pain at first. But by the time he was a hairbreadth away from Sara, he couldn't ignore the agony or the smell of his own skin boiling.

He yanked his hand back and cradled the burnt flesh. A growling sob tumbled out of his chest. They were real. They were his. He could tell. No one could read people as well and as quickly as he could. He could tell!

"I'm sorry," he whispered. "I thought I was strong enough. I thought I'd bought you enough time. When I told you to run, I thought I had them distracted! I swear, I—I'm so very sorry."

The images watched him silently. Could they even hear him?

"You see with your own eyes."

Guardian Pejhrafer stood behind him, sorrow dripping silently down his large features like a pair of streams across a mountain-side. "Death is no end, only a change. Their spirits live on, happy. And I can return them to you."

Arssen stared at the images, unwilling to lose one second with his family. Jemma smiled up at him and his heart plummeted. He beamed back at her through a film of tears.

He whispered to the angel, "At what cost, Guardian? I'll give you my life as long as you give me a day with them before you collect it."

"Hm. I require no price," Pejhrafer returned, voice rumbling. More bluish light curled out of the cracks in his skin with a soft *whoosh* in the silence. "I long abandoned my more useless tasks and became my own superior. And as such, I can task myself with nothing more than the comforting of those upon whom the world has spat."

"What's the price?" Arssen demanded. His eyes blinked at the flames, transfixed.

He felt panic well up inside as the two pale lights flickered in a sudden cold breath of air. He had no illusion that his time was running out.

"I am not a master of death. That title belongs to others. I can only restore your Jemma and Sara with the cooperation of their current keepers."

"Who?" Arssen could only imagine one answer to the question —he just waited for the angel to confirm it.

"The Cry."

The flames grew long in a second burst of wind, and the images of his family vanished for a horrible moment. Arssen didn't move, didn't breathe. The fires flickered and sputtered until the gust abated, then the images returned. Sara seemed to see Jemma in the flame next to her for the first time. Her eyes grew wide and panic froze her lovely features.

Arssen's heart caught. They weren't together. He had always imagined that his wife and daughter would at least be together in death. But if death meant isolation, then life was the only time they had together.

He cried out, cursing Crown Mind and any other god he could think of. "Stop stalling!" he howled at Guardian Pejhrafer. "I agree. Whatever it is, I agree!"

"Fill their ranks of the dead." Pejhrafer gave a great sigh as if the words tore his heart out on the way through his throat. "Give them easy prey. Then they will care less for the spirits they lost, and there will be a balance of sorts. Tell them where the nearby human resistance is."

"My friends are in there. Mother."

"Yes."

"Will they be safe?" Arssen turned to face the angel directly.

"No one is safe in this world," Pejhrafer stated. "Not you, not I, not them. The only ones who need not fear death are the dead."

John...the man grieving over his lost son. The warrior who protected his wife. Vanders...the woman Arssen had thought might someday replace an irreplaceable woman, but who now stared at him with only blame in her eyes. Salik...the killer who could take care of himself if only he stopped taking on everyone else's burdens too—ah, the poor old fool. Ursa…

Stay and burn on the inside, or leap towards the other side on only hope?

Arssen stared over his shoulder, tears slipping over an agonized scowl as he saw the pale shades of Jemma and Sara shiver: the only lights in the endless night around him.

THE SUN'S RED ANGER THRUMMED AGAINST THE FOGGY MASS IN THE SKY as Arssen stumbled up to the entrance of the rebel's caves. The Earth itself wasn't burning yet under the heat, but it would be soon. Daylight had arrived in all its fury.

Arssen half-expected his group to be waiting for him outside of the caves, and he sniffed. The air smelled of distant mildew. Odd. Arssen frowned as he realized that the memories of the walk there had just faded. Where had he—? It didn't matter. Shaking his head, he strode into the first cave without being stopped by any guards.

The reason why was quickly evident. The headquarters had been abandoned. V'lair must have moved his civilians and remaining soldiers to a safer distance from Melimard.

Arssen shuffled through the guard's quarters. A few abandoned uniforms lay strewn about on the floor. Three lay stretched out on the beds of their owners as if the guards just couldn't have been bothered to take the outfits with them. Arssen smiled slightly. The sight was kind of funny.

Then, he checked out the small sinkhole that had served as the kitchens. He snatched a cauldron of burning soup off the embers of a fire that someone had forgotten to extinguish. Careless. He poured himself a bowl of the gamey stew and ate as he walked. The tasteless food was nonetheless hot and soothed his shrunken stomach. He glanced about the place. Another uniform had been left in careless disarray over a second cook-fire, burning with a horrible smell.

Arssen stifled a giggle. It was just ridiculous enough to be funny. Hilarious, even.

The armory, the forge, the civilian caverns were the same. Candles that had been left burning now lit his way as he walked and slurped soup. Bunks had been shattered, a few broken swords and chairs lay around the floors, and more sets of clothing had been tossed about the rooms. Two child-sized tunics lay stacked on a larger one. A derisive laugh came honking out unconsciously. Slobs. He couldn't imagine what they had been thinking.

The underground air was soggy and thick, but he was used to it now. Some of the passages between caves were pitch black, but each bout of utter darkness relieved him like a cool shower. He couldn't quite figure out why. His eyes just seemed to hurt less.

Finally, he stepped into V'lair's old chambers. The cave was filled with a weird buzzing that tickled his ears and made his skin itch. He absentmindedly swatted his arms.

Uniforms and garments of all kinds lay scattered and thrown about the floor. The place was a scavenger's dream. Some clothes were hanging over the four-poster bed, which was now only a two-poster bed. Others were draped over the table and the remaining chairs. Rubble scattered over the floor and a far wall had partially caved in, half-burying more clothing. He frowned in confusion. But the frown dissolved in the unrelenting humor that had seized him that morning, and he burst out laughing.

Trying not to chuckle himself into a heap on the floor, Arssen picked his way around a pair of John's green and brown pants and over one of Ursa's ugly dresses. He noticed V'lair's armor laying in pieces near the center of the cave, and he imagined all the people running about the northern hills in just their underwear. He doubled over in another fit of helpless giggles.

Arssen took one more step forward when his feet shot out from underneath him and he landed on his back near a discarded chair. The fall hurt, but he couldn't stop laughing.

He stared at his ragged shoes and the red cloth tied around them. He couldn't see what he had slipped on. The red cloth should have added grip to the red soles of his red shoes. What had—?

Not red uniforms. Not uniforms.

Red.

red

red red red red red …

"Haaaahhh!"

Arssen bent over. Eyes glazed. Scream raging everywhere. Terrifying scream.

His scream. Not laughing anymore. He felt a second one coming.

"Aaaaaaahhhh! Aaaaaahhhhhhhh!"

He screamed and screamed until his dry throat crackled. He was sprawled out amongst hundreds of corpses and he screamed as his mind flirted with sanity. No Jemma. No wife. No life. Not here.

"Aaaaaahhhhh!"

Mother crushed. Salik slain. V'lair torn into a dozen pieces and scattered. John, Vanders, fingers intertwined in death. Red on the floor.

Red on the wall, Red in the hall.

Red on Arssen most of all.

Another laugh bubbled upwards and he choked it out. He interrupted it with another scream. When his breath gave out, he shook with silent mirth as he turned on the chair next to him and ripped it to pieces with his hands: his red hands … *red red red red red red red*

RED. He tossed the splinters and chunks over the dead bodies. It was the only thing he could do. The best thing to do. No, just the only thing to do. Yes.

Among the human bodies were massive skeletons, completely bereft of flesh. Some were whole, but others were not. The angels. Silvery stains covered the floor around each of the giant bodies and could have just as easily been the residue of some supernatural killing blow as the final remains of some Gray Ones. Whatever madness had occurred earlier, the angels and humans lay side-by-side in silence now.

A wail shook the cavern. Not his. Arssen whipped around.

The young angel, Guardian Varrador, stood in the dim entrance to the cave. He leaned heavily on the stone wall as if he had run miles to make it here. The power that danced across his skin faded and surged to the rhythm of his heaving chest. His face was warped nearly beyond recognition with hate and despondency as he stared at the massive tomb.

He wailed again. Then he fixed his unsteady gaze on the one living body in the room.

"Arssen, son of Ursa," Guardian Varrador hissed. His eyes flared and his voice rose to a roar. "Arssen, son or Ursa! Arssen, son of Ursa and Uruh! Arssen, husband to Sara! Arssen, father of Jemma! *I know you*."

Arssen stared. The names he heard no longer meant anything. Red was all that was left. Eat and sleep and Red. The desire to speak had abandoned him. No words. No thoughts. So he listened.

"I follow orders. I scout. And I return to this? This is my reward for unquestioning obedience? To outlive my legion and be the last? To arrive too late?" the angel bellowed.

And then Guardian Varrador gathered himself up. He rose and the light around him gathered until Arssen could have been looking at a living thunderstorm. "But I hear them. I will always be able to hear them. They knew what you did. The Cry sang it to them as they feasted, and now their bones echo it back to me."

Guardian Varrador took a long step towards Arssen with

clenched fists the size of ax heads. But then he stopped, shaking. Misery dripped across his features.

"What deal did you make?" he mumbled. "What treasure did they promise? Wealth? Comfort? Where is your reward? We are pledged not to harm, and I will not betray my Lord on your behalf. But by Crown Mind's heart, I swear that you have received all the reward that the betrayers will grant you, and even that is not punishment enough!"

Arssen followed the angel's gesture around the room of slaughter. His eyes fixed on the body of his mother. A wretched cry broke out of him and he hid his face. Oh good. All gone now. He stilled.

Varrador growled somewhere off to the side. There was a shuffling noise, back and forth across the floor. Mumbling. And then something that startled Arssen as he hid behind his hands. The angel sang.

The song was not a human song of words, but more akin to a birdsong. Arssen heard animalistic sounds in the song, paired with human syllables and noises that he could only just detect in the distant edges of hearing. The song filled the cave air, the Earth above it, and the Earth below it.

Whether from his own careful thought or through some more diabolic art, the meaning seeped into Arssen hours after Guardian Varrador had abandoned him in the cave.

No curse upon the Man
   Not more than he bears
   Set upon his bones long life
   Set upon his spirit long life
   Set no more harm upon this spirit
   May Crown Mind judge this spirit

But may his soul live again
   And each spirit dwell like me

Alone in guilt unquenchable
Adrift without loyalties
A bane to each family
As alone as he has left me

AFTERWARD, HE HAD HISSED IN THE COMMON LANGUAGE, "MAY YOU always ruin those you love."

But Arssen slept that night with the song still thrumming in his head. In the morning he awoke with the words still buried in his mind. They made him smile. They sort of rhymed.

After all, nothing could touch the dead. And this world never failed to make dead the living, regardless of songs. He wouldn't make it out alive, but for the rest of his days, he would run for his life all the same. He would eat and drink and sleep and wait for his wife and daughter.

The traitor angel's promise to bring back his family might be fulfilled someday. Or it might not. But one thought had imprinted itself in his head, a certainty entombed in the laws of time:

Every minute would bring him another minute closer to a family reunion, one way or another. So he waited.

EON 3 - BACK IN CONTROL

Now, Marty J. Bowman was not a wise man. In fact, he wasn't even that smart of a man. He admitted that. But he was shrewd, and he knew his business, and that's why he was getting tossed more job offers than he could juggle in two hands. Honestly, the thought made him a little giddy. But just a little. He did, after all, have his professional pride to consider, and he had until after the presidential election to make his decision.

That pride had carried him far from his original cloudy college days at the University of Oregon. After his first internship at a local advertising firm, Marty had always refused to accept any job that didn't take him a big step forward. "Life is too short for small steps" had been his senior quote, and was a phrase he repeated often, much to the annoyance of his close friends. "To take big steps, you have to stretch until it hurts," he'd said. And he'd stretched into his first full-time job writing copy for that firm, stretched into a bigger agency south in San Francisco, and stretched into the position of official speechwriter in the Gary Henson presidential campaign.

His friends still wondered how he had been so unfairly lucky as to receive that tap on the shoulder. Marty shrugged it off, figuring he'd have to be as crazy as a politician to know exactly why he'd been hired. Then again, he hadn't spent his life building up his social capital for nothing.

The wind was hot and dry when Marty stepped out of his '93 SVT Mustang Cobra. Unlike the inside of his car, which he had filled with new car smell every few weeks, the outside world smelled like exhaust, in every meaning of the word. He wrinkled his nose, gently shut the car door, and marched into the office building where the Henson campaign was headquartered.

He managed to make it into the elevator without looking anyone in the eye, since he had already had his fill of icy stares. But it didn't last. Just before the double doors of the lift closed, a janitor stumbled in and dragged a mop and bucket with him. The man gave Marty a nervous smile and nod before looking after his pail of dirty water.

Marty gave him a polite nod in return and stared straight ahead. He noted with displeasure that the janitor had tapped an even higher floor number than his, which meant the whole, painfully slow ride up would be awkward. He patted his head, a sign he was stressed. Then he felt a few hairs out of place.

"How do I look?" Marty demanded of the janitor.

The grungier man gave him a long glance with a surprisingly thoughtful frown. After a moment, he replied slowly, as if he were picking each word fresh from a garden somewhere.

"You have kind eyes with a lot of laugh lines, so you're either generally happy with your life or you've lied to yourself long enough to fake it. You got wrinkles earlier than you should've, and you look stressed. By your suit, you're a guy that likes to dress up, but you also don't care about fashion so much that you need new duds every year."

Marty wasn't sure how to react.

The janitor continued, unfazed by Marty's nonplussed expression. "No wedding ring, so no girl. You could be a sleaze that takes his ring off to pick up secretaries, but you've got a decent poolside tan and you don't have any tan lines from a ring either, so nix that.

You're clean but careless. You like making a scene more than making friends, huh?"

Marty took a deep breath. "The hair," he ground out. "How does the hair look?"

"Oh."

The janitor spit in one hand and patted the top of Marty's head with it. Marty turned as red as his Mustang.

"Gotcha covered, Mr. Bowman," the janitor said cheerfully.

Just then the doors opened again and an attractive woman and several of her coworkers hopped on the elevator before Marty could curse at the gormless floor wiper. The janitor brightened as he saw the floor they were on and hopped out, mop and bucket in hand, even though he was nowhere near the floor he had chosen. He waved at Marty as the doors closed.

One of the women gave Marty a friendly, "Good morning."

"Isn't it just," Marty returned.

AS HE EXPECTED, THE UNPLANNED SPIT SHINE SEEMED TO BE A GOOD indicator of the direction of his day. Henson himself was in the campaign office instead of en route to New York for the TV interviews he had scheduled. The thirty-six-year-old presidential candidate had parked his derriere on an intern's desk. To all appearances, the two seemed to be having a serious conversation about the failed reboot of *Get Smart*.

Henson was wearing a brightly colored, $15 windbreaker over his Armani dress shirt. He kept sweeping his floppy dark hair out of his face like he was on Dawson's Creek, a habit that had admittedly worked very well for him on the campaign trail. Clinton's Paula Jones affair had cost him his presidency two years ago, and the country wasn't about to elect another white male Democrat unless he was everything Billy-boy wasn't. Gary Henson fit the bill.

If he won, he'd easily be the youngest and least mature American ever to sit in the oval office. If he lost, his twin brother would be in power.

That alone was fascinating enough to bring voting numbers to the highest they'd been in a century, never mind the scandals. Politics had become interesting dinner conversation. The two Henson twins, Gary and Ben: two opposites, locked in a sibling rivalry that had reached unprecedented heights in their knock-down, drag-out, kick-in-the-teeth fight for the highest office in the land. It made the campaign office an odd blend of heaven and hell for Marty.

He, by the way, had his own problems with this overinflated visibility. While most of the other men and women fighting the good fight in the campaign office just gave him a polite smile or nod, a few of them were personal friends of his from back in college, other members of the profession, his circle.

And as of a week ago, his circle had unanimously agreed that Marty's name was mud.

He stepped past Sandy's desk and decided to try anyway. "Morning, Sandy. By the way, nice job wrangling those computer jockeys yesterday. Someone had to straighten them out. How goes the new ABC ad?"

Her long lashes didn't so much as flutter at the sound of his voice. "We'll see soon enough," she replied brusquely. She continued typing away at her keyboard, her unswerving gaze making it clear to him that she considered the encounter over.

He slouched away to his desk, not bothering to strike up a conversation with Dexter either. The event planner would be busy enough to ignore him outright.

Just then, Henson noticed Marty and excused himself from his conversation about defunct comedies to strut towards his speechwriter. His eyebrows wiggled expertly over the crazy smirk that had famously accompanied some personal sniping against the other contenders back in the primaries. Marty found the corners of his own mouth lifting despite his black mood. Moron.

"Bowman!" Henson crowed, shaking his hand. "It's a beautiful day in L.A.!"

"Which you would know since you are not in New York," Marty Bowman said with as much respect as he could muster.

"Hah! Yes, you'd be amazed how many people have mentioned that to me today."

"I wouldn't be. I really wouldn't be."

Henson rolled his eyes heavenward. "Believe me, I threw every ounce of grace and patience I had into those negotiations. Fox has another thing coming if they think being fourth best of four networks means they can boss around the democratically elected."

"They're Fox and you're a Democrat," Marty said with a weary shrug. "Sometimes I think they're just a little biased."

"If you think they're bad, you should rewatch what NBC did to my brother and the rest of those elephant schmucks. It always cheers me up," Henson chuckled, eyes bright. "Still, at least I didn't miss this weather by being stuck in that megastorm New York has going on."

He paused. "'Megastorm.' Is there any way we can use the word 'megastorm' in any of my speeches? Because if we can, then we have an obligation as Americans to do so."

Marty shifted in his chair uncomfortably, longing for a date with one of the office's coffee pots. "Would you bother reading it if I wrote it?"

"For 'megastorm,' I guarantee you a full minute of fully rehearsed, immaculately pronounced speech reading."

"Your supporters would think you'd lost your mind," Marty warned.

"Just because I appreciate a good word?" Henson grunted. Then he glanced back at Marty and grinned again. "Or because I actually recited one of my speeches for longer than three seconds?"

Marty jabbed a pen in his direction. "Bingo, sir. So, do you have anything particular to discuss, or are we just shooting the breeze?"

Henson wandered around the little separate office that Marty now called home. It had a potted fern on the desk, a window, and a door he could use to shut out the noise. The office was small, but an oasis of calm away from the heat that the interns faced in the open design of the main room.

And until last week's debate, this lovely office had belonged to

Sandy. Last week, Gary Henson had sent the media into a roaring frenzy by revealing that his opponent, his twin brother, had probably had an affair with his own sister-in-law. His wife's sister had confirmed this after a quick phone call. Her mental state rendered the admission legally worthless, of course. But that was a technicality. What followed wasn't so much a spark of controversy as it was a firebomb. The pre-election polls burned with the news.

And all thanks to Marty's personal sleuthing. Marty had caught the first hint of tension in the family. Marty had called around until he had gotten through to the elder twin's sister-in-law. The recorded details went straight to Gary.

So now Sandy worked with the rest in the main room and Marty was the undisputed office pet of Gary Henson. Funny how that worked.

Oblivious to Marty's swirling thoughts, Henson turned with a bored look on his sharp features. "I'm thinking golf. I know this one place with a hole twelve where you can *just* sink a hole-in-one with the right club. What about you? Too tied up today, or can I count you in?"

Marty stared blankly for a moment, picturing all the actual work he had piled up to process. But life was too short for small steps, so he nodded.

"COME ON! STRING BEAN, GIVE US A BREAK!"

With an exaggerated sigh, Marty slowed down and let his friends catch up with him. It was a rare, beautiful day of sunshine on the college campus. Walking at someone else's pace had never been comfortable or fun. Was it his fault he was the only one who worked out?

Sandy trotted up to his elbow and swatted him on the arm.

"Hey! What gives?" he demanded.

"Because I know your face," she said, sticking her tongue out at him. "You aren't, like, faster because you 'work out.' You have longer legs than us, string bean. That's it. End of story. Shut up."

Dexter laughed from behind them. "That shows you to think, and have a face, and all."

Dexter's girlfriend, Jean, made a face at him, too. He leaned in for a kiss but she pulled away and thrust her nose in the air.

"And that's why I don't date," Marty said with a snort.

"Because you're a smug little weenie?" Sandy smirked.

"Ah-ha-haha-haha. I don't see you with a man at your elbow, genius."

She bounced up onto a nearby bench and sat on the back, planting her dirty shoes on the seat. A large, flowering something-or-other was in full glorious bloom nearby. Marty could feel his eyes watering already as he crossed his arms and stared his challenge at his younger friend.

He was the oldest among his four friends by a full year, even though they were all sophomores at the university. And Marty looked oldest, with a more mature face and a long, slim form that was useful in Ultimate Frisbee but had also sowed the seed for his unfortunate nickname.

"Maybe I don't need a 'man' to enjoy life," Sandy said, folding her hands in her lap primly.

"Maybe I don't either. Check and mate," Marty shot back.

"You don't need a man? Good for you!" Sandy laughed.

Marty sighed. Acing a test was one thing, but teachers gave an hour for those. Sandy was a raven-haired word witch who could outtalk him even on her bad days. He just wasn't good at speaking. Sometimes he wondered if getting her out of his hair for a semester would be worth the trouble of creating a fake corporation, inviting her to intern with them, and then convincing some friends back home to fabricate an office environment to send her to each day. An entire duplicitous internship would be legendary.

It was worth a thought.

"And now you're trying to figure out where to banish your best friend," Sandy said, shaking a finger at him. "Shameful."

"*How* and *why* do you do that?" he demanded.

"Because it's fun, and because I know your face. Did I mention that?"

Jean and Dexter hung back, looking through one of Jean's textbooks. Dexter took the time to smirk at them, though. "Get a room, y'all."

"Y'all!" Jean, Sandy, and Marty all jumped on him at once.

"Come on! Give it up, y...ou people," Dexter protested. "I'll have you know it is a legitimate second person plural with—"

"—with culture and reasons and uses. Yes, yes, it's very cute," Jean interrupted him, nuzzling against his shirt collar.

"I'm surrounded by the uneducated fools of the world."

Happy to have the collective wit of the circle aimed at someone else, Marty affected a southern drawl to outshine Dexter's and said, "Why, that's why we all got ourselves to college! We getting ourselves learned but good, y'all!"

Dexter was about to snap back when little carrot-topped Christina ran up.

She was wheezing for breath and her eyes were squinty, a sure sign that she was upset. For a moment, Marty thought she was going to sprint right past them. Instead, she slammed into him and threw her arms around his chest.

She immediately began tugging him back the way she had come. From anyone else, the behavior would have been weird. But this was Christina. She had been as reserved as an owl until she had gotten to know the rest of the circle, then she just seemed to assume they were as good as family. Christina gave him another hard jerk to follow her.

"Whoa, man!" Marty protested. He tried not to fall over. "Where's the party?"

"Neddy fell," she whispered, her eyes huge and leaking down her pale face.

MARTY KNEW HE SHOULD HAVE BEEN AT WORK. HE WANTED TO BE AT work. He should have said no. He had writings to write. He was not a schmoozer, not a socializer. Getting in more work alone would have gone farther to convincing everyone else he wasn't some kind of pet hitman. In fact, he was a real copywriter and speechwriter.

But it was a nice day, at least. Some salty wind blew in from the coast and made him feel peckish.

He whacked his golf ball with all the finesse and power of a drunk bull. Now he had taken another big step back. Now he was sunk. The ball gently curved back to Earth. Or rather, to water. *Plop.* Yes, he was sunk. Just like that shot.

"You wouldn't have to keep taking penalties if you took your time and aimed, but man, do I wish I had your arm!" Gary Henson laughed.

"Thanks, I think," Marty said.

John Lemar laughed loudly. As Henson's faithful campaign manager, he had also abandoned the office for this impromptu outing. He was as tall as Marty but older and wider with a shock of gray hair that flapped in the wind like the wing of a seagull.

"I thought you spies were all good at golf, drinking, and poker," John wheezed, eyes glittering in the bright Californian sun.

"Mmm," Marty replied. That showed him.

While John and Henson continued to joke around, Marty found himself only throwing out an occasional retort. Mostly he just nodded and smiled. Fencing with wits, like golf, had never been his sport, but that wasn't the problem. A few weeks back, he would have slapped the Queen of England to be invited to eighteen holes with Gary Henson and John. Now, he just wanted to hide in his new office and bury himself in grammar and syntax.

On the seventeenth hole, their stomachs were all snarling and fit to be stuffed, and only John, who particularly prided himself on his golf game, was still taking a leisurely amount of setup time for each shot. During one such stretch of preparation, Henson sidled up to Marty with a smirk.

"What do you think?" he whispered, gesturing with a club to John as the older man wiggled back and forth and peered down range at the twin sand traps straddling the hole. "I can fake a sneeze like you wouldn't believe. Let's see if a few strokes off his game can ruffle that slab he calls hair."

Marty grunted. Juvenile.

"Competitive, sir?" he said. "Sounds like capitalist talk. If our constituents could just hear us now."

"Everyone's a weekday capitalist, man," Henson said. "But isn't this what the dream's about? Equalizing everyone? You know that some people are just born normal, like me. You can't throw losers on pedestals overnight. Sometimes it's smarter to knock the big boys down a few pegs instead. Make it fair. How many times have you written the words 'equal footing' in the past year?"

"More times than you've read it," Marty ventured.

"Hah! But we're going to lose our chance, he's about to swing."

By the way John's club was hanging in the air, he was indeed about to finalize his shot. Marty's stomach said "lunch," but his sense of debate said, "just a bit longer." So, he called out just before John could swing.

"John! Watch that cross-breeze!"

The campaign manager froze and looked up at a nearby palm. He turned to Marty slowly and for a moment he seemed to consider firing the speechwriter. Instead, he smiled and gave him a thumbs-up before starting his excruciating preparation ritual all over again.

Henson giggled and swore under his breath. "Brilliant, man, brilliant," he added. "And are you really trying to use my own politics against me? I'm Gary 'the Good Guy' Henson, or haven't you met my supporters?"

Marty leaned against a tree and massaged his ankle before replying. This was easily the longest time he had spoken directly to Gary Henson at once. Guilt and issues aside, he was nervous. Impressing the man was one thing, and his smear job had done that. But befriending the future president? That was worth more than all the job offers he had gotten in the past week combined. Henson knew how to reward people who impressed or amused him.

"'I don't rabble-rouse'," Marty quoted. "'I only invite the truth to make an appearance.'"

"Oh that's good," Henson said. "Who said that? You should throw that into one of my debate speeches."

"I, uh, did. Months ago."

"Really now."

"It was that primary debate when you tore through Gore."

"Hah! Yes, that was a good night," Henson said, grinning. "I was feeling the beast within and had to let him out. No offense to your speechwriting."

"Just don't let out your inner beast like Clinton did. I'm still surprised that you've made it this far as a single man. The stability - "

Henson interrupted with a flap of his gloved hand. The man rolled his muscular shoulders as they watched John bouncing on his toes and trying to get a bearing on those tricky cross-breezes.

"No ball and chain, no infidelity scandal," Henson said simply. "Out with the old and distracted, in with the young and dedicated."

"So if I were to ask you to double-date with me..." Marty said with a laugh.

"Unless Madonna's free, then you and your date would be stuck with the most handsome third wheel on the East Coast," he replied, tiny crow's feet softening his face as he did.

Marty took the chance to look at the man, to really look at him and not just a passing glance. Although Gary Henson and his brother were identical genetically, they had orchestrated their appearances to be as different as possible in the past year or two. The younger brother by minutes, Gary took the hairstyle of a teen heartthrob and the personality to boot. Yet, he was still grinning and joking even without a camera in his face. If anyone could smile at the world from the peak of Mount America while the world aimed its biggest guns at him, Henson could.

"I wouldn't have the time until after the election, myself," Marty said.

Henson harrumphed as he rolled up his $100 sleeves.

"Have a real whip-cracker for a boss, huh? Me too," he said with a glint in his eye. "I keep telling the guy, if he tries to wind me any tighter, I'll turn into a Swiss watch."

Marty snorted through a repressed laugh. "That kind of oddness might just get you into the White House, Mr. Henson."

"'Mr. Henson?' Man, it's either Gary or El Presidente," came the reply. "You can call my brother Henson. Those military types love last—chhheeeeeuuuw—names. Excuse me."

A roar of dismay broke the gentle ambiance of the golf course.

"I said, 'excuse me,' John," Gary Henson called out with wide eyes. "You know these summer allergies are killer. Just killer. Who knows when hell will break loose?"

John grumbled all through the hike to the sand trap.

As they approached the last hole, one of the caddies from the pro shop drove up in a golf cart and waved them down, yelling, "Phone call for you, sir!"

Gary frowned. "I just can't get a moment's peace, can I?" he mumbled.

But the caddie handed the note he had brought to Marty, instead. Both Gary and John raised their eyebrows at him.

"You can take it in the shop," the caddie advised him.

Maybe one of his friends was calling to apologize for shunning him. That would make his day. He opened the note and stared at the name in silence.

A Mr. Ben Henson for Mr. Marty Bowman

JUNIOR YEAR SHOULD HAVE BEEN THE START OF NEW THINGS, MARTY had thought. Everyone was older, wiser, and had more to lose as academics heated up and the threat of getting booted out into the real world began to loom in the form of internships and rumors of internships. Dexter was thinking of proposing. Christina was juggling two part-time jobs at the local watering hole and K-Mart to pay tuition. Yet some things seemed the same.

Racing Ned to the hospital: that was one of those things. The man of the hour was passed out in a pool of beer-flavored vomit on Marty's back seat. Marty gripped the steering wheel in a white-knuckled ferocity that Sandy kept nervously eyeing from the passenger seat.

"You didn't need to come," Marty told her, breaking the long silence. "I can drive him myself."

"Well, you didn't need to drive him," Sandy returned, her usual vigor dulled as she glanced back at their comatose friend. "I could have gotten my car."

"Someone had to. Check if he's—"

"He's still breathing," she interrupted. She glanced from the back seat back up to Marty's face. "I know your face, string bean. I'm worried, too."

Marty ground his teeth as they came to a stop at a flashing red light. They were the only car at the light. Minutes could have serious ramifications for Ned. Yet Marty still stopped completely, since it was the thing to do at a flashing red stop light. The windshield wipers groaned in protest as they sprinted back and forth across the glass, revealing empty streets. The rain-slicked road reflected streetlights back out of a mirror world beneath the asphalt.

The car lurched forward again as quickly as Marty dared. A *splot* indicated that Ned had taken a nosedive into the pool again, a possibility confirmed by Sandy's wrinkled nose. The smell of recycled alcohol would soon become as permanent a fixture in the old Ford as the patchy seat upholstery. At that thought, Marty slammed his palm against the steering wheel and growled.

"He's such a loser! Why does he do this to us?" he demanded.

"It's not like he's *trying* to mess with us," Sandy said. "The guy did spend an entire night in a tree when we told him it was our frat's rite of passage."

"That just means he's a moron, not loyal. Who looks at our circle of friends, male and female, I might add, and says to himself, 'You know, I bet that's actually a frat?' And yes, I do know he's a moron! Who doesn't know that he's a moron? He's made a career of drinking himself to death."

"What if he just wants to be liked?"

"By who, those Kappas? If we're not good enough for him, then...I don't know," Marty said. He groaned and rubbed the bridge of his nose with his free hand. "You know, we're too good for him."

He didn't take his eyes off the slippery turns, but he thought he saw Sandy slump back into her bucket chair.

"Maybe we are. So what?" she asked. "Why are you the first to bail him out if you hate the guy so much?"

"I don't hate him."

"I know." There was a long pause as passing streetlights played havoc with the internal lighting and with Marty's own sleep-blurred vision. Then she continued. "Have you ever noticed that you are always the one to do stuff like this? Me, Christina, Dexter, Jean—we all hang out with Ned more than you. But whenever he goes off the deep end, you're paying his bail or giving him the Heimlich or driving him to the stinking hospital before the rest of us can finish rolling our eyes."

Marty sighed loudly, trying to sound as annoyed at the questioning as he felt. She was always doing this. "Yes, I know. And no, it's not some stupid hero complex. Someone had to, okay?"

"Yeah, that's what you always say. So why are you doing it for someone you don't like?"

Another red light. This one was enforced by cross-traffic. The old Ford squeaked to a halt before the white line, and there was another little *splut* from the back seat.

Marty turned and looked Sandy straight in the face. She was cute with her eyebrows down, like a spoiled princess. He figured if he ever tried that dating thing one day—like he'd ever have time—then he'd see if she was still single. For now, she was still a brat.

"I don't know," he said. "Read my face. You keep saying you're so good at it. Tell me why I'm wasting my nights because I've got no clue!"

Sandy searched his face from between a dense forest of eyelashes. She nodded to the light, and Marty started forward as he saw green blazing up from the mirror world under the wet pavement. But there was also quick movement. White light. Right heading left.

He slammed the brakes on, throwing the Ford into a short skid and throwing his unconscious friend in the back to the floor. None too soon, either. An ugly white coupe all but chopped off their bumper as it shot through the intersection. Its horn blared at them.

Marty wheezed as his heart started beating again. By habit more than by thought, he pulled his car forward out of the intersection.

"He had a red light! He runs a red, nearly kills us, and then *he* honks at *me*?" Marty bellowed.

Sandy was making little woofing noises as she clung to the passenger side armrest with a death grip. She looked like she wanted to say something, but couldn't unclench herself to do it.

They continued on slowly, no one behind them to rush them forward on the dark road. Marty's first impulse was to smash something in place of the other driver's head, but everything around him in the car was only four bad seconds from disintegrating anyway. He had to let the rush of energy that trembled in his hand fade away. It left a prickly void in his muscles that stung with dissatisfaction.

"Gah."

He threw the car over to the shoulder of the road under a yellowing streetlamp, startling a slumping Sandy back into squeezing the remaining life out of the sad, stained armrest. He jumped out of the car and felt the cold rain drown any good spirits that might have survived his pitiful evening.

There were a few shops and a grocery store up ahead, and a gas station just behind them. But because of the time and the weather, the only sign of life was the weedy light glowing in the ad-riddled windows of the gas station. If something had happened to Idiot

Ned, there was probably no one in there smart enough to help them.

Marty's gasping brain couldn't pump out the name of the ER room or the address, even. He was driving by memory. But they were only a few minutes out. Then the stress could end and the silent grudge-holding bonanza he had planned for his friend would begin, with relish.

He threw open the back door. The good news was that Ned—the short, tanned gym rat—was now out of the stale puddle of used beer and nachos on the back seat. Unfortunately, he was now crumpled up in a painful jumble on the floor. His left knee streamed red under the leg of his shorts from where it had planted into the car jack Marty had behind the passenger seat.

"Hey! You okay?" Marty slapped his friend's face. "Hey! Come on, man! Don't do this to me, Pipsqueak."

Most days, that name would elicit a rough, "friendly" smack, or at least a growl. But Ned's eyes didn't even roll around underneath his closed lids. That couldn't be good.

Marty grabbed his friend under the arms and dragged him back onto the back bench, avoiding the vomit. He plucked a Kleenex from a box on the floor. Rummaging around in the pocket on the back of Sandy's chair, he dug past pencils, erasers, sharpeners, a calculator, and about $100 worth of textbooks. In the grit at the bottom, he found his target.

He folded the tissue and pressed it against the cut in Ned's leg, then rolled the rubber band he had found past his friend's shoe, sock, and a mad thicket of leg hair to pin the tissue over the wound.

Then Marty put his ear over Ned's nose until he heard and felt a whisper of breath. He relaxed.

"You can puke in my car, you can bleed in my car, but you can't do both, Pipsqueak," Marty growled. "Ah, I hate my life."

As rain pattered against his back pockets, he looked up to see Sandy smiling at him with something mushy in her shadowed features. He hated mushy.

"What?" he said warily.

"Because you have to," she said.

"Excuse me?" he asked.

"Why do you waste your time on people you don't care about?" she said. "Because you have to. You can't stand to be like everyone else and walk on by. You can't kick someone when they're down, you have to pick them up."

He slammed the door and then dove back into the front seat. Groaning, he slicked the water out of his eyes and slid the car into drive.

"Don't get mushy, Sandy. No one likes a girly-girl."

"No worries, string bean," Sandy said, a giggle creeping behind her tone. "You were the one who asked. I'm just here because you'd be sunk without me."

"Yeah, right," Marty said. But he breathed more easily as they pulled back onto the empty road.

MARTY PLAYED OUT THE HOLE WITH HIS BOSSES. WHEN THEY WERE back in the pro shop to settle up for the rounds, he took pains to avoid running into the caddie who had mentioned the call. There was an obscure chance that Ben Henson was angry enough to have waited the fifteen minutes. After all, you don't accuse a man of cheating on his wife with a disabled woman and then just have a friendly chat with him the week after.

He drove Gary back to the campaign headquarters through the early afternoon L.A. traffic. The sky was as blue as it was bright and blistering, and the trees swayed invitingly in the wind outside the steaming car as the Mustang's A/C struggled to banish the heat. But his mind was on the call. The political potential of chauffeuring the president-to-be was lost to silence.

Back at his desk in the busy office, Marty brooded. He glanced over some copy for a new Nevada ad that one of his contacts in that office had sent him. He stared at the words without seeing.

He opened up WordPerfect on his office computer and started hammering out lines that had nothing to do with the campaign.

pros:
improved relations with Gary Henson, John
Lemar, professional circles that value dedica-
tion and ingenuity
no personal mention by media so no public
backlash
possible in with next president: favors,
friendship, maybe future political position
job offers
so many job offers
(that's a little weird now that i think
about it)

Then he glanced up and down the short list. His
brow furrowed. Short meant simple, so why
didn't this feel simple? He dove into the
second list.

cons:
now shunned by Sandy, Dexter, Ned, Christina—
and maybe a few other people here and there who
didn't like my methods
POSSIBLE public backlash
could become media boogeyman
BEN HENSON

His fingers stopped typing and he stared at the white screen. As
innocuous as those little black squiggles were, he couldn't bring
himself to expound on the Ben Henson point. Writing it in all caps
had helped. Really, it said it all.

But why couldn't he type anything else out? "Ben Henson"
what? *Revenge? Political enemy?* Or did he just not want to type out
family life ruined, or *marriage wrecked,* or... something. He knew
what he'd done. No surprises. Everyone in the office knew too, and
they weren't horrified by it. He was overreacting. Pointless guilt.

After all, Ben Henson was a young warhound: a grizzly bear that tore opponents to shreds and could take shots without blinking a beady eye. He was not as quick as the Republican challengers he had beat. He certainly didn't have his brother Gary's fluid wit. The man rarely let himself get drawn out into scrapping with Gary during the debates and depended instead on stubbornly sticking to his talking points and the issues. He seemed a little obtuse, but the man did know how to shrug off petty arguments.

Yet a week had gone by and he still hadn't shrugged off the dirt that Gary had buried him under–shovel provided by one Marty Bowman.

Marty tapped on his keyboard absently, glowering. He flipped on the screensaver. The flying toasters were strangely relaxing and easy to watch as they fluttered through the boxy screen from one who-knows-where to another. Toasters, toast, food, lunch…He should take a lunch break. He glanced down at the ad copy lying on his desk.

Work first, lunch later. He still had a reputation to maintain, and he wasn't as hungry as usual. So he dove into the papers and lost himself in the language. With one read to absorb, one to peruse, and one more to dissect, he felt familiar enough with the radio bit to have written it himself. But if he had written it, he would have asked Dexter to slap him. The script was dry and unengaging and more fit for Ben's campaign than Gary's.

With a grunt of distaste, Marty tore the ad to shreds with his red pen. He had long ago stopped feeling bad about a brutally honest editing job. Friends and coworkers who sent him stuff like this knew what would happen to their beloved pieces and expected nothing less. He considered himself a forge that separated the good metal from the slag.

Christina had told him for years that he should consider a better analogy.

A knock sounded at the door and a frowning Dexter stepped into Marty's office. The blonde man had never hit that growth spurt he had prayed for, but he had grown wider since their college days.

He resembled a young Saint Nick when he smiled. He hadn't smiled much lately, though.

Marty eyed him warily. "Dexter. Do the event planners need help with something?"

"No. But you can help *me* understand why you just took half a day off to play a game you always said you hated," Dexter replied, a sardonic smile twisting his thin lips. At the moment, he would look very out of place giving gifts in a red suit.

"Okay…Well, when the boss says jump, we jump," Marty said with a shrug.

"Really? You're riding the 'down with the Man' train after that stunt you pulled?"

"What would you do if Gary Henson came to your desk and told you to play a game of golf with him?" Marty snapped. He glowered at his old friend. "Turn him down? I'd love to see that. Life's too—"

'Too short for small steps.'" Dexter sighed and rubbed the bridge of his nose, a sure sign that he was sleep-deprived. "So I've heard. And if I was merely invited, as I assume you were, then I would tell him 'thank you but I'm up to my eyes in scheduling conflicts.' I thought we all agreed that hard work was the way to climb the ladder, man. Not backstabbing and brown-nosing."

Marty felt a twinge in his stomach as he noticed the dark bags under his friend's eyes. He motioned to the chair in front of his desk and pushed an unopened can of Coke over to that side of the desktop. Dexter stared at it blankly for a moment. Then he offered a nearly imperceptible nod and slid into the wooden chair, although he ignored the offering of soda.

"Is that why I've been on death row, here?" Marty asked him in a low tone. "Because I have been digging through everything about this campaign—though I hadn't thought about the corporate ladder thing—but I haven't been able to figure out why you—"

"You 'can't figure out'?" Dexter said, tired eyes widening. "Let me stop you there, man. You're smart. Always have been, and not just about school and your writing. You're smart enough to know you've done something wrong, so don't tell me some sudden brain drain has left your moral compass spinning. You know I'm no saint..."

"Remind me, which statue did you dress up in a bra, wig, and makeup during the homecoming game?" Marty challenged.

Dexter didn't smile, but his face relaxed and he blew a hint of laughter out between his teeth.

"Like I said, no saint. And let me remind you which string of a man helped me sneak into the girl's dorm freshman year," he said.

"Could have been anyone."

Dexter's face grew serious again. "That was the only time someone convinced string bean to get off the pole. You even called your foster dad about that and cried. I mean, everyone feels guilt sometimes. But you always had Guilt with a capital G, you know?

"I always thought that was weird and unhealthy. But it was consistent, and it was you, and we could count on you to be you," he said. He rolled his eyes. "Please, don't let me speak in front of an audience until I get forty winks in. But my point is, you got down off your pole. You got down in the dirt."

Either Dexter's tired ramblings were nonsense, or Marty's ears were no longer on speaking terms with his brain. He wished his friend would contain his premise to a single sentence: preferably, a simple one.

"How come Christina hates my forge analogy but lets you throw around metaphors like that? You'd think her husband wouldn't be able to get away with so much as a simile," he teased.

Dexter shook his head, another scrunched grin disfiguring his warm features. "Forget it. I try to level with you, but you just avoid, avoid, avoid. Let me know when you plan to grow up and fess up, Mr. Bowman. I'd like to see my friend again when you find him."

He got up and left without another word.

"That doesn't even make sense," Marty barked at Dexter's back, to no response. For a moment, he thought one of his friends might have come to his senses. Obviously, it was a fool's hope. The guy had barely sat down before he'd decided Marty was some kind of lost cause and jumped right back up again.

What had gotten into everyone?

After glaring out the open door for a long moment, he turned back to the Nevada radio ad. The phone rang with a *brrrt. Brrrt.*

His hand was on the receiver when caution caught up to his conditioning. *Brrrt. Brrrt.* It was probably someone in the campaign office. They could walk over and talk to him face-to-face. *Brrrt. Brrrt.* But if it was someone from one of the other offices, they might need him. Then again, since when did the speechwriter get important calls? *Brrrt. Brrrt.*

He should answer. But he had voicemail. He could listen to the message. *Brrrt. Brrrt.* They'd leave a message if it were important. He withdrew his hand from the receiver as it rang again. Some days, phone calls came laden with gifts like the voices of old friends or job offers. Some days, it was a round of Russian roulette. *Brrrt.*

Ringing, and…voicemail.

He breathed again and returned to his ad editing.

Another knock on the doorframe startled him. This time it was John Lemar, and he had his campaign manager scowl back in place. That, or he was still steamed about Marty's part in throwing off his drive.

"Conference room," John rumbled, scratching at his sunburned nose. "The other boys have some ideas about how you could write more towards Mr. Henson's style, so chop-chop."

Marty smiled back politely, fuming behind his teeth. Any fool knew that Gary Henson's style was to ignore his speeches completely. But if the campaign manager and his stooges weren't so certain that Gary would choke without more talking points for him to disregard, Marty wouldn't have a job.

He followed his boss's boss into the conference room, nodding and pretending to listen. Handling co-workers was as important as the actual writing in this job. Marty played his part well enough, although his head still bounced around his conversations with

Sandy and Dexter. It gave him a headache that he was sure this meeting would exacerbate.

State manager Luis Ricardo was waiting for them along with a few other members of the campaign that Marty recognized by face but not by name. Mr. Ricardo had a tiny smudge of ketchup at the corner of his mouth from lunch, which nobody was kind enough to point out.

"Hot day, eh?" Mr. Ricardo said in his quiet voice. He turned to stare daggers into John. "Good day for a golf game, Mr. Lemar?"

John grumbled to himself as if the very thought of it was painful.

"Fortunately, it was a quiet morning with no fires to put out, so you chose a good day for...Wait. Except for the New York interview that Mr. Henson skipped, the budget meeting and the California poll meeting that you missed, Mr. Lemar, and whatever our speechwriter should have been doing when he was caddying for you both." Mr. Ricardo's face was empty, but the dark eyes within it were weapons.

John held up his hands in surrender. "If it helps, Mr. Bowman was invited along to play. It was just Gary getting to know his campaign team. After he went above and beyond on that sister-in-law angle, Gary felt like rewarding the man."

Any fool could tell John was just trying to placate the man, but Marty couldn't help feeling pleased anyway.

Mr. Ricardo glanced at Marty and jerked his head towards an empty chair. John and Marty both obeyed meekly. If a stranger were watching, he would never guess that John was the boss and Ricardo was under him.

"Look, Mr. Bowman," Mr. Ricardo said as the lights dimmed in the room and the projector warmed up. "Mini-vacations aside, I have nothing but respect for your work. You write well. That's why we hired you. And the way you sapped Mr. Ben Henson's defenses like that has been the biggest single shakeup in this election. The polls don't lie. I'd love to keep rocking our opponent while he's still off balance. To do that, I need you to keep feeding our Henson the right ammo."

Marty grinned and nodded. He felt like a child and was happy that the darkness hid the pride that was bubbling free. It was about time that someone sensible told it like it was.

"So what can I do to help?" he asked. "I'll doubt Senator Henson has anything dirtier left to find."

"Mr. Ben Henson," Mr. Ricardo emphasized, "is already bleeding. A second clean shot would be a miracle—one we can't base our strategy on."

On which we can't base our strategy, Sandy would have corrected. The thought made Marty's smile fade a little.

Mr. Ricardo continued, pacing towards the front of the conference room while one of the other men got a video loaded into the player. As the VHS rewound, Marty recognized the debate as the most recent one: The Debate.

"The truth is that Mr. Henson is not the kind of man who likes to sit still and take orders, even from his own campaign team. And the people love him for it. He's a terrible politician and a worse debater: the man has all the poise of a drunk penguin. But it's working. And last Saturday, he actually used some of the material we gave him. Word for word. So, we need to pick out what he used, when, and how. And you can give us more like that. Take what is ours. We need to reign in our raging bull before he gets himself in too deep."

What was it with people and metaphors today?

Mr. Ricardo motioned to the man running the A/V system and the debate started playing the debacle over again, right after the moment when Gary had hit Ben with the scandal. The volume was low, but it might as well have been thunder in the silent conference room, the crowd's shouts making Marty's hair bristle and his skin prickle.

In the film, the twins were behind the two podiums on stage. Gary had an almost pained, holier-than-thou expression spread across his features and Ben just looked shocked.

"This isn't news," Gary protested as the moderator tried to talk him down. *"Is it? You've been seeing her for a while, bro. It may not be common knowledge, per se, but—"*

"Mr. Henson," the white-haired moderator told him sternly, *"please just answer the question."*

"I did, man!" Gary said. *"'Protecting the family unit' is about protecting every definition of family, whatever people take it to mean. Three husbands, one wife? Protected! Two wives, no husband? Protected! One husband and wife and previously-agreed-on side action with your sister-in-law? It's—"*

"Sorry," Ben interrupted. His face had steeled over. *"I was under the impression that the best candidate the Democrats threw at me would care more about issues and less on baseless lies, intended—"*

"What's baseless about it?" Gary demanded.

"—intended to project their own party's failure in Clinton onto me!" Ben spoke over him.

By now, the crowd's growl created a backdrop for the moderator's unheeded warnings. The two brothers were both ramrod straight in their suits. Ben was zoned in on his twin, working his jaw in the bright lights. Gary seemed to be trolling for eye contact in the audience as he made his case, throwing out some of the phrases that Marty had fed him the morning before the debate.

"This is relevant! I am just pointing out the hypocrisy of claiming to represent an outdated form of family while doing 'your own thing' in your private life. This isn't Cuba! Our representatives are held to the same standards as each citizen, and that's how it always should be, brother."

As Ben blustered through a slow comeback, Mr. Ricardo spoke up.

"He used your 'hypocrisy' line. Just like he used your exact phrasing when making the original accusation. Keep watching for when he connects the sister-in-law scandal to his points."

Marty murmured his assent with the others in the room.

"Yes, yes, I couldn't agree with that more," Gary was saying. *"But are you denying it?"*

"Yes," Ben said.

"Yes?"

"Of course I deny it."

"Even though it was Connie herself who told us?" Gary asked him. Then as the moderator got onto him again, he turned back to the audience and held out his hands in a placating gesture. "I know I sound like some kind of political monster, dragging my brother's name through the mud or trashing his family. But that's my point: if his family is okay with it, we all should be! Tolerance is about not judging others, yes? Who was it that said, 'judge not or else you might be judged'? Someone famous..."

Half of the audience applauded at that, and some even laughed out loud.

"He butchered that quote," Marty grumbled under his breath.

Mr. Ricardo had good ears and glanced back at Marty. "Perhaps, but he got your point across. Now he's the man who loves and accepts his brother instead of a sniping backbiter. That's my point, people. He's using mostly his own words but he's keeping the basic script."

"Shh. This part," John mumbled through a mouthful of a scone that he must have smuggled into the room.

"Christ also told off a mob of self-righteous politicians who were trying to kill a prostitute. He said that only someone without blame could throw the first stone," Ben Henson said. He had his smugly mild tone back, and there was some applause from the mindless Republicans in the audience.

Gary snorted as if offended. "Sorry, but did you just call your sister-in-law a prostitute?"

The audience roared, some in laughter and support, and some in outrage.

John chuckled, a snuffly sound. "I loved that line. Our boy doesn't miss a beat."

"He needs no jokes written for him," Mr. Ricardo stated. "But he does need a frame to hang them in. And that's what we should watch as we finish this clip."

In which to hang them. Marty shook his head. He had created a Sandy in his head. He banished thoughts of his circle and focused on the meeting.

Marty laughed and cringed his way through the rest of the debate along with the others on the campaign team, pointing out places for improvement as they went. And all through it, there was a subtle sensation inside him. He kept his head straight because he knew that he could point to a presidential candidate's biggest win in a debate and say, *mine*.

ESCALON, CALIFORNIA WAS TINY WHEN IT HAD BEEN ESTABLISHED, AND it was still tiny in 1979 when Marty moved in with his newest foster family. The big, two-storied house was covered in faded yellow siding and looked more like it belonged in the middle of Kansas than Escalon. Then again, Escalon looked more like it belonged in Kansas than California, so maybe the house had just been transplanted with the rest of the two-square-mile farm town via Wicked-Witch-tornado.

Marty leaned out of the window of Mr. Baker's old pickup truck to see without the fanciful distortions of the muddy windshield. Also, fresh air was preferable to the smell of Mr. Baker, who had driven the entire time in a cloud of tobacco without giving his new foster son a glance.

"There it is," Mr. Baker stated. He did that: said each of his sentences like it was the honest-to-God truth and there was no point in denying it. Then again, he had so far only said the kinds of things that were the honest-to-God truth.

"It's large," Marty said to be polite. The child placement people were big on politeness.

"Bakers were here since before the town was," Mr. Baker mentioned.

He undid Marty's seatbelt (as if Marty wasn't old enough to do it himself) and slid out of the truck to stretch his back. Marty got his own door, to prove how big he was, and jumped down. The ride had been bumpy in Mr. Baker's ancient vehicle, and he was glad to have his shoes on solid ground again, even if that ground was just a packed dirt driveway. He stretched through the pain in his back-side and glanced around at his latest home.

The world seemed very open here. There were more fields than trees, and lots and lots of cloudy sky high above his Yankees ball-cap. The house was the tallest thing within spitting distance. He thought he saw an old barn and a newer toolshed behind the house, and he stared at the old metal implements lying about the patchy grass yard. Were those for horses? How old were these people? He almost expected Mr. Baker to yell, "Ma! I'm home with the boy!"

Mr. Baker stomped his work boots against the ground a few times to knock off excess dust. Then he raised his hand to his mouth as if to amplify his voice and shouted, "I'm home, Ma!"

Marty collapsed into a fit of giggles.

As Mr. Baker walked past, he gave Marty a searching look before offering him a 'tour of the spread.' Marty nodded. He just hoped he wouldn't get in trouble for laughing. The last thing he needed was to break his own record for Shortest Time with a New Family. The current fastest time was fifty-two hours.

'The spread' wasn't really worth a tour. They had cows, some bulls, a few more cows, and hay. The hay was primarily to feed the cows. The different fields were fenced off as if the cows had anywhere better to be. One of the big old animals was nuzzling against a stumpy tree near the fence, and Mr. Baker walked right up to the fence as if he wasn't outweighed by a lot of pounds of beef. He asked Marty if he wanted to see it up close.

Marty absolutely did not. He shook his head quickly to make that clear. He could get stomped on, sat on, eaten to death, or some-thing worse. He wasn't even as big as other foster kids his age, much less a huge cow.

"Come on...Marty," Mr. Baker said, as if he had to build the name on his tongue before spitting it out. "She won't bite you. You had best get used to them if you'll be living with them."

"I have to sleep in the barn?" Marty cried.

"No. No, you don't," Mr. Baker said slowly, looking somewhat confused. "But you will be staying on a farm that has cows."

"Papa!" came a voice with a funny accent.

A little blonde girl in overalls ran up from the house and threw her arms around Mr. Baker's waist. She peeked out from behind him at Marty.

Mr. Baker's wrinkles faded as he looked down at the girl and patted her shoulder. "I was only gone for a little while, child."

"It seemed like forever," the girl gushed with her foreign lisp.

Marty glared at the girl, disliking her immediately. He knew other kids like that in the system, the kind who would kiss up to grownups to get their way. The unfairness of it always made him mad. The blonde girl just stared back at him with big eyes.

"Who's that?" she asked.

"Hope, this is Marty," Mr. Baker said. "He's going to stay with us for a while."

A while? That didn't sound good.

Mr. Baker patted her again and she unsuctioned herself from his leg. He continued, looking Marty in the eye. "Marty, this is my daughter, Hope."

"I'm from *Ukraine!*" she said, pronouncing the country with gusto.

"I'm from *here*," he shot back.

She ignored his challenge and dove under the fence with the speed of a squirrel. She walked up to the nearby smelly beastie and bowed to it. With either bravery or stupidity, she petted it on its pale brown side.

"Meet the cows!" she cried. "This one is Cuds Clompf...I think. Or maybe this is Cuds' sister, Betsy Clompf. Isn't she cute?"

"I guess," Marty said, not disguising his doubt.

"Being careful keeps you healthy," Mr. Baker warned Hope.

"I know," Hope said, nodding. She looked at Marty. "Meet Mrs. Clompf, Marty! Come on..."

"I don't want to," he insisted. "She smells."

Hope rammed her fists onto her hips. "You're mean. She does

not smell! She's nice!"

"Marty just got here. He might be hungry," Mr. Baker told her.

Marty was feeling increasingly invisible. Apparently, only cows and annoying girls from Ukraine mattered on the Baker farm. He sulked and leaned against a fence pole.

"I am hungry and I can meet a cow whenever I want to," Marty clarified. "They're everywhere, right? I just don't want to today."

"Not today at all?" Hope pouted, another little trick that Marty was used to hating on other kids. Then her eyes lit up and she giggled. "You're scared of cows, huh? Marty's scared of cows!"

"I'm not scared!" he barked. His cheeks flushed.

He joked to himself about going for the record, but he was tired of going to new places and wanted to stay here for a while, at least. There was enough space in Escalon to avoid annoying little Ukrainian girls. So, he would have to do his best to be polite again. He made himself stop frowning.

"Stop arguing, you two," Mr. Baker said. He didn't sound mean, but he did sound serious. "We'll have a late lunch."

"But Mama and me already had lunch," Hope said.

Mr. Baker snagged her up from the cow's side of the fence, lifted her over, and sat her down gently while she squealed and giggled. The gruff older man and the blonde adopted kid seemed to love each other like real family.

Marty scuffed his shoe against a fat little mohawk of grass in the dirt, trying to uproot it and ignore his new foster family. He couldn't even get here in time to eat lunch right. Of course. Then Mr. Baker cleared his throat and Marty had to look up.

"We'll have a second lunch with him, then," Mr. Baker said. "He can see the cows later."

Hope clung to his hand as they both started walking towards the yellow farmhouse. "If he's not too scared," she teased.

With *him. He* can see the cows. *He's* too scared.

Marty couldn't quite place how he knew. But he had the sinking feeling that, record or no, he wouldn't be here long. He buried his hands in his pockets and trudged behind the farmer and his kid.

. . .

EYES BRIGHT, MARTY FELT INJECTED WITH SOMETHING LIKE GRANITE as he walked back to his desk. He could take any punch and not flinch, or run up a wall like a superhero. There was no other feeling quite like working hard and then sitting back as the rewards and recognition came trotting back. He could almost imagine that this was how farmers could stand their jobs.

So, when he came back to his desk and flipped on the answering machine by habit, he was startled by how quickly Cloud Nine could dissipate.

"Mr. Bowman," the message started, "this is Claire from Congressman Henson's office. The congressman would like to meet you for dinner tomorrow in Los Angeles to discuss our respective presidential campaigns. Besides his secret service detail, the congressman will come alone and hopes you will show him the same courtesy. Since we have already tried to call three times, we took the liberty of reserving the Swordfish Room at Taste of Venice on Center Street for dinner at seven. Please do not bring any cameras or other recording devices as the congressman appreciates his privacy. We extend you the same courtesy. Again, that's the Swordfish Room in Taste of Venice at seven. Thank you and have a great day."

Click.

The sound of the phone on the other end of the line hanging up might as well have been the pop of a pistol's hammer for how Marty reacted. He didn't move or put down the phone. Instead, he just stared at his corkboard of schedules and memos without seeing any of them.

"Why can't you leave me alone," he hissed into the silence of the office. "Blame your brother. I'm just doing my job, you soulless prick."

But the corkboard remained silent. Jerk.

And the fact remained that a man who might be quite furious with him—a man who had served in the military for years and still had many friends in the Pentagon and even Langley—this man wanted to meet him alone. What could go wrong?

The better question was why Marty shouldn't just forget he'd gotten the voicemail. His finger hovered over the delete button, brushing over the cool surface of the tan plastic knob. He should tap it. A little too much pressure was all he needed. Just...oops. He should.

He shouldn't. Marty leaned back in his swivel chair and groaned in synchronization with the groan of his chair.

After a few breaths, he tried to go back to Gary's script for his next interview. The CBS meetup would be a doozy, and Mr. Ricardo had told him to write in several loose structures for recovering from shots about Ben's adultery. While they had no problem with the enemy cooking in the water he had boiled, there was a danger that the media would fixate on the scandal to the point of ignoring Gary Henson completely.

At least, that's what John and Ricardo feared. Marty very much doubted that anyone could ignore Gary Henson completely.

He typed up and deleted line after line to find a good opening. Nothing seemed sticky. The words he wrote left an acrid smell in his nose, and one-by-one, they died as silently as they had been born.

Growling, he pushed himself away from the desk before he clobbered his keyboard. He got up and found himself walking back to Sandy's desk. He snagged a little aloe vera plant in a pot that she had left in the office, as a peace offering. He pasted a smile on his face and straightened his suit jacket.

Marty managed to sneak up on her, which meant that many fewer seconds of judging. He finally cleared his throat. When she started, he said "Hi" and slid the potted plant onto her new desktop.

"You forgot your friend," he mumbled, abruptly finding it diffi-cult to think.

Sandy shot him a strange look, then turned the aloe vera around and studied it.

"Actually, I left it for you," she said with a crooked smile. "It was growing gnats and I thought you could use some friends."

"That's. That's cute," he said, forcing a laugh and smile.

"And if you end up getting yourself *burned*, you can always crack open a stem and help yourself," she pressed without looking up, sorting through a pile of faxes on her desk.

"Alright," he snapped. "Just look at me and talk like a human being for a moment."

"Well, one only puts a bridle on a horse."

He felt the last of his goodwill slip away. He was in trouble and coming to her for help, and she couldn't stop tripping over her own clever tongue.

"Enough with the double talk, please. Sandy," he said with forced calm, "when did I ever treat you the way you're treating me? When have I ever treated anyone like my friends are treating me now?"

She spun around to face him, making him jump.

"You treated Ben Henson's family that way," she replied. "You found some old newspaper articles, made a few calls, and smeared a man's name. You've never even met him and you told the world he was having an affair with a handicapped woman! What about that don't you find repulsive, Marty?"

"I find the whole situation repulsive," he stated. "But that's why the man shouldn't get away with it! We can't have another Clinton, another Nixon. America—"

"So help me, if you try a patriotic line, Marty…"

Sandy scowled and tried to thrust the potted plant back in his hands, but he folded his arms behind his back and returned her frown. The pout that tugged at her lips wasn't cute anymore.

"Then how about a cliche? *Don't kill the messenger*," Marty returned. "Which, by the way, was our incoming president. All I did was—"

"How dare you—!"

"No!" he interrupted her. "How dare Congressman Henson! The only thing I did was expose the truth behind a man who acted like a saint in the light and saved his dirty deeds for behind the curtain. Some people would call me a hero for warning people what they were voting for. I pulled back that curtain."

Sandy met his gaze then, and for the first time in days, she didn't look angry or accusing. She looked very tired.

When she didn't immediately snap back, Marty felt the old familiar flood of guilt come back. He was still right, but he shouldn't have snarled like a dog, no matter how Sandy treated him. Feeling exhausted as well, he dropped into the empty chair at the desk across from hers.

"Sorry."

Sandy nodded, but said, "But not for what counts. That's the problem."

He groaned into his hand. Then a thought occurred to him.

"We're not a bullheaded bunch," he said. "But the only person I've seen Dexter and Jean and Christina and Ned all rally behind is you."

"They used to 'rally' behind you, too," she replied, sounding as disheartened as she looked.

"You're the one who ordered everyone to avoid me," Marty said.

He sighed. He didn't wait for a reply, nor did she offer one. With a stiff nod, he walked back to his new office. Only once he got there did he realize that Sandy had somehow slipped the aloe vera back into his grip. Instead of setting it back on the desk, he chunked it in the wastebasket and enjoyed the sound it made. Then he went back to work.

CHRISTINA'S SMILE WAS CROOKED BUT SWEET AND KIND OF CHARMING. And Marty seemed to see it every time he looked up during the Wednesday dinners these days.

Wednesday dinner had been orchestrated by Sandy. Since graduation, the girl had emerged as a sort of leader of their little circle of friends—at least of the ones who had moved to the L.A. area after college. So, when she had practically mandated that everyone walk away from their internships and new jobs on Wednesday evening and meet at her place to eat together, no one argued.

It was early fall and the air was warm enough that Marty and Ned were still braving the crowds to hit the beach on Saturdays, so both of them sat in their chairs gingerly that night. Marty made sure his shirt didn't touch his poor, toasted back too much.

Christina sat next to him and watched curiously. "What are you doing?"

"Sunburn," he mumbled through a mouthful of chips and salsa. "Forgot the sunblock last week."

She rubbed his leg sympathetically.

Dexter took a different tack. He slapped poor Ned on the back and grinned when his friend yelped. "Someone should push you two buoys further out to sea, dude."

Ned looked like he was going to pull an Old Ned move and toss Dexter out of his chair, but Jean fixed them both with a stink eye. They cooled their jets just in time, too. Sandy brushed in wearing a sundress and carrying a plate of burgers from her apartment's kitchen.

She recited a prayer, ignoring atheist Ned's uncomfortable look as the rest of them bowed their heads. It was short and to the point: Sandy's specialty. Then they dug into the spread.

"It's crazy how expensive apartments are around here," Jean mentioned for the fifty-first time that week. And for the fifty-first time, five voices chimed in to emphatically agree and complain.

"Rooming with someone else who works helps, but only a little," Dexter said and nodded at Jean. He twisted the band on his finger uncomfortably, as he did whenever he talked about being married.

"It would be easier if I had a roommate," Christina said. "The only place I could find was this trashy two-room place. You wouldn't think it would be so hard to find someone else looking to save money!"

Marty looked around at his friends, who were glancing at each other with something like poorly repressed amusement. Maybe there was some inside joke he was missing.

When no one answered, he said, "Well, the family I'm staying with—sorry, Sandy: *with whom* I'm staying—they'd probably be happy to see me out sooner rather than later. How much is rent?"

Jean slapped her hand over her face.

Christina beamed at Marty and tripped over her words to get them out fast enough. "Not bad at all, really. I'll show you later. And there's a great pool. And we'd have our own washing machine. And each bedroom with its half-bath. I mean, we both have half-baths. There's a full bath off the living room! It's weird but cool. You could come over on Friday and take a look."

Behind Christina's back, Sandy was shaking her head emphatically and Dexter was mouthing *no*. Marty snorted to himself, confused. But Christina looked excited.

"Sure, Friday after work is good," Marty said with a half-grin. What was wrong with the group sticking together?

"Yo, Sandy, mind if Marty and me use some of that green goo you have for sunburns?" Ned asked loudly.

"Good idea!" Sandy said. "You two go before you finish baking. It's in the bathroom."

Marty gave Ned a look but followed him through Sandy's bedroom anyway. They had just rounded the corner when Ned grabbed Marty by the shoulder and said, "Bad move, string bean. Bad move!"

"What?" Marty gaped at his friend.

The impressive cords of muscles in Ned's neck bunched as he peered up at me through bleached strands of hair. "You know, you're smart. But you're a moron. A girl is practically drooling over you, and you just offer to move in with her? Are you insane?"

"Drooling over me?" Marty whispered. "Come on, man. She's known me for years!"

"And liked you for years."

"Oh please. Look at those other guys she was dating!"

Ned wrinkled his nose. "And they never worked out. And you

were always nice to her. See where this is going, idiot?"

Marty leaned against a wall, grinning and panicking all at once.

"Nah, you're yanking my chain. She knows I don't date. Dating's for hormonal idiots. Like you."

"Don't make me benchpress you, string bean," Ned grated the nickname out slowly. "And you're pretty high and mighty for someone who's about to share an apartment with a single girl."

"Huh." Marty stared out the bedroom window at the city lights in the distance. "Maybe I should date her. You know? She's nice. She's cute. Saying no would kill her."

"Dude..." Ned shook his head. "Sure, she's great. But do you like her? Could you imagine any future with her?"

Marty shrugged. "I don't...Maybe. It's weird to think about."

"Exactly," Ned said. "It's just not you, dude. And that's cool. But as much as you hate to rip the hook out of her face, you have to throw her back or she'll slowly suffocate."

"What?"

"Fishing. That was a fishing analogy."

"Leave the analogies to the writers, musclehead," Marty said with a roll of the eyes.

Ned suddenly looked around, darted into the bathroom, and returned with a bottle of aloe vera. He squirted some into his palm before tossing the bottle at Marty.

"Quick, before Christina gets suspicious," he said, rubbing the stuff on his back under his shirt. "So what are you going to do?"

Marty applied some to himself and hated how the goop glued his button-down shirt to his skin. It made his flesh crawl, but it was also strangely cool. He had to get himself some of this stuff. He also had to think fast.

It wasn't exactly a tough decision. He pictured the redhead's adorable face, imagined holding her close, maybe kissing her. It was a riveting idea. Riveting, however, was also how he felt about skydiving some day. And driving a Mustang.

But either of those things he could walk away from without one of his best friends crying and hating him. Even without being in the situation, he could feel the old familiar roots of capital-G Guilt tangling themselves around him and slowing everything down.

"I guess you're right. That'll be a fun talk," he replied ruefully. "I'll see the apartment with her on Friday and let her down then. I guess."

He tossed the bottle back to Ned and headed back out to the living room where the others were. Ned paused him with a grunt.

"Don't do it because I told you to, string bean," Ned ordered. "Do it because you like Christina too much to break up with her for real."

"Yeah… Right." Marty started to walk out again.

"Yo."

Ned stared at Marty until Marty met his gaze.

"You're a better man than me, if that helps," Ned stated. "I've been pulled aside like this too, and I never listened. A smart guy listens. A smart guy changes when something's wrong, and I ain't ever been that smart."

"But you survived, and that's what matters," Marty said, patting him on the shoulder.

Ned's face scrunched into fourteen kinds of pain. Marty's eyes widened apologetically, but he also had to snicker.

"Thanks," Ned groaned. "And if I don't kill you first, you and Christina will probably both survive this, too. Now move, before this aloe stuff kicks in and I kick your skinny keister."

Marty moved.

ALTHOUGH THE SUN WAS BRIGHT AND THE WEATHER COOLER, MARTY stumbled through the next workday like a zombie. He'd had next to no sleep. Every half hour had spawned another bizarre yet unmemorable nightmare or another hour of heart-pounding wakefulness. His body felt like it had been used to mop up a spill, rung out, and thrown in some cosmic washer.

No one important interrupted his work that day. Gary Henson was away to campaign in some breadbasket state along with John.

Mr. Ricardo was otherwise occupied. That left Marty with eight incredibly long hours to write and plan–or, more accurately, to endure internal torment over what to do about the dinner that evening.

The three dollar white, plastic clock on the wall in his office was analog, but it didn't audibly tick. He had only noticed that once before now. At the time, he had been grateful for the peace it afforded him, especially compared to the racket of the main room when the interns were making cold calls.

But today he found himself constantly checking that worthless little clock. It seemed incredibly slow. He stood up on his chair to make sure it was working twice since he had no ticking to convince him time was really moving. The day would end too soon, but at the same time, he couldn't wait for it to be over.

Gary's next broadcast speech was for a live rally in Alaska, of all places. Joke after joke came and went. The words were doing cartwheels and somersaults across the screen as Marty tried to type, a parade of terrible anecdotes and platitudes that should never have been given life at his fingertips. Most of them got the ax. Others would go on to live a full life on a document that would, at best, be skimmed over, and would more likely be left to return to sawdust in the iron clutch of a binder somewhere. Either way, no harm was done. Writing while distracted could lead to embarrassment and a visit with the boss in an ad agency. Working for a presidential candidate would have been so much worse, but Marty knew Gary. He was more worried about the other Henson at the moment.

Thud. He tapped his forehead against the desk and groaned.

"This is all garbage," he growled at the computer screen. He glared until the speech blurred. "Why aren't you working?"

After another few minutes of staring bullets through his poor word processor, he brought up a new, blank document. His fingers moved of their own volition. He stared down at his hands in a dull fog of surprise as years of practice did their work on the sticky, gray keyboard.

He found himself building a second pros-and-cons list, and he didn't like it.

pros: Success

CONS: YOUR SOUL

MARTY SNORTED AT THE MORBID ANALYSIS. A FAMILIAR TUG WAS pulling at him from somewhere behind his stomach. The sensation felt like strings that led to every finger and toe from under his skin, leaving him a helpless marionette to the character weakness he had suffered from since birth.

A small sob, more of a hiccup than anything, rattled him. He quickly rewrote the analysis before his eyes started watering—or something else as stupid.

PROS: SUCCESS, JOB SECURITY, FINANCIAL SECURITY, HELPING my boss, revealing THE TRUTH, life's too short for small steps

BUT HIS PUPPET STRINGS GOT YANKED BY THE SOFT VOICE OF GUILT again, and he added:

CONS: HATING YOURSELF, NAGGING FEELINGS, SCREWING THE $&*#^^%@(poOCH MOROn*

HE QUIT THE APPLICATION WITHOUT SAVING AND GLARED AROUND THE office as if expecting the aloe vera or one of its friends to tell him off. Flicking the mouse into the corner of the screen, Marty glanced back at the plant and wished he had left it in the trashcan. Then he jumped and cursed.

He moved the mouse again, dismissing the flock of flying toasters that had glided onto the desktop and tearing through his saved files. Twice. Thrice for good measure. But, with a falling feeling inside, he was certain of it: he'd erased his entire speech, except for a few uninspired opening lines that he had saved.

Hissing, he started again. And this time, he didn't let his mind wander off into a corner to sulk.

By the time he had saved the final draft, he was almost afraid to look at the clock. Sure enough, the silent murderer of minutes had slaughtered its way to half-past five o'clock. Everyone else had left him alone with the crew of short, Spanish-speaking cleaners. The clock went into the trash.

Marty stood. A wave of dizziness nearly knocked him into the wall, and he only steadied himself by grabbing the raised corner of his desk. He had no clue from where it had come. His stomach threatened to send him to the office bathroom with a case of seasickness.

He was terrified. Not necessarily of facing down the man he had accused, although that was rocking and rolling in his gut as well. It was the deciding. Once he chose to go or not, he'd be out of the woods. As long as he saw door number two's glorious escape to the comfort of his apartment couch with a pot of spaghetti and the TV soothing him into a stupor—as long as he had a door to freedom, the choice would pummel him into a useless blob.

He had felt that way before: each time he had kept Ned from poisoning himself in college, each time he had had to refuse to settle for a family that didn't really want him, every time he was stuck between the pretty option with the ugly end and the ugly option with a pretty end.

He wasn't even sure which was which, though. He needed someone else to close the right door for him.

That was his only explanation for showing up on Christina

Riley's front porch.

Christina's house was a beautiful little place with a small front yard, orange brick on the sides, and a big old tree of some kind shading the late model Toyota Carina in the driveway. A cracked concrete walk dissected the front lawn and led him up to the shade of the front porch. Sunset was still a few hours away, and the weather was perfect for lounging about a yard like this. Sometimes Marty regretted missing out on a place like this.

Christina answered the door and Marty hiccupped. Her red hair had been tamed into an elegant updo, she wore a long, flowing black dress and bright red lipstick. She looked excited until she saw who it was, then her face fell.

Marty felt his already fractured soul shiver at the look on her face. In a word, ouch.

"What do you want, Bowman?" Christina asked in an exasperated breath. "My husband's supposed to pick me up for Date Night soon."

"I..." His voice quavered and failed. He made two attempts to speak again, but couldn't. Marty's eyes began to burn in panic and embarrassment at her seeing him like this.

"Marty?" she asked, her pale green eyes searching his face. A small but real smile appeared on her face. Despite whatever Sandy had told her, Christina was still concerned for him.

Something clicked over internally. Marty's breath came in gulps, but he managed to fight down the...whatever it was, long enough to speak. He couldn't remember what he wanted to say, exactly, so he phrased it a little differently than he had planned.

"I'm meeting with Ben Henson at seven and I don't know what to do," he blurted out.

Christina's nearly invisible eyebrows flew upwards. "How did you schedule that?"

"I didn't. He did."

"Oh." A touch of scorn colored her voice again. "So, ignore him. That's nice and safe."

"You know I can't," he mumbled.

"Oh?"

"I owe him this."

The disdain faded, and her expression changed almost imperceptibly. Marty would have called it relief, but he wasn't reading people well lately.

"Oh. Yeah. Yeah, you do," she said. "So why are you here?"

"I know Sandy put my name on everyone's no-call list," he said, taking a deep breath, "but I have no idea what to say to him, and you're the nicest person I know. I could use nice. To be honest, I didn't really know I was going through with it until I told you."

She almost smiled, and the knot in Marty's intestines loosened by a fraction. "Why?"

He peered at her suspiciously. "Why what?"

"Why meet with the man you threw under the bus?" she asked simply. "Sandy said you were so sure you were in the right. So why?"

He felt his guard come up again. He was in the right, after all. He just made a choice that helped Gary and let justice be served to —Right. Right…

"I don't know if he deserved it or not," Marty said, having to pull each word out like a rotten tooth. "But his wife, his kids, his sister-in-law; they didn't. Happy? So, that's why. I need to…I don't know. So…yeah."

"So eloquent," Christina tittered. "I see why you were tapped to write speeches for the Democrats."

He managed to glower through her cuteness at the little twerp hiding underneath. He needed help, not cheap shots from a snobby Republican. "Christina."

She glanced at her watch as he squirmed, and then gestured into the house and stepped back into the air conditioning.

"Come on inside," she offered. "If you can admit all that, I can spare a few minutes. Let's see if I can't write you a better script for the big interview, string bean."

Marty scoffed. But he followed her inside and closed the door behind him.

EON 4 - SPILL BLOOD
ON FIRE

When consciousness finally returned, it found Anori freezing but alive in the soft embrace of a snowbank. The boy opened his eyes with difficulty. Almost immediately, the swirling snow in the gray mass of sky above him spun him back into the world of darkness.

Darkness.

Anori whimpered a little as his skull throbbed. Had his father been knocked down with him? Or had the great man slain the barbarian Mountain People who had attacked?

A large figure appeared out of the silent snowfall. Anori's hand clutched around for his club in the snow, but the man came closer and offered a hand in friendship rather than aggression. It was Scira. The huge, hairy blond man was of the Tundra People like Anori and his father. He lifted Anori up to his feet, where the boy rocked back and forth unsteadily.

It wasn't the snow that made him sway. Anori had galloped and tunneled and danced through heavy snow drifts since he could walk. Whether ice or powder, he had been born on it. And it would not betray him now, on the night of battle against the barbarians.

"Metwell, young Anori!" Scira roared with a warrior's manic

grin: one part relief and two parts excitement. "The Mountain People fled like bank mice, and we have answered their fear with death."

"Have you seen my father?" Anori cried over the moaning wind.

Scira shook his large head, and two pounds of snow fell from his bush-like mass of hair. "The fighting was thickest in the crevices where they had some shelter from our javelins, so that was where *I* fought them."

Anori glanced around and saw several barbarian bodies twisted and motionless in the snow, but there was no sign of his father and his furs sticking haphazardly out of an iron chest plate. Anori did find his own club, though, and snatched it up. The battle may have been over, but there could still be Mountain People lurking about the wastes. He hefted the heavy blunt weapon in his hand and felt safe again.

At least, he felt safer. He wouldn't feel fully secure until his father was lugging his big two-handed sword next to Anori's side.

A howl from some brazen wolf slipped in and out of the snowflakes. There was an evergreen wood nearby—the great cursed southern wood that was protected with walls of blown snow and filled with dark magics—and apparently, the hunters of the night within that shadowy world of trees wanted their share of the war spoils.

The cold didn't bother Anori, but he shivered at that sound.

Scira noticed. "Spooks, they may be. But their howl is a good omen to us today, for it means none of our twice-cursed foes hide in the forest. Our flank and our path home are both clear."

Anori nodded, and his woolen hood slipped off the back of his head. Scira grunted and spun him around like a toy. Anori felt the woodcutter's huge hand searching the back of his head, and pain lanced through his skull. The pangs were dull and throbbing, growing to blinding needle pricks when one of the rough fingers found a lump behind his right ear.

"That could have been a killing blow, boy," Scira said. "Be glad the barbarian who dealt it thought it was and did not check his work while you were in Darkness. We will get you bandaged when we regroup."

"The gods smiled at me," Anori said dutifully, just happy that Scira stopped poking his hurt head.

Scira's bearish smile came back and he clapped Anori on the shoulder. The man walked over to another pair of surviving Tundra People, his sword glittering on his back in the fading light.

Snowmelt had flooded Anori's boots and numbed his feet past the point of sensation. His fingers were better protected in his thick gloves, but he kept stretching them around to shake off the chill that had invaded while he had been lying on the ground. His head still snarled at him with each movement. The pain made him sniffle, and his nose ran a little. He was glad his father couldn't see him.

Anori continued to hunt around the rocky fields above the narrow valleys in which most of the fighting had taken place. The dead were numerous and included both the invading Mountain People and the defenders. The sight did not nauseate him as much as it once had but pressed down on his whole body like a fallen tree. Neither side had won that day. But at least the Tundra People were the ones walking away.

As he grew used to the throbbing in his head and tipped over less and less as he walked, Anori realized how thirsty he was. He slipped a worn sheep's stomach pouch out of his coat and drank the last dredges of water that he had brought with him from the well in his village. It was a big pouch, but the march from the Riverlands village to their southern border had taken two days.

"Anori."

Scira wore a grim look as he summoned the boy. The woodcutter had gathered with several others behind a snowbank. The moment Anori realized they were standing over half-a-dozen bodies, he felt like he had been submerged in snowmelt.

He didn't need to see. He stepped forward anyway.

Anori would have liked to have said that his father died

surrounded by the pitiful remains of fourteen muscular Mountain People. Real war didn't work like that. But he was proud to see his father's sword buried in one of the barbarians that had fallen nearby, and it was also a small comfort that he had fallen alongside friends instead of cornered alone like a bank mouse.

He stared down—close enough to confirm—not close enough for it to seem real. Or rather, it did seem real. Factual. Bad, but not demanding tears.

Anori spat at the barbarian corpse nearest to him. At the smallest sign of life, he would tear the murderer apart. He and his kind were responsible.

His father, a butcher, was the only other one left in his family. Anori was a man now, one of thirteen summers, but he had lost his mother to illness years ago and now barbarians had stolen away his father. No, he wouldn't cry. He wasn't sad. He was angry. He would hate those responsible until they had paid the price for the evil they had brought the Tundra Peoples.

The master of the war party, Freki, walked up to the warriors as they mourned silently. The man was not as tall as Scira, but he was strong, fast, and well-practiced in warfare. Freki had been fighting off invading barbarians for more years than Anori had been walking. The war master also had several wives and even more children, including several daughters that Anori had been forbidden to speak to by his own father after he caught Anori mooning after them.

Freki's shaven face seemed cursed into a perpetual frown, and even with the battle over, he glared about the field with a grim twitch to his mouth. He stopped for a moment in front of the four fallen Tundra People.

"Where they have fallen, we cannot reach them until we too go into Darkness!" Freki yelled over the wind hoarsely. "As always, now. Leave the meat for the wolves and take some blood to throw into the victor's pyre. We must leave this place before the weather does what the gutless Mountain People could not!"

The other men grunted and nodded. For a second time, a wolf howled from where the night had already fallen.

Anori moved as if a doll, controlled by the actions of another. Deep in a damp corner of his haversack, he found the ritual clay vial and pick. He handled them with all the care he could manage between numb fingers. Ready, he waited on the adult warriors.

Each living member of the village found the worldly remains of a man they had known in life and used the sanctified tools to gather fresh blood from those who had died. Many had to use the pick to produce enough essence to fill the vials.

Drawing his hood over his head again to shield him from the wind, Anori watched in silence. He had observed the sacred duties of the living before, but now he watched hard so he could do it himself. Few considerations, if any, were given for the corpses. After all, a body was not a person. The real person had been thrown into the snow and wind upon death, to be bound to the world as a weeping ghost and mourn their own passing for all time.

The only salvation from that fate was to spill the fallen's blood on a sacred pyre to be built upon their return to the Riverland's village. Every warrior was taught to fill the vials and bring them home. The act was one of honor, respect, and the hope that others would do the same for you once you were hewn from your body in battle. The dour-faced men, many bleeding profusely themselves, took care to fulfill their obligations before they had their wounds bathed and bandaged around the healer's fire.

As soon as Scira finished with the three vials he had collected, he approached Anori. "It is your turn now, young Anori," he said. "Take the first step to free your father. No man as valiant and hard-working as Heliis should roam as a phantom."

Anori continued to stare down at his father, studying him. The man still had his hood up and his eyes were closed. He could almost be asleep. But Anori couldn't ignore the dent in his father's helm that demanded he stare at it. There was no question.

At that thought, Anori finally began quivering.

Scira patted his shoulder clumsily. The man wasn't crying—didn't cry, never cried—but Anori saw his face crumpled as he looked down at the scene. Scira and Anori's father had been an unlikely pair: woodcutter and butcher. But both had enjoyed fishing from the river near the village when they could, a pastime that they had become surprisingly skilled at in recent years. The two had often earned extra food for their tables and for trade with others.

Anori wondered who would fish with Scira now.

A slight rumble shook the ground, and the Tundra People stopped mid-ceremony. All glanced around nervously. In the southern plains, as in the lands of the Mountain Peoples, ground-shakings were rumored to bring down trees and destroy caves. But this one stopped as quickly as it had started.

"That ended quickly," muttered Scira.

"Maybe it was the barbarian's ghosts fading from this world," said a nearby warrior with a club at his waist. "Anything as weak as them wouldn't make much of a noise while leaving."

That drew a few tired smiles from the other villagers, and they returned to their tasks.

The young warrior leaned down with the vial nested in his glove. He steadied his hand with measured breathing, and then he finished the work that he had sworn to undertake.

He completed the ritual with a murmured prayer into Darkness and capped the vial.

"You will rest soon, Father," he promised. The words were lost to the wind, but for now, they would be enough.

As he turned back to Scira, Anori felt his legs fail. He would have collapsed if Scira hadn't caught him. As he flickered in and out of consciousness, he felt the jostling motion of being carried while the giant woodcutter ran through the snow.

"*Juuta! Juuta irlenger Anori!*" the man cried for help.

Anori only heard it as if from underwater in the river back home: a distant shout from some imaginary place. His head lolled and bounced. He heard the howl of the storm and the growl of a beast and the rustling of his hood against his numb ears. He thought he saw a large gray timber wolf with black fur on its flank lope over to the fallen warriors.

And then he knew he was falling into Darkness, and he hoped it would just be a visit.

WHEN ANORI AWOKE FOR THE SECOND TIME THAT DAY, NIGHT HAD truly fallen on the snowy fields of the north. The war party had found shelter in one of the hundreds of caves that pockmarked the unforgiving terrain and started the healer's fire. The tall, blue flames flickered eerily against the narrow walls of the cave. Wounded villagers lay around the fire on makeshift mats of tough ice grass, watched over by the few warriors who had only others' blood on them, rather than their own.

Ilmut presided over the fire. Ilmut, the village healer. Ilmut, the witch-woman. She was strong enough to carry a haversack filled with her poultices and potions, and canny enough to repair all but the gravest of wounds. She leaned close to the fire, blowing a fine powder from her hand onto the snapping logs.

Anori soaked in the sight of her lips parted over her palm, her dark eyes staring intently, and the exotic contour of her face in the weird light. More than once he had dreamt of being injured in a brave battle against the barbarians and having her gentle care bring him back from Darkness itself. She would realize how courageous and powerful he had been, become entranced with his charm despite his youth, and forsake the lonely path of a witch-woman to create a new tribe with him.

Then he realized that he was halfway through that dream already. He carefully brought his hand up to his head, gritting his teeth. Poultice. Anori groaned. Ilmut had tended to him and he had missed it.

Faster than most men, Ilmut darted over to him and knocked his hand back down to his side. She frowned over him, her stony features reducing him to a puddle of snowmelt.

"Do not move! You should be resting, not destroying my work," she hissed.

She reached into one of the smaller packs at her belt and pulled out a pinch of dried herb: dreamstone, they called it. She reached down to force it into his mouth.

"No! I will rest! I will rest!" Anori cried quickly, wide eyes set on the disgusting sleeping aid.

The finger pinching the concentrated dose of dreamstone hovered over his lips for a moment before retreating. "Good," she told him. "Lay quietly, or I will return."

Anori nodded again. The pain flashing through his head at the motion made him wince.

Supernatural luck must have shone on their few remaining hunters, since dinner had been somehow caught and cooked since the fight. The warriors had roasted a summer boar and were stuffing their gullets with the meat. Ilmut had seasoned the catch with some of her own herbs, by the overpowering smell of it. Gorging was encouraged after battle. Actually, it was all but necessary to fight the fatigue from both the battle and the preparatory purge. Village warriors emptied their stomachs before the fight to prevent nausea and to keep them light on their feet.

Anori's own stomach growled audibly at the smell of the food, but his head still throbbed despite the healer's ministrations. The pain ground the edge off his hunger. Instead, he distracted himself by watching the lithe healer's movements in the firelight.

Before long, Freki stood up with his right arm wrapped in bandages and his blackened javelin in his other hand. Exciting stories of kills and rallied charges hushed to a dull murmur then sputtered out completely. Every man watched the war master as he paced. Anori had been in battle once before and knew what to expect now. Freki began to speak, his voice low.

"The Mountain People in the barbarian lands to the south once scorned the Tundra People and our beautiful fields. They left us alone and hoped we would freeze in the snow and the rivers of ice.

But we alone could tame the great North. We alone took possession of it and made it ours."

"*Feli, Freki,*" the villagers said, Anori among them.

Their leader continued, his eyes flashing blue in the light of the healer's fire. "The barbarian Mountain People grew jealous of our prosperity. While we flourished in the North, they withered in their caves among their unfarmable plateaus of rock. And in their jealousy, they sent their hordes of archers and swordsmen to take what only we could tame."

"*Feli, Freki,*" Anori agreed in time with the rest.

"But after their cowardly attacks in the night destroyed the village at the Lake, survivors warned the Tundra People of the barbarians' treachery." Freki's voice shivered and crackled with restrained emotion, and his brow dipped coldly. "Every village sent their best warriors, who drove themselves through the night in their fury. The Mountain People learned to fear the rage of the North the next day. The living retreated."

"*Feli, Freki!*"

"And yet the barbarians came! When our storms are calmest and most bearable to the weak Mountain People, when our fields bear their finest fruits and grains, they came! And still, they died in droves as the Tundra People beat them back with hammer and club, sword and javelin!"

"*Feli, Freki!*"

"And when they took the village at the Elder Grove and seized eight witch-women, the village of the Riverlands met them first!" Freki thundered. He prowled around the healer's fire like a trapped wolf. "The village lost fine warriors but saved many at the Elder Grove and forced the Mountain People into retreat. And finally, the witch-woman of that village divined the day of the next attack. The men of the Riverlands marched for days to meet the filthy thieves and murderers right at the southern border. They slaughtered their archers in ambush and trapped the rest of the Mountain People in gorges. Not one escaped! And every warrior of the Tundra People that fell in Darkness brought two of the barbarians with him!"

"*Feli, Freki!*" Anori yelled hoarsely, his voice added to the cry that tore through the cave.

"Let the night fear them, those warriors of the Riverlands, those mighty among the Tundra People! And may Darkness itself be sealed for a fortnight in testimony to the great gift of Mountain People it has received!"

Shouts of agreement burst forth from even the weakest in the dry, warm cave. Freki finished with a savage flourish of his javelin, the war master's teeth bared in a mixture of pain and pride.

Ilmut's lips moved as she whispered an incantation and threw a handful of something into the flames. The fire flared up with vibrant green tints amongst the blues. The scent of something sweet and pure filled the cave, mixing with the scent of the savory boar meat.

Anori felt the healer's fire was bathing them in some mystic power even as he watched. But he couldn't bring himself to cheer with the others, not with his father wandering the world as a weeping ghost.

Old Scira sat down next to him as other warriors danced around the outskirts of the cave, avoiding the wounded under the steady eye of Ilmut. Scira showed the young warrior one of the sacred clay vials. The smooth gray surface of the finger-sized container caught some of the blue-green firelight and looked truly enchanted. A bit of hide stretched over the top kept the precious lifeblood inside.

"Metwell, Anori," he said. "My neighbor is in here. What's left of him, at least. The poor man never married and didn't have anyone else to collect him, so… Well, he was a hard worker and a good farmer. He will be missed in the mead hall. As will your father, my small friend."

Anori's face would have wrinkled into a pout at the moniker. But it was difficult to care while his father's own blood vial cried out to him from within his haversack.

"I miss him already, right here," Anori said.

Scira sighed and watched the celebrations. "Battle is a blessing mixed into a curse, always. It isn't the strong who survive, or the smart, or the swift, although all of those can help. It is the thin edge of fortune that we can alone thank for walking off a battlefield with our blood still in our veins. Your father knew that and came anyway."

"Because he was brave," Anori said. "But he should have stayed home! He should have stayed with the Tundra People who were protecting the village! Then I could tell him all about the fight when I get home."

Scira pondered this for a moment, running his rough fingertips over the blood vial. A ruckus broke out on one side of the cave as the village tanner and a fisherman debated the superiority of a javelin over a war hammer. Some villagers watched with vague interest. Anori and Scira were not among them.

"You fought alongside Heliis during the battle, yes?" Scira asked. "How many times did you save each other's lives in the fight?"

"I don't really remember." Anori sniffed, breathing heavily through the effects of the healer's soothing mixtures. "I smashed a barbarian on the head when he tried to sneak up on Father. And he killed two of them that ambushed us behind that boulder pile."

"Then what makes you think *you* would have survived if you had fought alone and your father had stayed behind?" Scira said slowly, his eyes above his beard sincere.

Anori stopped. He thought about that a moment and then felt something deep inside him crush the blood out of his heart and leave it dry and aching. He looked up as his eyes filmed over and his throat stung.

"Me. It was my fault that he is dead!" he choked out. His breath came in gasps.

"Don't be absurd, boy!" Scira gaped at him. "The only one to blame was the gutless filth that did him in."

The man took a long draw from a wineskin and hiccupped. By the smell of his breath, Scira had started drinking as soon as the battle had ended, although it was anyone's guess as to whether it was in sorrow or celebration. As Anori batted the tears out of his eyes, he noticed that Scira's were bloodshot already.

Whether because of Anori's outburst, his excessive movement, or some sort of sixth sense for the opportunity to catch him in an embarrassing situation, Ilmut appeared. A frown bent her lips like a drawn barbarian bow, and she looked generally cross. Brushing her pale hair out of her face, she reached into a pouch on her belt. Anori didn't so much as breathe through his mouth for fear of getting dosed.

The witch-woman must have seen the pain in his face, though. She held his head still with one hand and unwrapped the bandages with the other. Her work was both quick and careful from years of practice with the mystic art of healing.

As soon as air struck the back of Anori's head, he cried out in pain. His hands clenched involuntarily and he bit back his shout.

Ilmut grunted at the sight and did something out of Anori's field of vision. There was some rustling close by. He expected more spikes of pain to shoot through his head and neck, but there was only a dull, cold sensation that creeped out from his head. More rustling pricked his ears.

Then he heard Scira gasp out loud. "I had no idea the wound was so deep," he slurred.

"Give me enough room to work, woodcutter," Ilmut said.

"To survive such a blow…It must have been a gift from the wondrous beyond! From the Darkness itself!"

The pain retreated like a barbarian attack: only after a good fight, but still retreating as sure as it had come. Still, Anori couldn't relax while Ilmut was working on him.

"Is that–? Is that the brain?" Scira demanded.

"Quiet! You'll upset the young warrior, and I. Am. *Working*."

Scira stood up and yelled for the entire cave to hear. "Champions! Warriors of the Riverlands! This young man suffered today for our victory. We all have lost friends, and some have lost brothers. But he lost his father and just near lost his own head to the barbarian filth!"

The village tanner stopped arguing to nod sympathetically. Several of the others also grunted and looked at Anori as if he was a lost and bleeding timber pup, while the war master and the healer merely watched the woodcutter yell. Anori was too weary to be embarrassed.

"But his father, Heliis, was a great man even in death!" Scira shouted. "A great butcher of both goats and barbarians, who saved his son's life one more time. And Anori, he survived the same killing blow that downed his father."

Scira fumbled with his wineskin and poured a little in his cupped hand. He clenched his fingers around the potent drink and lifted his fist in the air. The other warriors quickly followed his lead.

"To Anori!" he roared. "May he and his father's ghost never know strife again!"

"*Juumi Anori*," the villagers chanted back.

"And to the Tundra People," War Master Freki added, his good arm raising his fist of wine. It trickled down his arm like blood. "May we never stop throwing barbarians into Darkness!"

The dust and pebbles on the ground rattled with the response, and Anori winced at the noise. This was the most energy that most of these men would expend in the next few days of rest, save for that on the march back to the village.

"*Juumi Anori! Juumi Tavt Ilina!*" they cried. Then each man flung whatever drops of wine that remained in their fists to the ground, completing the salute.

Anori felt his heart glow: a startling sign of life in its crumpled condition. Perhaps Ilmut's ministrations were helping him faster than he thought. He felt light and airy and numb, as if he were floating in the river back home instead of laying on a stony cave floor in the southern wastes.

A smile wriggled over his face and he aimed it at Ilmut. "You are a beautiful Tundra People," he mumbled.

Scira heard his delirious mumbling and laughed. He winked at Anori, saying, "You will have to try your skill at fishing once we get home. Your father would have been proud to see you netting grayscales alongside his old friend. Metwell, young warrior." Then he wandered off to find a corner of the cave that would be perfect for drinking and sleeping.

Anori looked to see how the witch-woman had reacted to his bold proclamation. A rare smile lit up Ilmut's face. She was amused. She thought it was funny.

Anori realized he didn't mind. Amused was good. At least he had made her smile, and that was the least he could do after she saved his life. He felt his eyelids falling of their own accord. His entire body was relaxed and cold, despite the healer's fire less than a wolf's leap away. He couldn't fight off sleep, much less a wolf right now. Besides, cries honoring his name and the sight of Ilmut tending to his head wound was not the worst thing to fall asleep to.

So he smiled, and he slept.

HE AWOKE TO A SOUTHERN GROUNDSHAKING.

The cave was lit like twilight in the forests by the remains of the fire. Smoke and dust filled the air as Anori's eyes flew open, and a loud rumbling noise split his head like an ax. The war party shouted over the sound of the groundshaking. They grabbed what they could and fled as stone and snow fell in piles from above. One chunk of ice the size of a cave bear's head struck the ground near where Anori lay and rolled to a stop against his foot.

That was message enough for him. His head wracked with pain at each movement, Anori managed to stagger to his feet and grab his haversack. He made it a few steps. Then a wagonload of debris struck his outstretched arm and knocked him to his knees.

He noticed Freki at the mouth of the cave, directing the escape and refusing to leave yet. Anori would have welcomed the sight of Scira coming to his rescue, but the bearish man must have already made it out.

Anori's legs had been pinned by the rock, but just beneath the knees. He scraped aside rubble until he could pull his legs and feet out of the newly formed scree. His haversack had been half-buried as well, and he frantically scratched at the pile until he found a strap and yanked it out of the stones and snow.

He tried to run towards the cave entrance, but his head still spun and the ground shook violently twice more, knocking him to his legs. His entire body screamed in pain. His legs barely registered his commands and wobbled as he forced himself forward.

The other wounded had already fled or been carried out of the death trap. The grass mats surrounding the fire, and even the fire itself, had been buried as the groundshaking brought down the roof of the small cave. It was only he and Freki left, and the war master grabbed his arm and dragged him out into the early morning light.

He gasped in pain as he pitched forward into the snow.

The air was filled with flurries in the bright day, but not from the sky. The ridge of hills nearby still shook, and fallen snow from the previous day's storm had been tossed into the air again to float down to where the Tundra People waited in fear.

A fellow warrior helped Anori stand. The world beneath their feet still growled, but the largest shakings had subsided. And then there was one last rumble. The cave roared like a beast and belched forth dust and stone shards as it collapsed, leaving the land silent once more.

And then Scira stumbled out of the darkness—bloody, pale, and covered in dirt, but alive.

Shocked, Anori hobbled forward and grabbed the woodcutter's arm. Scira grimaced, now bereft of two front teeth. As they walked back away from the cave, Anori wasn't sure who was helping who walk.

"I'll never drink strong drafts again," Scira grumbled. "If you nearly don't wake up when the world falls down on you, then you drank too much. Never again…"

"If I had known you were still in there—" Anori apologized.

"You should still have marched out of that accursed cave," Scira growled. "I won't have Heliis' son and blood both lost on my account."

Others ran over to help them sit on a dry patch of ground. Ilmut looked as immutable and untiring as ever as she moved from warrior to warrior, checking for new injuries and examining the ones that she had already treated from the battle.

"The witches among the Mountain People have cursed us!" cried one villager. He cradled a broken arm and looked ill.

Anori listened as the others started mumbling. Some had wide eyes and gaping mouths, especially the younger warriors. Others glared about contemptuously at whatever barbarian witch-woman might dare show her face, muttering a few impotent curses of their own.

"Let them curse us," Freki said with iron in his voice, "for it means they can do nothing more to us with their bows and swords. We left none alive to track us or describe us to their witch-women. They will be unable to follow us with even their magics as soon as we leave the border. But it is also well-known that the gods have little love for the mountains. They often split entire peaks just in spite. Is it not also entirely plausible that one of the gods of the Mountain People is bringing devastation down upon them for their failure in battle, and we are only feeling the flurries on the edge of the storm?"

Anori felt heartened by the war master's confidence, but most of the others seemed doubtful. Glancing around at their weary faces, he understood. It was difficult to feel blessed by the gods' fortune when your freshly-stitched gashes had been torn open by the land itself.

His own legs stung from where they had been buried. A gentle probing revealed no broken bones or broken skin, for which he thanked his father's ghost. Perhaps he was looking out for Anori, even still. Confident that he was no more injured than he had been last night, Anori moved on to check the content of his haversack for damage. He pulled out his sheep-stomach pouch, still dry, and checked it for holes. Both it and his half-empty sack of mixed rye and lard were fine. He also found a strange little clay circle that he didn't remember packing.

Then Anori recognized it as the lid from a blood vial. He looked for the grass-padded pouch that his vials were snuggled inside. The ritual tools were gone. So were the extra blood vials.

So was his father's vial, except for the cap.

Anori screeched, blind to everything outside his haversack, including his own injuries. He tore through his pack and emptied everything onto the patchy grass. There wasn't even a sign of a stain. If it had broken and leaked into the haversack, he could have at least thrown the stained material into the fire at home. Now there was nothing.

Tears stung his eyes as he pawed through his small pile again and again. Frustration and fear and anger and self-loathing kept cycling through his pain-wracked mind.

Other villagers watched silently. Only the occasional moan from a wounded warrior and distant birdsong in the not-so-distant forest interrupted the quiet that lay heavy on Anori's hunched shoulders.

"The vial. I...I don't know where it *went*," Anori stammered between sobs. He looked up at Scira, but the large woodcutter looked like he had just watched his fishing friend die again. Anori felt his throat fill up with the pain of everything, the unfairness of it all, until it choked him.

He cried bitterly by himself as the other villagers separated themselves from him. Even the witch-woman would not approach to check his head wound. He had condemned his own father to wander the world as a cursed phantom forever, and sentencing someone to a fate worse than death was a crime worse than murder.

One by one, the villagers left to prepare for the march. And Anori wept alone.

HE DIDN'T KNOW WHETHER HE WOULD DIE OF THIRST OR COLD FIRST, but Anori suspected his crushed heart would fail before that. He had tried without success to claw his way back into the cave, to unbury his father's vial. But after his gloves had become torn and soaked and his fingers numb, he had to admit that even if he had been strong enough to move the ground itself, the vial had somehow been lost without its cap and there would be none of his father's blood to recover.

And now he sat and stared in a stupor. His village had abandoned him: Scira, Ilmut, the rest. He would live in the snow for as long as he could, and then—

"Anori."

The voice was devoid of both compassion and disgust. War Master Freki stood behind Anori with his haversack and his javelin slung over his back.

Expecting the worst, Anori turned and bowed in respect. A javelin prick in the neck would finish what the barbarians had tried to do. Such was a Tundra Peoples execution. He was terrified of facing the Darkness, but better now, as justice, than later while torn apart by beasts or slowly freezing.

A thump startled him into opening his eyes. A small, sharp knife with a bone handle had landed at his feet. He looked up, confusion contorting his impish features.

Freki motioned to the knife. "Restitution or punishment: which better pleases the gods, Anori?"

"Huh?" Anori stumbled over the words as he picked up the weapon.

"Do you think the gods above would prefer that you be executed, banished? Or do you think they would rather your father's ghost be released in the holy sacrament of blood in fire?" Freki asked quietly.

Sensing a trap, Anori shook his head. "I don't know."

"Neither do I, young Anori, but we can find out."

The young warrior looked up with a sharp, bird-like motion at the answer. The war master's jaw was set into its usual frown, and he cut a rather impressive figure as he stood ankle-deep in snow with his dark brown bear furs billowing out from under his iron armor. His hood almost completely draped over his bright yellow hair.

"You will retrace your steps to the battlefield above the fissures and collect fresh blood from your father's worldly body," Freki stated as if it were a matter of history and not a command. "You will do this alone, just as you lost the original blood vial alone. You will return to the village, alone. If you are swift and there is not another storm, you will be able to follow our footsteps back to the Riverlands. If not, follow the water and the woods and the sun when it shines."

Anori nodded mutely. The war party had been led by the war master's wisdom and mystic knowledge of the lands, not by a mapmaker. Returning alone without Freki's guidance would be far more difficult than the man seemed to think. He shivered slightly and pulled his fur closer around him.

Freki looked away and frowned at one of the decorations of the leader's ornate armor: a long trail of reddish hawk feathers that acted as a trim to his bear fur coat. The elegant fringe seemed to miraculously survive each battle that the war master took part in, despite his berserker fighting style. As long as Freki walked away from each fight with his coat and armor intact, it was more evidence that the gods themselves favored him.

Freki grunted. "You understand why you must go without help?"

"It is my duty alone," Anori said, mirroring the lofty way his father had spoken of such things. It was how he would have done it if roles had been reversed.

"It is your responsibility, yes," Freki said. "But as war master, I share the responsibility of every warrior under my command, living or fallen. I am beholden to help you. However, the ground-shakings threaten to crush our heads, many men are gravely injured, and I have other blood to spill on the fire at home. My burden to the many is greater than my burden is to just your father. So you must go."

Anori understood, but the words still felt as cutting and icy as a dagger in the snow.

"Then go," Freki demanded. He pulled two more objects out of his coat and placed them into Anori's fumbling hands. Another pair of unbroken ritual vials were wrapped tightly in a small woven cloth, and a full waterskin sloshed around in his hands. "Go. Follow the edge of the woods back south, and do not let the world keep the ghost of your father. He deserves better."

THUS, ANORI FOUND HIMSELF WALKING BACK TOWARDS THE LAND OF the barbarians with no one as a companion and nothing for a guide. The birds were louder now, sounding off in the wake of the groundshaking. The sky was a clear, frigid blue sea in which the red hawks and northern terns darted about like minnows.

The land itself was pale and uninteresting to his right: a cauldron of snow and stone, hills and fissures, gray and white and brown. There were few plants that could survive the year-long blanket of snow in the largely unprotected lands.

To his left, the forest seemed to absorb all the light that hit it. It was a giant, unforgiving blackish mass of branches and trunks and needles. The brush on the outskirts of the forest caught blowing snow until a wall of white blocked everything beneath the lowest branches. Tales that floated about the Riverland's mead hall told of another world in the everlasting night of the woods: a hideout of faeries, of hunter-beasts, of tiny villages that could fit within a single human home, even of massive snakes with wings and legs that roared like bears, all beyond the wall of snow.

Anori didn't know if he believed those stories. Some of the old men telling them had been half-asleep with drink, after all. He believed in what he saw, but he also couldn't shake the feeling of a single ant crawling down his back that he got when he heard those tales. They had always seemed grand and fantastic while sitting in the warm safety of the mead hall with his father and friends.

Now he walked alone through the wild. Now the stories seemed less wondrous.

He trekked a while that morning, seeing nothing living but the occasional bird in the sky. And when the lone lark or tern was replaced by a distant cloud of spiraling birds of prey, he knew he was nearing the battlefield at last.

By now his legs were sore, and whatever potion Ilmut had used on him must have faded. His brains thundered in his skull with each plodding step. He felt his eyes burned in their sockets. For the first time, Anori wondered what he would do if a barbarian were still alive on the field. He was not in any condition to fight.

The thought paralyzed him. He could all but see the second troop of Mountain People in their green-stained goat hides and helmets with ram horns embedded in the caps. They would be gathered around the fallen, performing some unspeakable ritual on the dead while they stared with pale, unblinking eyes out of shadowed faces. They'd chant and growl and screech in their weird, cursed tongue...

Anori slunk closer to the snowbank that piled against the treeline as his blood pounded through his head. His body felt heated from a fire within. He imagined tightening his grip on his club until his fingers burned and setting upon the Mountain People he'd find there. His training dictated that he would be killed quickly by multiple enemies, but not in his mind now. He would swing his weapon like a madman. Fueled by righteous fury, Anori would spin and flail too fast to be caught, slaying dozens of the goatherders. He could almost feel the give under his arm as his club broke their evil bones.

He'd return to Darkness tenfold what they took from him.

A young timber wolf with white and gold fur leaped out of the wall in front of him. Anori hiccupped and fell backward into the snow.

The creature stopped and stared at him with dark eyes, its legs splayed out as if it were as surprised as he. Its muscles were tensed beneath its soft coat and its chest heaved with sharp, quick breaths. And the moment that the young wolf saw Anori flinch, it fled into the fields of snow towards the battlefield.

Anori stood up, dusting the snow off his pants in disgust. Silly wolf.

Now keeping his distance from the wall of snow, he angled around until he had a good, safe view of the spot from which the wolf had appeared. Anori wasn't certain what he had expected, but he found a small dark hole through the packed slush that must have been dug out a long time ago. He wasn't sure if it was the wolves that had originally created the passage. Maybe it had been a faerie, a fire snake, or some other fiend that had first tunneled out of the dark world of these southern woods, and the wolves had just adopted the tunnel.

Either way, it was an oddly eerie sight. The small black hole would have been a tight fit, even for Anori, and looked to be the length of two tall men before opening up to the greenish dusk of the woods.

He continued on to escape the sightless gaze of the forest.

As he hiked through the snow, he kept his own eye on the wall. Several times in the next bit he saw more holes. Most were no bigger than a mouse hole or a snake den, but he had no desire to peer into the black gaps and see who was home.

His eyes followed tiny prints from the holes. Things—small rodents like rats and weasels, it seemed—had come and gone since the storm last night. The prints disappeared into the deeper drifts.

Then, several realizations struck Anori like a tree branch: animals were active, so they were hungry, birds in the sky meant they already were or soon would be on the ground eating bodies, and the heavy snow from last night might have buried his father's fallen form anyway.

Any fear or anger at the prospect of seeing the Mountain Peoples on the battlefield burned away. He ignored the pain in the back of his head as he jumped through the tall snow drifts towards the circling birds as quickly as he could manage.

"What if I'm late?" he mumbled to himself under his hood. The empty tundra did not answer.

The heavy snowfall from the previous night's northern storm made any movement difficult. Running was nearly impossible. Each step plunged a boot into the snow that threatened not to come out again. Anori growled through heavy breaths as he pushed through the drifts, willing his boots to stay on his feet where they belonged. If one came off, he would have to run without it.

Soon he recognized the canyon-like fissures opening up to his right in the boulder-strewn field. A small avalanche on a nearby hill had changed the landscape in the night, but he was certain he was still in the correct place. The birds and the four-legged meat-eaters were there.

Chest heaving, Anori charged onto the field. He held his trusted club at the ready in case one of the scavengers felt bold enough to find live meat. Fortunately, most of the large, ugly birds ignored him. Anori spotted the snowbank he needed to reach and felt his heart race. If he could retrieve his father's lifeblood quickly, complete the ritual, ask the gods for forgiveness… He had a chance. He might somehow find his way home and release his father. Anori wondered if the weeping ghost watched him now.

He rounded the corner of the icy mound just as he had the previous night. Instead of seeing several empty bodies, he saw scattered snow, torn bits of clothing, and a few bones.

Anori felt his limbs give way and he fell to his hands and knees in the snow. His muscles shuddered in protest. He didn't notice.

His father was gone. A hole in what must have been a sizable covering of snow had been dug up by creatures with claws. There was blood and mud and snow melt all tossed up together into a horrible sludge. There was no flesh, no bones, and no clothing left. Only the armor remained.

Several birds of prey crouched over the nearby slain barbarians, or what was left of them.

Anori retched. And as soon as he had control of his throat again, he screamed.

"Why!" he screeched at the gods in the sky. "Why? Why are you doing this to me?"

The words were so loud that they tore his mouth like the cold as they came. The birds scattered.

"You can't do this to me! You can't do this to me!" he cried, sobbing hot, angry tears. "Give me back my Father! You can't do this to him! He doesn't deserve it!"

His thoughts spun and wheeled in his head, dropping only to pick at his agonized mind and take off again. He couldn't pick through them enough to form more coherent words. But he had too much boiling to not say anything, so he screamed a long, wordless threat to the world.

Finally, Anori ran out of shout. He paused to breathe and felt his lungs burn as frosty air rushed back into them.

Gulping down air hard, he looked down to see a very startled wolf cub with a small bone in its mouth. It looked like a finger bone that had been licked clean. And snagged around one end was a scrap of white rabbit fur, the kind that had covered his father's sleeves.

Anori's club soared through the air towards the little wolf before he realized he had decided to throw it. The cub leaped away from the projectile, and it landed harmlessly in the snow nearby.

He snatched up his club, but the wolf cub was long gone. Hands shaking, Anori peered over the mound into the bright white snow after it. He spotted it near the forest. The cub had run to a fully grown timber wolf with a swath of black fur on its side. The parent wolf stared back at Anori, red staining its mouth and throat from its last meal.

All Anori saw was the red. He recognized the timber wolf from the previous night as the first onto the battlefield. He had no doubt as to what that last meal had been.

Parent and cub both loped over to the snowdrift barrier that cut the fields off from the woods. They both slipped into a hole in the wall. They were gone.

"Just like Father," Anori mumbled. He stared down at the ruddy spot his father's body had rested over. "Gone."

He stood still for a moment, his emotions swirling. He began to realize just how much the bandaged hole in his head throbbed in pain. Then his watery eyes narrowed and he snarled, releasing a puff of steam.

"I failed you, Father. But if I can't save you, I can pay those filthy animals back for you. I'll do it, Father. For you."

He wasn't expecting any kind of answer. Not a whisper in the summer air, not a brush of snow against his feet, certainly not the weeping ghost of his father to appear before him. Any of those things would have had him shriveled into a sniveling ball at this moment. Instead, he imagined the words of approval that he needed and set off for the hole in the snow wall. It would be the last hunt of his life.

In the short walk to the silent wall of white, Anori pictured the faces of the other villagers from the Riverlands if they ever heard that he and his father's souls were lost. Scira was shocked and tearing up. Freki was frowning as usual. Ilmut stared dispassionately. His younger friends back in the village looked confused and sad. All were wondering the same thing: What kind of warrior lets his father's soul wander, lost, without a fight?

An angry one, Anori decided. And he was furious. Furious at the Mountain Peoples for their evil. Furious at their witch-women for stealing his father's blood away from him in the cave with their groundshaking. Furious with the stupid beasts that would eat a great man like his father. Not only had they ruined his life, but they had also ruined the afterlife of a man who had managed both his trade and raising his son without ever complaining or falling to drink. Anyone that knew him would agree: Heliis deserved better.

So Anori found himself staring at the pale fluff surrounding the narrow, dark hole into the weird world beyond the sunlight. Tales he had heard warning children from entering the woods murmured fresh in his ears.

The tiny passage looked like the first obstacle. He leaned down and squinted inside, managing to peer through to the dim light beyond the massive barrier. An occasional vine or thin branch stuck through the walls of the snow tunnel. But at least there were no twists and turns that could leave him face-to-face with a wolf or worse.

The thought of crawling in after the wolves seemed ridiculous now that he was examining the snowdrift. Yes, he could still see their scratch marks on the snow on the bottom of the tunnel. Yes, he could probably fit through there, even with his iron chest plate around his torso. But the hole was small and cold and would leave him helpless if he was attacked.

He paused a moment, remembered, and set his jaw. Head still pounding, he leaned down into the narrow tunnel and had to stop again as a wave of dizziness struck him. His injury was letting him know just how severe it was. He didn't have long to complete the hunt.

Anori gritted his teeth through the sudden dance that the world was doing on the other side of his eyes. He squeezed his eyes closed and wriggled into the hole. The passage was just large enough for him to fit his shoulders and head through. With a little effort and working of his shoulder blades, he managed to shimmy inside with his whole body. Only when he opened his eyes again did he realize the tunnel was nearly night-black anyway.

"Don't close your eyes in the dark, Anori," he quoted his father. *"Don't crawl through a river, don't cut yourself before a cave bear, and don't close your eyes in the dark."*

Maybe it had been childhood ramblings that his father had liked to recall or maybe it had meant something profound. Either way, his father had said it often. The phrase seemed appropriate now.

Anori focused on the pale green light at the other end of the tunnel until everything stopped spinning. Then he wriggled through the surprisingly hard-packed hole. After a long few moments, he slid out the other side and fell to the ground below.

The other side of the barrier was a mass of brush and prickly vines that he suspected were what the snow drift had originally formed against. He fought his way through the tangle on hands and knees. At one point, a thorny bramble snatched his hood back off his head and he had to stop and readjust it. He wasn't about to risk one of those long, green needles sliding into the gash in the back of his head. But in less time than it took to crawl through the snow tunnel, he was out the other side into the forest proper, where there was little to no underbrush.

He brushed the snow and tree needles off his pants as he got to his feet. That's when he noticed the rough grey table, the two chairs, and the hooded man sitting under the towering trees.

The forest itself looked nothing like the rare stand of trees up in the Riverlands. Here, the trees had many broad branches and plenty of needles and leaves, unlike the kind of stunted, mostly bare trees Anori was used to seeing. The occasional bird call was louder than the wind in here. The sky was nowhere to be found behind the canopy overhead. Anori felt more like he was inside a cave or a hut than under trees. Dim green light tinted this new world, and the duskiness along with strange clouds of mist prevented him from seeing very far in any direction.

And there was that man at the table.

The table was less a table on closer inspection and more a slab of stone perched on a small boulder. The chairs were the stumps of two trees that must have been chopped down years and years ago. The stranger sat on the far side of the table, perched carefully on one jagged corner of his stump. The man wore strange material that was smoother and thinner than furs or even hides. The clothing was orange with black patterns like spider legs stitched into it, and a black hood drooped low over the stranger's face.

A twisted, square piece of iron sat in the middle of the table. A tiny fire burned inside and lit up the surrounding forest. Anori stood just outside of the ringed glow that the small fire inside the metal cast, and, wary, he waited there.

The stranger motioned him forward with a single finger. Anori silently declined.

"*Mlingtho'phit?*" the stranger inquired in a strange tongue.

Anori didn't so much as flinch. He didn't recognize the stranger's language and wondered if the man had wandered up from south of even the Mountain People. There were rumors that there were lands there where snow could not reach.

The stranger did not seem taken aback and switched to a more guttural type of speech. "*Enakik adag?*"

Anori hefted his club and adopted the fiercest glare he could manage. He didn't know the words, but he recognized them as part of the barbaric language of the Mountain Peoples. This man was an enemy.

Yet the stranger continued asking short phrases, and each sounded different. None were familiar. Anori slowly lowered his club when the barbarian's language did not come up again. Maybe this man was just—

"*Olis vumut?*" Hunting wolves?

Anori flinched as he recognized the language of the Tundra Peoples.

"Who are you?" Anori demanded.

"Tundra boy," the stranger said, nodding. But it sounded more like the stranger was identifying Anori than himself.

This time Anori raised his club and scowled. "Who are you?"

The man did not answer but gestured forward again.

At first, Anori was determined not to make the first move. Committing to a swing before your foe was a smart way to get sliced, impaled, and beheaded in battle. Besides, he didn't trust a stranger who wouldn't show his face from beneath his hood, or one who spoke the language of the barbarians.

But as if hearing Anori's thoughts, the stranger tilted his head back and made eye contact. The man, if it was a man at all, had a serious face and skin the color of a sunset. Over the skin, he seemed to also have a black stain of some kind covering everything but the areas around his nose, eyes, and mouth, shaped so that he appeared to be grinning wildly even while frowning at Anori.

"You hunt wolves, yes?" the stranger asked again. "By now they are back at their den and might not leave again for a time. Whether you intend to go in after them or not, you no longer need make haste."

"How would you know?" Anori asked. He was still flushed and breathing hard from the sight of the battlefield, and one target was as good as another right now. He needed revenge.

"I am the Watcher," the stranger said, "the Keeper of Light and Safe Paths. You are treading a dangerous one, yourself."

Anori sprinted forward and leaped on top of the stump across the stone table from the stranger, his club at the ready. The stranger twitched to face him but didn't attempt to attack. After a long moment of neither one moving, Anori settled down on his haunches but kept his club held tightly if the stranger tried to draw a weapon of his own.

"So will you help me hunt?" Anori asked.

Another moment passed. The man's golden face under the black paint calmed. Anori waited patiently while the stranger looked him over.

"Not as such."

"Then you are just in my way," Anori said, frowning. "I need to leave now, so goodbye."

Anori turned in his seat and stood up to leave.

"Have a hot drink before you leave," the stranger said calmly.

Turning with a scathing glare back to the stone table, Anori started. A pair of steaming clay mugs had appeared on either side of the metal fire-holder. The stranger picked up his and took a long draft.

"It is just hot water, I'm afraid," the stranger said. "I'm the Keeper of Light and Safe Paths, not of hospitality. My choices are limited."

"Where did these come from?" Anori asked suspiciously, keeping his distance from his cup. "I was watching. You didn't put them there."

The stranger hunched and relaxed his shoulders in an odd gesture–Anori wasn't sure if it was aggressive or not. But the stranger kept his face mostly visible beneath the thin black hood. And despite Anori's good eyes, he had yet to see any daggers or other hidden weapons on the stranger's person. So he liked his chances if it came to a fight.

The Keeper of Light and Safe Paths took another long slurp. "You are right not to trust me, but trust your nose. You need the water and the heat. You are not well for a man alone in the wild, one on a hunt with nothing but a club."

"I have a knife as well!" Anori exclaimed.

The following silence made his ears burn. His words seemed sillier and more childish the longer they sat in the thick, foggy air. The small fire in the iron container flickered and cast tongues of light across Anori's chest.

"*Drink*," the Keeper of Light and Safe Paths ordered.

Anori drank. A sniff and a brief taste revealed no hint of poison, so he relaxed and finished off the clean water in a few gulps.

"You don't like answering questions. I don't either," Anori said, feeling a little more generous as warmth spread out from his stomach. "And thank you for the water. But you may be a barbarian, or a madman of the wild, or a creation of my injured head. Wait, how did you know I was injured?"

The Keeper of Light and Safe Paths' brow rose like a banner. "You just told me."

"Before that, you said I was an injured hunter. And how did you know I was hunting the wolves?" Anori questioned. His voice was still strong, but he was beginning to fear that this man was not a man at all but some trick of the fae.

"I already told you, did I not?" the Keeper of Light and Safe Paths replied.

"You did not!" Anori yelled.

"I did. I told you I was the Keeper of Light and Safe Paths."

"That's not an answer!" Anori was angry and confused and frustrated and wanted to sink his club into some wolf skulls in the name of his poor father. This conversation made his head hurt worse.

"You are impatient to be off, and that impatience will lead you off the trail into woods that you will never leave," the Keeper of

Light and Safe Paths stated. "Tell me exactly what you seek, and I may be able to tell you how to find it."

Anori forced himself to breathe more slowly until the pain in his head lessened.

"Why should I trust you?" he asked. "You are not of the Tundra Peoples. And I can track the wolves myself."

The Keeper of Light and Safe Paths grunted. "Can you? Have you tracked under the endless boughs of these northern woods before? There is little snow in here. Have you thought about how to find your way out again after you reach your quarry?"

At that, Anori's indignant response dissolved into a hiccup. He wanted to fling out that it didn't matter, but he was worried now that he had thought about it. He clamped his mouth shut.

The Keeper of Light and Safe Paths leaned over and knotted his fingers together with an expression of primness: a look difficult to pull off when perched on a stump in the woods like an imp. His gloved hand swiped through the air and he snatched up the iron fire-holder by a handle. He peered into the heart of the fire-holder and blew slightly until the flame flared up and brightened their little section of the woods.

"So, Tundra boy, what do you seek?" the Keeper of Light and Safe Paths asked again.

"I am Anori, and I will kill the wolves that ate my father," he answered, his voice wavering slightly like the tiny fire in the iron holder.

"Revenge it is."

Anori heard the faint disapproval. He glared and said, "Father was a great man and his soul is lost because of those wolves. The only justice I can give him now is to kill them!"

"Ah, yes. 'Spill blood on fire,' isn't that what you believe?" the Keeper of Light and Safe Paths narrowed his eyes in interest. "Lifeblood poured out and burned in a sacred, cleansing hearth in the warrior's home to free their soul from the world. And yet," he spread his arms wide, "aimless violence."

"It's a start."

The Keeper actually smiled, and his features matched the painted expression on his face.

"That may be true. Can you think of no other way to treat the situation?" the Keeper of Light and Safe Paths asked. "Is there no way to still save your father?"

"There's no more blood," Anori mumbled, head hanging. "I need blood, but it's all gone."

"Gone is relative." A gleam flashed in the man's eye. "Where's the blood, Tundra boy?"

"It's gone."

"Where's the blood?"

"Can you not understand me now? It is gone!"

"Where's the blood?"

"The wolves ate it!" Anori yelled in frustration.

The Keeper blinked. "So burn the wolf."

"That–"

Anori stopped. The ridiculousness of the idea hit him and he started laughing. Then he pictured himself sitting on a stump across a stone table from a hobgoblin in the woods and laughed even harder.

"Burn the wolf?" he giggled. "Just drag the wolf home and toss him into the ceremonial fire?"

"Is it forbidden to burn an animal?" the Keeper of Light and Safe Paths asked.

"I don't know…No, but who would? It would be a disgrace," Anori protested, still chortling to himself.

After a moment, he added, "Father's blood might be cleansed if it is even still within the wolf. But the blood might be too tainted, or have become possessed by the wolf and lost its power, and I'm certain no one would allow me to throw a whole wolf into the sacred fire!" He started laughing again.

The Keeper of Light and Safe Paths did not answer. Maybe he was embarrassed at making an ignorant suggestion, or maybe he was just thinking. Anori looked up from laughing into his sleeve and—

Gone. The light had faded from the forest and his empty mug had vanished along with the stranger.

"Faeries!" Anori cursed, leaping off the stump and spitting out as much saliva as he could to rid his mouth of the foul water. It might have been cursed. Or it could have been an elixir like Ilmut brewed.

Anori couldn't believe he had sat and spoken with the faerie stranger for so long. The man had refused to answer questions and had clearly been magical. The tiny fire burning without wood was evidence enough of that. And Anori had drunk his water!

Anxious to be away from that place, Anori dashed back through the brambles over to the hole in the wall and stared out through it to the bright daylight outside this weird world. He breathed the fresh icy summer air that drifted into the tunnel. It calmed him. But just as quickly, he realized he had his back on a whole forest full of monsters and magic and wolves, and he dashed out of the branches and vines to face the darkness again. His nostrils were flared and his club was ready.

Nothing. The woods were empty. But the knowledge of how quickly that could change kept his limbs tense.

The mist was blowing in thicker. Clouds of the stuff wafted through the woods, obscuring trees for a moment before passing on. The air was thick and warm in Anori's nose. Fortunately, the unnatural clouds did not obscure his view of the wolf tracks, which were fairly plentiful in the soft dirt and mud that lay bare of snow or grass there between the trees.

Still wondering at the strange imp he had spoken with, he grimaced and patted the back of his head. Then he realized he was touching his bandage. The wound still hurt, but much less than it had minutes ago.

He touched his still-moistened lip, frowning. Could…? No.

Shaking his head, he followed the trail as it wove between trees and knolls. The path must have been walked many times before by more than just wolves. Anori had only hunted with his young friends before today, and that had mostly consisted of futile attempts to snag powderfoots in clumsy yet elaborate deadfalls. Tracking was a skill that most every villager learned at a young age to help put food on the table. However, tracking small prey through snow drifts was nothing like looking for wolves in a forest. The obnoxious presence of fallen leaves and needles complicated the task, and the lack of visibility in the mist meant that Anori had to stay alert, lest something else hunt him.

BEFORE LONG, HE RAN INTO HIS FIRST REAL DIFFICULTY. IT WAS something he had anticipated, but he still ground his teeth as he stared down at the long, meandering hot spring pool.

The water bubbled quietly from deep within the ground some-where. This spring and others like it were responsible for the rela-tive warmth of the woods and for the clouds of mist that drifted among the trees. The area that the wolves had walked through was both narrow and shallow, but the trail didn't come out directly on the other side.

With some reservation, Anori slipped off his boots and tied them up against his haversack. The dirt beneath his face was icy. Still, he moved slowly and carefully as he slid his foot into the water.

His foot immediately warned him that he had thrust it into burning embers instead of spring water, but he grit his teeth and held it down until the pain faded and he could feel the actual heat. He stuck his other foot in and went through the process again. The shallow water was filled with soft mud and smooth stones and felt wonderful once his half-frozen feet had thawed.

He tried to walk quietly, but every move splashed like a small waterfall in the relative silence. Anori winced. Any soothing effect the warm water had was blotted out by his nerves being tied up in his search for wolves, giant snakes, and faeries.

The banks of the spring-pond yielded no hint as to where the wolves had gone. He bent almost double as he trudged through the water, as much to lower his profile to predators as to better spy prints in the mud. He smiled a little at the funny feeling of mud between his toes.

A *crack* split the air as loudly as steel-on-steel. Anori dove to his stomach on the nearby bank to avoid the sound of landing in the water. His wide eyes frantically searched the mist. Nothing was visible. He had almost relaxed when he heard a distant rustling against leaves and stones. The rustles continued a moment, then stopped.

He waited.

Several long moments passed. He had counted slowly to ten many times since he last heard the noise, and he warily rose to his knees. Whatever it was, it was gone. It could have been one of the large carrion birds resting out of the wind, and he had startled it into leaving. Maybe the noise had been the wolf itself. Either way, he was now confident enough to stand again.

Anori glanced down before he did and became confident that he had also found the continuation of the game trail. Perfect. The chances were against it, but perhaps the gods favored his quest after all. The proof was right there, scratched into the soil.

"*Jumi, Anori,*" he whispered to himself.

He ripped a fern leaf out of the ground and brushed the water off his feet before shoving his warm toes back into his boots. As he stood, he could feel movement return to his legs. He pictured the empty hole where his father had lain and let his determination and goal grind away the other fears and distractions that had risen.

"Find the wolf, kill the wolf," he chanted to himself as he crept down the game trail as it meandered downhill into a deep vale.

"Find the wolf, kill the wolf," he said. He mulled it over as he hiked, and finally decided to add a third goal. "Find the wolf. Kill the wolf. Burn the wolf."

The villagers and other warriors might laugh and mock him. There was just as good a chance that they would scorn his attempt as blasphemous, sacrilegious. But if there was a chance they'd accept it, he would try it. Surely Ilmut would understand.

As he muttered to himself, Anori's heart grew warm with hope.

Bloody revenge and a chance to save his father were as welcome as a shield and a javelin.

His feet propelled him forward quickly towards another spring-fed pond at the bottom of the vale, this one far larger than the last. He kept glancing downwards to find the next hint of wolf tracks and to be sure his own feet didn't betray him to an exposed root, a slick patch of mud, or a layer of shale. The animals had not taken much care in hiding their steps. Hunters, either Tundra Peoples or Mountain Peoples, must have never entered this wood and taught the wolves to fear.

A full grove of thick-trunked needle trees covered the bottom of the hill. Anori had to slow down as he wove in between the close trunks, and as he did, he thought he heard the howl of snow and wind overhead. But no flakes reached the floor of the woods if there really was another storm blowing into the south.

Anori leaped from root to root. He would just begin to fear that he had lost the trail when he would see another set of claw marks or half a paw print in the loam. He panted as his muscles stretched and strained. All this activity in the relative warmth of the woods was working up a thin slick of sweat under his heavy coat.

But even in his rush, he paused under a tree with golden fruit. He had searched for berries before in the tundra, but he'd never seen anything this large. The scent stopped him more than anything. Sweet and mellow and something that strangely reminded him of a fresh loaf of bread, the smell made his mouth rebel against him. The bright yellow fruits were stripped from lower branches but still present at the higher limits of his reach.

His stomach grumbled at him, and he realized how empty it was. His head was still healing. He knew he needed strength if he were to survive his upcoming fight with the wolves and their cubs.

Anori picked a few with some difficulty and tried one. When the first nibble didn't taste poisonous, he devoured as many as he could stomach. The last three he slid into his haversack for later. He found himself licking the last sticky remnants of juice off his glove and regretting the speed at which the fruits had vanished. His stomach felt slightly swollen and unhappy, having been empty for so long that it had forgotten what to do with food.

Still dwelling on the odd savory flavor of the yellow fruits, Anori stumbled out of the grove of trees into the thickest cloud of mist yet. The pond he had seen while running downhill was even bigger than he had expected. It sprawled down the vale floor and was filled with old, knotty trees that swelled up from the brackish green surface like ancient monsters in their own right. The trees looked evil and angry, and Anori wouldn't have been surprised if they had been grown and twisted by faerie magic.

That's when he noticed the Keeper of Light and Safe Paths.

At the water's edge stood an old statue. The moldering stone monolith looked to be a human if the human were three times taller than any man Anori knew. Perhaps it really had been scaled to its sculptor: a frightening thought. But time and wind and water had eroded all but the beak-like nose of the face away, and only an outstretched hand pointing away from the pond retained any of its original detail.

The Keeper of Light and Safe Paths crouched high on the shoulder of the statue, his face hidden by shadows and his hood. One hand gripped his iron fire-holder. The other was outstretched, pointing in the opposite direction that the statue pointed.

Anori warily approached the eerie sight. The Keeper was motionless, save his head, which swiveled slowly to track Anori's movement. Distant birds and frogs made ripples of sound through the silence, but otherwise, Anori only heard his own footsteps and his pounding heartbeat in the fog. He could now see occasional stones left embedded in the ground as if placed there to mark some forgotten path. The game trail snaked nearby it and traveled to Anori's left, where the statue pointed.

To the right, the stones continued straight into the dark pond. The occasional stone stuck out of the water. Each one looked smaller, slipperier, and farther apart than the last as they trailed off into the pale mist that smothered the pond. And that was the way that the Keeper pointed.

Anori walked up to the base of the statue and stared up at the odd man in his black and orange clothing, perched on the statue like a vulture. The Keeper made not a sound. The wolf tracks continued on to the left along the game trail, but the Keeper of Light and Safe Paths seemed adamant that Anori take the other road.

After glancing down both paths, Anori scoffed and padded down the correct path, to the left. Anyone great enough to build a monolith that large must have known which way to have it point.

He tensed as he walked away. He wasn't sure that the people-less man, if he was even a man, wouldn't attack him for ignoring his instruction. The Keeper of Light and Safe Paths might be very touchy about his self-proclaimed role in this weird forest.

But all he heard was a disappointed click behind him like he remembered his father making when Anori occasionally carved up a sheep the wrong way back in the village. His father would gently take the knife out of his hands, pantomime the correct way to pare the valuable parts from the animal waste, and stay with him until he could say he was proud of how fast Anori learned. Even after Anori became a man, his father still knew how to get him to grin with the right praise when he deserved it.

The memory had struck Anori unexpectedly, and he found himself tightening his fist around his club yet again. The weapon was unyielding in his hands. He felt a growing urge to show the wolves who had eaten his father just how unyielding it was.

He turned with his eyes watering angrily. The Keeper was gone, although the warmth of his fire could just be seen fading down the dangerous path into the lake.

"Let him slip and bang his head," Anori muttered.

The words sounded cranky and petty in the foreign air, but he didn't have the vicious words he needed to tear through the Mountain People, rip the wolves asunder, and crush this whole miserable world of trees and mud. The thought of doing so made his face twitch into something like a grin.

If Anori had met himself in those dark woods, at that moment, wearing that expression, he would have certainly attacked on sight.

THE ANCIENT STONE PATH CONTINUED TO WIND AROUND THE LAKE between giant trees that must have been as old as the civilization that had built the road. The giants had great leaves the size of shovelheads. In places along their base, some past peoples had carved shapes and squiggles deep into the smooth bark. If there were scenes of battles or celebrations, like Ilmut and Freki would carve in the hut doors, Anori didn't recognize them. The strange symbols were in clean columns up and down the trunks. Maybe they were the scratches of birds or animals, but Anori had a vague, uneasy feeling about them.

Smaller and younger trees had grown up over the path under the canopies of the mammoths. These were stunted by the lack of sun, though, and were easy to skirt around or brush past. Some sort of tree vermin chittered above his head. He would see flashes of the creatures' white fur high in the branches and long twigs as they danced and fought amongst each other.

Anori jogged as quickly as the pain from his head wound allowed. He had no desire to meet one of those small white creatures or anything else that lived in this cursed place, and the wolves were certainly ahead of him. If he trusted the Keeper of Light and Safe Paths, which he didn't, then they might already be holed up in their den.

He was so caught up in his worries that he nearly missed the signs. The wolves had followed the old human path between the tall trees for a while, but the road continued up and out of the vale ahead. Their prints in the soft loam had started circling back around the large green pond.

Eyes were everywhere.

Anori's pace slowed to a creep before he settled down into a narrow hollow between a tree's large roots. The feeling that he was being watched had invaded his mind without warning. The feeling was immeasurably unnerving, and Anori jerked his head one way after another in an attempt to spot who or what was stalking him.

Several torturous moments passed. He couldn't see anything, not even any sign of anything. The sensation of being watched faded enough for him to ease himself out of his hiding place and continue after the wolves.

As he passed a fallen tree, he again suspected he was being stalked. Anori stayed on his feet this time. He swung his club around wildly, turning several times as he sensed something was behind him and ready to strike. He found nothing but faint dizziness.

And again, the feeling faded. Glancing around, panting, he continued on.

By the time the third rush of terror hit, he was exhausted and collapsed on the ground. His breath came in heady gulps. But this time he had his own suspicion about where these sensations were coming from. With shaky hands, he opened his haversack and took out the fruit he had eaten so quickly earlier. He gave the soft yellow flesh a sniff.

Anori wasn't sure what he had been expecting, but he felt his neck prickle as soon as the scent hit his nose. He flung the fruit away. His head was still reeling as he forced himself onwards with labored steps.

Like some child, he had eaten poisonous fruit without even noticing. And if not for these accursed wolves, he wouldn't have to be in this awful place, scrounging around for food among the faeries. They were to blame.

The sensation of fear faded as he walked, but the process was slow and uncomfortable. He could have sworn snowmelt was dripping out of every pore of his body. He shivered and focused on how he would approach the—

The wolf den was right ahead of him. He saw it: a cave. The timber wolf and its cub were both right ahead of him, standing well outside the opening.

He was shocked by his luck. He also wasn't certain that he

wasn't still having dreams during the day, like with the eyes. But afraid of being smelled by the powerful predators, Anori dropped into the dirt and watched them closely.

The elder wolf was near the lake and seemed to be growling at the pup. Anori had no idea why. Maybe the little vermin wouldn't go take a bath or drink with its parent. The pup toddled up to the cave entrance despite the grown wolf's protests. The adult made no move to go up after it but stood tensed and snarling silently.

Anori knew the safer plan of attack was to ambush the adult. That was where the danger was, and surprise would eliminate most of that danger. It was basic warcraft. But he was closer to the pup at the mouth of the cave than the mature timber wolf, and he judged he could sprint over and kill it before the wolf could reach him.

One would be down. There could have been more pups that had defiled his father's memory, but he had seen this one. This was the one that deserved a reckoning. He needed to get to it before it disappeared back into the cave.

His thoughts ceased. Planning ceased. Anori couldn't blot out the image of the worthless wolf baby eating his father's shattered bone.

He braced his feet against a root and charged.

Anori's legs burned and he could practically feel his surging blood pound against the thick bandages packed against his head wound. A wave of pain threatened to topple him. He lurched forward, stepping on a pile of fallen leaves that crackled like fire.

The young wolf finally turned towards him. It paused, sniffing the air in apparent confusion. The mature timber wolf snarled from the bank of the pool and charged through the mist toward the threat to its offspring.

Anori made it there first.

"For you, Father," he whispered.

His first strike would have crushed pebbles into dust, as fueled by inner fire as he was—and it did. The swing missed the still pup as he misjudged the distance in his dizziness. His club smashed the nearby rocks and sent shards of rock flying. He whipped it around in a backswing, but the wolf was moving now and darted towards the cave. Anori had to dive after it with the knowledge that he had one furious wolf behind him and more possible pack members in the darkness in front of him.

"No!"

He couldn't imagine how he had missed twice. But he had to take at least one vermin out of the fight before the other could bite his spine in half.

Anori raised his club halfway. He had had a split second to rethink his approach and decided to sacrifice power for speed and accuracy with a short swing, and the pup dodged again with the speed of a thing that preys on the weak. Anori was ready this time, though, and managed to graze it.

Before he could strike again, there was another snarl from behind him. At the same time, something massive loomed in the cave and, more than seeing it, he just sensed it and assumed it was a boulder until it lunged forward.

Anori felt agony.

The world spun around him in a nauseating blend of branches and dirt and mist.

A roar split his ears. He hit the ground and rolled to a stop. His head burned worse than ever. Movement was impossible. His legs refused to obey.

From where he lay, half-buried in leaves near the pond, he saw the two wolves loping off into the trees with a mountain of dark fur in pursuit. The monstrosity gouged the earth with claws the size of knives. A cave bear. The sight didn't make sense at first.

ANORI STARTED AWAKE. HE HADN'T REALIZED HE HAD PASSED INTO Darkness until he blinked some dust out of his eyes and found himself still stuck in leaves. Fortunately, the bear hadn't returned yet. Tundra People could kill Mountain People, angry hawks, and even wolves by themselves, but a cave bear the size of a village hut took a carefully planned ambush and as many warriors as could be persuaded.

With a quiet groan, Anori lifted himself to his feet. Blood trickled out of shallow furrows on his arm and shoulder. His armor had taken the brunt of the bear's claws, or else he would be dead.

Then he noticed the sticky feeling along his back. Apparently, the bear's claws had been stronger than even the ironmonger's work. He was alive, but the pain was so absolute that it was becoming an almost physical presence that walked where he walked and staggered where he staggered.

The pounding from his original head injury was now also paired with the thudding fear that the bear would return before he could leave. He had made it to the pond when he realized that he had left his club.

Thrown into a panic, Anori turned and took three shaky steps back toward the cave. He was certain the club had been knocked out of his fist there. A weapon was only a weapon to the Tundra Peoples, unlike more superstitious tribes, but this was a matter of survival. He couldn't see the club from where he was by the water.

But he could see the cave bear.

This beast was particularly massive. It had either lived a long life filled with many deer, wolves, and berries, or the creature had been granted its incredible girth by tricksters of the fae. It was brown and well-muscled and lumbering back into its home.

Going to the cave was out of the question. Staying to look for his club was, too. Anori had been beaten and clawed, smashed over the head, and abandoned. When the cave bear paused and sniffed the air, Anori hurried away along the water's edge as quickly as he could. His feet dragged and his head sent the entire world reeling at unnatural angles, but a draught of concentrated dread and stubbornness kept planting his feet in the ground.

One and another and pain. One and another and pain. One and another and pain...

Trembling, Anori finally succumbed to the demands of his body. He collapsed in a somewhat organized manner in the mud near the pond. He couldn't hear the bear, or wolves, or birds, or anything over the pounding in his ears.

Too broken to scream and too angry to cry, Anori sobbed in silence. After most of a day of tracking, he had lost his one chance in a short bout of clumsy, stupid, worthlessness. He had failed. He could not kill so much as a baby wolf. And it had to be incredibly young to wander into a cave bear's home.

Young and naive, he growled aloud the thought. Anori and the pup had something in common. Neither deserved to live, either. What would Freki say?

Once his breath had returned, he pushed himself into a sitting position. He was still bleeding, and that was bad. He was already too low on blood. Without really thinking or caring, he snapped off some wavy pondweed and wrapped it around the claw marks on his arm, tying them off at the end.

"I am not weak," he mumbled. He actually jumped a little at the sound of his own voice in the silence.

Glaring through blurry eyes at the bear's damage, he finished wrapping his scratches in the makeshift bandages. "I am not *weak*," he insisted through clenched teeth.

Finally, he slapped some mud over the bandages. He wasn't sure why. It seemed like the right thing to do, although he supposed he could just as easily be cursing his blood with some kind of worm venom as keeping it safe.

"I am not weak," he whispered, "but I am a fool."

"Misguided, a fool might be. But misguided, a fool does not always make," said the Keeper of Light and Safe Paths.

Anori's heart fluttered in shock, but his body was too weary to betray him. He turned around to see the Keeper standing in the pond nearby. No, he stood on the pond. No, on a rock on the pond. The stone path that the were-man had pointed to earlier. It lead to this spot on the shore.

"Why didn't you tell me about the bear?" Anori demanded, eyes watering. "You knew, and you didn't tell me!"

"Would you have believed me?"

"Yes, I would have!" Anori cried. Pain flashed in his vision and he cradled his head in his hands. "Leave, if you want to help. I don't need your dark magic."

The Keeper took a long step onto the shore, where he stood straight in his strange garb. "The future is always stepping closer to us, even when we stand still."

Anori didn't know what that meant, and he didn't care to ask. He slapped another handful of mud on himself and took special care to spread it all over his shoulder to avoid looking at or thinking about the strange were-man. His breath was returning in slower swallows now, but the pain was slow to recede. Even sitting still only did so much.

"You still must save your father's soul, Tundra boy," the Keeper said with a grim turn of his mouth under the wild beam of his painted face. "Do you know what failure is?"

"Be quiet, old man," Anori asked. Sitting bloody and beaten at the feet of a strange man did not make him feel charitable.

The Keeper walked over to a nearby tree and hung his small fire-cage on a broken branch. He slowly climbed into the lower boughs while saying, "Failure is not when your work has been interrupted. It is when a task can no longer be completed."

Anori was silent.

The Keeper continued to stretch until he was crouched in a crook of the tree, as he had crouched on the ancient statue. Then he cocked his head at Anori. "Have you failed?"

"Yes."

"Why?"

"I have no weapon and no trail. I will die out here. Alone."

"You are very grim," the Keeper stated. "But you've forgotten two things."

Anori knew he looked surprised, and he was too exhausted to worry about false hope. His father had loved hope, after all. With a burst of dizzying effort, he rose to his feet. "What? What did I forget?"

The Keeper blinked like an owl.

"You have forgotten what I told you: that I am the Keeper of Light and Safe Paths, a claim you already know to be true," he said. "Travel uphill until you reach the stream that feeds the pond. Walk along its bank until you find the wolf prints. You will find *naliis ii vumut.*" *Nothing but wolves.*

"What else did I forget, my club?" he said darkly.

"No."

Anori waited for the man to answer in his own time. The Keeper seemed to sense this, and a languorous smile spread across his face.

"You also forgot what *you* told me."

"What?" Anori asked. "Because if I said I was a great wolf hunter, I lied."

The Keeper shook his head. "No. I believe your exact words were, 'I have a knife as well!'"

Anori stared at him.

"You hunt alone, but you hunt with greater purpose than most," the Keeper said. "Let's talk about hate and let us speak of misery. This wood is not filled with faeries, dragons, giant were-beasts, and curses as some may tell you, but it is dangerous. There are ancient temples with treasures and teachings that could reignite wars. There are massive beasts that have lived too long and grown too strong. There are trees with inviting fruits that can enrage, confuse, or even kill those that taste them."

"I found some yellow ones that made me see eyes everywhere," Anori said as he rubbed more mud on himself.

The Keeper of Light and Safe Paths grunted.

"And yet as deadly as the world can be, a soul protected by a strong heart can endure everything," he said. "Your heart beats like an average heart: strong, then weak, then strong, then weak. If you are not careful and you encounter the worst while weak, your soul becomes as scarred as your body."

"Do you speak to everyone this way?" Anori asked. He threw out his arms wide, gesturing at himself. "I hurt. I bleed. I starve. What use do I have for fancy words about souls and hearts?"

The Keeper carefully lifted his small fire into the air, lighting up his face again. He peered into the iron cage and blew gently. The flame sputtered as if about to die then it flared up brighter. The Keeper turned his dark eyes to Anori.

"Be like the flame and endure," he said simply.

Anori's stomach clenched in hunger pangs, and it was one pain too many.

"Give me a weapon or food or a way out of this forest!" Anori cried, desperation settling over him. "Help me!"

The Keeper blinked again. "Do you think you would have naturally survived this long with that head wound? You have enough. We shall not meet again."

Growling, Anori fought through his pain to lean over, scoop up a handful of mud from the pond, and sling it at the mad were-man. Only, even as he straightened and threw, he saw that the Keeper had disappeared again.

"Good," Anori mumbled, chest heaving. Perhaps the strange man had healed his head. Perhaps not. The Keeper was annoying.

He glanced down at himself and wrinkled his nose. He had mud on everything but his face, and the mud stunk. Stunk wasn't even a strong enough word. It reeked. It was half clay and half rotting vegetation. A small, cold laugh that tickled hysteria rippled out of him. He would be the smelliest, toothless thing to ever attack a wolf.

Drawing Freki's knife, he clutched it between bruised fingers and vowed not to let it out of his grip until he stopped breathing. His stomach rumbled and he returned its gesture with indifference.

With no other direction to follow, Anori began the torturous walk up the hill. He still did not appreciate any form of cooperation with the self-proclaimed Keeper of Light and Safe Paths. Each step forward was painful, but each was also ever so slightly easier than the last. Perhaps the shock of the landing had made him overestimate the damage done by the cave bear earlier. Maybe tricky little faeries were healing him with their dark magics so they could better enjoy the fight between him and the wolves, should he find them.

His lips twisted into a bit of a smile and he muttered, "What do you think of me, faeries? Think I'll kill the nasty hunters of the night?"

He trod painfully until he found the stream. He heard it first in the form of a repeating, burbling noise before he stumbled onto the clear water's path through the hill. Unlike the evil-looking pond, the stream looked and smelled clean.

Greedily, Anori fell to his knees on the edge of the stream and practically threw water down his throat as quickly as possible. It tasted perfect. Only after his stomach was bloated, his throat was wet, and his thirst was quenched did he think about how much attention he might have just brought to himself, flailing as he did.

He slapped some more mud over spots where it had washed off, and even the mud from the stream seemed cleaner. Of course, he hadn't waited long enough to cover his injuries with this sweeter-smelling stuff. That was what the gods were doing to him: punishing him down to every little detail.

Anori continued to climb uphill until he found the wolf tracks. They had crossed the stream swiftly this time, crossing and exiting at the same place they had entered the water. Anori assumed it was because of their desperation to get away from the cave bear.

Sure enough, he also spotted several deep gouges in the dirt that could only have belonged to one thing. The prints stopped and turned at the stream's edge.

As Anori stepped over, he was leaving the bear's territory and entering that of the wolves.

His body was beaten, yes, but his mind was far worse. That delicate glimmer of life was torn and scarred by the events of the past days. It only wanted rest, and Anori knew it would only get that rest once he had vindicated his father. Then his suffering would mean something. Evil would be snuffed out and maybe at least his father's weeping ghost could wander the world of the living with pride.

So dull were Anori's thoughts that he tracked the wolves without real conscious intent. Even when he nearly lost the trail or became confused, he barely noticed.

Only when he found a fresh kill did he awake from his sleepless dreams.

Several vermin had been crushed and devoured by the brute and its spawn. There was little left but bones and some bloody skin. The sight alone would have normally had little effect on the young warrior, but now he bared his teeth and gripped Freki's knife so hard that his fingers threatened to go numb.

And when he found a small cave in a hollow a little farther up the hill, the boy's lips curled into a slightly manic grin. He was alert. He was looking, smelling, tasting the air. He was now fully and completely awake as his body begrudgingly energized him for combat one last time.

He was here.

This time, he didn't rush in like a fool. He backed out of sight and tested the wind. He shuffled to his right for a while until he was confident that low brush and wind would protect his presence until it was too late for the hunters to react.

Pain faded. He placed each foot and hand forward carefully to create no noise until he had crept into a shrub with flat, spicy fragrant needles. Peering through, he gazed over the hollow with a veteran's eye, albeit an angry and weary one.

The area was quiet. There weren't any members of the timber wolf pack currently outside the den, but the signs of their activity were plain even to Anori. Gray bits of fur were snagged on some nettles outside the cave entrance. Some snow had managed to slip between the thinner tangle of branches here, and there were wolf prints of all sizes in the snow and mud there.

There was also lots and lots of excrement lying around like small, stumpy logs. Some of the droppings left little of the night hunters' meals to the imagination. There was no sign of bodies drug back to the area from nearby kills, though. Anori wondered if another animal had originally moved his father's corpse.

The thought made him clench his teeth. He could only take it out on two animals, but he knew where they were.

He scrutinized the cave. It was more of a burrow than a proper cave, with an entrance not much larger than the tunnels through the snow drift wall. That hill was partially covered by a nettle patch that made approach from that direction implausible. There was no other good cover between his bush and the tunnel.

They came silently, without warning. A large, male wolf and several yearlings had crept into the clearing of the hollow. They seemed nervous, on edge, but they didn't look directly up at Anori. Yet.

Instead of flinching, Anori came to a stop as dead as winter ice. He held his breath and felt his flesh crawl for fear of giving his position away. Every needle and or twig under his stomach could betray him at a single shift of his weight, and he became very aware of everything he and his clothing touched. When he finally had to breathe, it was in pathetic little wheezes that were just strong enough to keep him from passing out.

The wolves crept forward. It occurred to Anori that one of the yearlings present had been the one who had first jumped out of the forest and alerted him to the tunnels. He couldn't pick it out, though.

With the pack leader and his spawn roaming about, Anori didn't dare move. His head itched.

There they were. The wolf matron with the black mark and the pup with the blood around its mouth. The younger wolf was limping slightly, and it was obvious that neither had escaped the cave bear completely unscathed. Anori felt his heart speed up at the thought. But he couldn't act while the entire pack was—

A yearling slipped into the den. Then another. Then the pack leader. Another yearling nosed about the entrance to the hole.

Anori felt himself tense. He had no plan yet, but if all of the predators except his targets were out of the picture even for a moment, he had a chance to get to the two wolves and kill or fatally wound them before the rest of the pack overwhelmed him.

His father wouldn't be saved, not if he was dead too, but a part of him had always suspected that that would be true anyway. At least he could butcher the brutes responsible for his misery. He could bear to be a weeping ghost himself if it meant the fire inside would be dimmed. At least he might be with his father.

The last of the yearlings bounced into the den, and the youngest hunter of the night sniffed around at some of the tufts of fur on the brambles. Anori should have been elated that his chance had come. He should have risen out of the bush in a righteous rage. He knew that he should.

But he was too busy being petrified as the timber wolf matron came sniffing his direction. Her dark eyes gleamed and her nose shone in the dim light. The nostrils quivered as the wolf tested the air for the intruder in the woods. Maybe it could tell the smell belonged to the creature that had pursued them. Or perhaps the matron just sensed something was wrong, like the other wolves.

Either way, Anori knew that he was a dead man. His numb fingers barely gripped the bone handle of Freki's knife as he watched the wolf's methodical approach.

It paused, only a few lengths away from the shrub now. Its nose was pressed to the ground. If it looked up now, it would see straight between two scraggly branches and Anori would be unmasked. He cursed the worthless shrub for not being healthier and growing more fully. He then cursed himself for cursing a shrub.

The wolf glanced up, its dark eyes staring straight into him.

Anori didn't blink, didn't breathe, didn't twitch, and didn't so much as think. He couldn't if he had tried. He just kept picturing the time he'd seen a timber wolf lunge at the throat of a goat and tear it out. Suddenly, he had to use all his self-control not to bring his hands up over his own throat.

The wolf's nose quivered as it stared at him. It raised its head. The matron glanced away.

Anori still didn't breathe.

Then the wolf walked around to the side of the shrub, still sniffing. Anori couldn't believe that it was still looking when it had clearly seen him. If wolves could track prey by smell, they should certainly be able to scent him at this range.

He risked a breath as his lungs moaned. It was slow but deep, and it filled his cold nose with a strange blend of the herbaceous evergreen he hid beneath and of putrid mud that he had slapped all over himself like a child.

There was no trunk or large branches between him and the wolf matron, but she was about to walk past him. At that point, he'd lose too much time while twisting around to face the foe and would lose his precious second of surprise.

"Please." He breathed the word out softer than even a weeping ghost could hear. Maybe it was a plea to the gods of the Tundra Peoples, or maybe not. But surely someone who appreciated justice could hear him. He gritted his teeth and tensed every muscle in his body.

He rolled to the side and lunged at the wolf. The knife was in his left hand, and his right hand clamped onto the back of the tundra wolf's neck the moment he impacted. He slammed the knife home.

The wolf didn't die quietly, though. It let out a strangled cry before Anori silenced it. He managed to knock it to the ground and avoid its snapping teeth and flailing legs, but he nearly had the air knocked out of his lungs when he was slammed into a partially-buried stone. He swung the knife a few more times into the hunter's throat. He held on until it thrashed one last time and surrendered to Darkness.

He had killed it.

Anori lay next to the dead wolf in shock and revulsion. Killing a human in war had become easy. The Mountain People were barely even human, and if he didn't stop them then they would slaughter him and anyone he cared about: Freki, Scira, Ilmut, the younger boys in the village who looked up to him. That kind of kill was less about killing, somehow.

But this attack was all about killing. It was what he wanted to do. Now he was realizing it was not something to be happy about or proud of.

A hard nip at his boots made him sit up with wild eyes. The wolf pup, the one that had taken his father's bone, had bitten him. Seeing Anori rise above it, the young desecrator fled to the den. Anori watched it go as he collected his scattered and burned wits.

He could chase it down now and finish his duty. The difficult part of the hunt was done—killing the scabby little bank mouse would be right and simple and satisfying.

"Don't close your eyes in the dark," he mumbled. "Don't cripple yourself when the world will do it for you. What would you do, Father?"

His indecision cost him. Anori watched the young wolf scramble into the den, its tongue hanging out and making it look ridiculous. His chance had disappeared. He could wait and use his mask of mud to ambush the offending animal, but the likelihood of being torn to pieces by the rest of the pack would increase to near-certainty. He was alive now. What was a dead runt worth, especially one that had been deprived of a parent as he had?

The wolf pack leader flew out of the den with a snarl baring its fangs. It was followed by the younger members of the pack, each smaller but still a grave threat alone. Together, they made a daunting sight as they advanced on the bush where the matron's body lay.

But bruised, scratched, injured, exhausted Anori had already limped away. He had wrapped the animal's heart and stomach in his hood and stuffed the bundle into his haversack. Then he had left.

Uphill was the only way he could hope to beat the pack. He had to climb as much as walk, but the steepness of the rocky ascent put some quick distance between him and the hunters of the night. Fog and dim forest life shrunk the world to just him and the cliff-like slope. Occasionally, a tree growing straight out of the hillside offered a decent grip and a short rest against its trunk, but otherwise, Anori felt his last eddies of strength fading from his limbs. He had abandoned his gloves to better grip the stone, and his fingers shook from fatigue and bled.

Anori heard a howl somewhere in the swirling mists behind him. He made the mistake of turning around and saw nothing but the dark fog and a few upper branches of the huge trees far below. Panicking, he flung himself up onto the next ledge—and promptly sprawled out on a plateau.

Shaking, he crawled away from the steep hillside towards some underbrush. The wolves would be able to smell the matron wolf's blood on him and were likely running up a gentler slope nearby. If that were the case, Anori thought, then they could be on him any moment. The tangle of vines and shrubs might buy him some more time.

Because the nearest section of undergrowth was made of nasty-looking nettles, Anori inched into a natural gap through the brush. He crawled on his stomach a ways. Once the thorns disappeared, he got up on his hands and knees to make better time.

Abruptly, the light all but disappeared. Anori's head bumped into a solid yet soft object and he stopped dead, whimpering slightly in pain as his head wound growled at him.

When the solid thing didn't attack him, he assumed it wasn't a wolf or cave bear and risked a glance. All he saw was white. The snow wall. He had found the edge of the forest again, and had stumbled on another one of the animal burrows through it. Had the Keeper of safe paths done this, or had it been pure good fortune?

Anori made record time through the tunnel. The darkness and cold and small space didn't even bother him in the face of being mauled by enraged wolves. He dropped out the other side and gasped for breath as the temperature dropped and he felt wind scouring his face again.

He lifted his head slightly to look back through the hole in the wall. Whether or not he had really escaped a land of faeries, fire-snakes, and temples of cursed treasure, he did know that he had survived bears and wolves and that unnatural man. That was one wood he would never visit again, magic or no.

A snarl sounded behind him from far back through the tunnel. He could hear the cries.

Throwing his legs into motion, despite just wanting to lay down and sleep, Anori ran. He saw the sun through the clouds and knew where North was, and he ran towards it. He wouldn't make it to safety before the wolves found him. But he had to try. There would be more than enough of his father's blood in the organs he had taken back from the wolf. The ritual could be altered, the right tools used later. If he made it back, he would see his father's spirit freed for a life beyond the grave. Even if he had to threaten Freki with his own knife to perform the ceremony.

His legs faltered and he fell headlong into the snow. The impact knocked the breath out of him. He could almost hear the pants of the pack behind him over the thunder in his ears.

The end was coming, but he had done his work. Revenge belonged to him and his father. Tears stained his muddy cheeks as he turned to face the timber wolves.

"Anori?" Scira roared. "What are you doing? Get up and run, boy!"

The Riverlands' youngest warrior started as he was hauled up from behind. Scira must have died on the trip home, and he was hearing his voice call out in the Darkness. The tugging was the wolves as they killed him. It was strange. He had expected it to be more painful.

The world turned dark.

"You, take his legs," Ilmut's voice snapped through the haze in his mind. "Follow Freki's trail back towards the village. I will discourage the hunters of the night in my own way, without your brute intimidation."

The thought that Ilmut had died as well made Anori a little sadder. Then he got a blast of Scira's breath in his face.

No, he was definitely still alive, at least for a little longer. He felt his body being hauled at a surprising pace through the air, and he wondered how many of the villagers had come back for him. The thought put fresh tears in his fading vision.

"I got the blood, Scira," he mumbled from dry lips. "I got Father's blood. Promise you will save him."

"Do not worry, my small friend," Scira told him quietly. "Ilmut trusted that black-hooded were-man to get us here, but I trust *her* to get us out of here. So let us just run first, eh?"

"We run," he agreed.

Then Anori slept.

EON 5 – TWO HEARTS BEATING

C lop-clop.

"Do the Naxos have any more news on the move?"

"Actually, Love, I do. I've been saving it for when we could all meet."

"All good, I hope. One more newsflash about shuttles losing air in deep space and I'm calling out sick."

"Calling out sick for a lifelong relocation?"

"I can be a very convincing fake. So, is it bad news?"

"Let's just enjoy the ride for now."

Sunset burned in the glass and metal windows of the surrounding skyscrapers in the lingering daylight. The weather was tame. The weather was always tame, though, so a better word would be "pristine." Prague's weathermen had outdone themselves today. After weeks of humidity and twenty-five-degree days, they had finally managed a crisp 23.34 Celsius. It was a day worth the time of Prague's elite.

Clop-clop.

People said that the entire European Union might stretch upwards to the capital in Madrid, but that the truly successful always rolled downhill into Prague. An experimental launch site called the Central Interstellar Dock had been built near the city millennia ago as trivial appeasement: a gesture from a centralized government that had long ignored Prague. For years, the dock sat in quiet obscurity. Then, private investors took over just before colonization took on a new meaning, and a 54-square-kilometer soft-launch site exploded into an international facility of over 550-square-kilometers. And Prague exploded with it.

Clop-clop.

Much of the city's ancient architecture had been lost to fire and storms in the past, but everything built since had been designed with the same styles and the same charm of the golden days of the past. Only the power-producing energy giants in their monolithic glass towers stood tall against the sky. And that part of town was on the other side of the Central Interstellar Docks. It didn't count as real Prague.

At least, not according to Mr. Jacqe Danni Kagir. He and his wife were enjoying a skyline unmarred by modern skyscrapers from a horse-drawn carriage.

Clop-clop.

Jacqe had been born in the Western United Nations to Pordre and Heidi Kagir. The two anthropologists had been studying in the province of Nevada at the time and quickly brought him back to Paris to raise him at home. He had grown up among universities and hydroponic wine platforms, where he had spent the first twenty years of his life as a remarkably passive, uninspired boy. He put minimal effort into his studies and spent all his free time alone in synthetic reality.

Then his grandmother had died of rapid-onset cancer. Jacqe had been incredibly close to her, even closer than he was to his own academically-obsessed parents, and her sudden disappearance from his life had stunned him. She had been a wholly sweet woman and had spent hours exploring the Parisian countryside with him during the long summer days. But after her death, he realized she did have her faults—like picking favorites. The fact that she left the majority of her fortune to him made that fact clear.

Afraid of disappointing her memory, he invested the entirety of his inheritance, became engaged to his long-time admirer Winni, and began climbing the steep mountain that was the world of finance. That was when he had begun to become Interesting.

Clop-clop.

He had found that not only could he deal with people, but he could also do it better than he could have hoped. Even better, he actually liked people. He made up for lost time by befriending anyone he could at work. "Nevau, how's your son liking the new melon diet?" "Hal, don't forget the SR conference next week! You will *love* the combat intelligence speaker." "Good morning, Ms. Fleur. Goodbye, Ms. Fleur." He let failed attempts wash off his back. Meanwhile, successful relationships grew on a foundation of sheer stubbornness, and Jacqe found that his social life began to bloom alongside his career.

Clop-clop.

Only now was he slowing down to enjoy the prosperity that he was bathing in—practically drowning in, as the case was. Abundance smothered him and Winni these days. Between his job as CFO of Integrated Nutrition Solutions, her comfortable position as sommelier for Landfall Imports, and their combined investment portfolio, currency had stopped having any real meaning years ago. Now it was just a way for Jacqe to tell how much his employers liked him.

Until last year, that is.

Clop-clop. Clop-clop-clop.

"Whoa, boys," clicked Herold, their driver from the Isles. He reigned in the pair of painted horses. They had reached the large ceramic circle built into the hill on the Naxo estate for landing craft.

The husband and wife let Herold open the door for them before stepping out of the handsome ebony carriage into the summer breeze. The carriage had been handcrafted under Jacqe's supervision and was one of his prouder accomplishments. The wood had been ported in from a rainforest on the other side of the galaxy where the trees naturally grew black. After the wooden vehicle had been crafted, it had been carefully preserved and lacquered to prevent age and the occasionally scheduled rainstorms from damaging the beautiful material. Jacqe had had it built for pleasure trips around the city.

After his aircart crash years ago, flying was far less palatable to his tastes. Besides, transportation was so frustratingly easy that he actually preferred using the old streets. Enjoying the view was a luxury, one that he enjoyed with Winni.

She slipped over to the smaller of the two horses and petted its neck, spoiling it with kind words and kisses on its nose. Herold sighed and shifted where he stood. Jacqe chuckled at the man's obvious discomfort over the flattering of his two equine employees.

"Don't worry, man," Jacqe said. "Winni wasn't named for naught. She won't let those beasts go astray."

"Small comfort when he noses me for attention every time I walk past," Herold muttered in his Isle brogue. One central language didn't mean one central accent, and his always made Jacqe's lip twitch.

Jacqe tipped him. It might have been unnecessary, considering his family employed the man, but it was the Interesting thing to do. Then he joined his wife at the edge of the platform, gave her his arm, and they walked up the long, stone road to the Naxo manor on the top of the hill.

Halfway up, Jacqe felt a twinge in his chest and paused, sucking in breath between his teeth with a wince. The growing sensation was quickly eaten by the rush of chemicals that flooded his body.

Winni turned to him sharply. "What happened?"

"Just a heart attack." Jacqe grimaced. "Either that or the wine you picked out had a sour note to it."

"I know, I know. They 'all taste the same.' But that was a thirty-year pinot noir from Desout, Love. The only sourness was yours. Leave the wine to me, and you tend to your heart attacks."

Jacqe grinned at his wife. Her angular nose was literally up in the air while she teased him, yet he stared. He found himself outright hypnotized by her mouth at times. The sarcastic, self-made woman had many virtues (and more than a few annoying features as well, like sarcasm), but some of the smallest things made him lose hold of his thoughts. The way the sunset burned in her wispy hair, how her lips curled when she was making fun of something, or the fact that she enjoyed shifting her body into forms that made him both sweat and smirk proudly in public.

As she was distracted by a vacation bird that had been startled out of a nearby shrub, he let his stare deepen. Her golden-brown dress held her well-endowed form snugly while billowing freely around her calves. She looked like a goddess out of the old millennia: a paragon of beauty and kindness that no man deserved, least of all him.

Some people looked down on him for marrying outside of the human race. Those people were jealous that they didn't have fyirn wives.

Then Winni's smirk faded and she frowned at him. "And if you have a heart attack while we're out on the new colony? The chems won't last forever, and living on that planet will be infinitely harsher than even a secondary country here on Earth."

"Like we said, I'll bring a large supply of chems," Jacqe said. "You worry too much."

"You don't worry enough," Winni retorted. "If I hadn't brought it up last month, you wouldn't have remembered to add your chems to the shuttle load at all."

"I had my mind on other things," Jacqe dismissed her. "I'm fine, Love. Really. Worry doesn't look as good on you as snarkasm does."

"Everything looks good on me," Winni tossed her head and posed, drawing a laugh from her husband.

They continued up the stone road, and Jacqe stretched his shoulders in the warm air. It was one of those summer days in which the air smelled good, felt good, and made the rest of the world look good. The Naxo estate was located on a hill fairly distant from ancient Prague, but still within the city's borders. The view of the land from here was truly something. Excepting, of course, those awful energy towers. They were not even vaguely Interesting.

The Naxo manor itself was much like its dwarven owners: sturdy, proud, and built to outlast humanity. With stone hewn from foreign quarries, the house had an otherworldly look to it that Jacqe could never quite define. The grounds were full of servers and their human controllers. The small army of robots and technicians was tending to the meticulously designed flower beds that meandered along the road and across the lawn. The beds had been placed just so to draw the eye to the centerpiece of the estate, the manor.

"Stefan, how are the upgrades treating you?" Jacqe called out to a controller he passed.

Stefan peered up at him with a grumpy frown. As always. He yelled back his answer despite being only a few meters away. As always. "No good! The power life is still unpredictable. This entire late-gen of robots has the same issue! They should know better than to patch power software with processing code."

"I have little idea as to what that means," Jacqe admitted with a cheerful smile.

"Apparently, neither do the designers! Och. If I have to change one more server's brain…" Stefan stomped off towards a server that was struggling to trim a tree with a radial beam.

"I was almost a server controller," Jacqe mused out loud.

Winni laughed. "Your parents would have had you sent off to a mine first."

Jacqe shrugged as they approached the grand staircase up to the manor's front doors. He always felt that, once past the technicality of the robotics, his admitted neurological need for order would have played well with that line of work.

They walked up the stairs slowly, enjoying the pull on their legs from the physical exertion. The slight soreness helped remind a body that he was still alive, Jacqe always told people.

Tick.

Or you could materialize from place to place like Miss Callee Pell Encqo just had. One moment the top of the stairs was occupied only by thirty-second-century Negrucian statues, and the next moment they were joined by a young woman with bright crimson hair, a midnight blue robe with frills, and a variegated purple and black hat with a peacock feather in it.

"Hullo, Callee," Winni and Jacqe said together. Jacqe kept his perpetually pleasant tone intact. Winni didn't disguise her snort of amusement.

Callee Pell Encqo was the fifth member of their colonization group, and the only human besides Jacqe. But *human* was a strong word for the exuberant woman. She looked like an average lady in her late third decade of life, but Callee was older than even some of the rocks in Prague. She was a holdover from the days when humans had reached for immortality with technologies that had long since been outlawed. Every one-hundred years or so, she had to have her brain reset like a common murderer, just to keep her fresh and sane.

It was immortality at a cost. Jacqe personally wouldn't wish it on anyone, and Calle might finally have come over to his way of thinking. Joining them on the planet meant no more treatments. Joining them meant joining them for life.

"Hullo!" Calle said, immediately analyzing Winni. "Blonde hair? Really? You have never seemed like a blond to me."

"Och, I like this color!" Winni protested in an angry tone. The gleam in her eye betrayed her, though. "It's infinitely as much silver as it is blonde."

"The highlights look fake, m'dear," Calle said dismissively. "But the hazel eyes are okay, I suppose."

Jacqe blinked, startled. He hadn't noticed that his wife's eyes were any less brown than earlier.

"They'll be green when I'm finished, so they'll match the hair and this dusty pink dress I practically stole from the tailor," Winni said. "I can't change genetics this perfect overnight, you know."

"Don't rub that ego of yours threadbare, now. And blonde over pink, I understand. But green eyes with pink?"

"When you see it, then you'll apologize. It's my outfit for the Midsummer's Ball. You're still coming, yes?"

"May I say something?" Jacqe broke in politely.

The two women stared at him.

"That's what I thought," Jacqe said meekly. "I always forget how awful you are together when you're normally such fine ladies apart."

"'Fine lady.' Have you met me, Silvertongue?" Calle asked.

"Really, Jacqe," Winni said, smiling.

Jacqe groaned as the front door to the Naxo manor slid open. A well-muscled human butler bowed them in and escorted them to the Naxos. They passed the ballroom, the grand dining room, the kitchen, up the main stairs (which were, incidentally, dwarf-proportioned and very easy on their legs), and past several overly-large bedrooms and through a washroom to what was little more than a walk-in water closet.

The room was just large enough for the metal table and cushioned chairs that had been squashed into it. Pipes and heaters overhead forced them to duck as they entered, and the walls were a good half meter thick. A copper dome in the center of the round table held a gently burning lamp that lit the ceiling and walls.

This was their war room: a place to plot their escape from their social lives and careers. The world of upper-class Earth had long since become insufferable. This was their rebellion.

They had too much wealth and not enough challenges left in life, but Esqetone Enterprises had a solution. The galaxy-wide metamaterials conglomerate had supposedly developed a new super mineral, something exotic and worth untold fortunes.

To promote new colonization efforts, and to revive the ancient golden age of exploration, they had hidden their entire first wave of the new metal under the crust of some uninhabited planet. The first Esqetone-approved treasure hunting team to discover and mine it would receive a ludicrous portion of Esqetone's profits. Hundreds of wealthy parties were sinking billions into spacecraft, ES equipment, and hired miners and explorers.

Thus, the Naxos' war room.

Already present were Suu and Lop Naxo, bundled into their pillow-wrapped chairs and hovering over steaming mugs of dark ale. Suu Naxo was the matron of the household, a grand specimen of dwarfhood with meticulously waxed limbs, a lush bush of onyx-black hair, and an imperious look that would have been at home on an ancient monarch. Lop was just Lop. He was shaved bald from head to toe, even though that fashion had faded several years back. He also had the largest private collection of weapons in the area. Lop prided himself on his armament room. Suu prided herself on every other part of the estate.

There were two other people in the room, but not living ones. Suu was projecting the three-dimensional images of her long-deceased grandparents from a device called a Redkat. The tangible recreations of the two old dwarves were run by AI that had once memorized their original personalities. Suu Naxo was conversing with them in hushed tones, and her Redkat grandfather kept trying to pat her on the head with a hint of a smile on his bearded face.

As the butler let Callee, Winni, and Jacqe in the door, Lop nudged her and she shut down the device. Her grandparents disappeared.

"A bit late, are we?" Lop mumbled. "I've already had two mugs of Rinner's port while waiting."

"Oh, we can smell them," Callee said as she slid into the seat next to him. Lop Naxo snorted into his mug, blasting fragrant steam out the top.

Winni sat next to Callee, of course, leaving Jacqe to settle uncomfortably into the chair between her and Suu. Neither Naxo spared Winni a second glance, as usual. Lop reached across the table to shake Jacqe's hand numb. The dwarf frowned fiercely, which was his version of smiling.

"Jacqe! Have you any news about the 1290 Despain repeater? Not that I'm expecting the fool to sell easily, but I have been designing a display case that would beautifully- "

"Not that old gun again, Emerald," Suu said. "Ask him about

the *move*. Like Grandfather always said, expedite important matters and ignore the rest. Have you news about the move, Jacqe?"

Jacqe cleared his throat and straightened the fashionable steel scarf around his throat. "Actually, I do."

"Do not tell me that Esqetone has canceled the treasure hunt," Suu groused.

"Surely not," Calle interjected. "There's too much interest. If anything, another team is trying to butt into our claim on Plenty. We can't be the only ones smart enough to expect Esqetone to hide a mineral motherlode on an ag-only planet."

"We put in our flight plans months ago. They better not," Winni said. She yawned and stretched in her seat, and her lightly-freckled skin practically glowed in the dim light. "Perhaps Esqetone's delaying the start of the treasure hunt again."

Suu pursed her lips. "As Grandmother would say, those with money care nothing for time."

"With how much we invested," Lop said with a shake of his head, "we'd better not have competition this soon. Or is this another update for our packing lists? Because if I have to bring any more spare clothing, I won't be able to fit my acroscyns in my cargo crate. We may need those for harvesting and self-defense!"

Callee scratched her nose, glancing about the room as if bored by the speculation. The woman had a minute-long attention span. Then her gaze seemed to pass right through Winni to rest on Jacqe's face, causing him to blush and avert his own eyes. Better not to be caught staring.

"We could let him actually tell us what happened," Winni suggested.

The others stared expectantly at him.

Jacqe cleared his throat again and dove in. "Firstly, all of us understand the deal, yes? This contest is bizarre and clearly a poorly-concealed attempt to encourage colonization of new planets, but the joke is on them because we want off this planet anyway. So we try to be the first to find this new mineral they synthesized, and we'll go down in history. When Esqetone gives the green light, we and all the other teams rush to find which planet they hid the treasure on, and mine it, and we're responsible for—"

"Are you really going to reiterate every detail? *Really?* Why?" Callee grumped.

"'Yes', 'yes', and 'dramatic effect'," Jacqe stated with a smile.

Suu toyed with her key-sized Redkat device as if aching to bring back the echo of her grandmother for a more stimulating conversation. Winni wrinkled her nose at them. Lop drank. Heavily.

"Barring delays, we would leave within the solar year and be on the planet the year after that. That's a long trip, but more importantly, it means that there's a two-year communication and supply delay after we arrive. To claim the treasure, our relocation to the lovely virgin shores of 'Plenty' will be permanent. We found the town that will thrive off this new synthetic mineral that Esqetone claims to have developed.

"Meanwhile, people back here on Earth will not like that. We all have our own shares of moguls, investment firms, charities, and employers who would rather we be bogged down here than free out there. It's a nightmare we'd best escape. And personally, I say the sooner the better.

"Who here is not tired of this life? All of us have come so far and achieved much, but Earth has become too safe, too ordered, and too...pristine. Whatever happened to an Interesting life? Callee has been a debutante for decades. Winni and I worked hard, fell into some fortune, and have fought boredom ever since. You and Suu," he gestured to Lop, "have had nothing but trouble staving off wealth prospectors, hungry investors, and the occasional anthropologist. We *could* move to dozens of planet Earths. We *could* visit one of the four cornerstones of the galaxy. We agreed this is the last great chance in the universe for actual adventure."

"Wait a moment," Calle interrupted. "Is this a long prelude to you telling us you gave us the wrong contest parameters? Because I can hear the 'but...' in your voice."

"My Jacqe admit he was wrong about something?" Winni said. "I may faint."

"Wake me up if he—heavens forbid—apologizes for something," Lop grunted while sliding back in his seat and closing his eyes. "Or better, record it for posterity."

"I do not know to what you are referring," Jacqe said, eyes twinkling. "I'm never wrong, just occasionally misinformed by those who are. Wasn't I right about joining this treasure hunt?"

"Enough of this. What are you about, man? Unless they push it back a third time, the launch is only months away. You said this was important. I even interrupted a discussion with my revered grandparents' memories for this, not that you would know anything about that," Suu stated. Her eyes were narrowed dangerously, and dark circles under her eyes shone from alabaster skin. She fingered the Redkat device.

"Well, I suppose the rest boils off to this," Jacqe said, eyes gleaming. "Esqetone officials called. We leave the day after tomorrow."

THE HUNT WAS AFOOT. THE FOLLOWING YEAR FLEW PAST AT A SPEED insignificant compared to that of their razor-class shuttle. Their target, planet Plenty, lay well outside of normal traveled space, and they had over half a light-year of empty void to traverse after passing through the Gespes .18060 string.

Navigation, flight, and maintenance were handled by artificials and late-gen robots, leaving Jacqe and the rest of the pilgrims to spend the majority of the time in Enhanced Sleep. The comfortable ES caskets minimized the wear-and-tear of the trip on the organic travelers. The African Alliance engineers who had built the shuttle had designed the ES casket to be ergonomic, self-sustaining pods that could double as life rafts in the case of a shuttle-wide catastrophic failure.

Once a month, the pilgrims were awoken from the Enhanced Sleep caskets. They peeled off the cuffs that handled their normal bodily functions, stretched out their legs, and walked around the shuttle for a day or two. They would discuss the views of the monitors that displayed the sights of interstellar space around them. They would mingle with the dozens of adventurers they'd hired, although the scruffy builders and miners were wary of their sponsors. They would laugh and groan and eat real food from the mountain of supplies in the shuttle's tail. Then they would say their goodbyes for another month and slip back off into a world of dreams in ES.

The last time they awoke, the shuttle was already entering the planet's atmosphere.

THE RAIN ON PLENTY CAME DOWN HARD AND CAME DOWN OFTEN. IN the beginning, this made everyone particularly miserable as the shelters were still little more than roofs and walls for the first month. The Esqetone shuttle had left them and the supplies on the planet after the first two days, hoping for a quick return home.

Early on, they had made the decision to start their search from the beach of a sheltered cove that was nestled in a small southern continent. Towering trees and vines grew everywhere they could find purchase, although grass and humbler shrubs did not appear native to the area.

A small mountain range was born from the bowels of the planet to the north of their landing spot and continued northeast, where the green, wooded slopes faded in the distance. That was their long shot. That was where they hoped to find Esqetone's great prize.

Fauna was almost as plentiful as flora. There were some birds in the air, but they paled in comparison to the hordes of bats and bat-like creatures that emerged to devour the local insect swarms at dusk. Giant fish, possibly sea mammals, boiled the ocean at the edge of eye's reach. And gargantuan species of moose that could have tripped over an Earth deer occasionally came down to the cove to bathe in the salt water.

Some of the hired miners brought one of the moose down for meat with one of Lop's antique hand cannons. They only managed to get to half the meat before they had a rancid carcass on their hands. They were almost happy to be drowning in the following monsoon, as it provided relief from the stench.

Winni never left Jacqe's side. In a world of mud and wet sand, they spent most of their time finishing and waterproofing the habitat. The blocky structure was small, lacked plumbing, and had only a small stove and a freezing unit as amenities. Winni cooked. At least, she tried not to poison them both while Jacqe ran about with almost childish enthusiasm.

After he destroyed the environment paste that sealed two panels when trying to hang a candle sconce, Winni finally put her foot down.

"Love, if you bring down that wall, I *will* make you stand there to block the rain and wind yourself," she threatened.

"You tell me the sweetest things," Jacqe said.

"That's why you chose me," she said, cocking her hip like she did when she was still a girl.

"I am simply trying to get us some light other than stove light. And since our power won't last forever, I thought we should make use of all the candles we brought."

"Oh, candles! Are the supply crates still submerged in the surf?"

Jacqe hastily slapped more paste over the crevice between the panels as spitting, sputtering rain driven by the moaning wind oozed through. He had to raise his voice to be heard over the whistle of the intruding weather.

"I believe the miners dragged them farther off the waterline," he called. "They should be safer now."

"'Miners' is a stretch, since they haven't even started mining yet," Winni grumbled as she eyed the frying eggs on the stove range. "When are we actually going to search this brave new world for the treasure, anyway?"

"I assume when Plenty stops raining on our parade," Jacqe said, smiling. "And the shuttle in two years will bring more supplies to assist us. But we funded the trip, we founded this team, and we will find this treasure."

"Because we know for certain it's here. Because we are so much smarter than the hundreds of other teams scouring the galaxy now."

Jacqe cast her a wrinkled look. "Our strategy was sound. This is a matter of prestige, of legacy. We won't live forever, so what else matters?"

"Come now, Jacqe," Winni said with a sigh. "It's not a matter of prestige, here. It's a matter of pride. What's the point of legacy without descendants to inherit it?"

"I thought you were kidding about children yesterday. Look at where we are, Love! How has *this* place changed your mind?" Jacqe asked.

Winni lowered her head deferentially, looked up at him through her bangs, pouted, and held her shoulders in a way that accentuated her curves. In other words, she was using every underhanded trick she knew.

"Do you really think I wouldn't make a good mother?" she murmured.

"That's not remotely what I said."

"What you say and what you mean aren't always the same thing, my love. Why have you always been against me having a child?"

"I don't... I mean, I don't want either of us to have a child. Especially here!"

Winni's eyes were large, angry, and hurt. "We deserve a legacy. Is this because you're afraid of having a fyirn daughter instead of a human son? Or because you think that a man who falls asleep while flying an aircart with his wife can't handle the responsibilities of a child?"

Jacqe froze. Then he snatched up his weather shield and marched out into the storm, mouth drawn into a taut line. What was the point of having that conversation? None whatsoever— that's what. He heard Winni calling after him but waved her off to let her know he wasn't angry, only disappointed. The door slid shut behind him.

Outside the boxy shelter, the driving rain pelted Jacqe and

threatened to soak through his weather shield. The clouds above were black and rolled about like great beasts. They squeezed and wrenched huge raindrops from each other in their fight for dominance overhead, burying the poor creatures below in the chilling deluge. Jacqe shuddered and tiptoed through the wet sand as quickly as he dared towards Suu and Lop's habitat.

This hunt did not progress as expected, he had to admit. They had imagined difficulties, of course, but nothing as constant and uninspiring as this rain. Very little exploring had been done other than to establish a safe perimeter around their part of the beach. Instead of prospecting and analyzing mineral yields, they spent most of the time just waterproofing anything that they didn't want to dissolve.

The storms had made their progress on the habitats equally disappointing. The oversized crates were little more than that—crates. They had yet to fell the first tree or pulp local minerals into usable metal, so Jacqe and the others had little to work with that they hadn't brought themselves. For how much room they had to live in, they might as well still be in the shuttle.

"May this cursed rain end by tonight," he growled to the sky.

Just as his weather shield became overwhelmed, he sidled up to the front of his friends' shelter and pounded on the front door.

A sleepy feminine voice called, "Who is it?"

"Jacqe!" he called back. "And I'm about to be soaked! Were you sleeping, Suu?"

The door slid open and the matriarch of the Naxo household gestured him inside. He hurriedly complied, noticing that even his friend's sleepwear looked elegant. Yet her hair was pulled into a tight web folded over the top of her head, a look that certainly had more to do with function than form. Suu's head lolled as if the weight of her evening hairstyle was too great to bear.

"Not sleeping yet, but what else is there to do in this climate?" Suu asked. She sat down at the tiny table extending from the eastern wall and poured him a mug of hot water.

He accepted it wryly, already missing the exotic brews that she and her husband would casually serve to even the meanest visitors back on Earth. Lop always had a few specialty drinks he'd share while he and Jacqe ruminated on the weekly fluctuations of the investment fields or what newest craze passed as entertainment, and his stock guaranteed an early bedtime. Suu had always had a less potent variety of dwarven and human brews shipped in from other planets. To her, hospitality had been a way to make her grandparents smile at her from across the Gorge—therefore, her mead cellar was something of a local legend back in Prague.

And now Jacqe had a nice mug of hot water. He could only imagine how disgruntled she was at being reduced to this.

After a moment of silence, Suu asked him, "So why are you here, Jacqe? Arguing with your *wife* again?" She studied him shrewdly from across the table.

He flinched, then quickly recovered his dignity into a shield of confidence.

"I can't imagine where her mind is lately," he stated. "She's not grumpy or angry. Yet she knows just what to bring up to frustrate me."

"Winni always had that gift," Suu said. She noiselessly sipped her own mug of water.

"It always seemed humorous before, but now I feel as if she's weaponized it. And I don't know why! We all knew that the beginning would be the roughest," he said.

Sip.

"Ah, I understand."

"You understand?"

"The answer to my first question. You are here to whine about your home life."

"Whining is for the passive," he stated. "I simply need to confide in people I trust on occasion."

Sip. Suu finished the water with disdain and turned the mug upside down on the tabletop in a dwarven fashion that Jacqe had always found amusing. She laced her short fingers together and studied Jacqe over them.

"Why don't you just shut her down?" Suu inquired, eyelids hung low. "That's what even I must do on occasion."

Jacqe squinted at the archaic turn of phrase. "I've never been one to talk over someone else. An Interesting gentleman does not order someone else to be quiet just because he doesn't like what they have to say."

He stood up and paced in small circles within the habitat. His mind worked best when his feet were moving, which was why he had insisted on taking many of his business-to-business meetings at Integrated Nutrition Solutions outside, walking around town or one of the city parks. Legwork helped a man think.

"You're pacing. You're worried," Suu observed. "I know it's been a few days since Lop and I visited you. Are things with her that bad?"

"Yes. No, of course not. It's- " Jacqe sighed. "It's her. It's you. It's Lop and Callee. I have not seen a smile since the day we landed! What happened to the adventuring souls that came treasure hunting with me?"

"Shall I read the list chronologically or in order of hatefulness?" Suu asked with no intonation at all.

Jacqe stared. "Honestly?"

"The miners clearly resent us and haven't so much as lifted a finger to help anyone but themselves. The water purifiers may or may not be faulty. The cursed rainfall helps with that but is stalling any construction or gardening or actual treasure hunting. Even the deer are large enough to trample us while we sleep. Shall I continue?"

Jacqe couldn't believe it. For years, he had known these people to brace themselves against tyrants in both politics and the workplace. His wife and three friends were all as cunning and determined as he could be. So why were they melting like sugar in the rain? He felt he didn't even know them.

"No need, I'm sure I can imagine half a hundred other horrors you poor folk are suffering," Jacqe said dryly.

Suu's look turned from tepid to icy in the space of a blink, but she said nothing.

Backpedaling, Jacqe said, "As you said, Suu, the water purifiers are all but obsolete with all this rain—which will also help if we have to set up our mining post away from rivers in the mountains. And the workers will eventually overcome their homesickness."

"Not only are they homesick," Suu said with a colorless laugh, "they're also sick of us. Lop has had little luck with them."

Jacqe chuckled back, the sound trailing off into a groan.

"Where is Lop?" he asked. "I could use a real laugh."

"My grandfather always said that laughter is the fool's panacea," Suu quoted. "But perhaps we should all find peace as we can in these days."

"For example, some find solace in dramatic acting."

Suu shot him a dark look. But it was the kind of dark look she normally saved for him, so Jacqe smiled and saluted with his mug in return. Just like home.

WRAPPING HIS WEATHER SHIELD AROUND HIM TIGHTLY, JACQE HOPED the kinetic projections would hold against the torrential downpour. The world smelled as wet and green as always as he tromped down the beach. The odor smothered all else until the human nose simply refused to recognize it anymore.

Jacqe stumbled. The sand beneath his feet had rippled after being beaten by waves and shuffled by the massive hooves of megafauna. That made jogging difficult. However, the miniature valleys and canyons in the sand were running brown with drainage that could snatch a wayward boot and drag the owner down with it. Twice he tripped, and twice he wiped wet sand from his face.

"This mineral better be capital-*I* Interesting," he growled. His words were ripped away by the storm.

He finally found Lop in an animated discussion under a wooden pavilion on the outskirts of the miner's village. This was the first time Jacqe had actually seen the log and mud huts that made up the village. He was startled by how well-crafted and large they were. His own leaky shelter could have fit into even the meanest of the adventurers' huts.

That seemed to be, in fact, the topic foremost on Lop's mind.

"Your father taught you, eh?" Lop said. "My own father was an ironmonger, but it was all ceremonial. He was born into money and did it just to waste away the hours. So as you can imagine, I didn't learn nearly as much as you!"

With a gleam in his eye, he nudged a taller man. The miner's mouth was stretched thin. Several other men and women stood behind him, apparently letting him speak for the group. Jacqe recognized him from the shuttle. The man had a full blonde beard and sharp, calm eyes that analyzed his surroundings with near-robotic continuity.

"Fascinating," the man replied. He did not appear fascinated at all.

"How long did it take you to build this shelter?" Lop asked, grunting and nodding at the roof over their heads.

Jacqe moved to stand beside his old friend.

The miner in charge cast him a careless glance before answering Lop. "Why are you here, dwarf?"

Lop frowned. "Attempting to be friendly. Perhaps I failed."

"Do you need the prints to build real huts? Replace those metal and plastic crates of yours?"

"Perhaps I was too subtle earlier. Neither I nor my friends have experience in construction."

"So you expect us to do your work?" a younger worker asked with a scowl.

Jacqe took a small step forward, his warm smile burning at their hostility.

"The name's Jacqe. And the request not unreasonable," he said. "We hired you, but we're all in this venture together. Your expertise could help us live more comfortably until the rain abates."

Lop nodded emphatically. "Isn't that in your contracts, friends?"

Jacqe winced behind his steady smile. He and Winni were both natural negotiators. Suu had been in management and knew how to make a difficult request. Lop, though? Lop was a self-proclaimed homemaker and a hobbyist. What he didn't know about motivational speaking could fill a book, and he would happily autograph that book for the people he annoyed. It's not that he was mean-spirited. He was just extremely practical and felt everyone else should be as well.

The head miner did not see it that way.

"Our contracts are to prospect and extract, *friend*," he told Lop. "We are here because we were the best mineral experts in modern Europe. If you come back and ask for assistance instead of demanding—"

"Listen now!" Lop demanded. "We're paying you! This is a simple matter, and you will be back to your puttering before the week passes."

Jacqe considered stepping in, but there were times you aided a merger and times when you made sure your name wasn't on record when it collapsed. Crossing his arms, he watched the scruffy folk in front of him seethe.

"Look, dwarf…" the bearded man began.

Then he paused, his face knotted in confusion. His eyes tracked something behind Jacqe.

Lop and Jacqe both turned to see Callee running toward them. Her bright red hair danced in a braid as she jogged, and she was clad in a sea suit, the bands of waterproof material baring her shapely waist. She carried her weather shield in one hand and the shuttle's radio in the other.

Even from that distance, Jacqe could tell something was wrong.

A marathoner, she was barely winded as she reached them. Her mouth was pulled thin. She held up the radio like a child with a golden egg. "The shuttle. They're—"

Then she went silent as the automated voice of the shuttle's mainframe hissed over the radio, breaking through a sea of white noise. The workers, Lop, and Jacqe also stopped speaking. The soft, droning voice of the shuttle system could just barely be heard over the pounding of rain on the shelter roof above their heads. Even the miner with the darkest scowl stopped grumbling as the only humans on planet Plenty struggled to catch the faint words.

"...into a spiral that...The shuttle has...appropriately...continues to drop. In..."

The automated voice crackled and jumped a few times like a hearth flame. Most of what came through was garbled by sheer distance. By now the shuttle would be well out of Plenty's solar system. Jacqe wasn't studied on the subject of interstellar communication, but even he knew that what few signals they were receiving were delayed and distorted by space.

"Try to clean that signal," Lop said, his broad features pulled tight.

Callee dallied with the radio array, but the signal grew only weaker.

"Let me," the head miner ordered, scratching his beard fitfully. Without waiting for a response, he snatched the device out of the younger woman's hands.

Callee looked startled and offended. Jacqe took a step forward to demand manners from the oaf, but the oaf cleared the connection first. They all stopped stone-still and listened.

"...cannot be recovered. The shuttle has been locked appropriately during this... event and will await recovery at a later time. ...currently unknown why the server power software failed. Awaiting signals...departure."

Jacqe's skin crept across his body. It had been a year ago since he had spoken to Lop's gardener about the man's servers, but it had been just over a month ago in his mind. The details escaped him, but Stefan had complained about power problems. A design flaw? Something was shutting his robots down.

The shuttle had been maintained by the same model of late-gen servers.

"What did all that mean?" the bearded man asked quietly.

They were artisans and experts in their field, the miners, but they weren't technicians. Jacqe could see the uncertainty in their careworn faces as they listened to the shuttle system repeat itself.

Then again, Callee and Lop wore the same expression: concerned but uncomprehending. Maybe the situation wasn't as simple as Jacqe thought. Maybe he was jumping to conclusions. He was almost never wrong and prided himself in that, but occasionally he was misinformed. It could be—

The shuttle's voice died mid-word. No. Not wrong.

"It means we're not getting supplies in a few years," Jacqe intoned, feeling his face go slack. His nerve endings buzzed and prickled. "We won't receive reinforcements. We won't hear back from Esqetone. As far as they know, we never even made it planetside."

"What happened to the shuttle?" one of the other adventurers demanded.

"Dead."

"Then send out an emergency call!" Lop cried. "Use the radio to—"

"Dead."

Callee's worry had melted away into a tranquility that even Jacqe didn't feel. Her dark eyes blinked slowly and evenly as she and Jacqe stared at each other.

"And us?" she asked.

"Dead."

"Wait, you blame *me* for this?" Jacqe asked with a lopsided grin. But his smirk faded when he saw Lop look away in embarrassment and Suu stare up at him.

Days had passed. The radio had resisted their efforts to clean the signal and the shuttle's voice had not sounded on Plenty again. As the sun set on the second week of silence, the financiers had met in Callee's habitat. Most of the friends were there anyway. Winni had disappeared for the evening. Perhaps she blamed Jacqe as well.

"Not blame, really," Callee inserted from her perch on her bed.

"But you have to admit, you were the one who wanted to leave the day the contest started. Not to say that it's your fault we're stranded!"

"I would say that," Suu stated from the tiny habitat table.

She wore her pinched expression with a plain, sturdy jumpsuit that had replaced her more delicate outfits. Many of those were like her charm these days: long gone. She kept scratching at her sleeves like a serpent attempting to shed a particularly thick layer of skin. And when Callee began arguing with her, Suu's unwashed hair flipped and bounced like a clutch of dead snakes as she animated each of her points with a jerk of the head.

Jacqe narrowed his eyes at those gathered as they continued to bicker. Each had come of his or her own volition, and each wanted a scapegoat for their current predicament. To think clearly, he tried looking at them not as friends but as leaders of industry: the same kind of cold analytics that had helped him survive negotiations on his path to CFO.

"Callee," he said, drawing the attention of the room.

She looked up at him, her face blank.

"You try to spare my feelings, which I appreciate, but let's have everything on the table," Jacqe stated, drawing himself up as if to prepare himself for the worst.

Callee's squirmed in discomfort.

"I wish you hadn't rushed us here," she said. "We were all expecting more months of preparation, and some of us needed that to get our affairs in order. Especially in light of the current, uh, predicament. You obviously wanted to escape Earth. That's fine."

"Esqetone changed the timetables," he corrected with a smile.

Callee rolled her eyes. "Yes, Jacqe. The contest obviously started sooner to make news. But we were in space for a year! A few weeks even wouldn't have made that much of a difference. You were the only one who wanted to rush things. Even Winni didn't want to go."

"Precisely," Suu said. "And if we had waited, they would have discovered that bilgy problem with the robots! And we wouldn't be here! Stranded!"

Jacqe tried not to let his annoyance show at the woman's little tirade. Lop patted Suu's hand. Jacqe used the opportunity to focus on him.

"Lop, you've always been a man of reason and facts," Jacqe said with a nod. "I understand that in times like this, we want to blame someone. But really now. What we need is to spend our energy planning ahead, figuring out where we go from here."

Lop shifted his weight back and forth, his eyes on the flickering candle set on the stovetop. He remained silent. By the way that Suu patted his arm, it was obvious that Jacqe was not the only one in the habitat who took the man's reaction as wordless agreement with the others.

"Now look," Jacqe said.

Callee cut him off. "You're right. We do need to get to work, not bicker. Blame, no matter how well deserved—"

"Humph."

"—No matter how well deserved, it won't help us. *We* have to help us. Can we survive if we miss a load of supplies?" Callee inquired.

"Eventually Esqetone will realize that something happened to the shuttle and send a rescue crew. Or at least send a new shuttle with more of our miners and supplies," Lop said, now eager to join the conversation. "I knew one of their corporate executors person ally. They may be bog-footed in legal rope, but they are no fools. Dead contestants would blacken their public eye. They'll organize a search party within the year."

Jacqe smiled. Now that was the Lop he knew. This conversation was more to his liking.

"The man is right," he stated. "Let's not worry about new supplies. We can't change that now. We need to work with what we have on-planet, and that was more than enough to bootstrap a mining town. We may not have new luxuries for a while. But wasn't the whole point of coming to escape the silk and milk lifestyle?"

"Perhaps we wouldn't have to be so far removed from it if you hadn't been so eager to escape some bad memories," Suu mumbled to herself.

The slight was just barely in his range of hearing and obviously intended to be lower. But once Jacqe heard, he couldn't ignore it. He smiled tightly at the dwarf. "Funny how your ancestors' influence doesn't stop rain or soften your bunk here. Missing your 'simple' pleasures, Suu?"

She slowly turned in her seat away from him. Pulling out her Redkat, she summoned the image of her grandmother and the two of them began having their own conversation of whispers. The memory of the old dwarf lady scowled at Jacqe.

Lop's eyes crinkled in amusement as he glanced between Suu and Jacqe. The man might as well have been watching sports— which was easy for a timid man who never stood up for himself against his imperious wife. He didn't know the sting of being ignored.

Disgruntled and wallowing in his own thoughts, Jacqe cleared his throat. "If we're past that, then let's discuss a plan of action."

Suu made some rough sound in her throat. Her grandmother shook her virtual head.

Lop excused himself to grab a candle from the supply crates outside.

That left Callee, so Jacqe turned to her. The woman bravely smiled.

She said, "As relatively comfortable as we're getting here, we need to make the trip to the mountains as soon as possible. This rain may never let up long enough for us to do it comfortably. If we want to find proof of Esqetone's treasure here on Plenty, we'll have to brave this weather."

"Unfortunately, you're right." Jacqe sighed. "And I don't like how comfortable the miners are getting on this beach. Those are pretty permanent structures that they've built."

"We could delegate pathfinding to the—"

"To the miners?" Jacqe laughed without humor. "They don't take well to delegation. And if we don't prove that we know what we're doing—that we still have authority here—well, we had better start locking our doors at night."

Callee shuddered. "Surely they wouldn't attack us."

Jacqe opened his mouth, but Suu abruptly laughed at something her esteemed fake grandmother had said. He sucked in his breath and let it out slowly. The gesture didn't help.

"Care to join us in reality?" he asked her.

"This coming from you?" Suu said, her face pulled into feigned surprise.

"Suu..." Calle warned.

"What do you mean by that, Naxo?" Jacqe said softly.

"You live in a shade of gray, between the darkness and the light. I do appreciate the past, yes. But you're delusional."

Jacqe breathed like a bull. He walked up to the woman and let his greater statue loom over the dwarven woman.

"I'm delusional? I'm a psychotic who led us all to our dooms?" he said. "Tell me just how *well-adjusted* you are for having conversations with dead dwarves. Dwarves who you think are some kind of gods, just because they birthed your mother..."

The matriarch of the Naxo family ground her teeth together, and the habitat went silent except for the clacking. She took her time gathering up the folds of her jumpsuit as if it were a robe. The woman stood. And she walked out.

"Oh look, you've driven everyone out of my house," Callee said with a heavy sigh.

"If I didn't love those two little fools so much, I'd strangle them," Jacqe replied.

Callee got off the bed and padded over to the table. The mugs of undrunk tea disappeared. She bustled about, cleaning up the evidence of the short-lived meeting. Jacqe did his part. He stayed out of her way, not wanting to violate the honor of her hospitality.

She glanced at him but didn't meet his eyes as she brushed past.

He frowned. Her blatant disapproval seemed unwarranted. He had kept his temper as well as could be expected. Hadn't he? And yet…

He needed to unify people more than anything, at the moment. It wasn't necessary for the sake of nicety. It was necessary because, despite what he said, he was well aware that they could die if they made too many mistakes here. Attempting to succeed alone was a mistake that even the biggest bumbler in the world of business wouldn't make.

"Callee," he said.

This time she made eye contact. The woman practically didn't blink, she was making so much eye contact.

"I…" he paused, suddenly doubting his analysis of her. "I wondered what you thought we should do next."

"What do you mean?" she dug.

"Despite the fact that everyone thinks I know everything, I do welcome advice, you know," he said, shrugging. He did not like the taste of the words.

She wrinkled her nose. Her eyebrows lifted in challenge. "I can't tell when you're serious or not."

"I'm serious about wanting your advice."

"So, the all-knowing Jacqe Kagir needs my help?"

"A tale for the ages, I know," he said.

She padded over to her bed, hefted her pillow, and chucked it at him. He dodged. Her throwing arm was significantly superior to his reflexes, though, and he caught a faceful of foam.

Callee giggled at his expression and went back to tidying the small room. Jacqe stepped forward and spun her around playfully, making her gasp as she was thrown off balance. She clutched at his arm to keep from toppling into the metal wall.

For a moment, the only sound came from the slow hiss of rain on the roof. He watched the candlelight play across her immortal features. When everyone else doubted him, Callee still trusted he'd come through. The woman had surrendered her long life to be with her friends. It was more risk than he could imagine taking, and he couldn't help smiling.

Callee beamed back. She pulled his head down to hers and kissed him hard on the mouth.

His thoughts flickered and sputtered worse than the candles. Jacqe didn't know *how* to think, much less *what* to think. Callee was surprisingly good at this.

That thought was enough to knock his guilty conscience back into gear and he gently pulled away. "No, we… I'm sorry."

Her eyes flashed, and she didn't relinquish her embrace yet.

"No?" she murmured. "Your smile said yes. Your kiss said yes. Why not shut up and listen?"

"But Winni," he protested.

"What about Winni?"

"I don't wander, Callee. I've always been faithful."

"Yes, you always were," Callee said. "But haven't I waited long enough? How obvious can a lady be? I followed you to the literal end of the galaxy."

Jacqe's head spun and nauseated him. He cleared his throat twice but still couldn't dislodge words from his esophagus.

Callee's face burned red and she pulled away from him. She walked towards her bed and said, "Just...just go. Now."

More confused than embarrassed, Jacqe made it to the door before he turned and opened his mouth. But there was nothing to be said. Bracing his weather shield, he stomped out into the new world with a scowl. The chilled, soggy night air complemented his mood. He picked his way over the dry patches in the yard between the habitats and three storage sheds, but he was still off balance and slipped into several dark puddles.

Neither Lop nor Suu was in sight. Jacqe was grateful for that since he wouldn't want them to see him like—oh. He hurriedly wiped at his mouth, rubbing Callee's pink lipstick off. She had brought some with her and worn it tonight. Had she been planning this? Her lips had been bright and soft and more...

He didn't understand women. He didn't understand Winni, much less Callee or Suu. In the world of corporate finance, men and women acted rationally. But outside? Light years away from civilization?

He slipped into his habitat, hoping that his wife was still out walking. She wasn't.

Winni wore her middle-aged skin very well, which was at least partially a result of her fyirn genetics. She was standing with her back to him. Only a towel, casually slung over her shoulder, covered any of her dusky reddish skin. Her body was more dramatically curved than usual—proportions that rarely appeared in nature, but that a shape-shifter might adopt to, say, drive her husband crazy.

Fyirns weren't human any more than dwarves like the Naxos were—that is to say, they didn't have the same genetics. It didn't mean they weren't people and couldn't love or befriend humans. Fyirns in particular had relied on interspecies relationships since the beginning. They were a female race who begot fyirn daughters and sons of the father's species. And to help overcome the natural discomfort most people instinctively had with marrying a member of another species, they had long-drift shifting abilities. Over a period of weeks or months, with enough calorie intake, they could change their own height, weight, build, hair color, skin color, or anything else they pleased.

And Winni had pleased to transform herself into a walking daydream. She stood as if she had been about to step into a shower, although the habitat lacked one. Her mouth opened into a perfect O as if startled.

His breath caught in his throat. Jacqe closed the door behind him. He didn't dare speak first for fear of breaking the spell.

"You shouldn't sneak up on a girl," Winni said with a pout. "After all, I'm not dressed."

"Winni…" he mumbled. For the second time that night, he felt his brain breaking and shorting like the shuttle's robots.

She turned slightly, showing off an inspiring vista before curtaining the view with her towel. "Yes, Jacqe? Hmm? Perhaps you should pick your tongue off the floor before speaking."

"Winni, Callee kissed me."

He blurted the words out before he could second guess himself. It wasn't his fault, but Winni should still know that it had happened. Offering the truth was his duty as a husband. But now that the sentence was just hanging there like an engorged spider on a web, he realized there might have been a better time and place for it.

Winni turned to face him. Her towel was wrapped around her properly now, but she let the corners gripped tightly in her fingers fall slightly to create generous décolletage. And then she laughed.

"The immortal girl? Well, of course, she's all over you," she chimed. "You're just so cute."

Jacqe watched her uncertainly. "You're angry."

"Why would I be?" she said with a dismissive shrug that caused the towel to slip another inch. "You are no longer a young thing, Love. And she is. She's no threat to me. *Should* I be angry?"

He stared at her, flabbergasted. She tittered at his expression and took several slow steps toward him. She reached out towards his face. Just when her fingers were about to touch his face, she pulled her hand back.

"Make me a mother, Jacqe," she hummed. Her towel slipped significantly.

"What?" he said, his voice husky. "Callee and I kissed. You should be fit to murder me."

"Perhaps it is just time to strengthen our relationship."

"No." He spoke more loudly than he intended. "Where is this coming from? Especially now! You never wanted children."

Winni pouted again, and again the gesture had nothing to do with being put out. "Why not now?" she drew out each word. And with each word, the towel dropped closer to her ankles.

For a moment, Jacqe's thoughts lost traction. For a moment, the stress and confusion of the day took a toll. For a moment, his brain had nothing to do with his thinking. For a moment.

Then with a sigh, a heave, and a great lurch forward, his age and wisdom took control again. They would discuss it like adults, not hormonal adolescents. Even if his brain was currently burnt out as badly as any hormonal adolescent's.

He said, "While on an alien world, it would be irresponsible for—"

"We're here because of you," she protested. "The treasure hunt was your silly idea. What did you think it would be like?"

Jacqe clamped his jaw shut to fight off the words that were building up behind his tongue. He thought of a second thing to say, then a third, and then a fourth, and then there were too many not to say something and he was talking and forgetting the consequences.

"I didn't think the shuttle would blow up," he protested. "I didn't think I would, for whatever reason, be held responsible for it! I didn't think that the miners would turn against us. I didn't think my rational friends would turn against *me*. And I certainly didn't think *you* would suddenly want a child when we can barely feed and protect ourselves here."

Winni sat back on the bed, and all the energy disappeared immediately. What had been rising in her like a snarling lynx had devolved into a pitiful stray cat.

"So, you have nothing to do with us being *here*?" she asked in a tiny voice. "Away from home? Away from good food? Away from our other friends and cars and batteries?"

Jacqe was still breathing heavily but felt as if he had fallen back to the floor alongside his wife's towel. He could yell at another yeller. But how could you yell at someone with tears pooling in their beautiful eyes? His own inner thunder fell to a distant rumble.

"I suggested this first," he admitted. "I asked you if you would come with me. I asked the others as well. I prepared as well as humanly possible. It is not my fault if something went wrong."

"It's not your fault if something went wrong?" Winni mumbled.

"Esqetone's engineers should have caught an error that large," Jacqe said firmly. "I don't know why they didn't. I'm as horrified as the rest of you, but I can't afford to curl up on the floor and cry. We have to stay strong and solve problems as they arise. We'll do it, Love. Won't we?"

He reached out and smiled in a way that he hoped projected confidence and vulnerability at the same time. But he had a feeling he looked more nauseated than anything else.

"It's not your fault if something went wrong," Winni repeated. She looked like she hadn't slept in days as she slipped into a robe. "It never is, is it?"

"Winni?" Jacqe said.

But she had already slipped past him into the night, disappearing from the small, dry safe space of the habitat.

It was Jacqe's turn to sit down heavily on the bed. No, he didn't understand women at all. For a moment, he considered running after her. Romantically, of course. Not in a drunken-wife-beater manner. But Winni had come to perfect hiding out on Plenty in the past weeks. If she didn't want to be found, an hour's hunt through the habitats and the miner's village wouldn't do the job.

No, she would come back when she was ready.

He let loose a long, pained groan and rubbed his eyes. "She kissed me, and that's how you react?"

Winni didn't show up again except briefly for lunch the next day. Then she disappeared again. But Jacqe couldn't bring himself to worry about her, somehow. He was sure she would be safe. Yes, there were still torrential downpours more often than not. Yes, the planet was completely unexplored and unsecured. Yes, it seemed the animal life was becoming more and more active, including some vicious long-fang cats the size of rhinoceri.

But she was a grown woman who could take care of herself. And that was that.

Something about that logic bothered him, but trying to figure out Winni always gave him a headache. So he kept his head low that day.

And what a day it was. Plenty's sun shone brightly through a rare cloudless sky. Salty gusts carried warm breezes in over the cool land. While the weather permitted, the Naxos were out getting their hands dirty doing repairs and tilling land, the same as the adventurers. Every breath Jacqe took hung thick with the pale perfumes of local flowers. Far out to sea, a line of black trickling across the horizon threatened the usual unfair fare later in the week.

But the dark clouds in the distance were tiny compared to the blackness dripping over Jacqe. A night's sleep had failed to refresh his friends. He had expected Callee to be a little distant, but she was as absent as Winni. Twice he saw her gathering wood or berries or what have you at the edge of the jungle, and twice she disappeared when he called out.

The Naxos seemed fully set against him. Suu must have finally dragged Lop into her blind, blame-tossing game. Jacqe had been so buried under the stuff that he was invisible today, apparently. Both Naxos had chosen the company of the traitorous miners over their old friend. They were clumsily trying to help work some survey scanners alongside the taller, brawnier workers.

As he watched the rough men ignore the frumpy dwarves, a rather savage grin wormed its way across his cheeks. Turn about, and all that.

Yet he was still alone and directionless. Esqetone had sent treasure hunt guidelines and manuals with them, but he had already flipped through their paper and leather volumes during days when the storms were at their worst. Each step had titles like *The Great Natural Wealth, Exploration and You*, and *Planning Your Hunting Party*. None of which particularly suited a lone colonist. Survival was a game best played with friends.

The brilliant weather further darkened the cloud that hung over Jacqe. He moped down the beach and listened to the surf hiss across the sand. Every day was one day closer to the end of their supplies, and he honestly had no reason to believe the corporate giant would mount a rescue effort for one team out of a thousand. They were on their own. And when he should be running the prospecting effort on this rare sunny day, he found himself useless.

A pariah. After finding more supplies missing that morning, he wasn't about to try to make friends with the miners.

So he walked. Angry, half-formed thoughts snarled in his skull. If bashing his own head open could let them out, it might be worth the pain. This wasn't his fault. Thanks to him, they were all in a new world—one far away from the corruption, boredom, and tragedies of the old one. They just had no courage to tame it.

And then Winni was next to him. Her face was badly bruised, her hair was disheveled, and her eyes shined with tears. Jacqe twitched, unnerved by the woman's sudden appearance.

"If I die, it's your fault," she hissed.

He took a half-step back, eyes widening. He nearly tripped.

But she was gone. He glanced around the sandy stretch, but she wasn't in sight. And there was nowhere she could have hidden either, unless she had become a crab and burrowed into the grit beneath his shoes.

Had it been real? Whether or not it was a portent of some evil, Jacqe wanted to dismiss it. His brain was baked. His soul had been waterlogged. He needed sleep. Anything could be causing him to come undone.

But he still took a hard look around for Winni. There were no trees she could have hidden behind, no tidal pools that could have cast a detailed reflection of her. Nothing in the area provided a reasonable excuse for what he had seen. And heard. He could have sworn it was her voice admonishing him. He lowered his head slightly.

Then he noticed. No footprints. There was nothing in the sand to make evident a living being's presence.

The muscles in his neck relaxed first, then those in his hands, and then from the back on down. Winni wasn't there. He just needed some rest. He closed his eyes and felt his heart pound. He hadn't had another heart attack since landing, but if anything could set the old time-bomb off, this day would.

And if he could survive in this world with a heart defect, then the others with their healthy bodies could certainly quit their whining.

He grunted and spoke to the humming breeze, "And I always thought alien wildlife would kill me…" But he trailed off as he squinted at a figure among the trees in the distance.

It looked like Winni again. This time, she didn't disappear. Her gait was unsteady, as if she had turned her ankle, and she hobbled along the edge of the heavy growth. She was wearing a long, grey dress like nothing she had brought from Earth.

"What are you doing, Love?" he mumbled. He started towards her.

She glanced behind her at something out of sight among the northern woods. She visibly flinched. A guttural, skin-crawling scream reached Jacqe's ears by the same time he saw her run into the woods.

"Winni!" Jacqe cried, his voice cracking.

There was no room for questions or resentment after that horrible screech. Jacqe ran after her as fast as his aged legs could take him.

The dark cloud about his head followed him into the shadows of the trees. What if she was badly hurt? What if they couldn't do anything for her? What was chasing her? What if their last conversation ever had been a petty argument?

Wheezing, he pushed himself as much as he could before he was forced to drop to a weak trot. Glimpses of her in the distance spurred him forward. Although not a runner himself, he was surprised he hadn't caught up to her yet. Molding their bodies left fyirns with less stamina and strength, and Winni did it often. So how frightened was she to be moving so fast?

And then, all at once, he found her.

He hadn't heard the roar of the stream until he reached it. Now, the water split the jungle in two.

Stream didn't seem like the right word either. The hissing, growling torrent wasn't wide enough to be a river, but it had carved deep into the bedrock. A huge volume of water tore through the crevice. Chances were good that it was fed by the constant runoff from the distant mountains. By the time it reached this part of the peninsula, tons of water had been funneled into the channel below.

And Winni crouched on a small rock formation midstream.

She looked terrified. Bloody scratches ran along her pale, exposed calves beneath the tattered gray dress. The tiny island she stood on had a flattish top with an old, twisted tree clinging to it. In turn, she clung to the tree.

"Winni," Jacqe gasped. He had come to a halt at the stream's edge. His knees knocked as badly as the pitiful clutches of air he had swallowed were knocking about his lungs.

"There are devils in the trees, Jacqe," she whispered. He wouldn't have understood her over the crashing water below them, if he hadn't been reading her lips. "Devils inhabit this planet. We've come here to die."

Jacqe was too winded to be shocked. "What are you talking about, Winni?"

"Monsters! Devils in the woods. Beasts outside of nature," she cried.

He glanced around him. There were tall, vine-laden trees. Beneath the trees were occasional bushes with vibrant green or yellow leaves. There was dirt, piles of soggy old leaves, rocks, and a bird or two enjoying the placid weather. But he couldn't find anything resembling unnatural beasts or devils wandering about the jungle.

"Winni, where did you see the creatures?" he asked, wheezing.

She shook her head. "Devils."

"Where, Love? Where?"

"They live on this planet. You brought me here to die."

"No one's going to die," he said. "Look, come back over here and I promise that we'll spend the rest of the day devil-proofing the habitat."

"They'll catch us first."

He grimaced. Whatever state of mind she was in, it would

complicate her ability to get back to safety. A glance around revealed no vines sturdy enough to use as rope, and no fallen branches long enough to make a crude bridge. Winni screamed.

He jerked as if struck by lightning and stared at the woman. Winni was shaking where she crouched, her eyes huge. Jacqe spun around wildly. Again, there were no signs of life bigger than a frightened green bird taking flight.

"What is it?" he yelled.

Then, she closed her eyes and began to cry. "Jacqe? Jacqe? I want to go home! To our home, in Prague."

He swallowed. His head was pounding painfully as if it contained a tiny war. Sweat threatened to suffocate him despite the damp chill that pervaded the jungle today. He realized he was shaking worse than Winni.

"Come back to me," he begged. "Come back and we'll make it work."

He twitched. Had he heard his name called? He thought he heard a shout, but Winni's trembling lips hadn't moved. More portents like on the beach, perhaps. More sleep-deprived fantasy.

Winni shook her head but managed to make it to her feet. She still clutched the tree. Instead of staring down at the roaring stream or out into the trees at imaginary devils, though, she stared holes into Jacqe. A flicker of irony itself played about her lips.

"Help me, husband," she called over the sounds of the stream. "I don't know how I made it across and I can't get back now. We'll both be stuck, alone, until you come over and save me."

He scoffed, staring at the distance between his bank and the tiny island. He didn't see how he could make the leap, much less a fyirn. He took a step toward the edge. A bit of shale and soil collapsed under his footfall, and he recoiled.

"Jacqe!"

He knew he had heard something this time. He looked up at Winni. She looked frightened again.

"Jacqe," she cried. "Please!"

His chest tore at the sound of her voice. She was his *wife*. Foolish or no, he had no choice. Right? Summoning his courage and a lungful of oxygen, he backed away from the edge to get a running start.

"Don't you dare!"

He tripped over a root at the yell. Callee was behind him, grabbing his wrist. Confused, he tried to shake free. What was she thinking? Winni was obviously in danger.

"Jacqe, a little help?" Winni called again.

"What are you doing?" Jacqe hissed to his friend. He eyed the crate of flowers she had been gathering.

"What am I doing? What are *you* doing? It's trying to kill you," she snarled. "What's wrong with you?"

"I am trying to save my *wife*, if you please."

"I don't please! I pleased with the others for years and years longer than we should have, because Suu sympathized with you. She supported you because she's obsessed with them too. But this is insane!"

"I'm slipping!" Winni said with a gasp that Jacqe could hear from across the stream.

She had indeed lost her balance somehow. One foot was dangling over the river, and the other had found shaky purchase on the slick rock face. If not for her white-handed grasp on the scraggly broadleaf... Winni moaned, helpless tears tracing paths in the dust on her cheeks. The saltwater revealed the freckles on her face.

"Leave her there, she's already dead. You'll just get yourself killed too," Calle insisted between her own gulps of breath.

Jacqe glanced at Calle. She was crying too, now. But he was too upset at her words to listen to the pang in his chest at the sight.

"*She's already dead?*" he demanded. "She's right there and we need to do something! Do you want me so badly that you'd have me kill my wife?"

"Jacqe!" Winni cried.

He braced himself to make a running leap.

"You killed her years ago!" Callee screamed.

Jacqe stopped. He felt the ice trickle upwards like a pervading frost. Some tiny, weak part of him had stilled his muscles, paralyzing him, making him listen.

"Why don't you remember, Jacqe? Have you really deluded yourself this badly? That's not Winni. That's not your wife. It's dying here without batteries and the evil thing's trying to take you with it. Don't. Go."

Jacqe stared at his Winni. She watched back from the rocky outcropping, chest heaving, limbs trembling.

"Please don't go," Callee said.

"I have to," he mumbled back, trying to thaw his legs out and start for the stream again.

"Oh for—" Callee snatched at his jacket, groping about until she yanked backward, holding something small and black. "This. This is her, you fool. This is her!"

"It's my wife!" he bellowed. "I won't- "

"The aircart crash," she interrupted. "Do you remember the accident?"

"Jacqe," Winni called.

But this time he almost didn't hear it. He stared at Callee, his face wrinkled. "Of course. It's why I had our carriage built back home."

"What caused the wreck?" she pressed.

"I…" He bristled, his eyes narrowing in offense. "I fell asleep. Embarrassing. I do not like talking about it."

"No. You don't 'not like talking about it.' You *never* talk about it. Why?"

Jacqe slowly shook his head. The battle in his head had turned into a world war, banging about his skull and setting off bombs at the base of his spine. He winced as pain lanced through his face. He couldn't clear his head. But instincts were still online. His wife was in trouble, he could help, and so he walked towards the island.

Callee spun him around bodily with a physique decades younger than his.

"Head trauma, broken spine, blood loss," she whispered, eyes as wide as Winni's. She was afraid. She was afraid of what she was saying. Jacqe didn't like it much either. "She never made it out of that aircart. And for years, we all played along with your game. Suu said you needed to recover on your own time. I waited years, Jacqe. Hoping you'd see the truth."

"Suu said what?" Jacqe snarled. He struggled to get out of her grip.

"She was wrong! She's addicted to her RedKat, just like you. Jacqe, what am I holding?"

He blinked. "My wallet."

"This is not a wallet," Callee yelled. "Why would you bring a wallet to an alien planet? You're lying to yourself again! It's your RedKat. This is Winni. And it's almost out of power. She's been disappearing lately, hasn't she? No real reason? It's just an image with her memories, and it's dying and mad. Don't listen to it."

With a burst of energy, he flopped to the edge of the torrent. Water below him flashed by at speeds that could rip a galloping horse downstream. Callee pulled back against his straining, but her physical strength was met with his sheer desperation.

"It's my wallet..." he groaned, fighting her. "Yes, it's useless. Foolish. Now let me save her!"

"Then I'll just throw it in the river," she challenged, cranking her hand back to toss it.

Jacqe broke. The pain in his brain halved.

"No," he gasped, lunging at her. He grabbed her wrist and kept her from tossing the device.

He wasn't crying. He was sure he wasn't crying. His eyes were watering so badly that he had to wipe his face clean on his shirt sleeve. Callee looked back at him with mixed pain and pity.

"I know," he mumbled. "I know it is. I know it is. Please..."

"Please what?" she asked. Her face was inches from his—one aged by decades, one young throughout millennia that she could no longer remember. "Please let you die?"

"I failed her once. Please. Don't let me fail her again. We're... Two hearts beating in..."

Callee's face softened between her angry red hair. "Jacqe... One's beating the other. For years you've just looked away. It's not what Winni would have wanted for—"

He slapped her face.

It wasn't as hard as he could have, but it was hard enough. As the loud report of the hit echoed over the noise of the stream, she dropped both his wrist and the device. He kicked aside the black box and ran back towards the trees.

Turning around, he braced himself to charge at the stream. He needed a full run to make it to her. She was still where he had seen it last, and its face was full of delight. She knew he loved her. He would prove it.

Pangs wracked his chest again, and this time he knew it wasn't emotional. Another heart attack. The chems embedded in his body rushed out to fight it, but it still took the breath from him.

He ran anyway. Somehow, he ran. Puffing like a man many times his weight, he swung his arms and willed his body to move faster. Physics fought him with every step. Another twinge in his chest. Another flood of artificial resistance. He nearly turned his ankle.

Callee wasn't close enough to catch him this time, and Winni smiled across at him, just waiting for him to rescue her. But why wasn't Callee up yet? And where was—

He saw the RedKat disappear into the water.

The thing was waterproof. It might last. He still saw Winni's image. He could still save her. He might make the jump.

But why?

Winded, hurting, tired, and crying, Jacqe obeyed his body and collapsed mid-step. He slid to a dirty stop not a meter from the stream.

"Winni. There's nothing left..." he wheezed, his throat sore and tight.

He glanced up through a hazy film at the RedKat projection's cold glare.

"I'm sorry. I'm sorry," he said, curling up in pain. A pathetic, weak lump of a man. That's all that was left.

Callee was on him in seconds. She pulled him up close to her and brushed bits of dirt, grass, and leaves off him. "I know," she murmured.

Winni faded, then came back. Blinked three times. There then gone then there again. Frozen in her position hanging off the tree, her image separated from the landscape and came flying at Jacqe and Callee.

She expanded and passed through them. Jacqe turned, his face pale and blotchy, but there was no sign of her on the other side. Shorted out and gone for good.

"Thanks for not leaving us, Jacqe," Callee said. She tried to sound upbeat. "The rest of this mess? Fixable. We'll find the treasure, here or somewhere else. Just don't leave us. Right?"

Jacqe saw the crash in his mind clearly now. Remembered. Wine from his wife's job. Daring each other to drive faster. Dark then light, blood then white, funeral then RedKat technician. And then forgetting. Rushing off from Earth to Plenty to forget completely.

He looked back at how his friends had acted in past years. How he had acted. What he had done.

Oh.

"I'm sorry."

EON 7 - NOVOCAINE NIGHTS

Lamb never considered himself to be living in a nightmare until he made soup-soup, which was an empty soup can boiled to eke out any remnants of flavor.

Not that Lamb was a stranger to being poor. Growing up in orphanages told him he was poor. Having his government food stipend beaten out of him by older boys told him he was poor. Taking slag work for misers' wages told him he was poor. But eating soup-soup? With all that metal taste? He wasn't poor. He was a prisoner, and the wardens had left them to starve.

He sniffed at the concoction as it bubbled and hoped to catch a whiff of something other than steam, rust, and the burning oil that it was cooking over. A little potato. Maybe...chicken? Lamb grinned and felt a draft through the tooth that he'd lost to a drunk years ago.

"Soup-soup's almost ready," he told Shack. "Want in on this?"

Shack lifted her tangled head of raven hair up out of her corner of the luxurious hotel room. She and Mossy had dragged their bazillion-thread-count queen bed to the far corner from the window and she had nested in the leather comforter like a bird. She swiped at her running nose half-heartedly.

"We ate yesterday. No, cause that's not food," she mumbled. Her normally bright blue eyes were clouded with sleep. "That's spit from the ropey mouth of his highness, Lord Scatmeow, no? Wake me when there's food."

"Wake me too," Lamb said wistfully, slurping at the brew. He could just catch the heartiness that must have been present in the original soup. "You want some, Mossy?"

He saw the manic gleam in her eye before he saw the rest of her in the gold-gilt bathroom mirror. She poked her head out of the bathroom. With a faint sniff, she peered suspiciously at the cookfire Lamb had started on the burnished copper dresser.

"That food?"

"Food indeed."

"This isn't like your carpet chowder, is it?" she said. "If so, I choose starvation."

"Have you tried sleep? It works wonders," Shack said with a wide yawn that showcased her straight, white teeth. Then she buried herself in the miles of crimson down around her.

"You tried not stealing a car? Works wonders," Mossy fired back.

She got a very rude gesture for her trouble.

Lamb shook his head at the two short girls and ladled the suspicious broth into a triplet of porcelain tureens he had stolen from an alcove down the hall. He slid one to Mossy and watched her down it quickly and burp. Slow slips suited him better. It let him imagine that there was flavor behind the intense heat.

There was a knock on the door.

No one moved. Each stared at the barricade they had erected two nights ago when they snuck in. They had leaned the extra queen bed frame against the door to keep out maids. Or worse.

The knock repeated.

"Is that from this door or next door?" Mossy whispered.

Lamb threw a hand over her mouth, not daring to open his mouth to tell her to be quiet. Shack's huge eyes blinked out of her blanket burrow. They had one knock left before Mossy's question was answered.

The third knock echoed through the hall.

Lamb didn't breathe, didn't blink. The pot of soup-soup hissed slightly. Then came a long, drawn-out, grating squeak of a door opening.

It wasn't their door.

The three prisoners expelled their respective breaths and clutched for their few belongings. Mossy grabbed her pillowcase of crackers, their emergency supply. Shack already had her collection of long mirror shards with silk wrapped around the ends. She also snatched up the jewelry box with House Mouse in it. Even the annoying little beast with the smug brown and white face seemed to know better than to make a peep. Perhaps it knew what was next door.

Lamb didn't grab anything. Like he was going to waste precious seconds on the soup-soup. If he had longer, he might try to bring his cooking setup. But things were easy. There were things in every room in the cursed hotel-prison. Only food and health had any real value here.

Lamb went for the bed they leaned against the door. The war between speed and silence made his thin arms shake as he eased the metal frame away. He hesitated, certain that his rattling limbs would knock the legs of the bed against the wall. *End of round. Thank you. Goodnight.*

Then Shack and Mossy were there. They helped him set the bed down quietly. About a minute had passed and they could still hear shuffling through the walls. Lamb took in a slow view of the hall through the room's peephole. Empty. Clear.

He eased the door open just wide enough to slip through. A glance showed the door to his immediate left yawning open. A maid's metal cart sat outside, a miniature wagon loaded with fluffy, white towels and sparkling glass bottles filled with various cleaners. Lamb didn't look too closely as he handed the door to Mossy, trusting her steady hand to keep it from creaking. Then he stood against the narrow space between the two rooms.

Everything screamed at him to run, except for a little shred of humanity that prison life hadn't squeezed out of him yet. That part forced him to stand between his two friends and whatever might creep out of the room. He waited as he felt the first girl slip past behind him.

Each second dripped down and down and finally off to the ground like blood from a wound.

And then Shack tapped his shoulder, having quietly closed the room door behind her. They were free. As fast as they dared, they padded down the long hall towards the next bend. Fortunately, the inch-thick forest of shaggy carpet beneath their bare feet did much to muffle their steps. Was that a noise behind them? Lamb refused to look around. And then...they turned the corner.

This had been their life for the better part of three years in Hotel Serestio. The so-called super-prison was an unfathomably massive facility that housed criminals from every level of notoriety caught by the League. Well, every criminal that they hadn't executed. Terrorizing, rebellion, murder, rape...No one walking these halls had gone that far.

In the beginning, they hadn't been walking the halls at all. Hotel Serestio was eerily beautiful and looked like an inn, yes, but it was a prison. Everyone had been locked in their own solitary confinement, in their own room, with their own three meals a day. With that level of isolation, one could only imagine how high the suicide rate was after the first few years.

But one day the meals stopped coming and the locks stopped humming. Lamb had walked out into the hall, unaccosted, and found his friends. And here they all were. In the network's largest prison, a planet away from all do-gooders. Untold millions of prisoners with nothing to do.

At first, Lamb, Shack, and Mossy spent their time in Hotel Serestio avoiding the worst prisoners. Some still feared repercussions from the League and minded their manners, but it didn't last. So Lamb and the others hid. And then the *things* came.

Like the maids.

There weren't as many prisoners now.

Lamb huffed down the hall. He was in worse shape than he had ever been in while on the streets of pissant planet Crux. There was little to do but hide and little to eat but the occasional salvage. Not much to build muscle on. In the last years, rumors had flown through whispers from prisoner to prisoner—tales of lucky schmucks finding kitchens and barricading themselves in with years of food at their disposal. Such stories kept people like them moving and hoping.

The three of them finally ducked into a hall bathroom lit by golden sconces over the sinks. They all piled into one handicapped stall and locked the thin white door behind them. The toilets weren't intrinsically safer than the rooms, as the maids checked them as well. But this one stunk of disinfectant. They had some breathing space before the next cleaning as long as they were willing to hug the commode for that long.

Lamb would have been terrified, years ago. But the prison was like having a never-ending IV of novocaine: it left everything numbed out.

"Gods…We're safe for a while. But bad news. I left the soup-soup," Lamb admitted.

"I would have made you do that anyway," Shack said, her nostrils flaring as she breathed.

Mossy didn't say anything, she just leaned her head against Shack's shoulder. The two of them could have been…

"So, your favorite color?" Lamb challenged.

"Purple," they both said at the same time.

"Hah, sisters!" Lamb said with a soft crow of triumph.

They glanced at each other in surprise. Then traded looks of disgust. It wasn't the first time Lamb had played the *Are Shack and Mossy Sisters* game.

"Who knows, who cares?" Mossy grumbled.

"Then what was your favorite childhood experience?" Lamb asked.

Mossy rolled her eyes, but Shack stared at the plastic stall wall thoughtfully. "I don't remember there being many mountains back home, but I swear I hiked one. It's pretty hazy. I don't remember much except the smell of trees. Maybe it was just a dream, no? Funny how dreams and memories stop seeming different after a while."

Mossy sat up and nodded.

"Pretty romantic answer," she said. "And here I was going to bring up the time we all got arrested because Shack tried to boot an entire car."

A strained chuckle escaped Lamb and he glanced away from the two girls. He didn't see if Shack gestured, but she certainly stopped talking quickly enough.

Then a voice drifted out of the stall next to theirs. "Trouble in paradise? Spare a morsel, or is it a bad time?"

Lamb was up on his feet with his back to the wall in a second. His pulse nearly drowned out the voice of the stranger. His fist curled around one of Shack's mirror daggers.

The only sign of the man in the stall next to them was a pair of feet. Like them, he was barefoot. Like them, gray, undyed slacks hung to his ankle bones. Unlike them, his flesh was a dusky red. Apparently, the League of the Trillion didn't grant favor to minorities like those rubies when sentencing people to life in prison.

"Who are you?" Mossy challenged. "Because no matter how tough you think you are, I'm betting my knife can still make pretty confetti out of any toe or finger you poke over here."

"Easy," the voice said. It sounded weary and bored, but the toes beneath the stall separator wiggled uncomfortably. "Don't mind me, I'm just a son of a gun. Like you. And I'm hungry."

"Aren't we all?" Lamb said. "But if we had food, wouldn't we have already eaten it?"

"Would you?" returned the voice.

A squeak from the hall.

The bathroom was suddenly bathed in silence. As they held their breaths, the low lighting of the sconce candles seemed too bright and revealing.

No other sounds came from the hall, but all prey knows that just means the predator is waiting, not gone. Lamb willed his heartbeat to slow. He forced his heavy breath to float from his lips instead of huff. The girls were better at going silent than he was, which was both a blessing and all the more reason to fear that he would be the one to finally get them caught.

Shack clutched the jewelry box with House Mouse in it. Lamb wished she would get rid of the rodent. He was a little time bomb liable to go off in a cacophony of squeaks someday, and then that would be that.

A minute crept out the door. Then a second minute. Then a few more. House Mouse peeked out of his box, wiggling his whiskers as he sniffed the air. The brown and white splotches on his face seemed to shiver. He stayed quiet.

There was another squeak in the hall, but this time it was followed by a steady stream of other old floorboard noises that faded into the distance as the thing left. After a minute of that, they finally breathed freely.

"That wasn't a maid," Shack mumbled.

"Too big," Mossy agreed, her eyes still flitting about the bathroom under the stall walls. "Maybe a janitor. Or cook? There have to be cooks, right?"

The other prisoner seemed to sit down on his commode and sighed. "It's a miracle any of us are still here."

"Speaking of which, you need to leave," Mossy said. "I'm going to want sleep tonight, and I can't get that while keeping one knife pointed at you."

"I was here first," the voice returned calmly.

"And I'm sorry about that, but she is right," Lamb said. He again placed himself between the women and this unknown in the neighboring stall. "There are more of us than you."

"I suppose I can appreciate that," the voice said. "But three days have passed since I had any food."

"We aren't sharing, so toad off," Mossy sneered.

There was a moment's silence, followed by, "So you do have something to share."

Shack pouted at Mossy. She said, "Oh well done, mortar-brain."

"Shack. Watch it," Lamb snapped at her. He turned back to the toes in the other stall and directed his words to them. "A couple of old soda crackers. That's all we've got. Emergency rations. We haven't had real food in almost as long as you, so please just leave. There's no need to spill someone's blood over this."

"Spill blood?" the voice laughed. "I prefer trading. I tend to live longer that way."

"What do you have that we would want?" Mossy asked. "Like I said, we have weapons. And you clearly don't have better food to trade."

"And we can get everything else for ourselves from the rooms," Lamb agreed.

Shack watched from the corner, still clutching her collection of knives. They had been her most useful contribution and had all but taken the trio off the menu for the rest of the prisoners. Now she was twitching like she would have to actually use one on this man. It did little to help Lamb's nerve.

"How about good news?" the voice said. "Very specific good news. Seems to me that's in short supply in Hotel Serestio."

"What sort of good news would be worth food?" Lamb asked.

"An exit strategy, perhaps? That would interest me, if I were you," the voice stated.

Shack, Mossy, and Lamb looked at each other.

"Give him some crackers," Lamb whispered as quietly as he could.

"Are you insane?" Shack hissed back, Mossy bobbing her head in agreement. "Why would we trust anything he says?"

"Why not?" Lamb shrugged. "I'd do anything to escape—wouldn't you?"

"Not this," Mossy whispered. "I'm keeping my crackers."

Lamb furrowed his brow. He hated to be the boss almost as much as he hated giving away their emergency soda crackers. But he hadn't had an offer like this before. He was tired and desperate, and why not? Why not believe this man was telling the truth?

"Okay," he murmured. "I've got a good feeling about this. It's my good feeling, so I'll only give him my share. What's left, you two split."

"Lamb, don't," Shack murmured, laying a hand on his bony thin wrist.

But he yanked free of her grasp like it was fire. Ignoring Shack, Lamb held out his hand to Mossy until she caved. Frowning like he had lost his gray stuff, she finally handed him the pillowcase.

"Fine. I'm going to trust you," he said, raising his voice so that the other prisoner could hear. "What you hear now is my making a toilet paper plate and setting the soda crackers on it. I am going to slide the crackers halfway to just under the stall wall. Half your side. Half ours. Give us the good news, you can grab them in peace. Try to trick us, and, well, I have a nice little knife right here."

"Trust, but verify, eh?" the voice said dryly.

In reply, Lamb pushed his makeshift stack of soda crackers until they were in place, just within reach of both sides. For a moment, he regretted his optimism. He remembered the joy they had felt when they had found the box of soda crackers hidden by some other poor unfortunate prisoner behind a vent. That day, they had been rich. Now, he was throwing a third of it away. His stomach growled.

Lamb forced himself to take a deep breath and left the crackers halfway between stalls. His knife, though, he kept in his lap. Not that the voice knew that. Sometimes a threat was enough. He hoped now was one of those times.

The feet shuffled in the other stall. Lamb could almost smell the drool.

"Fair enough," the voice purred. "There isn't a way out yet, but there will be one soon."

"Meaning?" Lamb pressed.

"Meaning I've heard things. Some rumors. Some bits and pieces from prisoners who had had direct contact with the guards back before the guards left. But mostly one indisputable source. A gammyn I met near an elevator bank. One of the lizard people themselves. From the League."

"Right, and we've spoken to the King of the North River who promised us three wishes in return for teaching him how to love," Mossy chirped.

The voice harrumphed. "Believe me, or don't. That's certainly your choice. But I *did* see a gammyn scout of some kind. He didn't want much to do with me, but he was watching for maids pretty intently. Apparently, we're going to have gammyn guests soon. A lot of them. And they will be wiping the floor with whatever they find in Hotel Serestio. That may include us, I'm afraid. The chickens have come home to roost."

"And that's...good?" Lamb asked. The voice was either a well-practiced liar or sincere, but so far Lamb hadn't heard anything worth lying about. Like actual encouraging news.

"Bad for everyone still wandering around the halls and rooms, maybe," the voice said. "But my League acquaintance let slip that they will be amassing in the lobby when they arrive. Maybe they'll forgive anyone waiting for them there. You could be evacuated before this prison becomes a slaughterhouse. I plan to be."

Lamb and the women looked at each other, saying nothing. What was there to say? Common knowledge had always dictated that the things that stalked the halls were guards. Guards left by the League when the normal guards had pulled out. And until now, that seemed like punishment enough.

Now the League might be sending in gammyn. Few creatures could do damage like the League's scaly-skinned half-breeds—they were the reason that the known universe remained under the control of a single government. They seemed to know everything and could appear out of thin air, and that didn't even scratch the surface of what they were rumored to do.

If the voice was right, Lamb, Shack, and Mossy were about to be in the middle of a war zone.

Or maybe the other prisoner was a lunatic. Or a liar.

"That is what I know. May I take my crackers now?" the voice requested.

A hand warily hovered over the makeshift platter on the tile floor. Lamb tapped his mirror dagger against the ground and the hand stopped.

"As long as you tell us where this lobby is," Lamb cautioned. "I've never heard of one before."

"If I knew where it was, I would be there now instead of trading crackers in a toilet. I'm still just looking for a safe stairwell."

Lamb groaned and considered scaring the man with a swipe of his dagger. Instead, he withdrew the blade and listened to his stomach whimper. The soda crackers vanished under the ruddy paw of the other prisoner. A frantic series of crunches followed.

Mossy winced at the noises. She patted Lamb as if to comfort him as his food disappeared down a stranger's greedy gullet.

Finally, the sounds of carnage ended with a soft sigh. "Thank you, my friends. Not enough, but there's never enough in this place. And I do love salt."

"Just go away," Mossy insisted, glaring at the feet.

"Quite so," the voice concurred. "Thank you for doing business like civilized people. Go and sell your newfound information to someone else for food. Or maybe look for the lobby like I am. Either way, fare thee well."

The door to the bathroom had tapped closed by the time that Lamb noticed the prisoner had left.

"Why did you give him your food?" Mossy asked, turning on him. "He didn't deserve it!"

"Mossy's right," Shack mumbled. "He got crackers. You got an earful of bad breath."

"See? She agrees."

Lamb huffed as the two women nodded at each other. In his experience, girls were like magnets. If they weren't repelling each other, they were glued to each other and repelling the nearest pole they could find. And he tended to be these two magnet's favorite pole to repel.

"A few stale crackers were worth the trade if he's telling the truth," Lamb said. "The question is, do we look into it? It's not like we have more pressing matters to—"

"Food," Shack interjected.

"Hide," Mossy said.

"Stay alive," they both added at the same time, as if it were an inside joke.

Both grumping and grinning at once, Lamb said, "Are you sure you two aren't sisters? What was the first birth party you remember?"

A raucous croak erupted in the hall. The hair of Lamb's scalp bristled and sent waves of cold trickling down his back.

There was a racket of motion and running feet outside, then the sounds of a struggle. Muffled. Almost quiet. A strangled cry fractured the conditioned air, followed by a cacophony of screams and cries. There were a lot of other noises that the Lamb couldn't bear to focus on too closely. One more wail was snapped in two, cutting it off.

It was the voice from the neighboring stall.

Lamb ground his hands into his forehead, not knowing what else to do. He wanted to block out those awful sounds. He *really* wanted to go out with every last knife and go to work. But past experience dictated only one result from that line of thinking, and he had just heard it. The answer was to hide.

Shack's face was stony, angry. But the storm in her eyes produced rain, and she shook with suppressed sobs. She clutched one of her knives in a white-knuckled fist.

Mossy just closed her eyes. She looked as if she felt the same way Lamb did.

But Lamb forced himself to move. He hissed, "Be right back." And against his better judgment, he slipped under the door of the stall and scrambled across the black tile to the bathroom floor. As he passed the row of dark marble sinks, he snatched a velvety red towel from one of the stacks.

He paused and listened at the door. The hall made sounds echo further than in rooms, and he estimated that the attack was far enough away that he could peek out a moment safely. Then he noticed that there was no handle on this side of the door, only a copper plate. Push to exit. That was bad. It meant instead of just his frowsy head poking out into the hall, the silhouette of the entire door could give him away.

That was almost enough to send him scrambling back to their stall in the far corner. Almost. But he sucked in a deep breath several times like he was about to go diving, held the last one, and then slowly pushed the lowest corner of the door with the towel bunched up in his hand.

Lamb's hand was shaking again, and the door shivered open inch by inch. He waited, but nothing stomped on or snatched at the wadded-up towel. Neither did any footsteps creak his way. He was safe for the moment. Breath locked and loaded, he poked his head around the door jam until his eyes were clear of the wall.

He regretted it.

There was a person behind another maid cart further down the hall. The figure was stooped over, cleaning the carpet. Lamb only saw a crisp white blouse sleeve and a glimpse of an orange rubber glove. Then he noticed the blood-soaked body towel.

The distant figure stood and walked back to the cart, carrying a pile of stained linens. It had a human body.

Human hands with protective gloves.

Human feet.

It was too bad it had a huge, black-feathered raven's head poking out of the neck ruffles.

The beak pointed straight at him as the thing dropped the soiled towels into a bucket at the bottom of the cart. Lamb froze. His shaking stilled in a wash of terror that went beyond movement. He stared at the cruelly-curved ebony beak.

The thing was cleaning up what was left of the prisoner.

That's all the maids did. They straightened empty rooms. They cleaned the halls and the bathrooms. They butchered human beings. What they didn't seem to do was eat, sleep, or die. This one appeared to have just finished dabbing a man off the elegant shag carpet.

It turned away, to head back towards the mess. It faced the wall for a moment as if studying a flickering sconce for dust, one beady black eye pointing down each side of the hall.

The maid hadn't seen him. He was safe. Lamb relaxed slightly and exhaled, shivering as his body took a desperate draw of air.

A half second after that, he remembered that birds saw from the sides, not head-on.

He vanished into the bathroom, shoving his wrinkled towel into the crack beneath the door to let it close slowly behind him. Perhaps the thing would just—

The maid screeched. The sound of running feet grew louder and louder.

"Hide hide hide," Lamb breathed as he threw himself into their stall. "By the gods, hide."

The women stared with bloodless faces, though they didn't shake as badly as he did. He shoved Shack into the crevice between the commode and the wall. Mossy took the hint and leaped up on the handrail along the wall for the handicapped. It supported her pale weight.

Lamb unlocked the plastic door and cracked it open enough to make the stall seem empty without revealing its occupants. Then they heard a bang as the bathroom door slammed open. Lamb practically flew to perch on the commode, his mirror knife at the ready. His wide eyes leaked dangerously. The overflow threatened to blind him, but he didn't dare move his sleeve up to wipe them clear.

Thud.

One of the other stalls was knocked open. Shack had her hands clasped over her mouth and her eyes squeezed shut.

Thud went the third door to their right.

Lamb's eyes searched the ground for a shadow of the approaching maid. Mossy looked disastrously close to toppling off her perch. She twitched slightly. Lamb threw his hand up and pressed her against the wall with his remaining strength.

There was a series of sharp raps from the sink area. He had a fleeting mental image of the maid pecking at the marble like an actual bird. For all he knew, it was doing just that.

And then a shadow crossed the floor. It stalked into the stall next to theirs with a *swoosh-swoosh* of crinoline. The movement ceased. Lamb chose that second to cease breathing. There was an odd trilling noise.

The thing reached down, the gloved hand holding a red-stained sponge. It scraped at the floor, cleaning up the crumbs of soda crackers that the prisoner had dropped along with the remains of the toilet paper plate. Shreds and pieces disappeared into a tiny floral dustpan.

It swept and scrubbed. Lamb's arm holding Mossy in place was sore and grew as heavy as a laden maid's cart. His right leg fell asleep and buzzed painfully. He barely breathed.

When he heard a small huff of breath from Shack, he reached across with his other hand and pinched her ear as painfully as he could. A warning. If they died because of her...But the sweeping didn't pause until the maid was done.

An hour after the maid had disappeared, they finally moved. Six hours and one uncomfortable nap born of sheer exhaustion later, they finally left the bathroom. By that time, they had come to a consensus.

"If there's a way out, we're looking for it," Mossy said for all of them.

HOURS PASSED. DAYS MIGHT HAVE AS WELL, BUT DAYS HAD NO REAL effect on Hotel Serestio. At least, you could never see daylight outside. Rumor had it, you couldn't see *outside* outside. They had never checked. Not since the first days after the abandonment from the League.

When they had first left their cells, they had wandered about with a small host of other prisoners. At that point, they had been happy to have human contact again. And, through rather horrible trial and error, the three rules of Hotel Serestio were drafted.

Sarcastic prisoner looked through a window and transformed into a screaming, drooling lunatic before offing herself?

Rule One: *You never look out the windows.*

Black-haired brute of a prisoner runs into a maid and gets himself dismembered and stuffed into the cart?

Rule Two: *Avoid the hotel staff.*

And Lamb still didn't know how the last one came about, but he had a vivid imagination.

Rule Three: *Don't get in the elevators.*

They followed the rules and were still alive years later. And they had seen what happened to people who didn't follow the rules, like the prisoner from the toilet.

Every day was made up of hiding and snatching the food from kitchens, dining rooms, and breakfast nooks. No one knew who was still making the food, but it kept them breathing. They were all starving, sleep-deprived, emaciated, pale, and constantly fearful for their lives. But they were still breathing. That was enough.

Lamb kept telling himself that while he tried to scrub away the memory of the man's screams. And those wet towels.

He shuddered. His thin chest rattled around inside his overly large shirt, and Shack gave him a sour look. She'd acted like a kicked cat since the bathroom. Lamb wasn't sure why. It wasn't like he was mad at her or anything since he had just pinched her a little to keep her quiet and alive.

"What?" he asked.

"You— Nothing."

Mossy turned away from the peephole where she was surveying the hall from their temporary shelter. "We're safe for now, but we still don't got a plan. How are we going to find a lobby?"

"Don't ask me," Lamb said.

"The elevators are the obvious choice if it wasn't for, you know, the rule," Shack said.

Lamb snorted. "Yeah, we're not going there."

"Fine. How about the stairs?" Shack asked, frowning.

"What stairs?" Lamb demanded. "These halls twist and turn forever. The last stairs we saw are months back in the other direction."

Mossy pranced away from the door and flopped onto the ground next to the dresser. She glanced in the miniature refrigerator without much hope on her face.

"I'm not going to just keep pushing forward like a blind beggar," she said. "That kind of mortar-brained move got us here in the first place."

The air crackled with the sounds of Shack grinding her teeth.

"Well, we've got the rooms, the hall behind us, which is maid-infested, and the hall before us," Lamb said. "I just wish we could move faster."

"Too bad we don't have a car." Mossy sniffed.

"Stop bringing that butt-end clown court into this!" Shack cried. "Please! I'm sorry, no? So just stop, both of you."

"I didn't say anything," Lamb stated with a shrug. It was kind of fun to see her squirm, though.

Mossy tossed her shaggy brown hair but stopped teasing. Shack flung herself on the room's huge single bed. Within seconds, she had smeared a little mayhem over it and constructed herself a new nest. A loud sigh floated out from the blankets.

"I second that," Lamb said. "We're running on sawdust and daydreams. A little sleep before we get moving, and *then* we make a run for this lobby."

"Fine," Mossy said. "I get the bathtub."

"You always take the bathtub."

She sauntered past and slapped Lamb across his back pocket. When he faked a lunge at her, she evaded with a hop and a giggle.

Chuckling softly, he shook his head as the younger girl disappeared into the marble-floored bathroom. Back on the streets, when he and the two girls had watched each other's backs for years, he had eventually come to see their feminine sides.

One day, Shack had become unbearably interesting. With her round face and messy hair, Shack wasn't a classic beauty. That had made protecting her from other men a little easier. But he still found himself obsessing. Fantasizing. Trying to find excuses to be alone and close to her. And she had seemed to like him too for a while. But painful hunger led to painful arguments when worst came to worst. The comfortable distance of friendship became preferable.

After almost a year, he had noticed Mossy becoming a young lady as well. Her playful nature balanced out her more aggressive tendencies. They managed to enjoy one quiet kiss in a bank's fountain one night. That was before she had helped Shack steal a car. Before Lamb had perjured in the hearing to save his friends. Before he had been tossed in Hotel Serestio alongside them for his heroism.

After being in prison, forget it. Thoughts of mushy moments and sweet words had died alongside hopes for a normal life—or a long life, for that matter.

So he smiled when Mossy felt flirty or Shack acted pouty, but he still laid on the opposite side of the bed from Shack's lair of pillows, sheets, and comforters. He didn't think twice about how he was alone with a woman, because he'd stopped thinking of both of them as women a while back. They were his only two friends, his only partners in this world and any other. That was more than enough.

He drifted off, grasping at memories of good times that hadn't yet faded. His body sank gratefully into the comforter and slowly relaxed until even his stomach stopped growling piteously.

Hours later, they awoke to voices.

Lamb blinked sleepily even as he tensed on all fours. Fortunately for him, Shack moved faster. She shoved him off the bed and dragged him with her into the tiny space under the frame. The springs pulled at his hair and scraped his ear. He started shaking again, but didn't protest.

From his corner near the wall, he was just an inch from being exposed. The bright side to that was that he could see the doorway through the draped corner of a translucent white sheet. His heartbeat threatened to pulverize his ribs when he saw that they had forgotten to barricade the door before sleeping. And now it swung wide open.

He couldn't tell who was out in the hall through the bright stream of light, but he heard the voices well enough. That meant prisoners. Cleaning ladies didn't talk.

"And here they lovely king bed with they east-facing window I tell you about," came a smooth, heavily-accented voice. "They fridge is cold for you feet, and they hot water in tub warms you poor arms. Take a look."

Three figures stepped into view. Two of them wavered back and forth as if they were ready to drop from exhaustion. The third was tall and looked like a professional wrestler with arms the size of Lamb's waist. He wore an odd, towering hat and seemed to be the speaker.

A noxious odor had wafted in with them, as if someone had brought some sun-bleached pork fat with them. Lamb dared to wrinkle his nose.

One of the two smaller figures spoke up in a piping falsetto, but it was in a language that Lamb didn't recognize. By the lilting drawl, Lamb assumed she was judging the room. Another male voice threw in his opinion in that same strange language. It was as if…What was this?

The couple, for they seemed to be a couple, staggered forward slightly and exclaimed in dismay at the sight of the messy bed. Lamb slapped a hand over Shack's mouth to keep her from screaming as the two walked close enough to be seen. He himself would have at least whimpered had his throat worked at the moment.

The two foreigners were dead. The man wore a three-piece suit and a top hat while the woman wore a faded blue dress that hid her feet. But their skin was bone white and missing in parts and pieces. Their heads lolled on limp spines. The man's lips had peeled back exposing overly long teeth. The woman's eyes were missing, leaving empty sockets that looked like they had been painted bright blue.

Yet their bodies still jerked and gestured as if alive. And the foreign voices continued to speak, although their mouths hung slack.

"That is they best part," the third, tall figure said, stepping forward. "They lived-in look makes you feel at—zooks! Who mess up they bed?"

He stepped into the light. Lamb's hand nearly crushed poor Shack's skull, he squeezed so hard.

The *thing* was a porter of some kind. It wore a smart vest and a shirt with the sleeves rolled up, which revealed unnaturally large and pale muscled arms bristling with wiry hair. It carried a trunk in each massive hand. And that was the most human part of it.

It had a horse head. Lamb hated himself for not being more surprised. He hated this life, this place, and everything else that made him used to the idea of people without people heads. But this thing's head, unlike the maids', kept craning around and looking at the walls, the floor, the ceiling, anything else but what the body seemed to be speaking about, as if no one had told the horse that it was expected to cooperate with the porter's body. Nestled under each arm was a glass container like the kind that held cheese in rich people's houses. Except these two containers held heads. Heads that looked familiar.

The living-dead gentleman motioned to his lady of the crypt and launched into what seemed like a scathing criticism of the curtains. His mouth still didn't move, just leer. But the male head in the right cheese-dome chattered rapidly on his behalf. Then Lamb realized that the healthy-looking, decapitated face would have fit the dead man perfectly, minus a few months of decay.

What?

"I beg you forgiveness," said the horse-headed porter, although the horse head was drooling at a spot on the wall at the time. "They room clearly been beset by hooligans. I shall check for hooligans."

What? No no no no no.

Lamb tried to scrunch back farther under the bed, but Shack wasn't leaving him any extra room. That infuriated him as panic flooded his system. He shoved his foot into her gut.

The porter set down the trunks with two heavy thuds and a suspicious sloshing sound. It crept around the bed as if to surprise anyone hiding on the other side. When it jumped around and found nothing but the end table, its muscle-bound shoulders slumped.

Gentleman Gore, as Lamb had decided to call the dead man, babbled on in the foreign language, slumping his head towards Lady Lurch in apparent disgust. Meanwhile, Lady Lurch was complaining about a little dust on the dresser. She shuffled backward so that she now stood between them and the door. If they had to run, they would have to slip through her cold, dead hands.

Lamb again scrunched back, hoping the dead things wouldn't see him. Maybe he and Shack could dash out of the room and the prissy corpses would just scream from their cheese-dome heads and back away.

Or the things would eat them. Gentleman Gore's fangs looked ready for gnashing.

The porter had given up on finding intruders behind the dresser and stepped out of Lamb's field of vision to check behind the curtains. He tensed. His one chance to escape might arrive in three…Two…

"*Yeeee!*"

Shack screeched and light filled the tiny dark space beneath the bed. The porter hadn't gone for the curtains, it had doubled back to the bed. The horse head's teeth had clamped on Shack's heel.

Lamb lunged out the other side of the bed as his thudding heart lay down a tattoo for Shack's wails and the snarled protests of Gentleman Gore and Lady Lurch. Lamb grabbed his friend's flailing hand. He missed the first swipe. Then he failed to overcome the creature's pull on her once he made contact. The porter's toothy grip felt unbreakable.

Lamb kept glancing up. The two would-be room-renters were still frightened by his sudden appearance from under the bed, but it wouldn't last. Even as he yanked on Shack's hand, he saw *frightened* grow into *upset* with just a hint of *murderously angry* thrown in for good measure.

They took a tentative step forward as they screamed at him. A few more steps would cut off his exit.

He did the math. If he couldn't save Shack, he could at least save himself. Lamb tensed and made one last, futile attempt to pull his friend free.

A new yell overpowered the rest of the ruckus.

Mossy sprang at Lady Lurch and drove her jagged mirror knife into the back of the dead woman's neck. The corpse went down, knocking over Gentleman Gore as she fell. Mossy sprang back, her weapon wrenched from her hand and her eyes wild.

Then Shack squirted out of the bed like a wet bar of soap. Her foot was bloody, but she managed to stand. "House Mouse!" she croaked.

The horse-headed mountain of muscle rose up, clawing his face on the other side of the bed. He flung the tiny body of House Mouse away, wiping at a bit of blood on its muzzle. To Lamb's shock, the little rodent seemed to have made a suicide run at the massive foe, sacrificing itself. And now Shack was safe.

"They hooligans are still here. I shall dispatch them for you viewing delight," the porter said. It bowed slightly towards the two dead customers.

The two dead customers that were springing to their feet, despite the knife still sticking out of Lady Lurch's neck.

Lamb was already running for the door. He flung it open as the porter charged them. Mossy ran through. For a brief second, Lamb considered slamming the door on Shack and leaving the trouble-maker as a roadblock. It would gift them a few seconds at the least.

Instead, he kicked one of the nasty, sloshing trunks lengthwise across the narrow choke point before the door and closed the door behind him only after Shack had limped out. His fingers had barely left the knob when a soft *thunk* was followed up by a deafening crash against the door.

Idiot thing.

Lamb didn't look back to see how quickly the porter had recovered from its face-to-face with the solid oak. Looking back got people killed. Instead, he all but picked up Shack and ran, half-dragging her despite her cries of pain. He reached Mossy as their bare feet pounded down the hallway. Mossy took a look at Shack's injured foot and helped Lamb carry her.

They dashed towards a maid cart in front of an open room. Suspicious stains trailed out from the room, but they didn't hesitate. They ran past and heard a squawk behind them.

At any other time, the sound would galvanize Lamb into a burst of speed fit to set carpet fibers aflame. But he had nothing left to give. He hoped it was a particularly slow maid. The grunting and panting of the porter behind them was encouragement enough.

"I'll—never—never steal another...Never—" Shack was gasping.

They passed countless doors, and the next turn in the hall still wasn't for another thirty rooms or so. They might lose the night-mares there. If they made it.

Suddenly Mossy yanked Shack to the left. Lamb almost missed it but managed to stop fast enough to join the others in the little side hall.

The room was longer than it was wide. Lamb briefly glimpsed recessed marble counters with folded towels and a broken cart in one corner, but the important thing was that it led to another hall. If they could get around that corner into the next hall fast enough, they could duck into a room and vanish for a time.

He saw a glint of steel to his right. Or…

With a soft hiss, he redirected his friends to the panel in the wall. The panel opened smoothly over a pile of discarded clothing. Behind it was a dark, metal passage that dropped straight down into oblivion. It was a laundry chute, like they had back home inside industrial plants to send filthy cloths down to washrooms in the basement. Except this one was huge. Big enough for even a fat human.

Lamb thought all this in the space of a heartbeat. Then he was moving. This wasn't a time to be chivalrous and hold the door to be sure the others made it. This wasn't even a time for explanations or discussions. The beastly staff were seconds behind them.

"Close up behind us," he breathed. And he got one leg up. He slid in.

Lamb went into freefall. He knocked against one side of the metal shaft, then another, all in pitch darkness. Shielding his face with his hands, he tensed, expecting to land and land hard at any moment. He hoped the others were behind him.

But not too closely behind him, or he was probably dead no matter how soft the landing was.

Bang.

Angry messages screamed up his spine from his tailbone. He had struck a slanted surface as the chute angled under him, and the impact knocked the breath out of him. He was sliding now instead of falling.

He heard two more slams behind him, one after the other. The first came with a yelp of pain, and he imagined that Shack had landed on her bad foot.

Blackness. Just blackness and the sound of his pants and shirt zinging across metal.

And then *poof.* He smacked into a pile of something soft. He had a moment to wonder why he had come to a stop while still in the chute, before two more-or-less soft somethings sandwiched him against the obstruction.

"Snakes!" Mossy's voice whispered in fear above him. "There's snakes here."

"I think that's Lamb making that sound," Shack wheezed. "I hit him pretty hard."

"Did either of you mortar-brains close the panel behind us?" Lamb hissed.

"I would have- "

"Great."

Mossy sounded offended. "I was two inches from being grabbed by that horrible thing with the heads on its belt. *Excuse me.*"

"So, they know we're down here," Shack surmised. Her voice, like theirs, echoed in the tight quarters. "But they can't follow us. Good thinking, Lamb."

Lamb didn't answer. He found himself frowning, thinking that if Shack had secured the room door before going to sleep like she was supposed to do, they would be safe now. He didn't give voice to that thought.

Instead, he probed the soft mass beneath them. He felt folds, loops, fluff, elastic, cloth, and buttons. All manner of laundry had been thrown down here. And judging by the fact that they weren't at the bottom of the chute, they seemed to have been jammed.

He made the mistake of saying as much.

"No-no-no," Shack whispered above. "No. Get us out, Lamb."

"He'll find a way," Mossy replied with more confidence than Lamb felt. "Just give him some space to work."

Shack didn't. She started squirming and breathing heavily. Despite her love of creating dens to sleep in, Shack did not do well in tight spaces.

"Stop it," hissed Mossy. "You're making things worse."

"Get me out of here," Shack moaned like she hadn't heard.

"Mossy, hold her still," Lamb said. The girl kept stepping on his shoulders, pulling his hair, and boxing his ears with her ankle bones. Just a little distracting. He ignored it as best he could while feeling the laundry clot for weakness. *Thud.* Heel-to-nose. He winced and said, "I think I can do this. Stop being such a—"

A shade of gray broke through the black. All three heads turned to watch a pale patch of light far above. They could then see that their chute branched upwards as other chutes connected to it. A panel on one of the other levels must have been moved, because they saw motion in the twilight before the glow blinked out entirely.

Then the laundry hit. All three yelled as wet towels pelted them. Only a few washcloths and socks and such made it through to Lamb, so he assumed that Mossy in the back had gotten the worst of it.

"No," Shack cried. "Get it off! We need to get—"

Smack. Lamb smacked her hurt foot to cut off the mania. He was almost as shocked as she was at the slap.

"I can do this," he repeated firmly.

Bracing his hands against the sides of the metal passage, Lamb kicked at a sunken corner of the mass beneath them. Nothing. He used Shack's weight against his shoulders to kick harder. This time something gave. A flurry of kicks made him feel like a spoiled brat mid-tantrum, but it seemed to work.

Without warning, they were sliding again. Wet laundry and flailing limbs filled the narrow passage.

After a long moment guiding his fall, Lamb started counting seconds. 1...2...

They passed what felt like another branch. 12...13...14...

Lamb scraped something that smelled like old people off his face. How many stories up had they been? They'd only ever used two flights of stairs in their time at Hotel Serestio. 46...47...

And then there was light. On a carpet of sodden laundry, they tumbled into a huge bin filled with the stuff.

Lamb lay there, stunned. The pile beneath him had cushioned his landing this time, but the sudden stop after falling had wrecked his balance. He could hear Mossy and Shack stirring behind him. He opened his eyes, blinked through the brown light, and listened.

They were in some sort of large, dim basement room. Hisses of steam and the grinding of gears provided ambient noise. It made

Lamb think the room had been built centuries before and ignored by both time and the League of the Trillion.

There was one creaking noise out there. Something out of the ordinary groans and clacking of machinery interrupted the repetition. Years of hiding from the things that infested the halls had taught him to recognize sounds of life.

That, and empty rooms didn't mumble to themselves.

"Dark horse over a metal fence, or a red one?" the mumbler was saying. "At night? Lost? Lost at night? Makes no sense. And is that a path or a river? Going up the river is different than down a dark path."

Lamb glanced at Shack and Mossy, who had untangled themselves and looked as wary as he did. He put a finger to his lips. With a painful, slow effort, he raised himself up so he could peek out of the bin.

A hazy form paced behind a steam vent in the corner. It appeared to be a woman hunched with age or pain who was studying something in her hands as she stumbled along. She continued to mutter under her breath. Not a monster, but not someone he particularly wanted to meet, either. Some survivors of the Hotel Serestio horror show didn't have companions to keep them sane.

"White knight, dark knight, gray knight?" she grumbled. "Gray night or white night? The gray? Another white night? Surely destiny be not so cruel. Perhaps a night in a shining armoire..."

The shadow of the strange woman walked off and the sounds of her mumbles faded. Lamb held his breath until he heard a door close in the distance.

Another minute of waiting turned up no more sounds outside the laboring machinery in the room. The trio pulled themselves out of the bin and eyed the large basement room.

"House Mouse..." Shack whispered. Her lip trembled slightly. "He saved me."

Lamb willed himself not to speak. But the will is wont to acquiesce to the heart's hurt.

"If we had barricaded the door instead of going to sleep, we would be safe hiding instead of running," he said, a bit imperiously, if he was honest.

"You mean me, don't you?" Shack asked, a look of incredulity on her face. "You're blaming me for that. For those two corpses and that horse thing getting in. Are you insane?"

"Don't worry, car thief," Mossy assuaged. "All of us should have known better. He didn't mean you specifically."

"Well *I* barricaded the door last time," Lamb said. "And Mossy, you did the time before that."

"I knew it," Shack snapped. "How are you that stupid and that mean, little boy?"

A retort came to mind—*so says the girl who thought she could steal a car*. But Lamb forced his lips closed more successfully this time and looked away. He wasn't sure where this frustration was coming from. But as painful as choking it back was, he knew enough stories about prisoner infighting drawing maids. Living was still too high on his to-do list.

"None of that matters right now," he said tightly. "We could have maids and who knows what else down on our heads any moment. We need to cover a lot of ground quickly to find a safe way out of this place. If we're lucky, we may even find a way to this lobby thing."

"So, we each search a different direction," Mossy said, motioning around at the endless banks of copper and brass machinery around them and the forest of old, gray pipes that seemed to hold up the ceiling overhead.

"Separating? We're smarter than that," Shack said, thrusting out her jaw. The ragged hair framing her face shivered.

"Don't flatter yourself," Lamb muttered under his breath.

He strode off, not waiting for an argument. They could mend hurt feelings after they were further from physical danger. Despite the frustration he felt towards his sluggish friends, a spark of excitement kept his bare feet padding across the stone basement floor.

They were down—further down than they had ever been before. And unless he was very deep underground, Lamb was closer to the ground floor than he had been in three years. Where there was a ground floor, there was a lobby, a front door, and a host of soldiers from the League.

At that point—if they even got as far as that point—League forces would either recapture Lamb and his friends or free them. Even imprisonment was better than wandering around and waiting to become "cleaned" by the daymares walking around the hotel. And better to turn himself in than to be considered a rogue and killed. Lamb doubted it had been the League who had let all the inmates out of their rooms years ago. He also doubted the League was happy that prisoners like him had survived their monsters for so long.

For who else would send monsters but monsters? The League maintained order at the claw-tips of their lizard-men, the gammyn. Facing them as criminals…

Criminals. Thanks to Shack. As Lamb prowled towards the far wall, he tossed a glance back at the young woman. He got a bad smell in his nose as he did and hunched his shoulders as she walked out of sight.

To this day, lying for her in court was the best and worst decision he had ever made. He had claimed in no uncertain terms that she had been with him at the time of the alleged crime. That was *before* the judge had mentioned that Shack and Mossy had been caught in the act, and he would have kicked an orphan in the crotch to have known that lovely little bit of trivia before committing perjury.

But it had been worth fanning his nose at the system…aye? It had been worth sticking up for a friend…yes? Doing what's right. Probably.

The ten years of imprisonment would have been definitely —*probably* worth it. But hiding and starving in the halls of a twisted hotel from the pit wasn't. Nothing was worth this existence. Scrounging on the streets and living in old recycle bins was better. No wonder Mossy was still bringing up the car theft years later.

Something grabbed Lamb. It yanked him into a thicket of green pipes.

Startled out of his thoughts, he made the deadliest mistake of Hotel Serestio. He hesitated. Two skinny arms held him in place away from prying eyes between two huge drum washers. One pinned his arms behind his back, and another clamped over his mouth. Lamb was distracted, then surprised, then hesitant to escape in case it was Mossy or Shack. That brief second should have cost him his life.

"Hsss-hsss-hss-hs-hs…" a feminine voice slithered past his ear.

He couldn't be sure whose it was. Most voices sound the same when all you have to go off of is "Hsss-hsss-hss-hs-hs." But it was enough to make his skin crawl.

He had prepared himself to go down screaming and swinging, but then he saw a shadow pass the spot he had stood moments ago. It was huge, had an odd head, and was carrying suitcases. With each step, it grunted and huffed.

The shape paused and turned to where Lamb was being held, and he figured that he was dead. One thing had snatched him, the other thing would leave his intestines on the floor for Mossy and Shack to find. He wondered if they would scream when they saw the mess.

But whatever had grabbed him didn't call out to the porter. Clouds of steam rippling with heat hung over them and they stood stock still among the pipes. Lamb saw a mental image of a squirrel he had once snatched for dinner back home. The creature had been caught away from trees and lampposts, burying a treasure in a gravel lot. It froze, knowing it couldn't escape, hoping that motion-lessness would save it. Playing statue hadn't saved the squirrel. Lamb doubted it would save him.

The porter took in a long breath of the steam, visibly relaxed, and continued on.

The second it had passed out of sight around a boiler tank,

Lamb found himself dragged bodily in the opposite direction. As sure as he was that he was about to be eaten by an insane cannibal prisoner, Lamb stayed limp. Fighting back would create a ruckus that would almost certainly bring the horse-headed creature back.

The woman, if it was a woman, finally flung him into a tiny side room and closed the door behind her, dampening the already dim light of the basement to a coffin gray. Lamb lay on his back, trying to orient himself. He tensed his legs to spring.

"Taking the quick path to a pauper's grave, eh?" mumbled a familiar voice. "Running ragged round the rock hasn't taught you to treat terrors timorously?"

Thssss... A hiss accompanied a small flame's birth on the end of a matchstick. In the tiny globe of light, Lamb saw the tall woman he had heard muttering to herself. She seemed neither particularly young nor old, just fully grown. She had likely been attractive before years of imprisonment had exhausted her. She wore the same bleached clothing that Lamb did.

Hers fit better, Lamb noticed. He decided he no longer felt threatened but was suddenly very aware of the smudges of black dust on his skin.

The woman held the light and listened through the door a moment. Once she seemed content that they were safe, she strode over to the far end of the little closet. The ground sparkled obsidian beneath her. The match revealed that the far wall was a slope of coal ceiling high. They were in the coal dump for the steamers in the main basement.

Lamb's toes went numb.

"Put that out!" he hissed. "You'll blow us all to the pit with that light!"

"It's not our fate to be blown to the pit today," the woman said with a sigh. "Believe me, I know fate. The name's Willow, Samanthene."

Willow, Samanthene trod over to a table that had been set up in the middle of the room. A rich red material had been draped over the little table, and it looked like a torn curtain from one of the rooms. She sat down behind the table when the match burnt out and left them stranded in darkness again. A knocking noise followed. Two gentle glows, one purple and one red, flickered to life on opposite sides of the table. The rich illumination came from two geodes. They lit a small stack of paper between them.

More confident that he wasn't about to die by coal dust combustion, Lamb approached the table. He eyed the crystals warily, having seen similar sights peddled by alley performers in the dark markets back home. "Were you a magician before you were thrown in here?"

"I made many, many, many modes of mischief. Not magic, not mage, not magician, not malpractice, mi'lord," she grumbled. "Arcane arts are for the asinine. And demons. Which you nearly knocked into, numbskull."

"Right," Lamb said. He wasn't sure how else to reply and was put off by the woman's odd mannerisms.

"Why?" she asked.

"What?"

"Why not acquire assurance that your acquaintances are also alive?"

Lamb ignored the stare she was threading into him like needlework. "They're smart. They'll take care... And what do you know about us? Have you been watching us?"

Samanthene tilted her head and frowned. She didn't look angry, sad, or upset as much as she looked like a law enforcer who had just caught him being foolish but didn't want to turn him over to the League for trial just yet.

"I watch everyone here," she murmured. "Ever since the creatures of the Pit arrived, I have been hard pressed to remain hidden. So many sad souls searching for something."

"Yeah, 'safety'," Lamb said with a grin. But if Samanthene was impressed by his attempt at alliteration, she didn't show it. He trudged on regardless. "Those things are monsters. I've seen them slaughter good people for no reason. And the League are monsters too if this is their idea of prison security."

The woman studied the scraps of paper laid out on the table, but briefly glanced up at that. "The creatures are not League. They are of crytholn."

"Is that another country? Because if they all look like that, I don't think I'd like to visit," Lamb said.

"Crytholn is the kingdom of the gray. The beings of the Pit. Demons. They attacked. Used evil magics to twist innocent workers into...abominations," she hissed.

Lamb studied her, but Samanthene looked like she was serious. Maybe she believed in all the religious gobble-gobble that the League tried to stuff down people's throats. Lamb saw how the horrors walking the halls could seem like bringers of the apocalypse, if anything could. So he just shrugged.

"Okay. Then I'm guessing the gammyn will definitely bring up that difference in theology when they get here," Lamb said.

"We dare not dream of that delightful day," she mumbled.

"Apparently, they're already on their way." He popped his neck back and forth. The knowledge that one of those beastly porters could open the door behind him at any time made him itch to find the lobby all the more.

She finally dropped the papers. Lamb caught a glance at some sketches of constellations, plant life, and what looked like a faceless, hairless man in a chef's uniform.

"How do you know?" she said.

"We spoke to a prisoner who saw a League scout," he said. "The scout warned of an incoming invasion. They're going to wipe us out."

"No," Samanthene whispered. "When the League of the Trillion went to war elsewhere years ago, they freed us to prevent their prisoners from all starving. If the gammyn are almost here, they are coming to wipe out the *creatures*. Unless... Well, perhaps the people too, if to prevent the possibility they possess us poor prisoners."

"So, it's all the same," Lamb groaned. "That's an even better reason to leave, *now*. I've been dragging my friends down to the lobby, since that's where the soldiers are supposed to be staging their assault. If we surrender before the fighting starts, we'll be safe."

She eyed him, squinting, and her nose crumpled. She pushed one of the scraps of paper towards him. He glanced at it and paused in surprise. It was a charcoal sketching of a young man with a grim frown and dark eyes—an eerily accurate drawing of him. Except the Lamb on the page looked angry and violent.

"That's me?" he asked.

"Astute. An artist, I am not. But beware, this belligerent boy be you," she muttered. "I believe you to be cursed."

Lamb swiped the paper up and studied it. His likeness was drawn on a background of swirled black shades and claw-like streaks. He didn't know art beyond what other street people would vandalize onto the buildings and bridges of rich men. But the picture looked...tortured.

"You're not well, are you?" Lamb said with a grunt. "Look, we'll sneak back out there, and find my friends, and then the four of us will—"

"For the love of Saint Slappy," Samanthene snapped.

She stood up straight. The confused look on her face had been replaced by a healthy glow. The withdrawn hunch in her back had disappeared. And her mumbling was certainly gone.

Lamb stared warily at the transformation, steeling himself to fight if needed.

"I really thought that old crone act would play better," she said in a voice tinged brown with disgust. She swept the scraps of paper into a tattered satchel. "Since you serve self-pity before sense, listen well."

Lamb took a few steps back in case things got violent. He wasn't sure what to think.

"I'm the kind of woman who knows things, and I show up when people need someone like me to knock some sense into them," she grumbled. "You gave me some free news, so here's some for you. The soul is a tricky thing. Not like the spirit. The spirit lives with the body, changes with the body, and goes to the great beyond after the body fails. You live. You die.

"But the soul is not attached to you. It forms the basic building blocks that your spirit grows from during your life. Like different crystals growing on the same rock after time has eroded the old crystals. Your soul continues after you move on. You could have a soul that's been used by a dozen different people before."

"I should—"

"Pipe down? I agree," Samanthene cut him off. She held up other sketches of his own angry face yelling, of him hiding under a bed, of him slapping a girl whose face he couldn't quite make out. "Your soul is stained. Somehow, something is haunting you. Hurting your heart. Ever feel horribly unlucky? Hmm? But when you die, you will find eternal rest. You *are* the sum of your spirit, not your soul. No matter how bad this life is, you have eternal rest to anticipate. Find some relief in that at least."

Perhaps the strange woman meant to be comforting, but she mostly just sounded coal-mad. Even if his spirit did survive death, he was quite sure he was headed towards eternal damnation, be it Hades, the Pit, or otherwise. She was babbling. He'd give her a few more seconds of his time before he walked out and found his friends, creatures or no creatures.

Her mouth wrinkled into a sardonic pucker. "This is important, nitwit. But a quick display to quell your questioning?"

He shrugged in reply, slowly easing himself back towards the door by wriggling his feet. It let him still face the deranged prisoner.

She picked up one of the sketchings. It was of a whiskered rodent nose poking out of an ornate jewelry box. A good likening of House Mouse in his natural environment.

Lamb stopped dead. Even a skilled stalker couldn't have seen the brave little pest of Shack's closely enough to draw that picture. How had she?

"I'm listening," he said in a small voice.

Samanthene didn't press her advantage. Instead, she laid the drawing flat on the wood table between the crystals. Grasping a corner delicately between two fingernails, she lifted it back up. Appearing beneath it, as if she were lifting a curtain instead of a thin slice of pulped wood, was a familiar jewelry box.

She tapped it twice and opened it. A curious brown and white face popped out. House Mouse had a tattered ear now but was otherwise far more alive than when Lamb last saw him.

Lamb emitted a gurgling sound.

"No, now you are listening," she said gently, proffering the box.

He stepped forward and took it as if in a dream, with no real free will of his own. He stared at the goddess, or demon, or prophet. He mumbled to himself, "And...now, I'm just numb."

"I imagine so, although not because I gave you a living mouse," she told him. "I don't know what took ahold of you, but your spirit in this era has gone cold. You are about to have a choice. You may mind your morose mentality and make others miserable, or trade your beloved resentment in exchange for a human life."

"I—look, I just don't get it."

"What else is there to say? Your soul is yours to care for," she huffed. "Don't darken it for any who will inherit it after you by letting your friend die."

Lamb swallowed. "Die? Which friend?"

Samanthene, or whoever she was, cleaned up the table as she spoke. She fastened the curtain around her shoulders like a cloak and slipped the sketches and one of the glowing crystals into hidden pockets.

"You warned me about the gammyn, so I'm returning the favor. *Quid pro quo,*" she added, her eyes sad and tired. "Some people believe their lives reek for a reason beyond their control. Yours actually might. I don't think that's fair. Too many eons have fallen to people's pride previously...All the more reason to hold on to those few beating hearts, yes?"

"Look, I get it. Souls, a friend in trouble, very dramatic," Lamb lied, eyes still wide. He held House Mouse close to his chest. "But if you know so much, just tell me what to do next!"

She created a small pile of splinters and wood shavings by scraping at the rough tabletop. Then she put away the other crystal, striking another match to light the coal room instead. She dropped the match near the curls of wood.

"I shan't do that," she said. She strode past him quickly toward the door, and he followed. "What I shall do is tell you what *not* to do. Don't step on cracks in pavement. Don't down duck dander— terribly hallucinogenic. Don't put all of your anger on. Don't lose loved ones."

And suddenly they were back in the creaking, hissing cavern of a basement. Lamb's dull, sleepwalking state vanished as he sensed the presence of danger nearby again. He blinked rapidly to clear his vision.

Samanthene closed the door to the coal room behind them quietly, then walked in the opposite direction of Lamb's friends and, hopefully, the door out. Then she tossed a last whisper over her red-cloaked shoulder.

"And don't dally as my deadly distraction detonates...Oh, that one was bad, Sam..."

She vanished behind a huge washing cylinder.

Lamb glanced at moving shapes in the other directions, at the monsters in the steamy mists. He looked down at Shack's beloved pet in his hands, and then back at the rusty metal door in the concrete wall. She had lit that match for a reason. Oh. Distraction.

Lamb didn't run as much as he strained against the steamy air to get away from the coal room as fast as he could. He found the miniature forest of pipes again and ducked in there, hoping he had put enough columns and heavy machines between—

Thoom.

The floor shuddered. It had been sharp and quick, with a brief but massive tongue of flame blowing out the door. As the echoes faded, screeches filled the room as a veritable flock of maids rushed past to find the source of the explosion.

How the strange woman had timed the explosion, Lamb didn't know or care. She could have been just another supernatural nightmare. But no, the monsters only took. She had given. He now had a certain jewelry box with precious cargo back.

Besides, a distraction was a distraction. As the maids danced about the burning coal room, working themselves into a frenzy, he slipped away.

Panting, Lamb weaved between the dark and lifeless engines. Some massive generators hummed as he passed. He slipped by another coal room next to a roaring furnace the size of a corner store. He had to skirt its open maw because the belches of cinders threatened to singe his shirt. His eyes flickered about like roving lamps, searching for a sign of Mossy and Shack. They could have been hunted by the porter that he'd seen earlier.

His bare feet slapped the cement floor in his haste. Stealth mattered less than speed, considering how many of the animal-headed things were down here. Despite his credo, he glanced back once or twice to see if the maids were following him yet. But since he was winding through the machines, he didn't have a very long line of sight. If something saw him, it would be too close for him to escape it.

Lamb had just padded around a small mountain of crumpled towels when he heard a sharp *kkhck*. Mossy had invented that noise as a way to locate each other, as it was an awkward sound that most other prisoners or monsters wouldn't make. Sure enough, Mossy peered out from amongst the laundry.

"What happened?" Lamb hissed to her after joining her in the pile. "Where's Shack?"

Mossy was all eyes. She wasn't crying, but she looked as stricken as that squirrel Lamb once caught.

"She left," she said with a voice like glass. "We were just splitting up to look for the door. But she said that we were better off without her and she was really sorry and she left us."

"She just walked away?" he said, his face rubber.

"She hates us, doesn't she?"

Lamb looked at her. Having left the soup-soup, he hadn't eaten since the day before last and he was feeling it. His body was sluggish and shaky. His brain kept trying to nap on the run. His fuzzy head told him to yell, ignore people, and go to sleep somewhere. The news about Shack exacerbated it.

With effort, he shook his head slightly. "I don't know what she's thinking. But she's an adult. We can't force her to—"

"To what? To care about living? To stay with us?" Mossy hissed back. She cast him a dark look.

"Are you sure you two aren't sisters?"

"Not the time, Lamb. Really not the right time."

"Well, what does Mossy say we do, huh?" Lamb prodded. "There's no reason I have to make the call. What do you think?"

She didn't reply.

"You hesitated," he pointed out. "*She* was the mortar-brain. If she doesn't want to find the lobby with us, maybe that's her guilt finally showing up. Of the three of us, she's the one that deserves to be here. She dragged you down with her. You constantly remind her of that."

His own exhaustion cut his monologue short. He slumped deeper into the pile, hoping he had enough towels stacked over him to hide him from prying eyes.

Mossy's eyes still filled her face, but now they shimmered in the light from the distant furnace. "So, we should just go," she mumbled.

"She made her decision. We should respect that," Lamb said through a heavy breath. "We need to get out while the maids are still distracted. I saw fifty of them around a burning coal room. Well, a whole clutch of them."

A pained groan trickled out of the young woman. But she also gave him a tiny, almost imperceptible nod. The two unburied themselves and peeked around the corner of the nearest wash drum.

"We didn't find any doors before we split up," Mossy warned in a whisper.

"Let's check the direction I went," he replied. "The way out had to be over there."

They started creeping along the wall, avoiding the bits of scrap metal, spare pieces, and broken stone that littered the floor. Kicking one could cause enough noise to bring something running.

"At least you found the stairs."

Lamb shook his head. "Actually, there was this woman who…"

He stopped and Mossy smacked into his back with a soft *oof*. He heard her skitter back into hiding somewhere. It was a smart move. He would have done the same if one of the girls had stopped dead in front of him while sneaking. But he hadn't seen a monster this time, at least not that sort.

He ground his teeth and shifted his weight. He shifted it back, tensed to continue moving but wavered in place.

"To the pit with her," he groaned. "We're going."

He stalked back and yanked Mossy out of the crevice between washers that she had found. She staggered after him.

"Which *her*?" she hissed, her eyebrows in a bemused knot. "Where are we going?"

"Both *her*s! If we all die, they'll regret it," he snarled. Then he turned and headed back the way Shack had supposedly disappeared, grumbling the entire way. Mossy followed.

The huge basement washroom with its churning mechanical energy gave way to the ghoulish silence of narrow back halls and storage rooms. The walls were stone and mortar, and the floor was cement slab. Rusty pipes sprouted from holes in walls, only to have been hacked to an early, brown-speckled end. The place stank like sewage.

Add in some roads, crime, and screaming tenants hanging from upper floor windows, and the place would have been indistinguishable from Lamb's old home city.

When Hotel Serestio had been a fully-functioning prison, these smaller rooms might have been used by the human staff. They crept past bunk halls, miniature kitchens, break rooms, conference chambers, and offices. All were covered in a layer of dust three years thick. Many were still locked.

Lamb and Mossy checked the unlocked rooms for their friend, but to no avail. In looking, Lamb was shocked at how bare the rooms were. He imagined most of the niceties and comforts had been taken when the place was abandoned, but even then the cold, windowless closets were far from the palatial overlord halls he had imagined the orderlies had occupied. Compared to this, he'd rather have been in one of the prison rooms.

His stomach growled angrily and he winced. Hunger was really making itself known. At the wrong time, a gastric grumble could scream as loudly as alarm bells.

Then their winding hall ended in a T-junction with another one. After assuring himself that they weren't in immediate danger, Lamb checked for footprints, oil, or any other disturbances that might have indicated whether Shack had chosen left or right. Nothing.

"We're splitting up," Mossy said.

"No," Lamb insisted. "That's how we got into this, remember?"

"Except I'm not planning to go hide like a baby. I'll be coming back," she said with a sniff. "Are you?"

He studied her stubborn face and huffed. "Fine. Just be careful, got it?"

"Well I *was* going to dance the Midsummer's Shake with one of those handsome horse-butlers, but now that you—"

"Mossy. I mean it."

She stared into his eyes for a moment and her sarcastic veneer splintered slightly. With a nod, she padded off to the right. She disappeared around a corner while still fidgeting with her mirror knife.

With a deep breath, Lamb charged to the left. Time was fading behind him and the lack of maids in this part of the hotel had emboldened him to throw stealth to the wind. The hall took a quarter turn right. The next few minutes were spent darting from one locked door to another and peering through the narrow glass panes that separated the end of his nose from long-abandoned shadows. Between the grays and blacks, he saw computers and lamps that had been old and outdated even when he had first come to Hotel Serestio. There were no cobwebs, no rat spatter, no other signs of life. Only muted tombs of lost work.

That's when the hall started winding. Instead of neat and orderly corners, the hall weaved back and forth like a weekend drunk. Or a drooling psychopathic. Not only was the hall not straight, it wasn't flat either. Everything was an uphill climb or a downhill stumble. The cement underfoot had frozen mid-undulation on the slopes, allowing him to walk carefully.

"What's wrong with this place?" he hissed out loud after slipping down a particularly steep incline.

He passed more locked rooms with black iron doors and smoky windows, and then Lamb came to a final stair. It was a proper stair this time, instead of a cement ramp. At the top was a pair of elegant wooden double doors. So, of course, he listened at the top step before charging through. He was rushed and had nerves tauter than power lines, but he wasn't suicidal yet.

His head filled with the pounding of his own pulse and the strange white noise that whispered whenever a body puts his ear to anything solid. Besides that, he heard only silence through the heavy door. He was about to turn away and chase after Mossy when he heard something human.

A quiet whimpering, crying, sniveling burble—a sad sound.

Shack. Lamb slipped through the door and found himself in a large office the size of three hotel rooms squashed together. It looked exactly how Lamb imagined the typical office for a corporate head should look: burnished metal shelves filled with heavy books, an oversized iron desk with an oversized throne behind it, plush carpets like upstairs but dark red, and even a coffin-sized fish tank to the side. The fish were long dead. Their skeletons had sunk to the bottom of the tank and only a few tattered strands of flesh clung to them, waving like seaweed.

A single overhead light buzzed at one-quarter power, unwilling to be shut down by the primary controls that had reduced the rest of this administration wing to emergency power.

If Lamb had to guess, the feeble overhead was the reason Shack had hidden here. It was the brightest thing he had seen since falling down the laundry chute. He couldn't see her, but the sobbing was coming from behind the desk. The huge chunk of metal must have felt as safe as a barricade.

"Shack," Lamb whispered.

The crying paused a moment, only to resume more bitterly and broken than before. The sound twisted his heart.

"It's your fault we're here, you know," he mumbled. "It's your fault. We all know it. You were stupid. I thought I was helping you. Maybe I was just...I lied for you and now we might all die here."

Unsurprisingly, the sobs continued. A master of diplomacy, that was Lamb.

"It's the League's fault for having such pointless, stupid laws. It's the city's fault for being insanely uptight about it. But it's your fault too! And I never got to say that because I felt like you were being punished enough but it wasn't enough and I needed to...to say that," he said in one breath. "You were a mortar-brain. But you're not the only one, okay? I am too. Gods know Mossy's certifiable. She's mean and teases you, but I don't...I never liked to admit that I was mad. But I was. But none of that matters anyway, because we need to get out of here. Our punishment better be done! We don't owe these pompous rats any more skin. Come on. Let's find this invasion team before they start sweeping the halls."

Lamb crouched uneasily near the door, unwilling to get closer and risk scaring her off. He heard a few sniffs before Shack's soft voice whispered back.

"You hated me."

"I didn't *hate* you! It was more— I was angry. I'm over that," he said, hoping she wouldn't drag it out. This was painful enough.

"You...forgave me."

"Yes, I guess," he murmured. "Just come back with us."

There was a happy sigh behind the desk.

"We were all happy," Shack said, her voice coming out of a whisper. "We were a team. I stole that vehicle. I was bad. Then you forgave me."

Lamb frowned. Shack sounded muffled and distant, like she was talking through her sleeve. He imagined her shirt was snotty and tear-stained by now, which made him feel worse. But she didn't have to make this so ooey-gooey emotional. This was past his tolerance for such things. He got up and walked towards the desk as Shack continued.

"I stopped being an idiot. You saw that and forgave me. That cheered me up because I knew you loved me then. I loved you two, too." She giggled.

"Shack, did you hit your head?" Lamb asked nervously.

He clutched his peace offering, House Mouse, a little closer. He leaned over the desk.

"Surprised?" yelled Shack as she sprang up behind the desk, startling him back onto the floor.

Except it was half of Shack, with her arms flopping about numbly with every bounce of her torso. She had nothing below the waist but gray. Her face had a huge smile frozen on it and her glassy eyes stared ahead. Widely. Unblinkingly. Frosted over with sickly blue that stained the skin around her sockets too.

"Gods!" Lamb screamed.

The apparition continued to flounce in place as if it were on a spring. And Shack might have been, for all Lamb knew. Her legs were gone, and a thick, shiny gray trunk grew out of the bottom of her gray prison shirt. Finger puppet. She was a giant finger puppet. On a monstrous finger.

"You got scared," she trilled. Except her mouth didn't move. It was the same muffled Shack voice as before, except now it sounded like someone throwing their voice for the amusement of a child. "I made lots of fun things out of the stupid boring people. They were scared. I liked them being scared it was fun I'll do it again."

"Oh, gods save me," Lamb wheezed, backing away as quickly as he could.

"You thought you should run and why not please pretty please lamby."

Lamb staggered to his feet.

"Scared" the voice whispered. "Scared?"

"Hah! Hah hah hahahaha hah ha hah hah hah!"

When the walls around him started laughing louder than the coal explosion, Lamb broke. He ran. He slammed the doors. He slipped down the stairs. He crawled up slopes. He fell off others. He ran.

The laughter still rang everywhere around him, along with the abominable imitation of Shack's voice. She was dead and puppet-fied. She was a final cruel joke on his existence. The dancing, laughing remains of a friend who had died thinking he hated her.

Then he was aware of a steady beating. Like a drum. Some kind of music? It replaced the fading laughter.

The doors he passed with their dark windows glowed with a faint, sickly light that pulsed in rhythm with the languorous, fell beat. He didn't dare look in the windows now. He might have seen movement in them out of the corner of his eye, but he couldn't look. He wouldn't.

Just like you couldn't look out the windows upstairs. Same thing? Was this thing the main thing that had made the prison mad? Was Lamb mad?

The soft rhythm started to grow.

He didn't remember getting back to the T-intersection. He probably ran. Maybe fell or crawled. Must have survived.

What Lamb did remember was stumbling into Mossy at the intersection where they had parted.

Mossy. Mossy and Shack.

"...found her," Mossy was saying.

He staggered backwards, regarding the spectre of his friend with horror. He spun around, but there was no sight or sound of anything following him. The bit of hall he could see was dark and normal.

He turned back. Shack still appeared to be human. And she had her legs. Lamb didn't want to take a closer look. For all he knew, this was another trick.

Shack, however, didn't seem any more interested in

approaching him than he was her. Her black hair was dank and stringy, her blue eyes red from crying, and her face blotchy. She erected a stony frown against him.

"I'm *so sorry*," she hissed, "that I'm an inconvenience to you. But this is *your* fault! We wouldn't be down in the basement, trapped, if you—"

Oh. It was the real Shack.

Then Lamb was smothering her in a deathly hug mid-sentence. He buried his face in her shoulder and tried to steady his own shaky breaths. He hiccupped instead. Or maybe it was a sob. Shack was too shocked to respond.

Just as he was about to pull away, assured that Shack was alive and normal, she gave him a quick embrace back. Her face was painted with ruddy splotches of embarrassment, but her expression was one of relief.

"I. Will. Never mention the car thing again," Lamb breathed, "because you have legs."

"What—"

"No time!" he hissed. He realized that he could still hear the beat behind him. It was getting louder in the distance, and now he was certain he could feel footfalls through the concrete floors. Something was coming.

Mossy stared at the corner of the hall with an open mouth. "Is that music?"

"Yes. Run," Lamb insisted.

They ran.

As they fled the cursed hall, Lamb realized he was still clutching House Mouse's box to his chest. He didn't trust himself to speak. Instead, he tucked it under his arms and vowed to hand him off to Shack the moment they were safe.

They entered the cavernous boiler room at the speed of hunted cats. They startled a maid walking out from between two long rows of machines with an armful of clean towels. The raven-headed freak squawked in either fury or delight. Lamb didn't glance back to watch it chase them. The maid was no longer his biggest concern. Oh, he was afraid that it would catch and dismember them. But he was much more afraid of being back in that hall or in that office with that...

For half a second, he risked a glance at his friends—at Mossy's bulging eyes, Shack's emaciated pallor, and the nearly identical flare of their nostrils. They were alive. He was alive and with them. He made himself think that, instead of...Anything else, non-specifically. Certainly not that pup—anything else.

Lamb thought so hard that he tripped over a discarded dress on the floor. He rolled on one ankle, twisting his body and throwing up his foot to try and regain his balance. Instead, he landed on his back.

His teeth clattered. He slid across the cement foundation for a second and saw the maid leaping towards him. Its sharp beak flew at his throat like the world's largest, ugliest shiv.

He was still holding House Mouse's jewel-encrusted box. Lamb rammed it upwards. Anything to keep that beak away.

Two howls of pain sounded. One tore through Lamb's throat, and the other through his ears. He felt like his arms were burning in that furnace he had passed earlier. Was he passing to the pit? Did you go to your eternal damnation arms first?

But the other shriek was that of the maid. The top half of its beak was dislocated and hanging at an awful angle. It kneeled not two feet away and fanned at the grisly injury with its rubber-gloved hands. Its beady eyes were shut as it keened.

Lamb noticed the jewelry box floating in front of the monster's face, impaled on its beak. As if in a dream, he reached forward with his left hand and plucked House Mouse from it. He thought the inferno in his arm would singe the entire limb right off. But House Mouse blinked up at him, traumatized yet unhurt.

Shack and Mossy dragged him away, screaming and crying and probably not understanding what had just happened any more than he did. Lamb managed to get to his feet and stagger with them. But he was spent.

And they found the stairs in the direction that the Samanthene woman had gone. The ruckus of a whole hotel's worth of pit-demons followed them up the stairwell. They had a good lead on all but the one that Lamb had bashed in the face, but it wasn't enough. Mossy and Shack had apparently downed their emergency crackers recently. They had energy. Lamb's body kept betraying him, pitching him forward or slipping on easy steps as they ran back and forth up the iron stair. And his arms couldn't support his weight when he did fall.

But they passed the giant green numbers on the doors. B6. B5. All the way to B2 before they heard a voice below them.

"They hooligans up there! Catch them in they stairwell. NOW. RIP THEM."

The porter's quaint accent wasn't so quaint.

Lamb fell against the railing and had to lean over it with his torso to catch himself hands-free. It worked, but it drove the breath from him. As he stared downward, he could make out a dark storm of raven heads and horse teeth and muscle and uniforms, along with a few unthinkables that he had never seen before that night. One seemed to have a human head but no mouth, a janitor's apron, and huge cat eyes that glowed green up at him in the stark industrial lighting.

With the help of the women, he continued on and thought nothing more of the sight. Perhaps the place really had fully numbed him out in the end.

"Don't stop, don't stop," the girls cried, throwing their weight against the nearest door. It was emblazoned with a giant:

G

Even as they fell through the other side and landed like a bunch of mortar-brains, Lamb turned from one to the other and cackled through a teary-eyed grin.

"Sisters!" he wheezed, kicking the door closed behind them with the last of his strength.

"Who cares?" they snapped at him.

"Who are you?" said a new human voice.

They were up on their feet in a second. Not because the reflexes of three underfed, exhausted prisoners were so keen, but because they were hauled upwards by their arms. Lamb gasped in pain at the rough treatment. Fortunately, the grip in his shoulder lessened to merely tendon-crushing levels.

He squinted through the bright light of the ground floor. They had entered between an elevator bank and a sprawling lobby, resplendent in golds, crimsons, and jet blacks. Couches and chairs and tables and complimentary computer desks. And soldiers, but not human soldiers.

Gammyn. The League was here in force, and they were armed to the teeth. Literally. The nearest gammyn gaped at them with sharpened fangs. They all had scales. Some had tails, some had wings, and most of them had talons instead of fingernails.

Lamb shuddered. The League had not seized control by shaking hands. The prisoner from the bathroom had been right after all. The gammyn were here and ready for a fight.

"Who are you?" demanded a nearby woman.

"Mossy, Shack, and Lamb," Mossy whispered, sounding awed.

"Your crimes?"

"I stole a car and dragged them into it," Shack said in a surprisingly clear voice. Her lip trembled though.

In that moment, Lamb fully and truly did lose hold on the last stock of resentment for her that he had set aside for a rainy day.

"Monsters behind us!" he cried hoarsely, jerking his head at the door to the stairwell. "Demon crow ladies and horse-headed men!"

That finally spurred the milling League soldiers into action. The three prisoners were rushed to the side where several other pathetic figures in prison gray fatigues were eating hot food and sitting on velvet couches-turned cots. Some strangely attractive gammyn tended to their wounds while another one quizzed them. How long had they been there? How many other prisoners were still alive? What defenses had the pit fiends built?

Lamb didn't understand half the questions. Many of them

pertained to an invasion of the prison that had supposedly driven the League out three years back. He answered as he could, but he had one very important query of his own. "Can we go home?"

Heads jerked around as screeches and chaos erupted from the stairwell. Dozens of angry caws turned to screeches of pain and panic within moments. More of the gammyn bellowed and surged towards the stairwell as one, meeting the tide of abominations spilling forth. One bird-headed body flew through the air, crashing through the elevator doors on the far wall before lying still.

A nearby League soldier roared, "Evacuate the prisoners, now! Form ranks!"

Their couch was lifted and carried like a pallet towards a series of grand brass doors that seemed to be the exit. They were jolted around by the speed of the retreat. The three humans clutched to the sides of their impromptu escape vehicle as more gammyn with bared fangs formed tactical lines behind them to intercept the waves of nightmares.

Lamb leaned against Mossy, squeezing his eyes to shut out the horrible sights behind them. He handed House Mouse to Shack as one of the soldiers tended to his arm, and the explosive smile on her blotchy face made his heart twitch. He kept a death grip on the tureen he had been handed. While much of it slopped out in their rush, he managed to down a spoonful of hot, flavorful broth that tasted nothing like an empty can boiled over burning hotel supplies. The screeches and wet, tearing sounds behind them grew louder.

They reached the huge brass doors, and several gammyn took positions on either side to drag one open.

"Don't ask how," Lamb mumbled to Shack as she stared at House Mouse. He glanced around for Samanthene, hoping she had escaped as they had, but the strange woman was not among the traumatized victims of the Hotel Serestio nightmare. "Just give that stupid little hero of yours some soup-soup."

EON 8 – CLOSER TO THE TRUTH

n the summer of 1952, Detective Jonathan L. Parks found himself declared a hostile witness in his own case. It was the State of Michigan v. Sidney Smith on multiple counts of home invasion, robbery, and arson, with one count of first-degree murder. To three of the four alleged crimes, Smith confessed. He was a common thug with a forgettable face, he claimed, but not a murderer. The closest thing the prosecution had to a witness to that crime was Detective Parks.

Jonathan wanted one last chance to speak directly to the defendant before he implicated the man in court. After hearing a lot of pitiable sobs and half-mumbled pleas, Jonathan came to mistrust his own memory. But when he tried to entertain the idea on the stand that the action was mere manslaughter, he was declared a hostile witness by his partner, Frank.

After the smoke cleared, Frank Barnhart was promoted to head detective of their Detroit precinct. Jonathan was suspended for several weeks, under suspicion of aiding and abetting. Smith did six years before getting out on good behavior.

By that time, the precinct had found a sort of new status quo.

Jonathan had regained some respect, and Frank often threw him some of the tougher cases, having forgiven the incident during the Smith case with the speed that his lambast-and-laugh-off personality afforded him. Among other officers, there lingered a rattling resentment against the older detective. Nothing solid. Nothing worth outright discrimination besides against the darkness of his skin, and that kind of talk he had mostly beaten into a pulp with his successes on the force. No, nothing but the underlying thought that the great Detective Parks had gone soft.

If anything, Jonathan's shooting of a would-be convenience store robber had only given traction to that opinion. Other policemen, particularly one Detective Hennessey, thought that Jonathan was desperate to prove a coldness he didn't actually possess. During the reports following that particularly messy robbery, Internal Affairs was particularly interested in his emotional state. Jonathan answered every question simply. In the end, his frustrated interrogator reported that the kill was clean. And yet, Jonathan never could shake the feeling that his friends and comrades were still just waiting for him to slip.

And then Sidney Smith was released in the fall of '58. He promptly ditched his new job, abandoned his apartment, and generally made the authorities aware that his good behavior only lasted as long as his prison stint. Another two burglaries left Barnhart and half the force casting nets and pounding war drums. Afraid that he would have a time bomb on his own hands, Head Detective Barnhart ordered Jonathan to pursue an unrelated report of gang violence down by the river.

While he was questioning Balkan toughs, some fool publicly fanned the flames of the "Smith case," calling the criminal out. One thing led to another. A house was torched, a woman was presumed dead, and Smith was found burned to death in his own inferno.

All of this had occurred not two days ago.

Thus, the dinner party.

Jonathan L. Parks checked his reflection in his rearview mirror outside of Detective Barnhart's old two-story place in east Detroit. He grimaced at the ripples in his skin and checked his teeth for debris. All told, not bad for a man of his age.

So he slid out of his warm car into the early spring mist, straightened his Chinese-tailored suit jacket, and walked around to the little backyard where the barbeque was already in full swing.

Nodding to a white man walking a hound past, Jonathan whistled into the stale air and made his way into the party atmosphere of the backyard. Electric lights on poles illuminated the tiny space even as the sun set. Those awkward, new, plastic lawn chairs were stuffed wherever they fit, but most members of the large crowd were standing around with drinks in hand. Most were younger than him. Most were more hip, energetic, and otherwise cheerful than him. Ah, kids.

He stood uncomfortably just inside the gate. A tight group of four in fancy clothing were chattering and blocking the path. Their excitement made their banal words carry past Jonathan's thin indifference.

"Of course, Billy Hoeft shouldn't be starting pitcher. Why else would they have put in Ned Garver last game?"

"To put on a show! Garver's flashy, and he's got that fastball that batters hate."

"Course they're putting on airs. They got the governor and the pope and the White Knight attending that one game."

"Oh come on, Harry. You know good and well no pope and no White Knight ever been in Briggs Stadium. Stop telling everyone they were."

"I can tell them if it's true! Why else would they have flashy Garver on the mound?"

"Because he's the best, that's why."

One of the women noticed Jonathan and he gave her a polite, short smile complete with reassuring nod. She gave him a polite, short smile back and returned to her loud conversation with her fellows.

Then another middle-aged man in a wrinkled suit caught his eye and approached. "Excuse me, sir," he said, "but weren't you one of the detectives on the Smith case with Frank?"

Jonathan looked the man over. Dark skin, kind face that was used to smiling, on the tall side, but narrowly built. Seemed harmless. He shook his head at the stranger.

"Detective, yes," Jonathan said. "I've worked with Detective Barnhart for years. But I wasn't on that particular case."

The baseball talk came to a stilted halt nearby. Without looking, he could feel curiosity burning into his back. The stranger in the suit continued to smile directly into his eyes with a confidence that was almost unnerving.

"Ah, but an observant man like you must know something about what went down," the man pressed. "At least more than us. All the papers have said is that they found a body in that house fire off Woodmont Avenue. And that firebug Smith is involved."

"The man stole things and burned houses down along with the evidence inside," Jonathan said. "I wouldn't be surprised if he were involved."

"You're a man who knows much and says little, aren't you, Jon?" the stranger said, frowning as if he could peel the juicy details out of Jonathan's brain with his gaze.

"*Parks!*" called a deep bass voice.

A shorter man approached with crinkled eyes, a starched suit, and short black curls bearing silver tips like frost. He didn't smile, but his eyes were large and bright in his face. He clasped Jonathan's hand in greeting.

"Hennessy," Jonathan said with a breath of relief. "Good to see you, man."

"Yeah. Come on, let's find a corner where we can hear ourselves think," Detective Hennessy said. He made no care to hide his remark from the nattering party-goers nearby.

Likewise, they seemed to ignore him. Nodding to them and to the unsettling stranger, Jonathan Parks squeezed past in his fellow officer's wake. Hennessy was short but built like a small panzer and unafraid of simply walking through people. It amused Jonathan to no end. He kept his mirth to himself.

They paused near the open screen door to the kitchen, and Hennessy peered up at him. "Where do you stand on next month's weekend graveyard?"

"Does it matter? They'll change it at the last moment," Jonathan replied.

"'Most effective department in Michigan'," Hennessy said with a shake of his head. "Course they will. But you and I should use the pull we have to stay clear. Not that you had the pull that you used to, before the Smith case, but I don't have lily-white cheeks neither. We two stick together."

"That we do," Jonathan said, tempering his annoyance in his smile. He knew from experience that Hennessy wasn't oblivious to what came out of his mouth. He just didn't care.

"Smith case? I've been meaning to talk to you boys about that. Strangest thing, eh?"

Jonathan twitched and looked up. He forgot why he normally didn't attend parties. He hated how quickly people were springing up on a body.

This newcomer was none other than their host, and Frank had a Budweiser- fueled, half-cocked grin on his face. Jonathan nodded nervously at his boss.

Frank Barnhart was as white as white came. He had this upscale little townhome in an otherwise grungy neighborhood, he had his all-American family in his wife and two children, and he loved to talk about said townhome and wife and two children. The man drank a few too many beers off the clock and was a little too bull-headed around the clock, but otherwise, he wasn't a bad sort.

Hennessy didn't see it that way. He and Barnhart did not get along, although, between the two of them, only Hennessy realized it. And by the frown pulling at Detective Hennessy's mouth, he was busy realizing it right now.

"A thief and his victim both burn up in a fire he set," Barnhart continued. "That'll be one for the books."

"This is Detroit," Hennessy said coldly. "I'm sure your story will be forgotten among all the other mundane cases that pay for our bread and booze."

Jonathan stayed silent and watched the men as the head detective turned to look at Hennessy.

"My story?" Barnhart said with a barking laugh. "Not all of us have your imagination for stories, Detective. Open-and-shut is...is as open-and-shut as they come."

"Difficult to argue with," Jonathan said without missing a beat. He eyed the mostly empty brown bottle in the man's hand. "Mind if we talk something other than shop? Because I just got off my beat and am ready to put my feet up."

Hennessy's scrunched expression precluded continued battle if anything did. But Barnhart, as usual, spoke first.

"You do look like you spent the day as a speed bump," he said with a grunt. "Guess I should get your sorry hide back off river duty now that the Smith...I'll talk to the chief tomorrow. But as far as talking shop goes, why do you think so many people showed up? People want to know the details before the official story hits the papers."

By now they had drifted inside to avoid the traffic of the back door. Standing in a corner of the kitchen with Jonathan and Hennessy in their suits and Barnhart in his fool turtleneck, they stuck out. Most of the other party-goers were dressed a little more comfortably. But Barnhart didn't care about normal. Hennessy always dressed like the world was watching. And Jonathan had a particularly lovely creature to impress.

A moment later, a different lovely creature approached: Mrs. Barnhart. Although she wasn't to Jonathan's taste, he couldn't help but appreciate how well the head detective had done for himself. The woman's eternal smile and sense of empathy forced everyone around her to like her. You just couldn't be annoyed, no matter what she did. Her ability to slap down her husband when he got too big for his britches didn't hurt either.

She patted Barnhart on his arm and looked back and forth between him and the partially-built cheese plate on a nearby counter. Finally, he got the hint and sauntered off. A boisterous show of chopping cheese followed, filling the kitchen with loud clattering sounds. Mrs. Barnhart smoothed her slightly frazzled hair and let out a puff of breath as she beamed at the two detectives.

"Sorry about that," she said. "I don't know what he said, but by Mr. Hennessy's face, I don't need to know."

"Don't mind Hennessy's face," Jonathan assured her. "I never do. It was just a little ribbing among professionals."

Hennessy took the moment to cough violently. He offered Mrs. Barnhart a pulled-groin sort of smile before returning to his brooding.

She looked at him and it was clear she wasn't fooled, but she nodded anyway. "Well, how have you boys been?" she asked them. "I know this Smith case has been rough on all of you at the station."

"The victim and the perpetrator both died," Hennessy stated. "After the initial legwork, there's not much left to do, ma'am."

"Nonsense. I've been married to an officer for almost twenty-five years. I know better than that. If the crooks don't get you, the paperwork will," she said with a light laugh.

Jonathan smiled and took a mug of hot coffee from the counter. A dozen more of the grey crockware vessels sat for other guests to find a second wind that night. He sipped from his and closed his eyes for a second. He personally thought coffee tasted the same way a dead polecat smelled, but he loved the way he hated it. The unpleasant sensation was a wake-up call by itself.

He opened his eyes and nodded to Mrs. Barnhart. His voice was too soft to reach other nearby inquisitive ears as he spoke. "So, Frank shared the details. Does he really plan to give the whole story tonight?"

"That's why so many came," she said brightly. "I don't know half of them well. Some are just friends of friends."

"I didn't realize every Clyde in Detroit cared about one more murder," Hennessy muttered.

Mrs. Barnhart smiled sadly.

Jonathan didn't say what he was thinking, that the chief wouldn't care for Barnhart spilling on a case that was still officially open. The police chief was notorious for his hatred of the press. Then again, the chief and head detective were so close that Barnhart would have to burn someone to death himself to incur any real punishment. And there was no point in offending his hosts. Instead, Jonathan smiled politely.

"What do you think really happened, ma'am?" he asked.

Hennessy clucked, caught Jonathan's patronizing glance, and decided to ease out of the conversation and into the den.

If Mrs. Barnhart had been hurt, she didn't show it. She pressed at a crease in her grey dress as she spoke.

"If you don't mind my saying so, Detective," she said, "only a busybody makes up her mind without sitting on all the facts first. I don't rightly know what to think. And I don't suppose me thinking one way or another has a bearing on the case, does it?"

"It still interests me. There's no official story yet, so why not hear your version?"

"Well I could, but I have some more drinks to prepare."

"And there is nothing I would rather do than help," Jonathan said, nodding gravely. "Lead the way."

She beamed at him and they joined Barnhart at the counter.

There, he poured cups of coffee and some drinks far stronger than that for passing guests. The missus and her husband kept throwing out different wild theories they had heard over the past few days. Jonathan grinned and groaned along at the stupidity of some of the concepts. The husband and wife were laughing over the alien conspiracy theory when a stooping man with more grey than brown in his mustache squeezed his way up to the kitchen counter between Jonathan and Mrs. Barnhart.

"I'll help with the drinks, dear," the man told Mrs. Barnhart. He had his back turned completely to Jonathan as if nobody were there.

Red flag. Jonathan sucked in a slow breath and pasted up a smile identical to the one on the new White Knight memorial on Belle Isle. Perfectly genteel. No hint of warmth. Solid iron.

"No need to worry yourself, sir," Jonathan said softly. "I'm helping with the drinks. You can just go enjoy the—"

"I was speaking to the Barnharts, mister," the man said without turning. "Unless they're paying you, then I suggest you go enjoy your coffee outside."

"Sammy!" Mrs. Barnhart cried, her smile wavering. "Detective Parks is a family friend."

"'Detective'?" the man demanded. Sammy turned and eyed Jonathan for the first time. "You, working with the police?"

"That surprises you, sir?"

"I didn't think your kind held much with the law."

The man's tone tickled Jonathan's gut. Despite his best effort, his smile soured into a bit of a sneer. He dropped to a stage whisper. "Actually, I work as an informant. You know, because of all my underworld connections."

"Parks," Detective Barnhart warned.

But this Sammy fellow seemed impervious to sarcasm. He squinted back and forth between the two detectives.

"Okay, okay. But how do we know you don't pass information back over to your gang pals?" Sammy demanded.

"For Heaven's sake," Mrs. Barnhart said. She had buried her face in one delicate hand that failed to hide the sanguine glow in her cheeks.

"No ma'am, that's a valid question!" Jonathan responded. His straight face stayed true only because he couldn't decide whether to laugh or roll his eyes at the short, richly-dressed old fool in front of him. "The chief planted a bomb in my car in case I ever wander off the straight and narrow."

"Parks! A word?" Barnhart growled.

Mrs. Barnhart refused to look at either of them as host led guest into a small laundry room and closed them both in.

As he stood there, Jonathan's mouth was pinched, and he felt a tremor in his spine. It made him want to scratch, or shudder, or clench his fists, and he wasn't sure which one first.

He had never been particularly badly treated. No more than the average man in Detroit, at least. But there had always been an undeniable feeling that he had been wronged. When he had been so wronged, he wasn't sure. When someone did sneer down his nose at Jonathan, he felt a strong sense of familiarity. He was life's punching bag, and he took every knock with a smile: that feeling stank in his nostrils like rotten meat whenever something went wrong. The urge to stand up and rebel against these injustices stroked at his old fingers and clenched on his spine.

But what injustices? When he tried to remember what had happened to make him feel this way, he couldn't touch it. The angry loneliness would eat him inside, burn him alive. But from where?

What was making him want to lay into the head detective right here and now? Barnhart had a reason to be upset.

And upset he was.

"What was that?" the head detective demanded. A vein on his head had turned a deathly shade of blue. "Wait. No. I don't want to know, so don't tell me. But Sammy is an old family friend, and next time you just...you speak to him, and you show the man some respect. Got it?"

Jonathan wrenched his face into a semblance of passivity. "Of course."

"Of course, 'of course'." Barnhart rubbed his eyebrows. "Everyone knows you and Detective Hennessy are under me. And then you go sassing an old man. How does that reflect on me? What kind of message does it send to people about my work? Our positions as civil servants?"

With a tiny sigh that barely escaped his pursed lips, Jonathan nodded. There was no rational argument that Frank Barnhart would listen to at the moment. The man's brains were drowning in the same stench that wafted out on his breath at every word.

"People respect us, so be respectable," Barnhart finished with a wheeze.

"Of course." Jonathan snatched up a full can from a nearby ice chest. He tossed it to Barnhart and hoped it was as flat as his voice was. "Beer for the road, boss?"

Barnhart fumbled the can, but finally mastered the feat of hand-to-eye coordination. He peered at Jonathan through narrowed, bleary eyes. Then, a broad smile slowly appeared.

"That's the Parks I know," he rumbled. "Now get out there and mind your manners, or else the missus will skin us both."

"Of course."

What he meant was *stuff it*, naturally. Or something stronger.

Barnhart opened the door and ushered Jonathan back into the kitchen. And just when Jonathan began to let himself breathe again, he turned the corner and saw a room full of cold eyes facing him. Mrs. Barnhart had vanished from the little kitchen and the warmth had gone with her.

He steeled himself and looked each of the other guests in the eye. Some were curious, hoping to see their host berate a subordinate. They glanced away quickly when he met their gazes. Other guests looked smug, and their sneers curled hard when he dared to look back at them. A few were outright angry. Perhaps they had heard him tease that old Sammy, or maybe they just didn't like the look of him.

One bitter face wasn't glaring at Jonathan. Hennessy had a flat, empty expression aimed at Barnhart that scared Jonathan more than the other faces. He had seen that kind of suppressed anger in more than one man, right before things went south. Ignoring the other looks and whispers, he made a beeline for the other detective.

"Easy, Hennessy," he murmured. "Let's find a quiet corner of the yard and some brews and wait for the main event, all right?"

Before the man could reply, a feminine voice interrupted.

"Mind yourself, detective. You giving Mrs. Barnhart a terrible time already."

He felt his face flush. Naturally. A man hunts for a beautiful creature, and the woods are empty. He stops to relieve himself, and the beautiful creature appears to watch in disgust.

"Ms. Susan," Hennessy said with respect, though a storm was still rolling in behind those dark eyes.

Jonathan turned to behold Susan Moore. In her late forties, she still had the figure of a thirty-year-old and the mouth of a teenager. If it wasn't controlled by the polished, precisely-machined inner workings that were Susan's mind, she'd be impetuous. She wore a distinguished yellow dress and had her wild, black curls cropped a little shorter than when Jonathan had last beheld her. It suited her.

However, as one of Mrs. Barnhart's best friends, it was clear that neither Jonathan nor Hennessy was suiting her at the moment.

"Don't 'Ms. Susan' me, you," she retorted. "I don't see you making things easier on the poor woman neither, moping and sulking around like a child."

"I do apologize for the scene," Jonathan said quickly. "A joke gone—"

"Joke?" she demanded, eyes crinkling at the corners. "That wasn't a joke and you aren't a comic. Now find a corner and lurk in it, like you two do best."

"Little fish only lurk when there's sharks in the open water," Hennessy mumbled.

Ms. Susan Moore rolled her eyes and herded them into the den, away from the other watching eyes. Seeing the troublemakers safely out of her friend's sanctuary, she spun on her heel and strutted off with a huff. Jonathan watched her walk away, his heart slowly returning to its normally scheduled program.

"Man, why you're sweet on Officer Moore's crusty old bird, I'll never know," Hennessy said in his low, distant thunder growl. "God rest his soul, I mean."

"I'm not 'sweet' on Susan, or anyone else," Jonathan explained. "We aren't schoolchildren here. I respect her, is all."

Hennessy grunted and lost interest in talking. Jonathan felt something like disappointment that the topic wouldn't be discussed further, but he banished the thought as silly.

For nearly half an hour, the two men drank and ate and watched the middle class bustle about the Barnharts' den and kitchen. No one seemed to know what to do with themselves besides stuff their faces and shoot the breeze. Then again, maybe that's all some people needed to do. Jonathan had never excelled at relaxing when work was much more fulfilling, but most people disagreed. They were enjoying the slow, meaningless pace of the party.

Perhaps the guests needed something relatively unimportant to distract them from the rest of the world. The Korean War had ended years ago, but things were still frosty with the Soviet Union. Newspaper articles hinted at signs of full-blown war. President Eisenhower seemed a little too set against the Soviets for most people's liking. And in past months, everything from car sales to employment had staggered for the first time since World War II. Jonathan remembered the Great Depression and reckoned that most other Americans did too, not that anyone would dare mention it now. There was plain speaking, and then there was a jinx.

There was also the uproar over the Lithuanian, the self-proclaimed White Knight. Jonathan doubted he was the only man claiming to be a god right now, but he seemed to be the most popular one. He had all but thrown the Russians out of the little spit of frozen land over there. Rumors abounded about this sign or that miracle he had performed, and the pope had declared the man a heretic, which made the White Knight all the more well-known. Catholics feared he would be the next Muhammad. Others like Jonathan feared he would be the next Adolf Hitler. It would be easier to ignore if dozens of their neighbors weren't leaving for Europe to join him.

So maybe these people did need the distraction of this party. Jonathan watched faces light up as they gossiped about this or that gang or other famous criminals as of late. To them, this was an oddball theme party. It was as funny to Jonathan as it was frustrating to see the dark stains of Detroit be treated like actors or musicians. But he wasn't about to inject himself into that mess. He just started his second cup of coffee in warm silence.

"I think I've finally figured it out," Hennessy mumbled into his own cup.

"Oh. You're talking again, Hennessy?" Jonathan asked.

The younger detective ignored him. "The chief, Detective Barnhart, and the rest, they don't listen to the facts on the Smith case because they don't care if it's solved. It's a big mystery for their parties. For their friends and their kids."

"That's crazy even for you," Jonathan said. "Why would anyone, especially Barnhart, want to leave a case unsolved? It's like saying a plumber would rather leave a toilet overflowing because he likes the look of fountains in the park."

"I tell you, that's the nicest answer I got. There's some not-so-nice ones, too."

"And what's that about not listening to facts? What facts? Your facts? You've got a theory to beat Barnhart's?"

Hennessy primly bit into the relish-drowned end of a hot dog and slid Jonathan a look. "And you don't?"

Jonathan pursed his lips. There was no point in sharing a pet theory.

"Uh-huh," Hennessy said. "I'm sure half the force thinks it's a closed case. The difference is that I worked it and they didn't. Barnhart isn't the only one to look into that fire and study that body. He's just the one who didn't follow up all the leads."

"You actually have a full theory? A working theory?" Jonathan said, leaning over with growing interest. Perhaps he wasn't the only one who had done his homework. "What?"

"Barnhart and the rest think that it was just another burglary gone bad, right?" Hennessy rumbled. "But I looked into how the fire started. I—"

"Discussing the case?" broke in a new voice.

The tall stranger from the backyard stood nearby—the one who had known Jonathan's name. He sat in a wooden chair nearby and leaned forward like a fellow accomplice. He was all smiles again. That, of course, spread a grimace across Hennessy's face faster than a body could butter bread.

"It's police business," Hennessy rumbled.

"Then why did Frank let slip that he might spill the story tonight if he has a few too many?" The stranger's eyes twinkled.

"What Detective Barnhart says is between him and his superiors," Jonathan said. "I don't need that heat from, well, 'the heat,' as kids call us."

"And if the records are still sealed from the public, then why are you two discussing it, sir? You gave me the impression that you were not on the case," the stranger reasoned.

"Again, not your business, *friend*," Hennessy told him. "We can talk because we trust each other. We might as well be partners out there." (Jonathan thought that last part a bit much, but wouldn't say so and hurt Hennessy's feelings, in case the man had any.) "We have to stick together, being the only men of color on the force."

Jonathan hissed between his teeth. His gaze darted about the room, and he hoped none of the very fair-skinned guests nearby had overheard. "Easy, Hennessy."

"It's tough in there for people like us, I imagine," the stranger said gravely. Jonathan stifled a groan as he saw Hennessy's expressive eyes ignite with the added fuel.

"Yeah, it's tough! Every promotion I ever earned on the force had to be ripped out of the grubby claws of those—Well," he amended, seeing Jonathan's iron look, "I never got what I didn't earn five times over. I've been transferred between precincts like you wouldn't believe, too, because these captains don't like my melanin."

"Have any of them told you as much?" the stranger murmured, leaning forward.

"One did. After a while, you learn the signs."

"Some are hateful, to be sure," Jonathan offered. "But if—"

"There's no 'but if' involved." Hennessy flicked his fingers as if banishing a foul smell. "You got stomped by the high-and-mighty too. Why do you think you weren't on the case, huh?"

Jonathan forced himself to keep cool. "Because I was too involved, I imagine."

The stranger looked back and forth between the two detectives a few times and seemed to do some quick arithmetic.

"You! You're that officer who let Smith get off easy the first time, aren't you?" The stranger whistled slowly. "What possessed you, man? Shortest road to getting blackballed."

"That's not why he got blackballed," Hennessy snorted. He downed the last of his coffee.

"I did what was right," Jonathan said, meeting their gazes easily. "I joined the force because I believe in the law. And law protects people until we are sure, *dead* sure, that they're guilty. We weren't dead sure then that Smith was a murderer, only a lousy firebug. But that hurt Detective Barnhart's feelings. So, when I wasn't demanding Smith's head with the rest of them this time around, he made sure I stayed out of it."

"And I make sure you stay in it," Hennessy said with a wink. He nodded to the other man. "When the others were gone from the crime scene for a few minutes, I let slip the fact that the evidence was otherwise unattended to our boy here. He got in and got out again, and Barnhart never knew."

Jonathan coughed loudly and made Hennessy flinch.

"Perhaps the less said, the better," Jonathan stated. "Besides, departmental politics can't be what you came to the party for, Mr...."

"George," the stranger said. He offered a wan smile as he stood from the old chair. "And I'll take a hint. I've taken enough of you gentlemen's time."

Hennessy stared at Jonathan while George walked off. Jonathan blinked back at the detective.

"What?"

"'What,' what? I was expecting you to be calling the man back, telling him you still wanted to chat and discuss your feelings," Hennessy countered.

"I don't always want to chat," Jonathan said.

"What? Couldn't be because he gave us a fake name, could it?" Hennessy said.

Jonathan gave him a startled look.

Before he could reply, a misty shadow landed on their corner. Frank Barnhart joined them on the wooden chair that George had left a moment ago.

Jonathan eyed the half a dozen or so others who also meandered into the den. He could feel his head buzz with the added presence of borderline drunk strangers now cramping the room.

Three women in red, yellow, and white pencil skirts were loudly judging some third party who had dared to pair a poodle skirt with flats. A young gentleman in a newsy cap was actually reading a partially wadded newspaper as he followed the group into the room, and somehow avoided colliding with anything. Two husbands and wives compared local supermarket prices and complained about the sudden inflation.

But they were all following Barnhart. Jonathan could spot a tail a block away, and these people weren't as practiced as the gang watches he normally tangled with. The guests were eyeing the host. Tension hummed in the house, and everyone else was talking too loudly to hear it.

It made his scalp itch. Inhaling slowly, Jonathan suppressed his annoyance with a gentle smile aimed at the man responsible for pulling him off a case.

"You boys weren't talking about the Smith Case, were you?" Barnhart said before muffling a burp with his hand.

Jonathan had stood up and thrown out "I'll be back in a moment" nearly before he realized he was stepping out of the room.

Perhaps he wasn't in the mood to hide his annoyance after all. He considered leaving the party completely. On the way out, he'd apologize to Mrs. Barnhart and avoid Susan. Patch things with her when they were both less stressed. Then he could just slide back into his car, go home, have a bath, and get over the fact that not everything in the world came to a neat conclusion, and justice didn't always prevail.

He paused next to a wall mirror and stared at the empty face in the scratched, flecked surface. Jonathan Parks. Crinkles at the eyes. Aged. Smiling. Weary. Old and tired. Groomed but flustered. A quirk dragged a corner of his mouth upwards...humor? Malice? If Jonathan had met himself near a crime scene, he'd have detained that character without hesitation.

With a sigh, he decided that he needed to look in mirrors more often, or not at all. He made his mind up on another matter as well.

It took a few minutes of searching to find Susan. Once he did, he waited patiently for her to finish her conversation before approaching. She was in the backyard, refilling coffee mugs as if she were a third host. He stood behind a cluster of 20-somethings with slicked-back hair and dark jackets. An early dew was already settling on the brown grass, glistening on their shoes. His own Gucci loafers threatened to soak through, and he shifted uncomfortably until Susan had emptied her pot of bean juice.

The intermingling smell of smoke and coffee had caused his stomach to start rumbling, and a trip inside for food began to seem worth the risk. He stepped forward and intercepted Susan. The sudden caution in her stance warned him off, but he ignored his gut.

"I misspoke earlier in front of Mrs. Barnhart," he confessed. "An impetuous reaction to a guest. How is she?"

"Always so formal, with your *petuous* and *misspoke*," Susan said, though she smiled slightly. "But you know Mrs. Barnhart. She wouldn't tell you even when she *is* embarrassed."

"A strong woman," Jonathan mused.

"A very strong woman," Susan corrected. "She has to be, married to a cop."

Susan started back through the crowds towards the kitchen

door and didn't seem to care whether he followed or not. Jonathan did, evading drifting guests.

"If she was fine, then why are you still angry at me?" Jonathan said with a short laugh.

"Angry? Who says I'm angry?" she tossed back without turning.

He noticed a nearby older couple staring, so he followed her more closely and lowered his voice. "Don't give me that, Susan. I can always tell when you're angry."

"It's usually whenever your big mouth is open."

"Well now, that hurts."

She turned and beamed at him. The smile was as fake and pink as a yard flamingo, but it still made him chuckle.

"I am serious!" he said, straightening his face again. "What can I do to make this—whatever this is—make it right?"

She dropped her forced smile, scoffed, and turned away. A bit of a rock in the yard tripped her and she nearly lost control of the tray to the amusement of those nearby. Jonathan leaped forward to help. But Susan snatched the tray out of his reach, nearly toppling the mugs on it.

"You keep your helpful hands to yourself, mister," she snapped.

"Susan…" he protested, then paused at hearing raised voices inside.

She must have heard them as well because Jonathan found the entire tray of empty mugs and the coffee pot thrust into his hands without so much as a "please." He followed her fluttering yellow dress like a ship following the rising sun.

Back in the den, Hennessy and Barnhart were discussing the case at a volume normally reserved for airplane engines. They weren't screaming, really. Just disagreeing. While screaming.

"How? How can you possibly be that stupid?" Barnhart demanded. Hennessy's nostrils flared. "Me, stupid? You're refusing to see the facts right in—" Barnhart snapped, "Is this another conspiracy theory to you, that imagination of—" "You are lazy, *sir*, and bull-rushed your pitiful idea straight to the chief!" "You're a *worthless* detective and an attention-grabbing piece—!"

"Quiet!"

Jonathan's roar drowned out both Hennessy's bass and Barnhart's snarl. All eyes turned to him.

"Please, sirs," he added in a conversational tone, breathing hard. He motioned to the two men as they stared from behind drawn faces. "Detective Hennessy, you're not respecting our host."

"Thank you," Barnhart said.

Susan stepped up next to him and turned on the head detective. "Detective Barnhart, you're not showing much respect to your wife, neither, ruining this party in front of your guests. And stop your fool yelling at that detective."

Jonathan was afraid Barnhart was going to take her back into the washroom as well, but the man grinned sheepishly and flushed even redder through his beer-rouge.

At that, a handful of the guests chuckled and some of the tension eased.

Hennessy wasn't done though. "Well fine, we can all be civil-like and solve this the way men are supposed to. And, all civil-like, I still say that your theory doesn't hold water, Head Detective."

Another voice broke in, calm and smooth like Tennessee whiskey. It was the nosy man again, George.

"Mr. Barnhart, I think you've kept us in suspense long enough. Who here would like to hear about the fire?"

A loud, giggling crescendo of *me*'s and *Yes, lets'* filled the room. Barnhart's chest seemed to double in size as he looked around. Susan and Jonathan found themselves pushed forward as more of the guests from outside tried to insert themselves into the den.

He was quite sure he would receive a withering glare if he dared to glance at Susan, so he watched the two other detectives settle into opposite sides of a worn yellow couch across the room. A floor lamp threw half shadows on them from under a lampshade so frilled it could have passed as a crouching terrier. They were making a right show of it.

Detective Barnhart cleared his throat, and the first act began.

"Right, this is the *official* report, the one that you'll all read about in the newspapers," he said. "You all know that the perpetrator was a notorious arsonist and thief. Name of Sidney Smith. We've, ah, put him away before. Not long enough, though. He got out and disappeared."

"How does a man like that disappear?" asked a man in a green cotton shirt that clashed with his black slacks.

"Unfortunately, it's not hard to vanish in Detroit," Barnhart said, his brow wrinkling. "He stopped checking in with his parole officer and left his last known address not two weeks after being released. We didn't think much of it at the time."

"Lot of ex-cons try to fade into the background after getting out," Hennessy rumbled. "You get caught, it's embarrassing, you hide your face a while. We wouldn't have cared if he hadn't been on parole."

Barnhart took over again, speaking loudly. "But then this little Italian family off Joy Road comes home after mass one Sunday and finds their back door busted. They smelled kerosene everywhere in the main bedroom, but it hadn't caught fire. All the wife's jewelry in the upstairs chest-of-drawers, gone. Good silver, gone. Even a small fireproof safe they had was missing, though we found that abandoned in the corner of the backyard later. Smith must have been scared off before he could crack it or bust it open. The crook had never tried safes before, but he'd never been that desperate either.

"And he hit another house two nights later. We actually found traces of the accelerant splashed on the rugs and on some drapes, but the owner came home before Smith was finished. Scared him off."

Jonathan grunted. "He actually saw Smith at the scene? I don't remember that victim being a witness in the report."

Barnhart cast him a magnanimous smile. "Potato potahto, detective. I'm trying to sum up a weeks-long investigation here."

Stifling an irritated twitch, Jonathan raised his hands in surrender and melted back into the crowd.

Someone asked, "What about the victim? Who died in the fire?"

"So, then we tried to track down Smith's whereabouts," Barnhart continued as if he hadn't heard. "Leaned on some local sources. Put out an APB on the man. Didn't help at first. Smith must have had something stashed away from previous robberies so that he didn't have to come up for air. The man torched and presumably robbed eight different houses and one cannery before we caught him last time, and since he always used enough gasoline to drown a whale, there are countless valuables that could be burned. Or could be in his pockets. No one knows. Of course, that's what the thug was going for.

"But years ago, when that ninth job led to murder—" Jonathan twitched at the word *murder* but didn't speak up this time "—the man, pardon the expression, got burned. Arson is one thing. Killing another human being is another, and not nearly as easy as you'd think. Smith obviously wasn't prepared for the emotional ramifications of murder—" This time, Jonathan swore that Barnhart looked directly at him when he said it. "—and happened to be seen by an off-duty detective as Smith fled the scene. Between his testimony and the small mountain of evidence I had accumulated over the fire spree, we had Smith in cuffs within the day. That's why he went to prison the first time."

In the brief dramatic pause following Barnhart's reminiscing, the sound of Detective Hennessy popping the bones in his neck was magnified. Magnified, and slightly disgusting. Susan snorted softly beside Jonathan.

"Yes, we were very proud of you, Detective," Hennessy said with a grunt. "But the man's question may be more pertinent to the current discussion. Namely, who died in the fire two days ago?" And before Barnhart could blurt out the answer, Hennessy stated, "A widow named Nancy Greene," into the attentive silence.

There were no gasps of shock, no mutterings of recognition. Nancy had been a fairly reclusive woman. She lived off of her late husband's savings, ate small meals in the silence of her own house, and, to the best of Jonathan's investigative talents, had only ever seemed to visit the public library or her one friend, a fellow widow named Mary Stout. Nancy would occasionally pick up groceries, fuel for her heaters in the winter, and oil and replacement parts for her ancient bicycle in the summer. She had led the quiet life of a retiree who is comfortable with solitude.

Her neighbors had described her as crotchety, though the news of the tragedy softened *crotchety* to *withdrawn and unassuming.* But still, Jonathan was surprised that not one person present recognized the name in this context.

Then George, or whatever his name was, said, "Nancy Greene. That wouldn't happen to be the same Nancy Greene who went cruising for a bruising on the radio?"

A few people's eyes lit up as the wonder that is the human memory shifted into gear.

Barnhart nodded. "She appeared on the Holloway Hour about a week after Smith was released, and she tore him a good one. One of her friends lost everything during his original spree. Nasty business. A lot of anger. And well-deserved. Shouldn't have painted herself as a target, though. Poor woman."

"Murdered by a madman," Charles Hennessy growled.

"Killed when the fire flared up, just like Smith," Barnhart corrected. "Robbery. Only."

"Murder. Suicide."

"You are kidding me, Hennessy!"

The two started squabbling again while the audience watched with breath held...Except for Jonathan, who groaned and turned to Susan.

"Do you believe these two?" he whispered.

"Yeah. Yeah, I believe them cause they act like that all the time. Who I can't believe is you, mister," Susan said. "Like you don't act just like them."

Jonathan frowned, hurt. "When did I argue with someone like that, especially with a fellow officer?"

Her mouth opened, eyes flashing. It stayed open for a moment. The flashing eyes darted back and forth across the room, searching her memory. Her mouth slid shut like the world's grimmest zipper.

"See? I mind my manners."

At that, she cocked her hip. "Fine. But you do have the opposite problem. You get yourself in trouble and then let yourself get stomped on—"

"By people like you, Susan Moore?" he asked with an innocent blink.

"I just put you in your place when you forget where that is."

"And what place is that?"

Again, she seemed confused. But Jonathan felt his own face flush this time. He hadn't been very good at flirting in school, and he was decades removed from that heyday.

"What?" she finally asked.

"You, ah, said you only badger me to put me in my place, and I was asking what place that was, and you were supposed to say—I mean, the general response would be something casual and flirtatious as well," he stammered.

He glanced around at the people crammed around them, but fortunately, they seemed to be more interested in the murder-thievery theories as opposed to an older man's attempt at coy banter. Hennessy was piling on evidence of premeditation. Barnhart stubbornly threw Smith's death as proof positive again and again.

None of that was new news to Jonathan. He ignored the argument for the living and breathing person before him.

"Are you trying to flirt with me, Mr. Parks?" Susan asked.

"Don't read into it," he said, blowing out of his lips as his stomach knotted. "I'm rusty."

"Rust makes it sound like you've actually used that tool before. You ever romanced a lady?"

"How rude, miss. I'll have you know I've spent hours and hours seriously considering the subject."

"Jonathan, you are a hoot," Susan murmured, shaking her head.

"But you got to know we're too old for games. And after Michael passed, I just don't have the spirit left to do that kind of dance no more."

Something in Jonathan's chest gave a tiny lurch and slumped against his ribs. He nodded and did his best to look stoic.

"I didn't think anyone could make 'no' sound so poetic," he said softly. At least, it was supposed to be soft. He actually had to raise his voice and lean in to make himself heard over the vehement conversation between his two fellow detectives. "As long as you're not saying no because you're hoping for a miracle."

"A woman's got a right to any hopes she wants," Susan retorted, the small smile fading from her lips. "But I'm no fool. If the Lord wanted to give my Michael back, he'd have sent an angel to that ambulance. Mr. White Knight can keep his voodoo to himself, thank you."

"Good," Jonathan said, backing off with a wave of surrender. "Glad to hear it. I just wanted to know you were handling it well."

"I can handle myself, yourself, or any other self that gets into my business, don't you worry."

He was mid-chuckle when he realized the room had gone quiet. The party guests were all staring at him. The suffocation slowly came around from the sudden attention.

"Now I didn't laugh that loud, did I?" he drawled, meeting a few gazes.

"Which is it, Parks?" Barnhart asked, burping slightly.

"Which...?" he asked in exasperation. The rest of the party was interrupting a rather important moment for him.

"I told him you had an opinion on the case, so spill it!" Hennessy rumbled. "Which one of us is on the level: me, or Mr. Head Detective here?"

Jonathan continued to note the mass of eyes staring at him. Mostly light browns with some blues and hazels tossed into the field. All curious now. He straightened his suit jacket and sighed.

"You know that my opinion can't be trusted," he said, voice

heavy with feigned regret. "Obviously I'm blinded by my history with Mr. Smith, fooled by his sob stories, hoodwinked by—"

"We *get it*," Hennessy interrupted, to a few titters from the others.

"Sarcasm!" Barnhart belched. "Yes. See? We get it. Now come on, even you can see that Smith wasn't stupid enough to murder someone while the entire city hunted him."

"Leading the witness!"

Jonathan shifted his weight, turned, and winked at Susan. This might be fun after all. So, she thought he let people walk over him, did she?

"Don't worry, Detective Hennessy. Contrary to popular belief, I am not that easily led," he stated, to the general discomfort of those around him. "Murder or failed theft, is it? Let me at least explain my reasoning before I give my answer, or else I'll never get a chance.

"Fact. The victim was the middle-aged wife of a deceased Ford factory worker. Work accident. Small payout from the company. She lived alone and kept only a tight group of friends. No church affiliation or other such organization that we know of, all of which made her a good target, right?"

He got a few nods. Some of the younger folk were clearly filled to the brim with facts already, but other grayer heads seemed interested enough to leave him control of the room.

He cleared his throat and continued. "Fact. The victim knew another, previous victim of Mr. Smith's. She was predisposed to dislike him, predisposed enough to rant against the man's reputation, sanity, and even his potential ancestry, all while on public radio. She definitely made herself a target at that point."

"But enough to kill?" Barnhart pressed. "You were the one who swore before a court that he wasn't a killer."

"I agree with Frank!" George called out.

"Thanks! Who are you again?" Barnhart said with a frown.

"In good time!" Jonathan replied. "More facts. Mr. Sidney Smith was the son of a local mechanic and had three sisters. He learned to appreciate the combustion engine from watching his father work on motors and gained an unfortunate love of sneaking into junkyards and setting old cars ablaze to see if he could escape. He claimed it was practice for if he were ever in a wreck himself. And yes, that story came from my talk with the man during his original trial.

"Even more unfortunately, his fascination with car wrecks and car fires clarified into a love of *setting* fires. When he didn't make it as a mechanic, he turned to a more exotic trade. Fact: he was a terrible mechanic but actually quite skilled as an arsonist. The thefts he carried out under the cover of the fires were more to fuel his habit than any—" Jonathan held his hands up at the resounding groans "—thing else. Sorry for that pun. Regardless, Smith is...*was* a man who lived for thrills."

"So what?" asked someone from the crowd.

He glanced about but couldn't see who'd spoken up. "That brings me to my first wild assumption: that maybe Sidney Smith didn't hit those houses after getting out of prison."

People started talking all at once. Not in shock at his brilliance, naturally, but a dozen different opinions in complete disinterest to his oddball theory.

"Let the man speak, for Heaven's sake!" roared George.

None were more surprised than Jonathan. But seeing that even Barnhart and Hennessy paused following the man's outburst, he continued while he could.

"Thank you, 'Mr. George.' It's not something I can prove. Just a working hunch," he proclaimed. "But if the Smith I knew had to choose between burning something and stealing something, he would have made sure he got his precious flames first. And yes, he may have been rusty after prison, but two botched jobs in a row? That wasn't the work of someone who torched a whole cannery back in the day and escaped."

"Who else would bother?" Barnhart asked. He sounded bored and a little frustrated. Having worked with and for the man for years, Jonathan knew the man missed the limelight. It was just how the detective operated. "We've not got a sniff of a copycat arsonist," he mumbled. "And what are chances that someone else would start right as he gets outta the big house? None. That's the chances."

Hennessy, still seated next to their host on the couch, wrinkled his nose at what must have been a glorious haze of beer breath.

"I agree!" Jonathan yelled, making those nearest him jump. Despite himself, he felt excitement drowning some of his politeness. People were actually listening to him.

"You agree," repeated Hennessy. "You think that he didn't try to burglarize and burn those other houses, and he didn't try to murder a woman he must've hated?"

"No, I don't agree with that," Jonathan said.

"*Hah!* Detective Parks, esteemed officer of thirty-some-odd years, disagrees with that assumption of yours," Hennessy crooned. "That man murdered that poor woman and got his due. It's as—"

"It was more likely manslaughter," Jonathan said, his voice just barely loud enough to be heard.

Hennessy actually growled at that, and Barnhart rolled his eyes.

"Not that worn-out sentiment. It's the trial all over again," Hennessy said.

"I meant—" Jonathan started, then realized he had lost the room. People were again ignoring him. He gritted his teeth, letting the slight pain in his gums stiffen his resolve. "I don't mean he accidentally killed her. She killed *him!*"

He held up his hands at the wave of protests. "No! Hear me out, gentlemen. Smith has the motive and the means to burn down Ms. Greene's house, yes. But what about the first two break-ins? They occurred between the time of Patricia Greene's public attack on him and her house fire. Why would he put every officer in Detroit on his tail just to steal some hard-to-hock necklaces?"

"For practice," Barnhart yelled. "For the love…Why's it gotta be so fancy complicated with you two?"

"Practice? Possible but unlikely. There was no value in it for a broke arsonist, entertainment or otherwise. But what if someone else, an amateur...? What if someone else did it? Someone might want to frame him, have him locked up again. Someone who hated him. Ms. Greene seemed almost too obvious a suspect in that respect, and that was a heavy crime to pull off for an older woman with no criminal past. She'd have to have more reason to frame an arsonist."

He stopped and took a draft of coffee. People waited. A toxic blanket of drink, sleepiness, and the stifling atmosphere in the room had shut down the conversation.

Briefly, he felt déjà vu. Surrounded by others, yet alone—almost feeling like a wall separated him from the rest of humanity. Jonathan tried to shake the sensation.

"We're closer to the truth now, actually. Greene was poor, living off a dwindling savings account with no income of her own," Jonathan said slowly. "Insurance fraud has a way of fixing problems if a body goes to the trouble of setting it up right. Insult a hated arsonist publicly. Fake his return to crime. Then burn down the house and play the traumatized victim while waiting for the insurance to pay."

"Except they found two bodies at this scene," Hennessy reminded the room. "Why was Smith there? Why didn't Greene live to collect on this insurance scam? Quite ineffective."

But Barnhart wore a deep frown. He fluttered his fingers at Jonathan. It took the junior detective a moment to realize he was being ordered to finish his theory.

"Without more evidence, I don't have that answer," Jonathan admitted. "Maybe she really did hate him enough to trick him into the house before setting fire to it. Maybe he actually did show up to confront her but at the worst possible time. You know we usually don't get full answers without confessions. Just one theory that fits better than the others. There's no doubt in my mind that she did it.

"When I did my own investigation, I noticed the kerosene heaters in the house. So, I hit the bricks until I tracked down the grocery that she bicycled to most frequently. The clerk wouldn't have remembered her at all, except that while other customers had been buying less and less fuel for their heaters with Spring coming, she had been stocking it up like she was expecting a second winter."

"Huh. Kerosene was used at the Italians' house," Barnhart said.

"...While Sidney Smith loved his easy-to-light, fresh-from-the-tank gasoline. And I'm willing to bet any man here that kerosene was used on the second failed arsonist attack as well. They were practice, all right, but not for Smith. Ms. Greene needed to figure out how to light a house on fire, and what better way than to resurrect her supposed attacker's crime spree?"

There was a moment of silence following that question. Jonathan had finally run out of steam, and everyone else was still processing it. He tried to melt back into the crowd behind him but found himself stuck alone in a small clearing amongst the sweaty forest of house guests. He did see Susan staring at him. If he wasn't mistaken, there was a tiny smile playing about her face.

He nodded at her. Proof positive that you could stand up for yourself without kicking other people's feet out from under them.

"So, I'm no policeman, but I have to ask," George finally said. "Out of all those details, how do you take away just that tiny answer, 'She tried to fool her insurance company'?"

Jonathan had been watching Susan, planning. Planning a campaign of gestures and kind words and dinners so complex that she couldn't help but give him a chance. He glanced around stupidly when he finally realized that the man had been speaking to him and was still waiting for an answer.

Jonathan Parks shook his head. "Don't get me wrong, whatever did happen that night, it was as big a mess as I hope to never see again. But everything comes down to one stupid decision, doesn't it? A single mistake doesn't define something as complicated as a life. But it can certainly end it. Yes, it can."

There was a brief, thoughtful pause, which was more than he expected.

Then Detectives Hennessy and Barnhart found their voices again and began debating details, comparing notes against

Jonathan's story. Susan and Mrs. Barnhart were whispering away in the corner, and the bevy of nameless guests around him broke back into their own storm of conspiracy theories.

Jonathan finished his coffee and whispered to no one in particular, "Take me home." He then followed his own order and left for home and a hot bath.

EON 9 – ALL THE FOOLS

The world of Mekrro burned. The streets of Mercy's Landing were masses of riots and slaughter, and the smoke of hundreds of fires mingled with the storm clouds above. And in the middle of it all, on a roof off the edge of the capital tower, Uunderspar, master and slave sat together. One was dressed all in dark hues and the other wore the gray of a technician. Both were covered in dark stains and were frail in their exhaustion.

"There's perfect harmony in the rising and the falling of humanity," the man in the black coat said. His own blood dribbled down out of the corroded holes in his armor under the trench coat. He licked his cracked lips.

And Delk0 stared at that injured man, sprawled against a collapsed beam on the landing porch. The doj didn't approach the mastermind. Even in Trip Mine's state, he might still have some torture left in those malicious bones of his.

Uunderspar shook beneath them. The second stages of the trap had been sprung. Trip Mine's bombs would finally do what the empire had failed to do. They would end Trip Mine.

The last faint wisps of acrid smoke and released sulfur floated into the red sky. The oily cloud dissipated. With that, the last sign of the fallen light ship had billowed away, away into the harsh winds of the firestorm that turned the surface of Mekrro beneath them into magma.

Distant mechanical screams filled the air. Shifting, amorphous shapes darted through the charcoal clouds ahead. Artificial lightning flashed with every exchange of fire. Did they know yet, those still fighting the battle above or on the grounds?

Did they know they weren't immortal anymore?

"This is harmony?" Delk0 wheezed. "This...madness? This destruction?"

"It's *bloody beautiful.*" A gurgle trickled out of Trip Mine as he fought to sit up straight. "But no. No. No! Perfect harmony is in the grand scheme."

"Enough with your 'grand scheme.' The 'grand scheme' ended everything," Delk0 said. "The empire burns. You'd have your allies tear the world asunder."

The pair, the last living organisms on the porch Uunderspar, both stared overhead at a metallic wail. The smoke-choked sky had opened enough to reveal a cluster of fighters, bombers, rippers, and AADs.

Two imperial fighters had slipped behind one of the rogues' rippers as they passed close to Uunderspar. The aircraft were so close that Delk0 saw the red fangs of the self-proclaimed King Dagon's emblem on the outmaneuvered craft. A legend among enforcers throughout the city and a close ally of Trip Mine, the muscled giant now swerved and phased back and forth erratically. It did little. Blast after blast of light and fire punished it from the forward cannons of the empire's automated ships.

As King Dagon's burning ripper fell past the landing porch, it was bisected by the continued onslaught. One half plummeted out of sight into the city below, while the other slammed into the tower with a thud that reached those on the porch. The imperials parted ways and disappeared into the roiling maelstrom of smoke.

"Lovely word, that," Trip Mine mumbled. Under his wide hat

brim, his dark eyes followed the descent of the King's shattered craft. "Asunder…"

Hours before the two stood on Uunderspar, Delk0 found himself alive yet again.

The darkness around him was broken only by a faint emerald glow from above. He was submerged. He drank liquid, breathed liquid, and felt nothing but liquid. His body was entirely relaxed. Only now, as he awakened, did his mind and spirit begin to fill the far reaches of his extremities. He could wiggle his toes a little. An eddy tickled his nose.

This was the fourth time he had been reborn during his stint as Trip Mine's butler. The occupational hazard of being the house slave of an occupational villain was the raids on his base of operations. And there was that one time that the man had made Delk0 a test subject for his latest explosive toy. That had been more humiliating than the raids.

But he struggled to remember how he had died this time. He knew he was Delk0, doj. It was a start. He worked for his master, Trip Mine. And he had died…How?

He had left the master's dinner in the safe room, tidied the bedroom, then secured the lab downstairs. Trip Mine had been missing for most of the day. Though he came and went at all hours as his various jobs demanded, so that hadn't been worrisome. Then Delk0 had gone to bed…

And woken up here. He must have died in his sleep. Perhaps the lab hadn't been as secure as he thought. After all, the master had some truly nasty surprises iced down there. Or they had been attacked again by a political enemy. Trip Mine had become more and more cold with the empire lately: dangerous, as they essentially controlled the world.

Regardless, the next step now was to wait for his crate to arrive back at Trip Mine's hideout.

People weren't born anymore, at least not on Mekrro. The entire planet was comprised of leadership and essential staff for the empire. Anyone who mattered had their soul bound to the Paradise facility on Jones' Island. When the living body was eventually destroyed, they were recalled and uploaded to their genetic duplicate on Jones' Island and shipped back to wherever the empire needed them.

As an artificial lifeform, Delk0 was always sent straight back to his master, Trip Mine. The man was a monster, a maniac. But he treated Delk0 and his other doj, 6Cin, as well as could be expected. When they disappointed him, they paid for it. When they performed as expected, they were ignored.

Every fourth moon or so, he would drag 6Cin along on a job. Delk0 rarely managed to probe her for details on what transpired, though she would always become much quieter during the days following one of those missions. Delk0 wondered if 6Cin was in transit back from Paradise as well, or if she had survived whatever had killed him.

"-*me?*"

What?

"*- can...listen to-* "

Delk0 heard a wavering call through the liquid. Strange. If he were conscious, he would have expected that his crate had arrived at Trip Mine's front step, probably a week or so after his initial death. But the metal sheath around him should have peeled away and released him by now. And he hadn't heard voices before.

"Hello," he tried to call, but there was no air in his lungs yet. He just managed to open and close his mouth like a worthless tuna.

He looked up into the warbling emerald light overhead and saw a new shadow. It moved.

"*Sorry...*"

The voice faded as the shadow vanished.

Delk0 had just settled himself to ignoring this anomaly when his body seized with an itch. Not just an itch. If every wooly sheep in the universe had been dumped in one pit, Delk0 could have rolled in it and been happier than he was now. His nerves rebelled. The sensation crawled into his limbs and fried his synthetic brain.

Even as the physical discomfort grew, his mind slid away. He felt as if he were being pulled by a current out of his physical body, and he immediately lost all sense of sight, touch, sound, everything.

He felt relief. Then fear. Then he was in a small room made of some kind of boards, with a desk, an ancient bed, and a human woman. When Delk0 tried to focus on anything, he became dizzy and the room faded completely. When he relaxed, he regained the vague impressions he was getting.

"...stop fighting! Don't make me throw you back like an undersized bass," came the fuzzy voice from earlier.

Obeying, he froze. The room floated around him like an image seen through the distorting heat of the desert.

"Better." The human turned around. She wore strange, loose beige pants and a vest jacket over long sleeves. She had a brown bowler, small compared to his master's more flamboyant hat. And her eyes were brown, unlike his own bright orange optics.

"Not here to talk, little one. Didn't want you here at all, but Willow needed to collaborate on this one. Knowledge and secrets together, apparently."

Delk0 floated.

The woman shrugged and shifted a sad brown hat on her head. The motion tousled her hair. *"Leave the work to us. All you have to do—"*

"Remember."

And there he was, elsewhere. There was grass underfoot. On Mekrro? And trees everywhere. What were trees? He wasn't sure, but he must have been around them his whole life. Just like his family. His beautiful wife and child.

But where were they? He seemed to be floating in the river. Just floating and waiting.

Then Delk0 felt something besides the faint currents in the lifeblood around him. Cold. Hard. Metal bars, all crisscrossed, rising from below. Raising him. He was sitting, then slumping, and now laying on it as he broke the surface. He spewed out about 6 liters of the embryonic liquid and stretched his limbs feebly as he looked around.

"Wondering if I'd find you here, mate," came a familiar drawling voice.

He looked up to see a tall man dressed in dark slacks, custom red and black body armor, and a leather trench coat over it all. He wore a wide-brimmed black hat over his dusky, clean-shaven face. Black hair and black eyes gleamed with sweat and joy respectively.

Trip Mine claimed he hadn't spent so much as five minutes designing his signature outfit as a rogue. And Delk0 believed him. It was garish and none too subtle. But the doj was still slightly calmer for having seen his master, as he was roughly hoisted to his feet and did his best to stand under his own power.

"This must be like coming home to you, huh?" Trip Mine said, turning away in the dim, verdant light.

Only then did Delk0 take stock of his surroundings. This wasn't home. The chamber he was in was chaotic, almost organically designed. Metal catwalks wound their way out of sight in every direction. Tanks big enough to hold small whales had been squeezed into every available space. Girders and titan archways supported the levels above them, and a peek between the catwalk and the nearby tank of lifeblood revealed more layers worming their way down through the metal cavern below.

"We're not…" Delk0 mumbled, then stopped at the foolishness of the remark.

"Right!" Trip Mine grunted, hands on his hips as he looked around. "This lovely hive of filth is the Paradise facility. Welcome back to Jones' Island, Delkie! Home of the dead. Birthplace of doj everywhere. Can't say I love the stench."

"Dojs can't smell," Delk0 repeated dully. He had to remind his master constantly.

"Don't care, mate. I sure can!" the supervillain called. He was already leaving, his long legs carrying him at a jaunty canter along the twisting catwalk.

Delk0 dutifully followed as they danced their way slowly upwards. The lights grew marginally brighter with each higher level they reached, and more and more of the lifeblood-filled vats seemed to contain mostly-grown occupants. Twice they dodged around transfer crates that were carrying newly inhabited bodies up to the surface of Jones' Island.

The simulated gravity current carrying the second one caught Delk0 and nearly dragged him off the path. Trip Mine snatched him back as the crate floated off into the canyon-like expanse between one side of the facility and the other.

Trip Mine grimaced and immediately let go of Delk0. He shook his glove as if he had felt the intense heat of the doj's naked arm through the leather. "You need clothes. Find some."

"Yes, of course," Delk0 responded, but he glanced around help-lessly at his alien surroundings. They didn't have suits on pegs in the depths of Paradise. By the looks of it, no living creature had been down here for years. "Where did you get your new outfit?"

"Ain't new. I came in to 'tour' the facility. You're just dead lucky I happened by your little bath *and* recognized you on my way out. And I do mean it. Dead. Lucky."

"You're here for the empire?" Delk0 gaped at his master.

Scoffing, Trip Mine turned and led them onwards. After half an eternity of climbing ramps on his new legs, Delk0 was relieved when they finally slipped into a cargo lift that took them up to Paradise's nerve center. They slipped down some office hallways. Trip Mine opted to sneak past a few doors with voices on the other side, and Delk0 suspected by the man's mannerisms that he wasn't supposed to be here.

The only people who approached Jones' Island, did so with permission from the Emperor himself, Dominum. The same Dominum who had created and controlled Trip Mine and his juiced-up criminal ilk.

Delk0 began to suspect how he had been killed.

But it was not the place of a slave to question the likes of Trip Mine. He…not the….

"Why do you act like the boss of me, mother?" Arssen snarled, causing Trip Mine to stop dead in his tracks. *"In front of everyone? You're worthless, Ursa, and I should have fed you to the Gray Ones eons ago. You insuf- "*

Trip Mine punched him in the face.

When the hall stopped spinning and Delk0 managed to pick himself off the floor, he thanked the dark gods that Trip Mine didn't have supernatural powers like many other villains, namely superior strength. Not that Delk0's nose was happy. As soon as he stood, Trip Mine shoved him against a wall and leaned in so close that his steamy breath slapped his slave's face.

"What did you say?" Trip Mine hissed, eyes narrow but unreadable.

Fearing a second strike, Delk0 whimpered.

"No, feed someone to what now? Spit it out, Delkie!" his master insisted.

Confused, Delk0 whispered, "Gray ones. Gray Ones? I don't know what I was saying. Software fatigue, or…Forgive me."

Trip Mine cast him a strange look and released him. Delk0 thought to ask him what it meant, but just then a noise down the hall sent the pair scurrying away.

The rage and hatred simmered in the back of Delk0's brain, fading but not disappearing. For the first time, Delk0 had a strange thought. He could kill Trip Mine.

Not that he wanted to. He didn't want to. He didn't. No. But so many people would be alive if his master would have just died years ago. Who knew what kind of good he'd do himself and others by taking on one last chore. His master's back was turned. The human wasn't even suspicious.

Delk0 shuddered and slunk forward.

Unlike the cavernous regeneration chamber below, the nerve center was fairly small, brightly lit, and simple to navigate. Trip Mine dragged them into the water closet the facility techs used on breaks. He scoured the staff lockers, breaking into one after another and mumbling to himself.

"Does no soul in this bloody place have a spare suit?" he mumbled.

Delk0 shifted his weight in discomfort, aware of his own nudity and how it was inconveniencing his master. But then his sensitive ears picked up a sound in the hall outside. Even with his human senses, Trip Mine already seemed to be expecting the intruder and faced the door as the newcomer walked into the water closet.

The Paradise tech froze as soon as he saw the pair of them there. Delk0 wondered what the human thought of an outlandishly dressed henchman of Dominum and a naked doj slave in his changing room.

"Who are you?" the tech demanded. His frizzy black hair bounced slightly as he glanced between the two of them. "You're not supposed to be here."

"G'day. Now, your suit, mate," Trip Mine drawled.

"No," mumbled Delk0 with a sick realization as to what was about to happen.

The tech had a look of incredulity splayed across his narrow features and kept shifting his weight from one leg to the other, obviously in bad need of the water closet's amenities.

"Wait, are you the reason coms are down?" he asked. "I told you, you're—"

Pfft.

Delk0 had looked away in time, knowing his master. But, horribly, the sound of the man's head was not as muffled as the retort of Trip Mine's armor-shredding pistol.

"And I told *you*, 'your suit'," Trip Mine said with a barracuda's smile. He motioned to the fallen man and looked meaningfully at Delk0.

The doj stood there, refusing. So, Trip Mine buried the toe of his shiny leather shoe in the fork of his slave's legs. The doj went down in a heap.

After he could stagger to his feet, Delk0 gingerly stepped over

and divested the tech of his outfit. It took some further encouragement, but he slipped into the attire and winced as the hidden bands
within the threads tightened to fit his slightly smaller frame. He
studied himself in the simple wall mirror and felt the iron-gray
jacket and pants did not complement his own phantom-white skin.
And that was to say nothing of the minor stains on the tall collar
which had not been there two minutes ago.

He couldn't help wondering if he shouldn't have bashed the
rogue's head in a few minutes ago. It would have saved a life
already.

"You don't like it? Sad squirts, mate," Trip Mine said. He spun
on his heel and made for the hall again, the tail of his black jacket
flapping behind him. "I had a lovely antipersonnel planted in the
doorway that I would have just loved to set off. I had to use Nibbler
on him," he patted his pistol as he sheathed it, "otherwise there
wouldn't have been enough cloth left to cover your wee robot bits."

"Thank you," Delk0 said automatically. He knew the proper
response, even though he doubted Trip Mine really would have set
off a bomb in Paradise. Jones' Island contained the only system of
its kind. If even one vat of lifeblood was cracked, every rogue
under Dominum's sway would have a new target. No one would
forgive a threat to the lifeline that was the Paradise facility.

With one last sad glance at the body on the water closet floor,
Delk0 followed Trip Mine out through the last few doors. A broken
window later and they snuck onto the external landing porch.
Delk0 got his first breath of fresh air in his new lungs. The damp,
cold atmosphere did its best to drown him with the torrential
waves of rain for which the planet Mekrro was famous. Thunder
shook the facility.

"I hid the *Ill Wind* on the back of the porch," Trip Mine yelled
over the howl of the wind. "Follow close! Stay low, Delkie and you
might just make it off this bloody rock."

Sidestepping the heavily-manned front door to Paradise, they
slipped between several parked military shuttles towards the
opposite side of the porch. While the wrenching beast of a storm

hid them visually, the plethora of physiological signals they gave off must have been sending up red flags to the guards' equipment.

"They will sense my body heat," Delk0 hissed.

The shadow of a man didn't so much as pause, but a caustic laugh did trail behind him. It and the sounds of their footsteps were quickly lost to the rain and a new cell of the storm slammed into Jones' Island. Delk0 hoped the laugh meant his master had a plan for the sensors.

Caught up in that worry and clad in the inware of the dead tech, he lost his footing in the gale. He almost lost sight of Trip Mine. He charged ahead in the tempest, blind to his own safety…only to run headlong into his master, ducked behind a Vanetail light ship.

Trip Mine didn't so much as flinch. He watched something intently. Delk0 picked himself up and craned his neck carefully to follow his master's gaze.

"Oh," he said.

There, on the corner of the launch porch behind a much larger transport and half-covered by a tar sheet, rested Trip Mine's personal ship. The *Ill Wind* was small and sleek, its power hidden by a rough and dented exterior. Its owner had made more than one desperate escape in it. Stolen from a black-marketeer Trip Mine had slain, the tiny planet-hopper was one of his favorite things in the world, after his black hat and his Ignitor.

And now the Emperor's minions were swarming over the *Ill Wind*, nearly a hundred meters away. The Paradise guards had pried their way into and seemed to be scanning every micrometer of the ship with their wand-like probes.

Delk0 whimpered as flashes of lightning burned the scene into their eyes.

"All in the grand scheme, mate," Trip Mine said, punching Delk0 in the small of his back and grinning at his hiss of pain. "We're taking the Vanetail."

Even as Delk0 watched, the light ship in front of them opened with a surreptitious hiss at Trip Mine's touch. The doj knew little about flyers, but he knew that you couldn't open one unless it was yours. Too much security.

His master was a skilled human, not an honest one.

Trip Mine rolled through the narrow door that had opened on their side of the Vanetail. Delk0's eyes darted left and right, as he was certain someone would have sighted them. The only movement nearby on the porch was that of pelting rain and the flapping tarps over the ships and stacks of supplies.

Then the guards around the *Ill Wind* began fanning out, no doubt looking for the pilot of the unwelcome craft. Delk0 dove into the Vanetail and the door sealed itself behind him with another soft hiss. Inside was dry and still and silent. The internal environment barely glowed brightly enough for him to find his way to the copilot seat behind Trip Mine. He slid into the chair at a jerk of the head from his master. With more soft hissing, the console beneath molded around his legs as the back of the seat did the same around his chest and head, securing him completely. He now saw what the ship saw, and that was the Jones' Island security force well within firing range with a slew of weapons on hand.

Delk0 struggled not to panic. "What now? How are we—"

VVVVIIIIIIIIII.

The insufferable squeal of the engine would have deafened him if he had been outside the ship. The Vanetail hopped into the air. But until it had adjusted to the weather, its location, and a dozen other factors, it wouldn't be able to take off for a few deathly seconds. And every guard on the porch looked their direction.

"They see us!" Delk0 yelled through the console.

All he heard was a low hiss and a pop. Then a crackling rumble shook the porch as a blinding white flash pulsed from the *Ill Wind*. Their stolen light ship was rocked backward out over the ocean by the concussion but remained aloft. He couldn't see anything still, but he heard short, throaty coughs burbling from Trip Mine.

"Your ship," Delk0 rasped. "They destroyed…"

Only then did he notice the Ignitor in Trip Mine's clutch. The device was little more than a short rod molded to the human's grip, but it had dozens of hidden pressure points and switches. It connected to untold thousands of pounds of explosive that Trip Mine neurotically hid everywhere he went, just in case he needed them. Only he knew the combinations to set off any of the traps, like the betabuster he'd just blown.

The *Ill Wind* had just experienced owner-assisted suicide.

Delk0 went mute. He watched numbly through their craft as they headed north to the mainland, hundreds of kilometers away. Jones' Island shrunk slowly as the ship gained speed and height in the storm. From here, he could see the scattered, twisted, and burned wreckage of machines and men left by Trip Mine's bomb. More figures like toys were running out from the main gate of the Paradise facility, but they'd be too late. The squat bunker of a building stretched for nearly half a kilometer back across the narrow island. The green emergency lights had flared to life as sirens wailed. The land mass itself was a band of black volcanic stone and massive, glistening crystals that was barely visible above the meters-tall waves.

One hulking figure, taller than the security detail around him, stepped out of Paradise. It shoved a few men aside and simply watched their light ship as they raced away. Delk0 felt his nerves crawl at the sight.

The cockpit of the Vanetail was eerily quiet. The console around Delk0's head neutralized the violent rocking of the ship in the gale as well. Though he could see they were being tossed about as they left, he couldn't feel the vertigo that should have been wrenching his brain into gruel.

His thoughts were broken by a deep voice like a cave in, which penetrated their ship's console.

"One called Trip Mine, I speak to you," the rumble poured into the cockpit. *"Kanal bids you return. Face your trespass and the consequence."*

Delk0's jaw went slack at the voice. His body shook within its confines as his nerves exploded into full fight-or-flight instincts. Trip Mine seemed shaken as well, but it was difficult to tell from just the back of his head.

"I don't...don't report to...*you, gorgeous*," Trip Mine ground out from between his teeth.

"Would you be shot down over the ocean? No. Return. It is the only option."

The poor doj frantically searched the Vanetail's programs. There was no other option. She was right. He was overwhelmed by the need to return and soothe the screaming in his head. He had to turn the ship around. But the co-pilot commands were blocked. His master wasn't having it.

"Turn us around, please!" Delk0 wailed, body shaking. "Please, master!"

"Shut it, Delkie! Grow a pair."

"Return."

"Please!"

Delk0's doj body, built to thrive in conditions of extreme pressure and temperatures, practically glowed as he radiated out precious body heat. His thoughts had tapered off to nothing more than the repeated urge to obey the order. Kanal, the mistress of Jones' Island, would not let them go. Every kilometer they put between them and Paradise worsened the tremors wracking him.

"Dominum made us. We enjoy a life beyond the rats that populate the worlds. So much freedom for so few laws. You broke one of those laws. Return. Trip Mine, return."

Their ship had made incredible headway. Being a light ship, it was built entirely for swift travel, even through the raging storm conditions outside the cockpit. They had made it over fifteen kilometers out of sight of the island when their speed finally, finally slowed to a halt.

Trip Mine groaned through the console. The gentle rise and fall of the hovering Vanetail belayed the tempest outside. The master's long, frustrated sigh wavered as the voice of this Kanal villain finally made him see reason.

"Kanal..." he growled, as if in pain. "Three."

"Trip Mine. If you—"

"Two!"

The fluid began to drain from Delk0 face, leaving it tingling. His hands gripped the console around him so hard that one of his brand-new capillaries burst.

"One," Trip Mine said.

"I do not understand."

"Boom," Trip Mine chirped through a smile.

Clouds in front of them glowed. Delk0 agreed with the rogue on the island, he didn't understand either. But he saw the world fly past them in a torrent of rain and light as Trip Mine had thrown them into an accelerated climb, nose towards the mainland.

Delk0 realized that the agony in his head driving him to return to Jones' Island had vanished. Kanal was no longer projecting her will onto them.

Noise. Even through the tightly encapsulated cockpit, a vibration like an earthquake shattered his fragile sense of safety.

"You can't sit back and watch your own masterpiece with one of those," Trip Mine called over the com. "Blindness. That's what I hate about atomics, Delkie."

A strange lightness filled him. Despite the warning, Delk0 turned his Vanetail-vision around to view the rear. A glowing, growing, howling plume illuminated the storm around it for kilos. The ocean burned with the power of a dying sun below them. Instinctively, he avoided looking directly at the new cloud.

"Welcome to life after immortality," Trip Mine murmured, choked with unshed tears. Then, of course, the fool started laughing.

"I BELIEVE THAT WE ALL FALL AT SOME TIME."

His master coughed up blood now between words. The rogue continued to watch the oily streaks of smoke from King Dagon's doomed vessel. His expression was unreadable under his hat.

Did he even realize that his fellow conspirators were dying? Or was he simply unable to fully accept the concept of aftermath? Of consequences? That would explain a lot of his past decisions.

"All of us were caught in the middle of the madness," Trip Mine growled into the acrid air. "Hunted. Spat upon. Cursed by both sides. And now you're like me, mate. Like me."

Delk0 looked up, blank-faced, to see that Trip Mine was watching him. He felt his abdominals tremble as he sneered back.

"Oh. Scorn, scorn, scorn," Trip Mine said. "End of the day, we both did what we had to do, with a little bit of what we wanted tossed in for flavor."

"You tried to destroy the empire. And not to save people either. Just to prove you could. I may be a slave, but on my worst day, I wouldn't even consider the acts you pull."

Trip Mine swept blood and sweat out of his eyes as he leaned forward. "You don't understand. The world has ended many times before. Each eon starts small, people get powerful and corrupt, sentient life destroys itself. Every. Bloody. Time. The emperor tried to stall the natural order. I put life back on course, is all."

"There's no conversing with a broken mind," Delk0 retorted. He shuddered as he spoke out of years of chained regrets. "I may only be a machine like one of your bombs, but at least I have my parts intact. The ghosts in your head drove you insane. The ones in mine just warned me."

Uunderspar rumbled again beneath them. This landing porch wasn't as large as the one on Jones' Island, but the emptiness of it made the space feel massive. It was their balcony seat for the fall of Mercy's Landing. This conflagration around them had passed 'battle' hours ago and was the start of a very fine, first-rate war to end all wars.

Delk0 prodded his broken ribs with a whimper of pain at the molten sensations within. No more repairs. No more restarts. This was it. For the first time since his decision, he began to shake. The aftermath of his own choices sunk into the dank resources of his mind and took root.

"Delkie…You hear voices, too?" Trip Mine murmured. But his

words were clipped away by the scream of nearby shifter ships spiraling in uncontrolled dives a quarter kilometer away. Trip Mine sighed wistfully and sunk a little lower into the growing pool of blood beneath him.

DELK0 FELT STRANGE. THEY HAD LEFT THE ATOMIZED JONES' ISLAND far behind and flew through the stormy night with nothing but clouds above and mountainous ocean waves below. There was nothing to break the silence but Trip Mine's neurotic mutterings, and Delk0 had lived with that for so many years that he could ignore it.

So, there was little to distract him from his own thoughts. His synthetic mind, built for sentient qualities over computational perfection, buzzed sporadically. He didn't know how to feel about abruptly being mortal. He had always assumed this hell would always continue in some form. Less expensive to revive a trained doj than build a new spirit from scratch.

So, what now?

What now, he pondered.

"What now?" Delk0 whispered.

The thumping, incantational hisses from Trip Mine's side of the cockpit paused. Delk0 went as still as steel as the mastermind's hatted head tilted. A heartbeat sounded. Another came and went. The hat tilted forward again as the mutters resumed.

Safe from his master's attention, Delk0's worry shifted. He hoped beyond hope that 6Cin was alive. If she had died with him, or since, then she had either been destroyed with the Paradise facility or her spirit had...Had what? What happened to the dead now? Perhaps their spirits floated around the Network forever, lost and forgotten. It was still freedom from the Dominum's tyranny, in a way, but the thought brought Delk0 no joy. Lost spirits.

Spirits. Two in his head now. Confusion and loss from one in a river. Anguish and guilt and hatred from the other. Both pressed in on Delk0.

He shook himself through the muddle in his head and forced himself to focus on his friend.

6Cin, with her high cheekbones and bobbed black hair. 6Cin, with her gently whitish-orange skin and bright sunset eyes.

And he couldn't deny that the two of them were partners. The two slaves of a madman, huddling down in the rogue's hideout for months on end while he was destroying who-knew-what in some corner of the world. They were friends forged through the flames of Mercy's Landing.

And who knew if he'd ever hear her voice again.

Delk0's thoughts drifted, snagged, bounced and popped like rubber like they had twice already that day.

"*Sandy,*" he said with a happy sigh. "*I was such a moron back then. Think of how much time we could have saved if I could've seen past the end of my nose.*"

"What?" Trip Mine called sharply from ahead.

Marty glanced over at the smartly dressed man sitting across the living room from him. "*Sorry, dude. Just husband-wife talk. You know how it is.*"

"Enlighten me, *dude.*"

"*Sorry about the sweet talk.*" Marty laughed, his face flushing a bit. *Sometimes I just can't… Well.* I feel… Eh?"

A moment went by as a whole new file of information downloaded itself into Delk0's personal folder. The data transfer was as massive as Delk0's whole personal history up to that point. And it was filed next to two others that must have appeared in the past twelve hours as well. Megahertz. His brain throbbed.

"Delk0."

The word was spoken without inflection, thoughtless, a mention in passing. Delk0 knew that tone. He shivered within the console as his eyes watched for the slightest twitch from Trip Mine. "I don't understand," he whispered.

An audible sigh replied. "Good, you're back. Thought I'd have to eject you, Delkie. Wouldn't that be a waste of a trip fetching you, just to let you drown? Bad form."

"I'm back?" he asked dumbly.

A grunt. "Course, you don't remember. How bloody original. If I have to run diagnostics on you..." Trip Mine ended with a sigh. No more was said.

Delk0 struggled to grasp what had just happened. It was like awakening from a dream. He had just been someone else, somewhere else, but couldn't remember any details. He had the unnerving impression that there were three ghosts in his head now, and they were watching his every move.

The feeling was short-lived, though. Within ten minutes, their ship had reached the storm breakers.

Massive columns protruded from the turbulent sea every kilometer or so. They ringed the entire continent of Vrendele like the fangs of a great primordial beast. Impossibly tall, the barriers of energy between them acted as a fence against the hundred-meter-tall tides of Mekrro.

Delk0 strained to get a better look at them as they approached in their light ship. It was the first he had actually ever seen of them.

Somehow, Trip Mine noticed his slave's goofy craning. He grunted.

"Each breaker is just under a kilometer tall," he said pleasantly, the tone unnerving Delk0. "Including what is buried below the ocean floor, any of them would stand taller than even Uunderspar in Mercy's Landing. If one of them were to, say, impact with a moon at a significant velocity, then, well, the moon would lose. The barrier actually converts the ungodly levels of force against it into energy to repel those same tides. Fancy, eh?"

Delk0 swallowed noiselessly. He needed a drink.

"They were built by the empire back when it first moved to Mekrro. They found all those lovely metals underground and wanted to park their flabby fannies on all that shiny goodness, but the planet had other ideas. So, out come the behemoths and up go the storm breakers. Took a better part of a century to complete the wall, but jolly ole Emperor Dominum is a bloody patient freak of nature. A single breaker took a hundred machines two years to construct. Each is designed with a core of the unbreakable stuff, but the rest is synthetic metals."

"How do you know all of that?" Delk0 asked faintly.

Trip Mine didn't answer.

"Crown, save me," Delk0 whispered.

"Crown Mind? He couldn't have saved you if I'd had a bit more fun," Trip Mine drawled. "But don't worry your little orange eyeballs, eh? The master plan doesn't include a dead breaker. Ah, but if wishes were vicious…"

Delk0 held his breath to prevent him from correcting his master's butchered phrase. He also sucked in his breath because the Vanetail had just rocketed skyward to skirt over the storm breaker wall. The glistening field between the nearest pylons just tickled the underbelly of their ship as they crested, a slight grinding noise and cockpit alarms making the doj's skin burn anxiously.

And then they were over the top and back at the much lower sea level surrounding the mainland. Behind them, the transparent barrier provided an unnatural cutaway of the ocean. Dark clumps floated against the wall.

Curious, Delk0 focused the Vanetail's telescoping view on the masses. They were fish. Dozens of fish, hundreds of fish, crushed by the inexorable force of the tide against an immovable barrier. The countless tiny bodies had been gathered by the currents. Now the sloppy masses gently rose and fell against the side of the storm breakers.

The sight disappeared, lost to distance as they shoved onward into Vrendele.

The great cities, including the capital, were centered around the mines in the middle of the continent. For now, the Vanetail passed over farms, fields, and outposts that fed and supported the seat of the empire. Here, the storm clouds were mixed with a new, unwelcome addition to the sparkling country's vistas: smoke. Great, billowing clouds of it hung like fungus over the southern fields and villas.

Vrendele was burning. Town after town was in various stages of riot and destruction. Some were little more than blackened craters. Others were physically untouched but held swarming masses of fleeing slaves and imperial bureaucrats.

"This was you?" Delk0 asked, jaw slack.

A long, low bout of laughter tumbled from Trip Mine's direction. When he spoke, he sounded pleased.

"No! Bloody bags, no. I'm good, Delkie, but not that good."

"Who else would or even *could* do this? It's horrible."

A beat passed, then, "The Emperor sent hundreds and hundreds of us into the Breath, you know. Hundreds and hundreds of loose cannons that he uses or kills at his pleasure. But even the best cannon backfires when neglected. Even. The. Best."

"Rogues always fight the empire. That's what they do," Delk0 reminded him.

"Dominum created us to create fear and drive people into his arms. I doubt he and his sick parade of sycophants are happy that their toys are pulling their empire down around their ears. This is war, Delkie. We've been waiting years for this."

War.

Then Trip Mine returned to his almost musical mutterings, but the Vanetail accelerated. The light ship carried them past a city or two for which Delk0 didn't have names. From the blurred sights he could catch at this speed, they seemed tiny in comparison with Mercy's Landing. Delk0 tried to imagine the chaos under their feet.

As singular as he was, Trip Mine was hardly the only unnatural maniac wandering Vrendele. No one seemed to know how normal sociopaths and criminals had gained their strange abilities, like Kanal's dominance. Delk0 and 6Cin had spoken to other dojs in the city while waiting in line on handout days. Even officials of the empire reviled the rogues, and the slaves of the city knew to ignore or outright hide from anyone in flamboyant attire. City enforcers and soldiers occasionally cracked down when one went too far, although that usually led to dead enforcers.

But as a slave to such a rogue, Delk0 couldn't help but overhear things. Discrete operations, government contracts, hits sanctioned by Emperor Dominum himself. And of course, the various mischief the rogues practiced to remind the citizens of the empire why they needed government protection. Apparently, one did not subjugate a hundred worlds without a left hand holding a dagger, and hundreds of loose daggers now ran unchecked in the country below their little Vanetail.

Delk0 held onto the thought that Mercy's Landing was relatively untouched. The enforcers in the capital were heavily armed and armored. Weaponized dojs, heavy air support, turret grids—anything was fair game for protecting the Emperor and his top lieutenants. Yet even as they reached the outskirts of the city, the sounds of distant explosions tore at his heart.

He closed his eyes for the rest of their trip, shutting out the wrong, wrong reality into which he had been resurrected. Poor 6Cin.

Within minutes, the Vanetail finally slowed and landed. The cockpit glowed a faint red to indicate their arrival. As the thin entrances hissed open to the left, Trip Mine practically laughed as he called out.

"Delkie, we're home. Well, home-adjacent. The Uundertower, really. Since King Dagon, Circle Assassin, and the rest of the normal crew are giving the empire stooges the ole bruisy-and-bloody, you're my backup. Grab a handheld, mate!"

Numb, Delk0 shrugged out of the console as the craft released him. He fumbled for the personal missile launcher that his master had indicated. The long, sleek canister was similar to those Trip Mine hoarded back in the lair, so Delk0 was familiar with the general concept of it, if nothing else.

His thoughts shuddered into place as the weapon melded with him. He blinked as targeting instructions flickered at the corner of his vision, ready to unleash the first rocket at the merest of inclinations. The slave forced himself to steady his raw impulses.

And just like that, his thoughts went astray again. He barely had enough time to feel horror at the loss of control before Anori felt—

Father's gone now, but at least he rested peacefully instead of wandering as a weeping ghost. Anori hoped to join him someday. Someday, but not any day soon. He had many years of fishing, fighting, and living first. And perhaps a return to that forest. The magic of that place still haunted him.

Phesssh.

A long, wispy hydrogen trail followed the missile off the side of the landing porch. Delk0 watched, stunned, as his errant rocket slammed into the sixty second floor of the national archives far below. The windows blew out of that building near where the missile had punched into the wall. Debris flew out to the streets below, including one humanoid shape.

Trip Mine roared and struck Delk0 so hard his vision swam. He struck him again in the ear, as if for good measure. "I should've taken you for a run years ago, Delkie! Ha!"

Nauseated by what he had just done, Delk0 struggled to regain control of both himself and the handheld. He couldn't get the image of the falling body out of his mind's eye. His breaths came swift and short.

Then his master shook him. The man's hat was pulled low over his eyes, but the dark orbs glistened in the shadow. A tiny smile mismatched the rest of his hungry expression.

"Right, listen up," Trip Mine said. "You're the heroic doj tech that caught me on Jones' Island, eh? You were sent to bring me back to Dominum and his lieutenants and to bring grave news that's meant for only their ears."

His head still pounding from the punches, Delk0 only nodded.

"This is the only way we'll get close to them during a time like this. Botch this up, we die. Act unsure or hesitate, we die. Insist on seeing a lieutenant for this. They'll be with Dominum, of course, but it's less suspicious than trying to see the Emperor directly. No one does that. I cut the communications to the Paradise facility, so they have no way to check their doj rosters to prove you wrong.

Trip Mine's gloved hand fell heavily on his slave's shoulder.

"This is why I saved you, Delkie," he said. "This is what you're good for. We'll make bloody history, you and I. I and you. Us. Eh?"

"Of course," Delk0 gasped.

The hand patted him twice and pulled away. Trip Mine moved in front of him and slumped in place.

"Keep the handheld on me," he demanded. "Insist on reporting to a lieutenant. Don't let anyone search me. Improvise! Once we meet our makers, I plan to do the talking. Then you may have to use that thing for more than just target practice."

The two started marching across the porch, and Delk0 felt his already prodigious body heat levels rising as he panicked. He doubted he could do this on a good day. But what choice did he have?

The landing porch was almost entirely empty. The dark grey metal shelf protruded out from near the top of Uunderspar and usually held over a hundred various ships and drones. Most of these seemed to be airborne at the moment, and the skeleton crew of enforcers was now very literally a skeleton crew. Hundreds of tiny craters and scorch marks pockmarked the porch, and still burning bodies lay scattered.

Delk0's hand shook as they passed one with the alabaster complexion of a doj. Murdered by one of Trip Mine's associates. Trip Mine caught the look and chuckled through unmoving lips. "King Dagon's a real artist, eh?"

Once inside Uunderspar, Delk0 felt even smaller than he had on the porch. Even this simple hall had a ceiling of at least ten meters. Thick tapestries padded the walls in reds and grays, the colors of the empire. Recordings of Dominum demanding order from his subjects loomed here and there, spritzing into existence as they passed and throwing his magnified voice throughout the tower.

"We shall not tolerate their misguided actions," Emperor Dominum's massive bust stated. His lamp-like eyes stared directly at them from five different locations in the hall, the recordings reacting to their presence. "Power through unity. Unity through power. These self-proclaimed villains and all who stand with them shall see the heel of the empire before we crush them underfoot today. Their arrogance is their demise in disguise."

As if unable to control himself, Trip Mine snickered softly in the following silence.

Recorded Dominum had good hearing. "*Kneel!*" he roared.

Trip Mine obediently leaned forward to his knees, acting the part of the meek prisoner. Delk0, on the other hand, threw himself prostrate on the ground and dropped the handheld.

"What is this?" came a much smaller, much weedier voice.

Enforcers had finally shown themselves. Five men in imperial red and gray lumbered up in their various forms, headed by a colonel in a normal sapient body. The enforcers looked angry. And they had just found a pair of walking corpses to take all that anger.

Delk0 froze on the ground, unable to move. He could practically hear Trip Mine's thoughts screaming at him to stand, play his part, but he couldn't stand anymore than he could dance the videtauchi at the moment.

The colonel audibly growled. Or maybe it was one of his more bestial minions doing the growling. He barked an order. Suddenly Delk0 felt himself lifted a full meter into the air by two of the enforcers. One currently took the shape of a massive ape-like beast with an extra pair of arms, while the other was in a nightmarish concoction of metal spines and mechanized limbs.

"I asked you a question, slave," the colonel spat up at Delk0.

It was probably the first time anyone had addressed him first while in Trip Mine's presence. Delk0's narrow chest heaved as he looked to his master for help that wouldn't come. The ruse required him to do the talking this time.

So, one word at a time, he grated out, "I bring word from Jones' Island. This is how you serve the empire, colonel?"

The muscled back of Trip Mine tensed under his bulky trench coat.

The enforcer colonel cocked a single eyebrow. He raised his arm and pulled a heavy gun out of nowhere, though he kept it pointed at the ground.

Well, it was time to go all in. Delk0 roared, letting his fear free. "This city is burning! We're under attack! I have terrible news from Paradise and a prisoner, and you're holding me here. Do you have any idea what the lieutenants will do to all of us if I arrive late?"

One of the other enforcers, mostly human at the moment but covered in metal plates and weapons, took two steps forward. He struck Delk0 so hard that the doj's vision flashed bright white and orange and red.

"You sackless shred of filth," he snarled, eyes glistening and mouth frothing under a soup of a dozen performance drugs. "You'll learn to speak better to your masters."

He raised his fist again. Then his eyes bugged out horribly and a patch of froth flew off his lips and landed on the tip of Delk0's nose. The doj's pupils dilated and he shook. The armor melted off the enforcer who had punched him as the man sank to his knees, screaming as he clutched his head. He now looked only human, his generated upgrades nowhere in sight as his concentration broke.

The colonel stepped forward and kicked his enforcer out of the way, a single long finger at the side of his own skull as he glared at the writhing soldier. With his conjured weapon, he motioned for the others to set Delk0 on his feet. They complied quickly. The colonel gave the doj and the villain a long, shrewd stare before nodding. That was when Delk0 noticed it.

The human's dark eyes had been obscured by a film of blood. When the colonel spoke, his voice was stilted. Unnatural.

"Yes," he said. "We will escort you to the Avicage. Emperor Dominum awaits you eagerly. If you lie, the great Emperor will delight in your instruction."

The man said instruction like most men said dismemberment. Not particularly subtle. But the drastic change in the colonel's voice unnerved Delk0 more than his words.

They were led further into the Uunderspar, minus one enforcer. His hoarse shrieks faded after a while, but not soon enough for Delk0. He gripped his handheld like it was his beacon home. They passed conference halls, grand ballrooms, lounges, dining rooms, barracks, and even a strange room with metal doors the size of a flier behind which a sound like a thousand wasps thrummed.

Every room was empty. Only an occasional squadron of enforcers ran or flew past, yelling through coms to their comrades on the ground outside.

"The Avicage," the colonel announced as they reached a pair of soaring crimson metal doors marked with the white sign of the empire.

"Huh. Smaller than I expected," Trip Mine said.

"Quiet, you," Delk0 said as fiercely as he could without risking later reprisal.

The enforcers backed away. The colonel gave one last glance over his shoulder as they vanished into the depths of the tower. The blood mist had left his eyes and dribbled onto his cheeks, and he looked both shaken and anxious to leave the vicinity of the massive door.

Delk0 spun back towards the Avicage door when he heard a humming noise. The towering sheet of metal seemed to be vibrating. He blinked, trying to focus on the immense slabs of bloody metal in front of him. His gut instinct said that the Uunderspar was being bombed from outside. But the floor and walls of the capital building held steady.

In fact, now the door had calmed as well. But comparing it to the walls, he realized that they were no longer the neutral plaster they had been. Instead, the walls were gray sheet metal with ribs of the same dark red as the door.

Trip Mine turned slowly and whispered, "Well this is rubbish."

Although careful to keep the handheld trained on Trip Mine, Delk0 craned his neck to look back down the hall behind them.

Except they were no longer in the hall.

The room was massive. And by the view through the transparent roof, he had a pretty good idea that this Avicage chamber was the closest thing Uundespar had to a penthouse. Shifter ships like dragons and giant ghouls flew out there. Raging bombers darted high above the roof. One burning craft had a bead on the transparent section of roof and headed straight for it. Before Delk0 could so much as gasp, streams of light from the turret grid reduced it to a few floating splinters which bounced noiselessly off the ceiling.

The Avicage itself was filled with weapons, armor, a wall of vault doors stacked from floor to ceiling, and five unamused occupants. Delk0's superheated core vented a little as four of the five figures stared at them.

There stood Black Sail, his pale and glowing body armor draped in funeral silks. His infamous whalebone mace lay in a display case nearby but vanished and reappeared in his hand at a gesture from the Emperor's archmage.

Genshou's huge, insectoid form shifted weight from foot to foot. She peered at them through dark green eyes, the last remnant of humanity visible under her crimson carapace, pincers, and talons.

Forge Master flexed his long, mechanical fingers and put one to his chin thoughtfully as dozens of various scanners and probes analyzed the intruders.

Behind them all swayed the ghostly shape of Morning Dew. The shadows from the nearby furniture stretched and wavered towards her, as if desperate to join her. Her scarred face oozed tears from eyeless sockets.

In the face of the empire's greatest men and women, Delk0 felt the lies die in his throat. But the four lieutenants of the Emperor were also the original four archvillains. For all he knew, some dark art of Black Sail's or one of Forge Master's neurological weapons had drained the courage out of him. His breath came heavy and strained.

If Trip Mine felt the same fear and reverence as his slave, he hid it. With a smile on his face and a click to his shiny shoes, the rogue stepped toward his masters and offered an extravagant bow.

"G'day. I apologize for the little incident on Jones' Island," he said. "Not my *finest* work, but—"

Emperor Dominum stepped out from behind Genshou and pointed a heavy finger at Trip Mine. Three glowing streaks like emergency flares flew into Trip Mine's torso and out his back, leaving smoldering holes in his trenchcoat.

With a tiny gasp, the great Trip Mine fell face down on the floor.

THE LANDING PORCH WAS ONE CORNER SMALLER NOW. THE BATTLE IN the skies had grown. More of the expensive shifter ships and even shape-changing enforcers had taken to the skies to eradicate the traitors. A bomber would be chased by a tentacle monster and several winged metal men, only to turn and blow the luminescent monster into a fireball, which continued to chase it. Crashed ships returned to the fight in various states of disrepair. Beings or vehicles, Delk0 wasn't sure which, flew around in the fray. One of the light-things in the shape of a snaking cylinder had been shot down and crashed into and through a corner of the Uunderspar porch, leaving nothing but a jagged hole.

Reinforcements from the dark, weird corners of the worlds had found the fight.

"Your friends won't win," Delk0 said softly, watching the massacre overhead.

"They won't *survive*, mate," Trip Mine returned. "There's a difference."

"You," Delk0 spat, "have no concept of pity. If you can't pity your fellow fools, at least pity the dying innocents."

"We're all the innocent now, eh?" Trip Mine said. His eyes were unfocused and his head listed. "When we're cut, we'll bleed. Every man alive is a victim of these times. Even us rogues. We were lost. Bloody fools, like you said. Dominum offered us the power to take back our lives. Once, we drank from that chalice, but now it holds nothing that we need. That power has sailed.

"Back then, we all sailed away. We returned made of diamond and steel. We were invincible tools in the fingers of the empire. But now that's ended, and we're all free."

As his master rambled, feverish eyes wandering, Delk0 stretched his legs gingerly and stood. The broad porch remained empty except for the two of them. They were toy figurines discarded in a war of titans. A single stray missile or bomb would end his life for the final time. No revival. No returns.

He briefly considered firing his handheld at his own feet and leaving on his own terms. But he wanted to be around when Trip Mine fell. As he grew tired of the human's chatter, he snorted steam.

"What do your voices tell you?" Trip Mine questioned.

Delk0 flinched. "What voices?"

"Come on, Delkie," his master drawled. "It's the end of the world. Embrace your inner madness for a minute!"

"I hear…" He hesitated.

"Out with it. All the bloody details!"

"Memories. Like I'm eating ghosts. Each time one hits, I remember someone else's life like I lived it," Delk0 confessed. "And then the ghost stays in my head."

Trip Mine's bloody mouth creased into a slow frown. For a moment, Delk0 thought the rogue would scoff, but then, "Ghosts. Lives. Do you remember words like Acrothon, gammyn, or Nierzon?"

Delk0 shook his head. "No. Why? How would you know—? Wait, yes! Gammyn things kept one of the ghosts in a prison called… Sare-ee-stow?"

Trip Mine might have looked horrified, satisfied, blanched, or anything in between and the doj wouldn't be able to tell. The man was covered in too many bruises and stains. But he didn't answer, either. He knew something.

Then a gust from a passing ripper hit. The rogue's hat blew off. Delk0 had seen Trip Mine's broad fedora fly off once before, and the man had snatched it back on with unnatural speed. This time, he didn't even glance at it.

The hat tumbled a few times towards the edge of the landing porch. Watching it, something clicked inside Delk0. It might have been his conditioning under Trip Mine's heel. It might have been part of his initial program to serve sentient life. It might have just been because the sight of the hat floating off into the burning streets below would have saddened him. Regardless of why, Delk0 trotted over and caught it.

Trip Mine glanced up as his slave offered him his hat back. A small, sickening smile slid up his smooth cheeks. He placed the hat back on his head.

"At least the old Delkie is still in there somewhere," he said hoarsely.

"I have always been me," Delk0 replied, sitting next to him. "But someone finally told me I could do something, so I did."

To his surprise, Trip Mine slowly clapped. "Here's to multi-personality disease!" he said with a curt laugh. "Here's to your ghosts. But between you and me, Delkie, only one of us knows who's really in your head."

On the floor, Trip Mine made a pitiful mewling sound as he clutched his bleeding guts. His defenses and shields had abandoned him, and Dominum's blasts had done their work.

Delk0 couldn't drop his handheld, though he imagined he should. His hands wouldn't move. His knees wouldn't bend. His manufactured body, as impressive as it was for manual labor, was still slave to his fallible mind. And that seemed to be completely out of order.

"Which ones are they?" Genshou trilled. For an armored mutant pushing three meters in height, she had a surprisingly pleasant voice. She didn't sound particularly interested in them, though.

Forge Master simply appeared next to Trip Mine. Delk0 flinched, but the archvillain ignored him. He picked up the fallen Trip Mine by the head, gave him another scan for good measure, and then reappeared back at a case of various rifles that he had been apparently perusing before the interruption.

"One of ours. No real genetic shift," Forge Master clicked out. His head was fully visible above his armor, but his mouth never moved. "Surprised he survived the Archon's Breath. Brains. Strategy. Saboteur. We've used that one against the Hokke uprisings. May be a mastermind behind our current revolt."

"That's *the* mastermind, Forgy-porgy," Trip Mine choked out. He seemed to be struggling to look debonair, but the grimace on his face and his weak legs betrayed him.

Genshou laughed softly. Forge Master didn't so much as blink twice as he hefted a rifle you could've loaded a dog into.

All four of the lieutenants looked vaguely annoyed by the grandstanding upstart and his pet doj. But as Dominum had brought the intruders here, the lieutenants seemed content to let Dominum handle them.

Trip Mine stumbled to his feet. With one arm crossed over his bleeding stomach, he lowered a finger at the Emperor. He intoned, "You made all this possible, old man. You can't kill and torture your own servants for fun and not expect war. My fellow walking monstrosities didn't take much convincing. Now you'll have to kill every last filthy son of a sot to stop this. Everyone hates you. Your entire empire is on board."

Then Dominum stepped forward, and Delk0 had his first real look at the leader of known sentient life. The man wore an ancient black iron chestplate, gauntlets, boots, pauldrons, and an angular helmet that revealed nothing of the head except but a pair of glowing red eyes like that of a possessed lion caught in the light. His huge, muscular arms were wrapped entirely in crimson bandages.

The Emperor looked to be in good shape for a centuries-old demigod.

"*Trip Mine.*" His voice didn't thunder through the skull like Kanal's, but it seemed to emanate from everywhere at once. "*Yes, I know you. You who collapsed the Necrim Oubliette without injuring a single prisoner. You who slaughtered every child in the town of Galloway with a single incendiary device. I know every last one of my servants, Trip Mine. Faithful, or otherwise.*"

And Dominium leapt forward, apexing meters above and slamming down towards Trip Mine.

At that moment, Delk0 seized up. Sobs wracked his body, and he was oblivious to anything around him.

"My poor Winni..." Jacqe hissed through the sudden pain in his head.

He had failed his wife. Falling asleep had been as good as murder. He had failed his friends and confidants, leading them to eternal damnation on some forlorn planet with no hope of return. And he had failed 6Cin. She was gone, he knew she was gone. It was like Winni all over again...

He sighed.

Delk0 forced a hard restart of the few mental processes he had manual control over. His positronic neurons shut down for the briefest of instances and came back to life. As he heard chaos around him, he slowly regained control over his faculties. Jacqe still sniffled in his memory, but he was Delk0 again. And it didn't erase the feeling of failure. He had never done anything right, whether he was a doj slave or a multi-billionaire human. He hurt people. Failed people.

Not that he had more than a moment of self-pity. The sharp hisses of his master's pistol Nibbler had faded. Dominum had lifted Trip Mine into the air with a single iron hand clutching his throat.

"Why are all sentients born arrogant fools?" Dominum asked, his voice shaking with anger. *"Answer me that. Because that is the only explanation for why every other generation attempts such a coup, ignoring the failures of every last attempt by their pitiful predecessors."*

"Somen's gotta chip on hees shold'r," Trip Mine squeaked out. "Wos matter? Wrong sida th' bed?"

Dominum turned and slammed Trip Mine across the back of an ornate couch between weapon cases, breaking the seat in half.

"I never liked that couch," breathed Morning Dew. She had floated unnervingly close to Delk0 and now casually commented on the destruction behind her without breaking her eyeless stare at the doj.

He wasn't sure if the mutilated lieutenant wanted to hug him, eat him, or vivisect him. At least she didn't seem to consider him a threat. The feeling wasn't mutual. He felt his gaze slipping to the targeting console in the corner of his eye, his arms tensed and ready to bring his handheld to bear should Morning Dew make a move.

Over on the wreckage of the couch, a hacking laugh floated up from Trip Mine's crumpled form. He feebly tried to stand, but Dominum casually scooped him up and tossed him across the Avicage floor, where he rolled to a stop near Delk0. The rogue still laughed.

"Complacency, mate!" he cried. "You killed yourselves years ago and didn't think twice."

"Slam talk," Forge Master stated. "Frippery. Empty words."

This entire time, Black Sail had been silently polishing his mace. Now, Delk0 noticed his twisted lips had been forming a long string of silent syllables. Delk0 wasn't sure what the archmage was doing, but it couldn't be good for their health.

Trip Mine was still focused on Forge Master's dismissal. "Empty? Me? I'm hurt. You don't hold a candle to my brilliance, but go ahead and try your brain at where—"

"*You came from Jones' Island,*" Dominum interrupted. "*Nothing in or out of these walls escapes me, my tool. You dressed your slave up in a technician's garb and lied to my men. You've visited Paradise without my express permission. So tell me before you perish, Trip Mine—was cutting communications worth what you learned of Paradise? Do you still believe you can defeat the lords of death and life after witnessing mankind's destiny firsthand?*"

"A speech like that, and you accuse *me* of frippery," Trip Mine said, dragging himself upright. Several long splinters of wood still protruded from his coat like quills.

Delk0 flexed his fingers around his missile launcher as Genshou and Forge Master began to approach them. "Master?" he hissed, stepping closer to Trip Mine.

"*Genshou, take back a perimeter on the streets below. Let our people see where true power lies,*" Dominum rumbled, red eyes fixed on Trip Mine.

"I've been waiting to hear those words," she trilled. The archvillain proceeded to snatch the massive dog-gun from Forge Master's hands.

"*Black Sail, you know your orders.*" The silent lieutenant nodded in response, never pausing his incantations. "*Forge Master, retake the northwest gate. The reinforcements from the first sector will help us with the abominations over in Nasran.*"

"You'll never make it that far," Trip Mine snarled, sounding genuinely angry for the first time that day. Blood dribbled from between his clenched teeth. "You won't even make it out of this room. Because I brought a weapon to this funeral pyre, and you still don't know what it is."

"Make him be silent," Morning Dew said with a sigh. "Too...lively for my taste."

Dominum raised a finger. Red glimmers of light flared to life around his arm, growing in size and brightness as they orbited his extended limb. He spoke as they sped up. "*After this is over, little tools, I shall enjoy killing you slowly. Again, and again, and again.*"

"You sure could, mate, but you'll have to wait for the fallout to fade first. Welcome to life after paradise," Trip Mine murmured. "Goodbye, Emperor."

This time, the burst of new memories hit him so hard and fast that it was over before he realized it had started. He was still Delk0 the slave doj, but he remembered another life, a short and horrible life. There were impressions of fear and pain and of a single missed chance to survive.

Dominum seemed to hesitate. His eyes widened slightly.

More! More memories struck him and made the world tilt around him. A youth spoke directly to him, over the threats of the Avicage. Lamb was suddenly smirking in his face. "*We like fighting, us. Fight monsters and demons and people who don't care about people. What about you, Orange Eyes? You up to a fight? Are you? Well?*" Was Lamb talking, or Delk0?

In that second, Delk0 saw Morning Dew flinch and his machine-forged reactions took over. He fired the handheld.

A bloom of fire engulfed the lieutenant and Trip Mine and Delk0 were both thrown onto their backs, all but deaf and with hot blood starting to ooze out of the shrapnel wounds on their chests. Morning Dew herself had slid back closer to the middle of the Avicage, near the other archvillains of the empire.

Trip Mine dragged Delk0 to his knees as Dominum's hellfire streaked towards them, and he croaked out a single word like a passcode. "Nierzon."

Hard, white light engulfed them. There was nothing but silence and that light around them.

Then Delk0's internal sensors went berserk, telling him that the ground was above then left then down then above then right then behind then up. His body was frozen within the light the entire time.

They finally tumbled free. The light vanished. Trip Mine and Delk0 were sprawled out in one of the halls they had entered, smoke and ruin behind them. At first, he thought they had tele-ported. But then he saw a roughly spherical hole torn through the nearby wall and a similar impact site on the wall opposite.

The doj felt like he had just been pulped for juice, but Trip Mine looked even worse. His face and throat were heavily bruised. Blood trickled out of everything but his eyes. The wounds in his stomach looked even bigger up close, and he could barely stand under his own power.

But a bloody, broken-toothed, gruesome smile gashed open his visage. He made as if to speak but ended up coughing instead.

Finally, he managed. "If only that shield had had the juice to protect me from the couch too, eh?"

"What happened?" Delk0 wheezed out, staggering to his feet.

"Don't you know by now that I never lose? The grand scheme is inevitable."

His master gestured up at the wall where they had finally struck. He followed the shaking hand and saw a dark shard embedded in the metal wall. Inching closer, he saw it. A chunk of exoskeleton protruded there like a massive dart.

"You killed them," Delk0 muttered.

"Orbital strike from the Felburg facility," Trip Mine said. "Stole the codes away from the empire years ago. Glad they still worked, or that would have been bloody embarrassing."

"You killed them!"

Trip Mine's grin faded. "No. I tore them apart and irradiated their corpses, mate. I burned them off the face of the planet."

A little voice in the back of Delk0's head spoke, one that was entirely his own. He could have prevented this madness. Back in the Paradise facility, Delk0 could have ended Trip Mine's song short of this horrifying chord. One blow to the skull. But no. And now this.

"Did you ever stop and think what that would do to us?" Delk0 whispered. He was past protocol and training. His legs shook.

"What *I* did to us? What about what *they* did to us! *To me!*"

"The empire will die with them," Delk0 stated, his brain running the probabilities. None of it was good. "They kept everything else in check! They gave us order!"

"*Yes!*" Trip Mine yelled, a dangerous gleam in his eyes. "Yes, there will be anarchy! Perfect, sweet anarchy. Yes, the worlds will fall. They deserve it! Dominum stopped the natural order of things for too long. The world has been screaming for death and rebirth, screaming so loud that even I could hear it!"

Delk0 took a step back, retrieving his missile launcher. He had always known his master was mad. But Trip Mine had usually maintained his composure and had his own sort of insane logic, whereas this wounded creature in front of him was utterly unhinged.

But Trip Mine wasn't finished. He crawled up to Delk0 and clutched at his stolen tech jacket. Delk0 felt repulsed as the villain wheezed bloody spittle in his face.

"You're just a machine, Delkie. I don't expect you to understand. I've been so many places and heard so many voices in the dark corners of the universe." His face convulsed. "You know what I heard, Delkie?"

He pulled himself up on Delk0's shirt further and whispered in the doj's ear. "Truth. I heard truth. Truth from beyond the grave, from the eras before. Every ten thousand years, something ends up killing the universe before it's reborn again. So why shouldn't it be me this time. Why. Not. Me."

Delk0 wrenched free from the human.

Trip Mine toppled with a look of betrayal on his ruined features. The doj opened his mouth to lambast the rogue, but then he saw the gaping head wound under the man's hat. His mouth slowly closed. Trip Mine wouldn't be walking this one off. He might not even know what he was saying.

"I'm going back to the old base," Delk0 said, his voice shaking. "Maybe 6Cin is still there."

"No. You're really not," Trip Mine growled. "What you are going to do is help me to the medical capsule in the Vanetail, so we can get off this monument to failure before my charges bring it down around us."

"Bomb the Uunderspar? You're delusional," Delk0 retorted.

Trip Mine pulled the Ignitor out of his coat and tickled one hidden pressure plate after another.

"Boom," he said with sudden calm. "You know me. Always prepared. Now come on! We have ten minutes before the grand scheme continues."

Delk0 stared at the man. "I'm not going with you."

"You are one in a thousand, Delkie," Trip Mine allowed. "But that thousand is still a slave race. You're a machine. Act like one."

Delk0 didn't budge.

Trip Mine's eye narrowed. "Now, doj. Don't make me order you."

An order would be obeyed to the best of a slave's ability, like it or not. It was the very lowest a doj could fall, acting without choice or thought.

Chest heaving, face pulled into a mask of rage, Delk0 stepped forward. He glanced back at the chunk of Genshou's chitin that hung on the wall. He pulled Trip Mine to his feet. And the two of them started hobbling through the grand halls of Uunderspar towards the landing porch.

In the distance, the towering Miner's Respite imploded. The center of the vast mineral empire beneath the city, the building had housed the thousands of lords and flunkies of Dominum who had brutally controlled the mining populace. Thousands of dojs had been built and worked to death in those tunnels.

The destruction of the Respite might have been symbolic. It might have also been a sign of more sinister happenings in the mines under the building. Either way, the empire's victory in Mercy's Landing looked less and less certain.

Trip Mine sank low on the porch, unable to keep himself up. He sighed heavily as they watched the distant fire of the Miner's Respite. He said, "There's no redemption for creatures like us, Delkie, the legs that nightmares stand on. But the legs rebelled. At least you and I both slaughtered those nightmares. Although, considering the insignificant tool that you killed, my work was a just little more...spectacular."

"You have always lived for spectacular," Delk0 said heavily. He pointed towards the column of black smoke that had replaced the tower in the distance. "Did you do that?"

"Sloppy work," Trip Mine mumbled. "All at once. No...no spectacle."

"Oh. I would have thanked you," Delk0 said. "For the dojs, you understand."

He turned towards his master and stopped dead. The silenced barrel of Nibbler shook decimeters from his nose.

"You've had that the entire time?" Delk0 whispered.

"Whole bloody time." Trip Mine grimaced.

A beat passed. Several followed. The porch shook worse now as more bombs in Trip Mine's final crescendo tore load-bearing supports out of Uunderspar's heart far below.

"What now?"

"Your ghosts. How many?"

Delk0 couldn't move, much less think properly. "How many?"

"How. Many. Ghosts?"

"Eight. But one doesn't talk."

Trip Mine started giggling. The sound was terrifying.

"'One doesn't talk.' I'll just bet little blighter Six doesn't talk."

Delk0 counted in his head. His core vented when he got to six. He faintly asked, "How did you know it was the sixth?"

Nibbler wavered, but Trip Mine was using the last of his strength to keep the gun in his slave's face.

"A wild guess. But I'm the bloody king of wild guesses," Trip Mine growled. "'I guess I should take this job.' 'I guess I should rig this bridge in case I need to blow it later.' 'I guess I should listen to what the voice in my head says. *He* seems clever.' He told me things that I verified years ago. One of them was a fascinating little bit of trivia about the world being tens of thousands of years old."

He shrugged slightly, wincing at the motion. "None of it mattered much to me. Not until *he* explained why I needed to design the grand scheme. Think about it. Even though the empire's best can only trace history back about nine thousand years or so, there are ruins older than that. Why?"

"Please put Nibbler down," Delk0 mumbled.

Trip Mine pressed the gun into Delk0's forehead, which stopped the shaking some.

"Ha, always the funny one," he said. "But think. How are there manmade structures older than the planets? No answer makes sense. But Delkie, we're all *recycled*. The planet, the Network, the universe, all of it had a big, fat reset button that the powers that be hit every 10,000 years or so when everything goes sad squirts on sentients. A few lucky ones are saved for repopulation. But planets, stars, everything else, boom. Destroyed and remade."

"And you, the master of destruction, are trying to help the end of the world along." Delk0 scoffed. "Because a voice told you. How did this voice know? Tell me that."

"*He* is outside of time," Trip Mine stated. "That's all *he* wants you to know. I thought *he* was speaking to you, too, until you told me how many ghosts you hear just now. Eight.

"Well mate, eight times the world was ruined and brought back. Eight great eons of history. This is the ninth. You're hearing your own ghosts."

A bombing run sent multiple shocks through Uunderspar. Delk0 grit his teeth until it was over, then shouted, "By that logic, is there one more ghost coming? The ghost of this eon."

"That's you, fool!" Trip Mine called back over the cacophony. "You are the you of this eon! They aren't ghosts, they're *you!* Your spirit is all Delkie, but you're running off a used soul. That soul has been in a different person every eon, so of course you see ghosts. Meet the ghosts of Delk0-past, mate. How'd they look?"

At that, Delk0 began to laugh. He had been so tense, so tired, and so angry at the world that he wasn't prepared for the sensation. He rolled over backward and shook with choked gasps and chuckles, ignoring the gun that Trip Mine now fumbled.

It was all crazy. All of this. But it just explained something.

Through teary slits of vision, he saw Trip Mine's gun hand slowly fall limp. He just watched his slave laugh like a man possessed.

"*Arssen!*" Delk0 screamed, rage searing through the mania. "Arssen! You did this to me! You got us all cursed! Rot! In! Hell!"

Arssen cringed inside his head. Whatever remained of the second era traitor began to wail, and Delk0's own eyes leaked lubricant.

"You knew Arssen?" Trip Mine mumbled. "No, you *were* that slobbering mad freak. All the bloody slaves I could have gotten, and I land with the father of betrayal."

When Delk0 could breathe again, he realized what his master had said. "I didn't tell you he was a traitor."

Devoid of energy, the man behind the empire's fall sprawled out on the ground. He rolled his head slightly to look at Delk0. "Come on, mate. A man's got to have some secrets."

• • •

THE TWO STAGGERED OUT OF THE TOWER TO THE LANDING PORCH, THE doj's hands grasping with waning strength at the dead weight of the other.

"The probability that we escape Mercy's Landing is unmentionable," Delk0 said, grimacing from exertion.

"Then don't bloody mention it," Trip Mine replied.

He was in terrible shape. His dusky skin had gone pale and clammy. Sweat streaked his face and mingled with blood. Every step forward put pressure on his abdomen, and now the mastermind of the rebellion had lost the willpower to ignore it. The flashes of pain through his rage were the only things that kept Delk0 from dropping him and fleeing.

But they had made it to the porch with no significant interruption by the enforcers. The shape-changing soldiers of the empire fought the war down below, attempted to find their Emperor in the ruins of the Avicage, or fled now that the highly centralized power of the empire had been decapitated.

"My people still hold the northwest gate," Trip Mine growled. "Once I'm patched up, we take the light ship through and gather our strength in Sector One. The rogues will abandon their posts here on Mekrro and then I'll push my magic button. *Boom.*"

"You would blow the northwest gate?"

"I'll blow Mekrro."

Delk0 nearly opened his mouth but suppressed the urge. Of course, it was at least within the realm of the possible. Orbital strikes on power plants. Core drills and planet busters. Taking out storm breakers around Vrendelle and Nasran and letting the sea reclaim the world. Trip Mine could slaughter billions in moments.

"What then?" Delk0 asked, his voice icy. "Rebuild? Be the new Emperor?"

Trip Mine shook his head slowly, wincing as he did. "Sentients can only keep Civilization alive for so long. It needs to die. I'm just helping it along, one planet at a time."

Delk0 glanced at the porch ahead of them. The screams of men and metal were audible out here as the city tore itself apart. But the

Vanetail still stood, silently waiting for them. He had hoped it would have been blown up or stolen by now. The loss would have made his decisions for him.

I never had my one moment like this, Jonathan told him from a lifetime away. Delk0 then remembered protecting a very different city, walking a beat, living alone for years. *But every day is filled with moments. This isn't that different, you know. It's not about standing up for yourself. It's about standing up for people who can't. You've got this, my man.*

"What?" he said under his breath. His head couldn't take much more of this. All these identities were shredding his mind from within. Had the dream woman back in the Paradise facility tried to drive him insane with these voices? Regardless of her intent, he feared it was working.

He was jolted back to reality as a long groan trickled out of his master. Delk0 carefully let him go. Somehow the man stayed on his feet as he examined his broken form. Delk0 stepped back.

"You'd destroy everything?" Delk0 said quietly. "The world will lose five depraved overlords and gain a slow death. Is that it?"

"Yes. You just can't understand the *need* for it." Trip Mine spat blood.

Delk0's eyes were little more than slits. He didn't know whether to laugh or cry. "Because I'm just a slave?"

"I'm following orders from a higher power, just like you'll follow mine!" he cried.

Higher power? At this point, Delk0 couldn't trust a word out of his master's mouth.

Trip Mine's arms snaked around his midsection as he doubled over. He breathed harder. With a glance around, he also seemed to realize that Delk0 had positioned himself between the villain and the Vanetail.

"Delkie? Get out of my way, Delkie."

Ca said no. Arssen wanted to see Trip Mine die, for some reason. Jonathan said forgive, but never sit back and let a man sin. Of all the other voices clamoring affirmation, he trusted Jonathan's most.

"No," Delk0 said.

Even facing a shell of the man Trip Mine used to be, he still shuddered through each breath as he willed his feet not to move. The missile launcher hanging from its strap around his shoulder dug into his weary muscles.

Trip Mine's broken teeth split in a snarl. "Don't make me order you. I haven't for years, but I'll order you!"

He was out of time. An order would be an order, per his programming. "I cannot let you kill more people, Trip Mine," he said with a gasp. "You ruined the lives of trillions? Fine! But you'll be lost like them. You'll be part of the pain they feel."

"DelkZeroNineNine, you will not shoot me and you will take me to that ship's medical capsule."

The words struck a chord. The will seeped out of Delk0's limbs and he stood there, ready to serve.

Trip Mine didn't throw him a cocky grin. He didn't spit at the cowed slave. What he did do was slump a little farther forward while some of the life left his eyes.

"Time to go, Delkie," he murmured.

"Master," Delk0 intoned.

Then the doj slid the handheld into position and fired a missile. The rocket didn't streak at Trip Mine but at the Vanetail.

The light ship's shield caught the majority of the blast, but the sheer force was enough to throw Delk0 and Trip Mine to the floor at this distance. The impact on the shields forced the entire craft to slide across the porch, and slowly off into space.

It disappeared over the edge. Even fancy light ships with medical capsules and interstellar capabilities didn't fly while idling in standby.

Delk0 turned back to Trip Mine. The man was stunned. His mouth was slightly agape, his eyes unblinking. The now-empty handheld clattered to the porch. Stepping forward, Delk0 took extra care as he lifted Trip Mine into a full carry and walked towards the edge of the landing porch.

"What are…What…?" Trip Mine struggled to speak.

"I am following my orders, master," Delk0 stated. "'Time to go.'"

Then Trip Mine threw his head back and howled into the night. Even in his current condition, Delk0 felt his core vent at the ghastly sound.

"DelkZeroNineNine!" he screamed. "I order you to lay me on this landing porch *before taking any other action.*"

He complied.

Trip Mine's howls shook his body. Eyes squinched shut, tears of agony running tracks in the dust on his face, the rogue laughed. "I'm going to die. I'm actually going to die," he wheezed. A grin stretched across his features, and his eyes were wide with mirth like a man possessed.

Judging from his memories of Arssen's insanity, Delk0 now wondered if perhaps he was. It would explain so much.

"But you'll die too, mate," Trip Mine hissed through his mad humor. "I hope I live long enough to see it."

A series of thunderous retorts shattered the world behind them. Delk0 swiveled and cried out as the topmost levels of Uunderspar shattered outward, a ball of flame leaping straight upwards as if the hateful spirit of Dominum himself had just been exorcised from his home.

"Stage one," Trip Mine said, his laughter subsiding into silent, sporadic shakes. The tears still came, though. "At least we can actually sit back and enjoy this one, Delkie. We've got the rest of our lives."

After long minutes of shuddering under the onslaught, Uunderspar had finally begun to tilt. The monstrosity didn't have much time now.

Delk0 felt his eyes watering with sudden fear and sadness. Now he could feel the porch tilting. Now he knew that he would really and truly die in the next sixty seconds.

He categorically didn't want to die.

Who was the woman in the room, the one who had stuffed other spirits in his mind? Why had she? Was it encouragement for Delk0 to stop Trip Mine from toppling an empire? If so he had failed. Or was it to stop Trip Mine, period?

A distant shriek of metal heralded the fall of the tower, followed by a single, massive concussion below. A saboteur's finale.

"Really, there's nothing, nothing left to say," murmured the voice next to him.

And with that, Trip Mine fell silent. Whether dead or dying, his eyes were watery and wide open. Open to watch the fire and thunder in the distance that blossomed out of ancient towers and impenetrable citadels. Open to watch the jagged teeth of Mekrro collapse inward and downward like cans. Open as the great tower itself shook slightly beneath them, lean towards the red setting star visible through the smoke on the horizon, and then almost soundlessly floated downwards beneath them with the grace of an ash mote.

His slide turned into a freefall. And then Ca, Arssen, Marty, Anori, Jacqe, Lamb, Jonathan, and DelkZeroNineNine cried out so that it tore the synthetic vocal cords. "I am free!"

OUTRO

Across the street from a Tudor home stood a woman in a scruffy brown bowler hat, loose beige clothing, and a vest. She leaned against a mailbox. The yard she hid in was largely shaded from the nearest streetlamp by a conifer hedge, and she stood just in the black edge of the shadows.

Inside the house, the Jager family was adjusting to their son's news. Outside the house, a steady rain still beat down on the world as if it would never let up.

A man with tight ebony curls stood next to her, frowning silently. "I liked him better back in Eights."

"Pish-posh, you only met him once at a party," the woman scolded. "Give him time to grow up again."

"I suppose. At least he has one single spirit running the show this time. No remaining memories from your work?"

"That was before. This is now. The extra memories died with Delk0."

"And the curse?"

There was no response.

Although rain was pattering down, it did not seem to hit the pair. Their hair stayed in place and their clothes remained dry. A dog barked and the two held their breath, turning all but invisible in the darkness of the yard.

The barking dog in question was a poodle being walked past quickly by its bundled owner. The dog-walker wore white pumps and *clik-clik-clikked* towards them on the sidewalk. She seemed out of breath and out of sorts. By the time she reached them, it was obvious that her snuffly poodle wasn't being rained on either. It gave two more obnoxious barks before its owner folded the leash, dog and all, up into the form of a paper fortune teller, which she tossed into the gutter.

"I've been looking everywhere for you," she said crossly to the shadows. "Bad enough I get the wrong address, but you two are ghosting on me as well."

The man and woman faded back into view.

"Ms. Willow," she said. "You gave us a fright. He's right across the way, talking with his family."

"About time the former fiend found a family, poor soul," Ms. Willow said with a sigh.

A new voice murmured behind them. "To be fair, his lives always *start* with a family."

The three all faded slightly as they spun around. One hooded figure carrying an unlit lantern stood in the middle of a glistening circle of toadstools near the evergreen hedge. His garb was orange and black, like some kind of Halloween decoration.

Yet another man joined the hooded figure from around the side of the house. He shook his head.

"That's morbid," he chided. "Varrador's curse only affects the one soul, not the spirits of any future family members."

"And how many majhran were cast out for using curses properly?" the lantern-man returned in a soft voice nearly lost to the rain.

"To Harvest Lantern's point, look at his soul's history. One tortured life after another," the hatted woman said.

The conversation fell into contemplation as the five strange figures stared at the house. Several lights burned in the windows, but curtains and blinds closed out the night. Yet the individuals across the street continued to survey the house as if their gazes could burn past the walls and windows to the reunited spirits inside the quiet house.

The rain came down harder.

"Ruth Cross," Harvest Lantern broke the silence. "Did I ever thank you for illuminating Delk0's past spirits for him?"

"I don't believe so, no."

"Ah. Good."

Ruth squinted back at him. "Childish. It was the best solution. Even if it did come from Willow."

Samanthene Willow snorted.

"Forgive and forget, my friend," the dark-haired man told Harvest Lantern. "A guide in the dark is the only way for a lost spirit to find peace. You know this best."

"As do I," Ruth Cross amended.

"And me," Ms. Willow chirped. "I always thought our three responsibilities overlapped the most out of any of us."

"Hsst!"

As Harvest Lantern hissed out in warning, all five figures disappeared completely. Two cars drove past, one tailing the other closely and glaring through its rear window with its brights. They stopped at the intersection a ways down the street and went their own ways.

"Rude driver." Ruth sniffed, returning to view.

The man at her side came back as well, checking a silver watch on his wrist. "I must return my attention to my duties at the ASU. I suggest you all make yourself scarce as well. Perhaps Delk0's sacrifice broke the curse on his soul, perhaps not. But we'll have plenty of years to observe."

"That's my line," Ms. Willow grumbled. "Or did someone make *you* the Mistress of Hopes and Hidden Truths?"

And then she was truly gone.

Harvest Lantern nodded to the others and disappeared into the evergreen hedge. Red oak leaves and speckles of snow flew out behind him, vanishing before they hit the ground.

"Take care, George," Ruth said. "Or John, or James, or whatever you call yourself this era."

"Jacobson, as you well know," the man grumbled as Ruth vanished.

He turned to the last remaining man, the one who'd been humming to himself the entire time while the others spoke. "It's up to you to keep an eye on this new spirit now, this Mark Jager. And just in case some of Ruth's memory handiwork remains, I wouldn't let him see much of you."

Then Jacobson vanished.

The man in the black hat and leather duster nodded and softly sang into the downpour. "*...tell you 'bout my dreams...*" He stepped out onto the sidewalk and made it half of the way down the road before there was nothing left but his shoe prints padding through the puddles.

A few steps later and they were gone too.

ABOUT THE AUTHOR

Creighton Halbert grew up poring over the adventures of the Pevensies and the fantastic imagery from Dr. Seuss's imagination. Interested in beauty wherever it can be built, these days he spends his free time writing, gardening, and living life with his lovely wife.

MORE FROM FOUNDATIONS - DARK PRISONER: THE KRUTHOS KEY

www.FoundationsBooks.net

D. Thomas Jerlo

~Fantasy~

GET IT HERE: https://www.dthomasjerlo.com/

A best-selling and award nominated author of fantasy and paranormal, D. Thomas Jerlo's novels hook unsuspecting readers into worlds of mage'ic and refuses to let them go until that last page is read.

Imprisoned for over a thousand years by the Diveneans of old, Lord Balthazar covets one thing: his freedom. Using his minion, Isafel, and an evil imp spawn called Ilio, they will search Etharia for the one thing that will set their master free and bring chaos to the lands—the Kruthos Key.

With underlords scheming to take the throne and demons roaming freely throughout the land, it's a race against time. But one Divenean still lives, and with the help of an ex-General there may be hope left.

But is it enough?

MORE FROM FOUNDATIONS - HELL COMPANY

www.FoundationsBooks.net

Get it Here:

https://books2read.com/hellforthecompany

Imprisoned for over a thousand years by the Diveneans of old, Lord Balthazar covets one thing: his freedom.

Using his minion, Isafel, and an evil imp spawn called Ilio, they will search Etharia for the one thing that will set their master free and bring chaos to the lands—the Kruthos Key.

With underlords scheming to take the throne and demons roaming freely throughout the land, it's a race against time. But one Divenean still lives, and with the help of an ex-General there may be hope left.

But is it enough?

What stands between humanity and the battle of Armageddon? A sword.

But not just any sword - the Fiery Sword that guarded the Gates of Eden after humanity was kicked out. Before the flood, it was stolen by the 23rd Demon kicked from heaven, who eventually married and imbued it into her human son.

But now she's dead, and it's starting to manifest.

FOUNDATIONS BOOK PUBLISHING

Our mission is to exceed the expectations of our authors and the reading community with an uncompromising commitment to quality, individualism and personal pride. We measure our success one book at a time.

You can find more great works in multiple genres including Romance, Literary Fictions, Thrillers, Suspense, Young Adult, and more!

Visit us at FoundationsBooks.net

www.ingramcontent.com/pod-product-compliance
Lightning Source LLC
Chambersburg PA
CBHW072338020726
47506CB00004B/926